Like a Tree

"Like a tree standing by the water, I shall not be moved."
— Traditional American Hymn

LIKE A TREE

A Novel

Calvin Kytle

NewSouth Books
Montgomery | Louisville

NewSouth, Inc.
105 S. Court Street
Montgomery, AL 36104

ISBN-13: 978-1-60306-036-3
ISBN-10: 1-60306-036-7

Kytle, Calvin.
Like a tree : a novel / Calvin Kytle.
p. cm.

1. Teenage boys—Georgia—Atlanta—Fiction. 2. Middle class—Georgia—Atlanta—Fiction. 3. Race relations—Fiction. 4. Atlanta (Ga.)—Fiction. 5. Depressions—1929—Fiction. 6. Georgia—History—20th century—Fiction. I. Title.
PS3611.Y85L55 2007
813'.6—dc22

2007015862

Like a Tree is a work of fiction. References to public figures are true to the public record. Resemblance to anybody else, living or dead, is unintentional. To verify and extend personal memory of the Great Depression I have drawn on contemporary journals and periodicals. For facts and background, I found indispensable the social histories of Frederick Lewis Allen and William K. Klingaman. — C.K.

Design by Randall Williams
Printed in the United States of America

To Elizabeth

1

After delivering a fruit cake to old Mrs. Yancey in Apartment 320, Damon Krueger stepped back into the dimly lit corridor. He skirted a small Christmas tree and was well on his way to the bread truck when he saw a door open and a man emerge, followed by a beautiful woman.

She was standing in the doorway in the light of a recessed ceiling lamp. Damon could see her clearly. Her hair was black and wiry, cut short to form a cap on an exquisitely shaped head. Her eyes were deep brown, accented by long eyelashes. Her nose looked chiseled and her lips were full. Her skin was unblemished, the color of a vanilla caramel. She was wearing a green dress that fell straight from her shoulders to the middle of her calves; it had long sleeves with cloth-covered buttons and a Mandarin collar. He was so taken with the sight of her that it was a moment or two before he brought the man in focus. Perhaps an inch shy of six feet, the man appeared to be in his late thirties. His hair was sandy and beginning to gray. Recognizing him, Damon gasped. It was his father.

Damon moved back, positioning himself against the wall where he hoped the shadows would hide him. His heart was pounding.

The woman was smiling sweetly. She was speaking too softly for Damon to make out what she was saying, but whatever it was his father was obviously pleased. He watched, holding his breath, as his father pulled the woman to his chest and gave her a long kiss on the lips. They embraced. His father then murmured good-bye and walked—Damon thought a bit haltingly—down the hall to the stairway. The woman stepped inside and closed the door.

A month earlier, Damon Krueger had turned sixteen. It was 1935, the sixth year of the Great Depression. Most of the population was living on hope, faith, and denial. Still, 1935 was not a bad year to be sixteen—if you were white, middle class, Protestant, and lucky enough to live in Atlanta.

A week or so before school let out for the Christmas holidays, Damon got a message from Skyland Bakery's route man, Andy Flaherty, with whom he had worked the past summer. Andy's new assistant had broken an ankle and would have to stay off his feet during the busiest time of the season. Could Damon take his place, at least for the few days before Christmas?

Damon could, and did.

THROUGHOUT THE THIRTIES Skyland Bakery was known to every household in northside Atlanta. Horse-drawn wagons moved down the friendly streets, stopping every twenty-five yards or so long enough for Skyland's salesmen, in immaculate white coveralls, to go door-to-door filling and taking orders for breads, rolls, doughnuts, Danish, cakes, pies, and almost anything else that could be shaped from dough and baked in an oven. The bakery's agents were recruited for their endurance, friendly dispositions, and kindness to horses. Andy was one of the best. He had the build of a center fielder—tall and lean with firm forearms and powerful legs. Incontestably Irish, he had brown hair and eyes as blue as cornflowers. He had the attitude of a man who'd been around and generally liked what he saw. Comfortably adjusted to a high level of testosterone, he was thirty-five but only recently married and still undomesticated.

Andy Flaherty was Damon's introduction to the blue-collar world, and Damon took note. Andy augmented his wages imaginatively. He collected the horse manure in ten-gallon pails and once he'd accumulated enough for a suburban garden sold it to the Atlanta Rose Fanciers for twenty-five cents a gallon. He sold about half the day-old bread at regular prices, pocketing for himself the company's advertised discount. He was very good at cultivating tips, especially from lonely widows. There was, however, a streak of Robin Hood in him. He kept a list of ladies on his route whom he knew to be in need; every Saturday he dropped left-over bread and pastries at their doors.

Damon was paid thirty-five cents an hour. His job was to help deliver the baked goods, feed and water May Belle, shovel up the manure, and sometimes hold the wagon while Andy was gone a bit longer than usual comforting one of the lonely widows. In some ways, Andy was a role model. He was cheerful, but not insufferably so, and he moved gracefully, without a shred of self-consciousness. He spoke plainly. Before the summer employment was over he had enriched Damon's vocabulary with words that wouldn't make it into Webster's for another fifty years.

"There's a new tenant in 320," Andy said when Damon joined him in the wagon that December morning. "And your old sweetheart in 209 has taken her nookie to Fort Bragg. Her husband got home from Cuba last week." He clicked his tongue and cracked the reins lightly. May Belle obediently picked up speed. "Other than that, not much change. Your old customers will be glad to see you." He turned in his seat and gave Damon a smile. "I am too."

Although his prospects were improving, Damon's father had still not found steady employment. He'd been among the first to register with the Works Progress Administration, the most ambitious of the New Deal agencies, when it opened offices in Atlanta earlier that year. He'd been turned down. The personnel clerk, who interviewed him with an air of kind dispassion, told him he was both overqualified and too well off. "We have to save the hard labor for the neediest." Seeing the disappointment in Doug Krueger's eyes, he put his application in a cardboard box marked "Hold," and went on encouragingly, "I'm recommending you for a job in administration. Come back in a month." But there was no job open when Doug went back a month later, and for most of that fall he'd worked as a meter reader for Georgia Power. Three days before Christmas, the Power Company reduced its crew of meter readers, and once again, Doug Krueger was out of work.

At breakfast on Christmas Eve, Doug told his wife Maude not to expect him for lunch. He was going to Decatur. There was a sudden vacancy in the DeKalb County Works Department and he would be spending most of the morning waiting to be interviewed for a job as a building-code inspector.

He and Damon left together in the Model-A Ford. He let Damon out at the corner of Ponce de Leon and Boulevard, where Damon would wait on the curb for Andy to pick him up on May Belle's first stop out of the barn. The morning was frosty, his hands were cold, and the wind cut through his light jacket. He gave his father a weak smile as they parted.

"Good luck, Daddy."

Doug caught the expression in Damon's eyes. "Try not to worry, son. The worst is over."

Damon looked at him, disbelieving. "You sound as if you mean it."

"I do. I have a feeling that 1936 is going to bring us a lot of welcome surprises."

Damon reached through the car window and gave his father an affectionate, almost patronizing, pat on the arm. Doug put the car in gear and turned onto Ponce de Leon Avenue. They didn't expect to see each other again until supper.

During an average week Andy traveled five contiguous routes, each covering a distance of between fifteen and twenty miles. On this Christmas Eve morning he was on Route One, which went through a nondescript neighborhood of high-rise apartments, low-roofed duplexes, and a few small frame houses, some of them built before World War I. Wreaths of pine and holly hung in many of the windows and on others were decals of laughing snowmen, sleighs, and flying reindeer. In this Depression year they all looked defiantly cheerful.

The route began on Ponce de Leon and Boulevard and ran south to the intersection of Monroe Drive and Piedmont Avenue. From there it turned slightly northwest onto Piedmont to Fifth Street, this time moving east to catch Argonne Avenue and the other side streets before reconnecting with Boulevard and terminating.

It turned out to be a strenuous day. A lot of the women had underestimated their needs for Christmas sweets, and by mid-afternoon Damon was winded from having been sent back to the wagon so many times for additional cakes and breakfast rolls. It was especially taxing when, as it seemed to him too frequently, the trips had him going up stairs to third-floor apartments and back again. He had just completed one such delivery when he spied his father.

Before returning to the wagon, Damon waited until he was sure his father had left the premises. He felt a little faint. His heart was still racing when he rejoined Andy.

"Are you all right?" Andy asked him.

"I'm just a little out of breath."

"You got to take it easy on those stairs," Andy said kindly. He gave the reins a little slap and May Belle moved forward.

Later, after he'd calmed himself, Damon asked Andy about the lady in Apartment 320.

"You mean the high yaller?"

"Who is she? Has she been here long?"

"She's got a funny name. Azurelee. Something like that. One word. She's been here the past month but she's leaving today. She's from Chicago."

"What's she doing here?"

"I don't know. She's a teacher, I think. All she told me was that she was on a short assignment at Spelman and she'd like a loaf of rye every Thursday and a coffee cake every other Thursday."

"She's pretty."

Andy laughed. "And smart. And tough."

"I guess that means she turned you down."

"On the second Thursday, I asked if she'd like a quickie."

"You didn't. What did she say?"

"She slapped my face and asked me for the name of my boss."

"You told her?"

Andy laughed again, teasing. "I gave her your name."

"You're kidding."

"Of course I'm kidding. I don't touch women like Azurelee."

"She's a Negro?"

"She could be passing. She's light enough."

"What else do you know about her?"

They had reached another row of apartments. Andy pulled May Belle to a halt and reached for his bread basket. "Just that she was born and raised in Chesterton."

Chesterton? Damon's heart started racing again.

ABOUT FOUR-THIRTY that afternoon, Maude got a call from Mrs. Norcross's cook Minnie.

"Miz Krueger? We forgot to order two pounds of butter mints." An embarrassed pause. "I know it's late, and I'd be first to understand how you'd be just too tired to lift another finger, but Miz Norcross says could you possibly add them to the order and have them here before noon tomorrow?" Maude considered briefly. She was indeed too tired. But then, Grace Norcross was one of her best customers and at five dollars a pound she'd earn an extra ten dollars, plus the dollar tip Damon was sure to get for delivering them.

"I couldn't help samplin' one of your Bourbon balls," Minnie was saying. "I was sorely tempted to slice me a piece of your date-nut cake, too, 'cept it looks too pretty to cut and—. Maybe you ought to make it three pounds. Could you, Miz Krueger?" A detectable note of anxiety had come into Minnie's voice. Maude suspected that she feared a scolding from Mrs. Norcross if the answer was no.

"I can," Maude assured her. "But I may not be able to get them to you before two o'clock. They have to have time to cure, you know."

"Two will be fine," said Minnie. "Thank you, ma'am."

"I GUESS," DOUG SAID, "this means we won't be going to Arabella's?"

She looked at the kitchen clock and made a quick calculation. "We'll go," she told him. "I'll do the mints after we get home."

"Maybe I could help you pull."

"I don't think so," she said, trying not to sound irritable. Pulling mints was tricky. The last time Doug had "helped" he'd stopped pulling only long enough to stoop and tie his shoelaces and the whole batch had been ruined.

She took off her apron. "Right now I'm going to take a short nap. What you can do is heat up the soup when Damon gets home and tell him I made sandwiches for him. They're in the refrigerator. Wake me after he's eaten. I need to talk to him." She saw a question in Doug's eyes. "You and I can wait. We'll get more than enough to eat at Arabella's."

They would be expected at Arabella's at eight, in about three hours.

She left Doug in the living room listening to "Amos 'n' Andy" and went to the bedroom, removing her smock as she went. She took a minute to take off her dress, then lay down in her slip under a thin cotton blanket. In a moment she was fast asleep. She didn't rouse until she heard Damon's knock at the bedroom door.

"Come in, darling," she said drowsily "Turn on the lamp for me. I want to see you."

He moved to the bedside table and switched on the lamp. He turned to her. "Are you all right, mother?"

"I'm fine," she said. Now she could see his face clearly. He looked worried. "You're tired, Damon. You need a bit of a rest."

"I'll lie down for a while before I get dressed. Ben won't be picking me up till after nine."

"I pressed your tuxedo," she said. He nodded in thanks, but his expression was unchanged. Troubled now, she told him to sit on the edge of the bed where she could get a better look at him. "Is something on your mind, sweetheart?"

"I had an awful day," he volunteered. "I kept running all day long, up and down stairs. I began to think every family in Atlanta lived in a third-floor apartment—that every one of them wanted a fruitcake and had waited till the last minute to order it."

"That reminds me." She told him about the order for mints. "I thought you might be able to run them out there after lunch tomorrow and still get back in plenty of time for Bertha's party."

He gave a soft sigh and rose to go. "Sure," he said. "I just hope there'll be enough gas in the car to get me to Habersham Road and back."

"The tank's at least half full," she said. "Your father got two dollars worth yesterday."

He gave her forehead a kiss and moved toward the door. With one hand on the knob, he hesitated and turned his head to face her.

"There is something, isn't there Damon?"

"Mother—" He considered whether to continue. Was there any way he could ask what he wanted to know without moving her to ask him questions in return that he'd rather die than answer? He took a deep breath and decided to risk it. "Mother, why didn't Daddy go back to Chesterton when he had the chance and work with Papa Krueger? Why didn't he take over the business after Papa Krueger died?"

She froze. To give herself a moment to think, she rose on her elbows and rested the back of her neck on the headboard. "Why?" she asked. "Why are you asking a question like that just now? Has something happened?"

"I've been wondering. I think about it a lot."

"Why don't you ask your father?"

"I have."

"And what did he tell you?"

"He said someday, when I'm older, I'd understand. What am I suppose to make of that?"

"Doug didn't go back to Chesterton and work with Papa Krueger because—because he wanted to be on his own. He thought he'd do better on his own."

It was no answer. "There's more to it than that," Damon said, his voice rising. "You know there's more to it than that. I've read Papa Krueger's obituary. He owned thousands of acres in Chester County. There were no fewer than five farms and Lord knows how much rental property. He had the big house on Dixie Avenue. He owned the store. He was a founder, a vice president, and a stockholder in the Bank of Chester. All that, and he left not one dime of it to Daddy."

Damon was speaking now out of resentment and frustration and a strong, unfamiliar sense of betrayal. He could no more control his voice than he could rid himself of the shock and confusion he'd felt earlier that day when he'd come upon his father in embrace with a colored woman. "Why?" he demanded, his voice breaking. "Why did it all go to Aunt Helen? What made Papa Krueger drop Daddy from his will? That's what happened, isn't it, Mother? What did Daddy do so bad that turned Papa Krueger against him?"

She frowned. "Let me ask you a question. Why is it so important that you know? That you bring up this particularly unhappy subject at this most inappropriate time?"

He felt his body sag in exasperation. "When is there ever an appropriate time? I think about it all the time. Lord, Mother. Here we are—a few years ago, before you started catering, we were scrambling to pay the rent, and barely managing to pay the bill before they turned the lights off, and some days with nothing to eat but rice and tomato soup. I used to go to dances and take my date to the Varsity at intermission and all I had in my pocket was thirty-five cents and I'd be scared to death she'd order something more than chocolate milk and toasted pound cake. If it weren't for you, we'd be on relief, for God's sake. Do you think I don't know how hard it is for you, even now? How it frets you, that every time the mortgage comes due you may not be able to meet it? And there's Aunt Helen and Uncle Dave and those silly twins To and Fro—"

"You mean Sue and Flo, darling."

"—and all the rest of that dumb family with money to burn, living in the house that should be ours, just because Aunt Helen had the good sense never to cross her father. What did Daddy do? If you know, why won't you tell me?"

"I wish you wouldn't take the Lord's name in vain, Damon."

"Or is it you don't know, Mother?"

She looked pained, defeated. "Your father was once a very proud man," she said softly.

It was all the explanation he was going to get, and with it she meant to put an end to the conversation.

"Okay," he said resignedly. "But tell me this much. What kind of man was Papa Krueger?"

For some reason she smiled, perhaps because of the change in subject. "He was a good man, a God-fearing man. Bald. Not so short or fat that you could call him roly-poly, but sort of round. One leg was shorter than the other. He wore a built-up shoe and he rolled a little when he walked. He was full of stories and little jokes. He was a cheerful man. They called him Brother Sunshine."

"I mean underneath all that. What sort of man was he? How would he have been to do business with?"

"Oh Damon, must you? I never got to know your grandfather. Doug had been gone two years from Chesterton when we got married. I never met either of your grandparents until Doug introduced me a month or so before the wedding. Doug and I were in South Carolina—in Hastings—and we would have had few opportunities to visit his parents, even if Doug had wanted to. One of the few times was after you were born, when we took you to Chesterton to show you off. Then a year or so later Papa Krueger had that accident and died, when you were two." She paused, realizing that she had missed the point. "I have no idea what sort of businessman he was, except that he was a successful one."

When Damon said nothing in response, she spoke to what to her was a more important concern. "Go a little easier on your father, son. He's not had a light time of it. He's not well. It's awful for him right now, being laid off only three days before Christmas."

Yes, he was thinking, but why was it so hard, even in these times, for his father to find a job? Was he really so sick he couldn't be depended on to keep it?

"—and he loves you," his mother was saying.

Damon stood in silence, reflecting. His mother threw off the blanket and stood up, meaning to go down the hall to the bathroom. "I have to hurry and get dressed now." She looked genuinely apologetic. "We'll talk about this again. When we're not so pushed."

He nodded. "I'm sorry, Mother."

She kissed him good-bye. "I'm so proud of you, son," she said under her breath.

"I'm proud of you," he said.

He reached in his right pocket and pulled out his pay envelope. "Four days' work. Eleven dollars and twenty cents. Here's ten toward next month's mortgage."

He leaned over, kissed her, and left.

She was on the verge of tears.

2

Maude Yoder was the only girl in her family. She had two brothers. Two other siblings, both listed on their death certificates merely as "female infants," had died of diphtheria before she was born.

Her mother was mostly English. Besides the fact that her maiden name was Fletcher and that she had been orphaned at twelve, Maude knew almost nothing about her history. The records on her father's side, however, were copious. Her great-great paternal grandfather had come to America from Hamburg, on a boat that had been hijacked by pirates who had stolen everything of any value. According to one family journal of unknown authorship, he had arrived in Charleston in 1728 "clad only in a croker sack." Sometime later he moved up to the North Carolina Piedmont, acquired land, became a reasonably prosperous farmer and an even more profitable blacksmith. He sired three sons, all of whom grew to adulthood, thrived, and multiplied.

Maude's father Joseph inherited his ancestor's entrepreneurial skills. In addition, he had a mind for learning. He worked his way through Catawba College, majoring in philosophy with a minor in business. After graduation he became a Lutheran minister, at different times—from about 1890 until World War I—serving rural congregations in North Carolina, Alabama, Georgia, and South Carolina. At the time Maude was born, in 1898, he was pastor of a growing church in Lexington, South Carolina. He was also the county school superintendent and an eager but intelligently restrained land speculator. In his spare time, which he seemed to have in abundance, he invented utilitarian devices. He held patents for a folding ironing board, a door stop and holder, a twelve-foot platform ladder for cherry picking, and a metal cinder deflector. He abandoned the cherry picker after the platform collapsed during a demonstration at the state fair and almost killed the young farmhand he'd hired to assist him. But at least three of his inventions were produced and marketed. The cinder deflector made him quite a lot of money. Installed on the windows of passenger trains, it caught the soot and cinders blowing from the coal-fired engines ahead; before its invention a lady seated by a window could not ride for more than a few miles before her hair was filthy and stiff as a board. The deflector was sold in volume to railroads and aggressively promoted to attract passengers "who want to stay clean while enjoying the view." The door stop was a pivoting brass contraption that screwed to the floor and could be activated by foot. It turned out to be particularly attractive to farm women who, their hands full of firewood or laundry, otherwise would have to stoop and put down their burdens before entering or leaving a room. The stops were sold by the thousands—one dollar each—by drummers throughout the South; in a few surviving farm houses they could be found still in use. In one divinely inspired project, Papa Yoder managed to combine profit with evangelism. He wrote a verse called "Let Your Conscience Be Your Guide," had it printed as a postcard, and sold it, a penny apiece, through the same network of drummers.

Income from preaching and teaching was enough to assure his family a subsistence living, and sometimes even a comfortable one. Beyond this his fortunes rose and fell with the fluctuating royalties from his inventions and the unpredictable returns from his land deals. In Maude's childhood the family seemed to move at least once a year, into a small and over-furnished parsonage when times were bad, and into a typically two-story frame house when times were better. The children accommodated themselves to the repressive atmosphere of a parsonage largely because they had come to understand that before another year was out their father would be able to move them into a house that carried no obligation to entertain the ladies' Bible circle or to decorate the walls with religious mottoes and pictures of Christ in thorns. Further, such a move held the realistic promise of indoor plumbing and separate rooms for Maude and the older boys.

Shortly after celebrating Maude's twelfth birthday the family was struck with an affluence that endured throughout the next ten years. Rights to the folding ironing board were sold to Sears Roebuck on terms that brought her father a dollar on every sale, and after the cinder deflector's successful acceptance by Carolina-Chesapeake Railways it was installed by the thousands in railroad systems west of the Mississippi. Hardly had he banked the first proceeds from these sales when a developer offered him fifteen thousand dollars for acreage near Lexington that only two years before he had acquired (from an appreciative and recently widowed member of his congregation) for something less than two thousand. The good Lord, he told his wife and children, as if he half believed it, was finally rewarding him for all his clean living and good works.

In 1909 the Lutheran synod assigned Joseph Yoder to an old established church in Hastings, a thriving commercial center with a population of 45,000, about fifty miles east of Columbia, the state capital. Feeling that he was finally settled for life, Joseph bought himself a Lincoln touring car, recruited a chauffeur and a staff of three Negro domestics, and moved with his wife and three children into an antebellum estate that occupied three acres on Woodrow Street. The main house, built of masonry and oak with a front porch dominated by four Doric columns, had twelve rooms, including an enormous kitchen and two interior baths in what had formerly been small dressing rooms. Rising at the rear of a spacious foyer was a wide staircase of solid walnut that led upstairs to the master bedroom, his wife's sewing room, a guest room, and three small bedrooms for the children. The living room and dining room were to the right of the foyer; to the left was the music room, which opened into Papa Yoder's library. Set almost in the middle of a flower garden in the big back yard were two detached cottages, once servants' quarters that the previous owner had redesigned and converted into a garage and tool shed.

This was the setting of Maude's adolescence, lived out as a pampered daughter in a stereotypically old and well-to-do Southern family. Her father, a physically formidable man with an acquired ability to charm, governed the household like a benevolent despot. His wife and children contentedly acquiesced, understanding that it was his nature to dispense all manner of blessings on those who pleased him and didn't cross him;

they had learned early that he was most pleased if they did what he asked of them and played their roles in conformity to his idea of the happy American family. As they grew older, the boys found ways to give assent without undue sacrifice of integrity and to do pretty much whatever they wanted to do, short of being drunk in his sight or bringing fallen women home for dinner. He was generally a tolerant if not indifferent father to the boys. His attitude seemed to be that if you fed and clothed them and saw that they got good educations they should be equipped to make it on their own. Not so with Maude. His was a world of fixed verities, overcast by a gracious God. He thought of himself as a gentleman and, in common with most gentlemen of his generation, he took it for granted that a woman's job was to bear the children, manage the household, tend the sick, and stay out of politics. But he held equally that women were to be adored and adorned. Few things pleased him more than to brush his wife's fine black hair every night at bedtime, or to surprise her with a new frock or a new piece of jewelry on no special occasion. He treated Maude with the same thoughtful, indulgent affection, taking it as a given that she should be shaped to his image of the perfect young lady.

But there developed a deeper and more satisfying dimension to his love of Maude when he discovered that she shared his passion for words and literature. He taught her to read when she was barely five. Not long after that, astonishingly, he found her diagramming sentences with the same enthusiasm that her brothers had for memorizing batting averages. Given an infallible memory and her intense interest in vocabulary, she usually beat the adults at Anagrams.

Whereas it had been the habit of his wife to read to the boys when they were children, he insisted that he be the one to read to Maude, and he took it upon himself to direct her reading tastes. Fortunately, she had an instinctive dislike for sentimentality and melodrama; small bites of Elsie Dinsmore were more than enough. By the time she was thirteen she had gone beyond Hurlbut's Bible stories and Louisa May Alcott and was deep into Jane Austen and George Eliot (he began to worry that she was developing a mind of her own when he failed to dissuade her from *Middlemarch)*. Proud of her precocity, he also encouraged her to write, happy that she asked him to review her homework in composition. Some of his lessons she would never forget: "One doesn't lay down, Maude; one lies down"; "Remember, honey, accommodate is spelled with two m's"; "Please, baby—there's an important difference between principal and principle." He was a good and gentle teacher. She won the district spelling bee when she was eleven and on three successive years thereafter. During her senior year at high school she was awarded the Palmer medal for excellence in English.

Maude's mother Mary was a slight, fine-boned woman of enormous energy who accepted her role as homemaker in good spirit. From her, Maude learned how to sew and cook, including some special tricks with pastry and leftovers. Mary, however, had been the daughter of a preacher and now, as a preacher's wife, she was tired of being what she called herself—"a second-class citizen"—and was determined that her family escape the pigeon hole her husband's congregations were prone to put it in. So she saw to it that Maude was dressed like other girls—"no Mrs. Astor's hand-me-downs"—and, by scrimping and saving and lopping pennies off the weekly grocery allowance, she was able to enroll her daughter in dancing school. Maude, she told her husband, was going to be neither treated like an object of charity nor honored—"or humored," she amended, with uncharacteristic sarcasm—like a little plaster saint for whom ordinary girl talk automatically stops whenever she enters a room. Later, when the royalties from his inventions started coming, to Joseph's astonishment she insisted that he take out a family membership in the Francis Marion Country Club. "If you can buy yourself a Lincoln you can surely buy your family a few normal pleasures."

"But a country club?" Joseph said, protesting. "Don't you know the Bible says we should eschew the company of money-changers?"

"Yes," she responded with a fire in her voice that he had rarely heard, "but I know nothing in the Bible that says we have to wear yellow homespun, live in closets, and associate only with born-again Christians."

"But Mary darling—"

"Don't 'Mary darling' me. I want Maude to be the belle of the ball. And I want our boys to be welcome at parties. I want them to meet girls somewhere besides Sunday School—girls who don't even go to Sunday School. I want them to know the latest jokes and the latest songs and to dance the Chicken Trot, or whatever it is they trot, and wear good clothes and play tennis and golf and, yes, maybe even bridge or poker. If that means we have to join a higher class—or, in your opinion, a lower class—so be it."

So the Yoders joined the country club.

Maude was not a rebellious child. She was inclined to do what at the time was expected of all young girls who had inherited a certain station in society or whose families, like hers, had a conspicuous amount of money. After high school, she went off to a two-year finishing school in Charlotte, where she studied art and music appreciation, European history, domestic science, literature, deportment, and elocution. She was graduated in June 1917, two months after the United States entered World War I. A year later, her anticipated debut was canceled when word came of the death of her oldest brother, Joseph Jr., in the battle for Chateau Thierry.

In such a circumstance, young ladies in Hastings of her station were expected, after a period of mourning, to join the Junior League, travel abroad for perhaps as long as a year, then come home and get married.

She never got to travel. Instead, she met Douglas Krueger.

He was the best-looking man she had ever seen. Though of only medium height, he held himself so erect that he looked four inches taller. He had the physique of an Olympic diver—broad shoulders, firm chest, slim hips, flat stomach. In or out of the sun, his skin was an even tan, edging toward pink. His hair was reddish blond, his eyebrows slightly darker, his eyes chestnut brown. If he had an imperfection, it was that his lower lip was a trifle thick.

She first saw him at the club, from a lawn chair with a good view of the tennis courts. He was in tennis whites. The sun was warm and bright, and whenever his chase of the ball carried him out of the shade his blond head lit up as if aflame. It almost took her breath away. He moved across the court with a grace that approached elegance. When he served, he had a way of lifting his left foot, resting for a moment on the heel, and then stepping back and bending at the right hip before tossing the ball high and bringing his racquet up. It was a purposeful gesture, a sort of polite warning to his opponent, and Maude was altogether captivated by it.

"Edna," she said to the girl in the chair to her right. "Who is he?"

"Which one?"

"The one at the net. The one with the champagne hair."

"Oh, that's Doug somebody. He's a friend of Strut Montague's. I think they may have been at Tech together. He's just out of the army."

"Where's he from? Was he overseas?"

Edna smiled, not at all surprised by the excitement in Maude's voice. "He grew up in Georgia, some little town near the Alabama line, I think. No, he never went over. He spent his whole time in the Signal Corps, somewhere in New Jersey."

"What's he doing in Hastings? Will he be here long?"

"Don't ask me. I've told you all I know. Except that he's a marvelous, I mean really yummy, dancer."

After the last set, Doug Krueger climbed the low embankment and came to her on the terrace. Strut Montague, his tennis partner, was with him, a burly young man whom Maude knew from their days together in dancing class. "This is my friend Douglas Krueger," Strut said. "We were Phi Delts together at Tech." She scarcely heard Strut, attentive as she was to the smiling figure who stood before her. She offered him her hand. He took it and held it. He spoke. "So glad to meet you," he said, and she thought she heard a choir of flutes. Flustered, she moved her eyes from his face and focused on his wrist. For a moment all she could see were the fine blond hairs, soft as down, against his bronze forearms. She wondered if his whole body was covered in down, and she shivered.

Five months later they were married. If Doug had been more persuasive, it would have been sooner. He had urged her to run away with him, but this she could not consider. "Papa and Mama have always dreamed of a church wedding for me, and Papa would be heartsick if he couldn't do the ceremony." So they were married in the main chapel of the Lutheran Church of the Redeemer, with Maude in her mother's wedding dress of silk and real lace, and four bridesmaids in pink chiffon, one of whom was Doug's sister Helen, embarrassingly overweight and nervous, as if the ceremony might demand of her more than she could deliver. And indeed it was a ceremony. There was Papa in his scarlet robe at the altar. There were Douglas and Strut, his best man, and across the aisle from them her surviving brother to give her away, all in rented formal morning dress, and there was the full church choir singing "O Promise Me" accompanied by an organist and a brass ensemble that raised the whole affair to the solemnity of an investiture.

Doug's mother had arrived two days before the event, a lady whose carriage and coloring left no doubt which of his parents Doug favored. His father joined them for the bridal dinner the night before, pleading the pressure of business for his tardiness, his manner conveying a certain ambiguity, alternating between his obligation to be amusing and a desire to withdraw, as if to distance himself from his son. He seemed to have memorized every clean joke in Captain Billy's Whizbang. ("What time of day was Adam created?' "A little before Eve." "Ho, ho, ho, ho.") He had a laugh that could rock Gibraltar, but then, disconcertingly, he would lapse into silence, the kind of hush that envelops a group of mourners. Maude didn't know what to make of him. She suspected that he would have preferred that Doug marry somebody else, or marry not at all, but exactly why he made her feel this way she could not imagine.

Doug's nature was to be open. There was little about himself that he showed any reluctance to disclose during the months after their somewhat impetuous marriage. The one exception was his estrangement from his father.

He wrote home faithfully once a week, but Maude noticed that the letters were always addressed to his mother alone. In conversation he never referred to his father except in answer to a direct question.

His love for his mother was almost overdone. Hers for him was so demonstrative that his sister Helen found it hard not to feel resentful. His mother lavished presents on him, and not infrequently her letters included a small check, fifteen dollars or so, enclosed without comment. Catherine Krueger was a tall, trim woman with Doug's coloring and erect bearing. Indomitably cheerful, she was convinced that she lived in the best of all possible worlds and was inclined to think the best of everybody.("If you can't speak well of somebody, don't speak at all.") She came for a visit sometime during the spring of that first year in Hastings, arriving with an extra bag that contained linen tablecloths, four percale sheets, a Paisley shawl, and a Beleek tea set. "My mother's," she told Maude. "Had them for years, gathering dust. Time somebody enjoyed them."

Catherine, then in her mid-forties, spent a week with them, much of the time helping Maude rearrange furniture and waxing floors. The Yoders took quite a liking to her. There were several pleasant daytime excursions in the Lincoln with Papa Yoder driving, ending with picnic suppers in Hampton Park for which Catherine insisted on preparing the potato salad and sweet tea. Beyond Maude's polite inquiry about his health on the day of Catherine's arrival, there was no mention of Papa Krueger during the entire week.

Their first two years together Maude would remember as the best of her life. Doug brought to love-making the same attitude of self-confidence that invested everything he did. He was a patient and gentle lover, more experienced than she would ever have thought him to be.

With a degree from Georgia Tech, he was working for South Carolina's biggest electrical contractor and earning a hundred and fifty dollars a month, more than enough to meet their basic needs, pay the bootlegger, maintain their club membership, and to put a few dollars out of every paycheck into a savings account. They had a Model-T Ford, a wedding gift from Papa Yoder. They lived in a rented three-bedroom, two-story house on Divine Place, across the street from Strut and Trudy and within walking distance of her parents' home. They were able to furnish the house comfortably, if sparingly, with a few contemporary pieces of Maude's choosing and several useful and handsome antiques donated by various members of their families. Among the antiques was a Hepplewhite drop-leaf dining table with matching shield-back chairs that had been left from the estate of Doug's paternal grandfather. Shortly after moving in, Doug built a workshop in the basement, complete with a lathe and a power saw, and displayed an appreciable gift for carpentry and cabinetmaking. Among the pieces he designed and crafted was a double bed with a frame and headboard of solid oak, carved in a random pattern of lotus leaves.

But beginning early in 1920 a series of events brought an end to these happy times and thrust Maude into harsh reality. In January, her brother Vincent, who had escaped the lethal epidemic of 1918, died suddenly of Spanish flu, which had returned in what the public health service had reported was a weaker strain. In March, her father slipped on the porch steps, fell, and broke his right hip. Two days later the wound became painfully infected. A week later he was dead. Equally as sudden, her mother had barely survived the funeral service when, apparently from grief and shock, she dropped dead of a heart attack.

About the same time Carolina-Chesapeake Railways found a way to improve the design of the cinder deflector without infringing on Joseph Yoder's patent, and Sears canceled the contract for the folding ironing board after adopting a slightly different and less expensive model from another supplier. The royalty checks stopped coming. Worse, when the estate was settled, Papa Yoder was discovered to have been both an excessively generous philanthropist and an impulsive, imprudent investor. Driven perhaps as much by guilt as by the Biblical call to charity, he had given twenty percent of his annual income to the Lutheran Church and had been in the habit of making sizeable donations to a number of schools and orphanages. Having borrowed heavily to finance land purchases, he died land poor. As a consequence, whereas his children had confidently expected bequests of a size to support them in comfort, there was hardly enough money to pay off the bank debts. About the only remaining asset was the Woodrow Street property, which when sold after the death of his wife, yielded Maude, the lone survivor, little more than five thousand dollars.

Their first years together were also ones in which Maude came to discover, if not always to understand, that Doug was a man of many parts but perhaps not a man for all seasons. Some of the discoveries made her love him all the more; some gave her a vague, indefinable sense of foreboding. On the surface, and certainly whenever he was in company, he was easy-going, self-possessed, charming, rarely moved to disagree, and never petulant. But underneath there were deep running passions and strong currents of resentment. To no small degree, he seemed to be in constant rebellion against authority and an unjust world. He had a congenital dislike for the born rich and a concomitant sympathy for the poor and hard done by. Maude saw both as admirable virtues, but sometimes he seemed to be too quick on the attack and too outspoken for his own good. In a man with his small-town background, such convictions were hard to understand. Certainly she saw nothing in his father to explain them. While his mother probably shared his attitudes, to Maude she appeared to be too passive, too reconciled to her station as idealized Southern Lady, to have ever said or done much to shape his rebellious spirit. Nevertheless, rebel he was and on occasion his suppressed anger exploded into a kind of cold rage that threatened to get out of control.

The first time she saw this happen, they were at dinner at the home of John and Alicia Sanders, a couple they had only recently met, a pair that in Maude's eyes represented a step above on Hastings's social ladder and therefore to be cultivated. The man, however, was intolerable. The beneficiary of an old South Carolina name and inherited wealth, he accepted it as his birthright to be arrogant, patronizing, vulgar—and drunk. As the meal progressed, between sips and burps, he talked as if instructing the unenlightened, expressing contempt for Woodrow Wilson, defense of Warren Harding, suspicion of Albert Einstein, and approval of an up-and-coming Italian politician named Benito Mussolini. Doug said little or nothing until the subject shifted to motion pictures and the virtues of *Birth of a Nation*.

"One of the only really good movies those kikes in Hollywood have made," Sanders said.

Maude gave a slight gasp. "I didn't know D. W. Griffith was a Jew."

"Oh yes," Sanders assured her. "His real name is Goldenson."

"I find that hard to believe," Doug said quietly.

Sanders turned belligerent. "Are you calling me a liar?"

"I just think you may be misinformed."

Sanders got red in the face. He raised his voice to a near scream. "Don't tell me I'm misinformed. Kikes have taken over Hollywood, just like they're taking over all the banks in this country."

Doug put down his napkin and pushed back his chair. "Forgive me, sir," he said, with exaggerated formality, "but if you say kike or nigger one more time I'm going to forget that I'm a guest in your house."

Startled, Sanders gave a nervous laugh. "Well," he said, "I didn't know I had a nigger-lovin' Commie at my table."

At that, Doug rose and signaled to Maude. "My wife and I want neither your hospitality nor your friendship. Come, Maude, it's time to go."

She didn't know whether to be embarrassed or proud.

A few days later, on the morning of his third anniversary with Poole and Company, Doug was summoned to Poole's office. He went, expecting to be told he was getting a raise.

Amos Poole was a tall, rangy man with a very big head supported by a short neck sucked into a massive chest. He was in his mid-fifties but his body was as firm and as hard as it had been when he'd played center field for a season with the Atlanta Crackers thirty years ago; he spent countless hours and took enormous pride keeping it that way. Vain and cunning, he could be relentlessly ingratiating to those who had something he wanted, ruthless to those who didn't want him to have it, and Ol' Boy Familiar to everybody else.

His dark brown eyes, separated by a fleshy pendulous nose, were set deep in their sockets. When he was angry they narrowed into a menacing squint. They were narrowed into a menacing squint when Doug entered his office. "Sit down, Mr. Krueger," he said from where he sat behind his enormous mahogany desk.

Mr. Krueger? Not a good sign. Doug sat.

There was a brass paperweight seamed like a baseball on the otherwise clean desk. Amos Poole had his right hand gripped on the paperweight. He looked as if with the least provocation he might throw it at Doug's face.

"Well, Mr. Krueger, what do you have to say for yourself?"

"Sir?"

"What the hell did you say to John Sanders that's got him telling everybody I'm harboring a communist?"

Doug frowned. "I guess I told him I didn't enjoy his company."

"That's all?"

"And that I'd knock his block off if he didn't stop saying nigger."

"My, aren't you the pious one." Poole's fingers grasped the paperweight more tightly. "Do you know who John Sanders is?"

"I know what he is. He's a bigot."

"He's an old and good friend of mine."

"I'm sorry to hear it."

"He's also chairman of the school board and vice chairman of the advisory committee to the state public works commission. Do you have any idea what his friendship means to this company?"

"I can imagine."

"He wants me to fire you."

"You want me to apologize to him?"

"That would be a start."

"I guess I could apologize for my show of temper. I could never apologize for what I told him. He's a stupid and mean-spirited man and Maude and I don't care to have anything more to do with him."

Poole's eyes almost disappeared into their sockets. His shoulders dropped and he sighed. "Write him whatever kind of apology you feel you can without sacrificing your goddamned integrity. I'll try to forget it."

"Is that all, sir?"

"Not quite. If I ever hear of you insulting a customer, a friend of mine again, you'll be on the street."

Doug gave a hollow laugh.

"What's so funny?

"When Betty called this morning and said you wanted to see me, I thought you were going to give me a raise."

"A raise?"

"This happens to be the day of my third anniversary with the company. I've had only one salary increase in three years. I've done everything you've asked of me, and I've heard no complaints. Why shouldn't I think I deserved a raise?"

"I don't hand out raises lightly."

"So I gather. I've also been thinking I'm underused. I have a degree from Georgia Tech. I thought I was being hired to do systems design. Too much of the time you've had me doing things an apprentice could do—stringing wire, rewiring old gas-fitted buildings, replacing blown fuses. I was hoping at least for a better assignment."

"As long as you work for this company, Mr. Krueger, you'll do what I tell you to do. If you're so dissatisfied, perhaps you should—"

"Quit? You're absolutely right." Doug took a deep breath. "I quit."

What rattled Maude when he told her was that he spoke in a tone of optimism hardly justified by their circumstance. At that moment she felt something slipping in her heart. For the first time, his expression of grounded self-reliance failed to reassure her.

"You mean you've been offered a better job?"

"I mean I'm no longer working for Amos Poole and Company."

He seated himself on one of the straight-back Hitchcock chairs, holding himself beautifully erect.

"Aren't you scared?"

"Why should I be scared? I'll find another job."

She stared in disbelief. He smiled.

"I'm sure," she forced herself to say. "You want to tell me what happened?"

The smile disappeared, replaced by a hint of defiance. "He gave me no choice, really," Doug said soberly. "I've been there three years and half the time he's had me doing all kinds of stinking chores that anybody with muscles and a strong back can do. He called me in this morning to scold me about what I said to John Sanders and after we got beyond that I told him how I felt. I told him I thought I was due a raise and a change of job assignment."

"And?"

"He said he was sorry I was dissatisfied."

"Had he promised you a raise?"

"No. But Maude—I've been working my tail off. Never a day off except for the week of our honeymoon, which I took without pay." He lit a cigarette and took a long drag. "And look what he's had me doing. I reminded him this morning that I had a degree in electrical engineering and that when he hired me I hadn't expected to be spending my time wallowing on my belly in dust or mud and fighting off spiders and toads."

"And what did he say to that?"

"He just squinted at me with those beady little eyes of his and said that as long as I was on his payroll I'd do whatever he told me to do."

"So that's when you quit?"

"Right that minute."

"And how do you feel now?"

"Relieved." He pulled his shoulders back in a gesture of pride. "I'd never have gotten anywhere working for Poole. He never intended to promote me. And I didn't for sure go four years at Georgia Tech to be a petty-cash man the rest of my life."

Her initial dismay was now diluted in a swift rush of sympathy. "I understand, darling. I do. I just wish it hadn't happened right now. And I wish you hadn't decided to quit before you had someplace else to go."

"Oh come on, Maude," he said peevishly. "What else could I have done?"

"I'm pregnant, Doug," she reminded him. "We've already had more than enough stress in this house."

Chastened, he rose, went to her, and gave her a light kiss on the lips. "Don't fret, lamb," he said. "I'll give you nothing to worry about. I promise." He move to the corner cupboard and brought back two glasses and a bottle of Scotch." Here, let me pour you a drink."

She shook her head. "Not now," she said and retreated into silence. He finished his drink quickly and moved as if to go for another. With an apparent change of mind, he turned back to her.

"Is there more, Doug?" she asked him.

He sat down again. "I don't know. Except that I think Poole may have been looking for a way to get me out of his shop. I think he's glad he didn't have to fire me."

"Why, Doug?"

"He may know that I found out about Cooter. And he's worried I may tell."

"Who's Cooter?"

"I should have said squeal."

Again, "Who's Cooter?"

"He's the chief clerk in the state procurement office. He handles bids and contracts. I had gone into Poole's office one afternoon to return some drawings. It was after quitting time and I was alone. The phone rang. It was Cooter, and when I picked up he obviously thought I was Poole. All he said was something like 'Under thirty-five thousand.' I said 'What?' and he hung up."

"Under thirty-five thousand? What did that mean?"

"I figured he was telling Poole how to bid on the contract for the new wing of Memorial Hall. Two weeks later, when we were awarded the contract, I was sure of it."

"So Mr. Poole's a cheat."

"I think if you dug deep you'd find that he's been bribing and conspiring and getting contracts illegally for years."

She sighed. She knew what he was going to say next.

"I'm glad to be out of there," he said. "If my father ever taught me one thing, it's better to be a crook than work for one. It's only a matter of time till Poole gets caught. When he does, God knows who he might bring down with him."

She sighed again. If Doug drew comfort from that thought, let him.

As far as she knew, before their marriage Doug had displayed no more than an indifferent interest in politics. Now he showed signs of a maturing social conscience, sometimes reacting to the day's news with an indignation that approached the passionate. He was especially upset by reports of race riots in Chicago, visiting the local library every afternoon for a week to read more detailed accounts in the Chicago newspapers. ("Troops were called in today to help quell riots here that have left thirty-one dead and more than five hundred injured.")

He joined the state Democratic party and campaigned vigorously for "the least offensive" candidates for local office in the 1920 primary. South Carolina, like the twelve others in the then Solid South, was a one-party state, so the race for president drew little excitement, especially since it was generally assumed that the country, tired of Woodrow Wilson's pieties, would go overwhelmingly Republican. Curiously, Doug would come home after canvassing a neighborhood not so much discouraged by most people's political expectations, so contrary to his own, as he was puzzled by them.

"People don't know their own self-interest," he lamented to Maude. "There's this poor guy on Blossom Street. With four children. He's ho-ho-ho for Roger Bondurant even though Bondurant's pushing for a sales tax on food and medicine. He thinks Bondurant must be a good man because he passes the plate at church every Sunday."

He went on. "A woman on Olive Street—she's almost forty years old and never voted before in her life—never allowed to vote before—and she's going to vote against Stew Mulligan. You know why? Not because he's opposed to higher salaries for school teachers and pasteurized milk, but because he had his picture in the papers standing on his head. He's too undignified to be in public office, she says."

"Poor dear," said Maude. "You really expect people to be rational, don't you?"

"Maybe. It doesn't seem to be any more rational in national politics. The party said thumbs down on Al Smith not just because he's a Catholic but because he's experienced and has a record on the issues. And they selected instead a mediocrity like Jim Cox whose main virtue is that nobody can tell where he stands on the League of Nations, and nobody can question his patriotism because he got a law passed in Ohio that bans the teaching of German. No wonder they put Franklin Roosevelt on the ticket. What does it matter if he's a playboy and can't even change a fuse? He's from New York and he's got a name."

"You look so bitter, darling. Would you rather be a Republican?"

"And vote for Warren Harding? God forbid. Though it might not be a bad thing to bring the Republican party to South Carolina."

"But if you hate politics so—"

"Hate politics? I love it."

And for a while it appeared that he did. Indeed, Maude briefly entertained the hope that Doug might have found his calling. But in November when the 1920 elections were over, there seemed to be nothing in politics to command his energies and by Christmas he had found a new enthusiasm: radio.

One day he came home with what looked like an oatmeal box wrapped in copper wire.

"It's an oatmeal box, wrapped in wire," he explained. "Shellacked. A few other things—brass tracks here, with slides, and an aerial. See? And oh yes, a piece of galena crystal."

She looked at him as if he were out of his mind.

"I've made us a crystal set," he said delightedly. "A radio."

"So?"

"Here, I'll show you." He handed her a set of earphones. "Put these on and listen."

He fiddled with a slide. Nothing. He fiddled some more. This time her ears were assaulted by static. He kept moving the slide until the static disappeared.

A moment later, quite recognizably she heard the last verses of "The Road to Mandalay," sung by a baritone who sounded as if he knew he was making history.

"My, that's thrilling," Maude said, returning the headphones. "Where's it coming from?"

"Pittsburgh. KDKA, I think. I tell you, Maude, in a few years there'll be radio stations in every town in America. It's revolutionary. Radio is going to change the world. It's going to change everything! It's as revolutionary as the printing press, as—-."

He stopped, arrested by the expression on Maude's face. Her jaw was dropped and her eyes were wide and brimming.

"I'm sorry," he said, blushing. "I guess I get carried away."

She kissed him. "Don't you know, Doug? I never love you more than when you get carried away." She kissed him again. "Let's go to bed."

In October Doug got a phone message from Helen that his mother had suffered a stroke. Her recovery was problematical. Could he come?

He and Maude left for Chesterton by the next train. They found Catherine in bed, weak, her left arm temporarily paralyzed, but able to talk and still sound in her mind. "Don't worry, darlings," she greeted them. "It runs in mother's side of the family. She had a stroke at forty-five and lived to be eighty."

Doug had difficulty holding back the tears. "I don't know what I'd do without you," he said, trembling.

She took his hand. "Cut that out. I'm not going anywhere, baby."

At that moment his father entered the room. It was only the second time Maude had seen him. He looked shorter, stouter, and pinker than she remembered him from the wedding. He reminded her of some amiable Dickens character, perhaps Mr. Dick in *David Copperfield*. She knew that he owned a combination furniture store and funeral parlor, and he looked the part. He was wearing his undertaker's black suit; there had been a memorial service earlier that morning. His face was fixed in a practiced smile, the kind that grieving family members took to be an expression of sorrow relieved by the comforting conviction that the deceased was "now at peace with his blessed Jesus." He smelled of formaldehyde and lilac water.

Seated in the coach on the way back to Hastings, Maude ventured to ask Doug about his father. "What is there between you two?" she said. "He seems like a thoroughly nice man to me."

"And I guess to every white body in Chesterton," Doug said.

She eyed him quizzically. "What do you mean by that?"

"Just that you have to know my father well to hate him."

For a moment they were silent. "You don't want to tell me, do you?" she said.

"No," he said, pained. "Not now, Maude. Maybe later." He turned and gazed vacantly out the window. "My father is a Klansman."

3

Three weeks after leaving Poole and Company Doug went to work for Poole's rival, an electrical contractor named John Akin. During the interview, Akin had asked him why he'd left Poole. Doug told him. Akin reacted without surprise.

"Amos Poole says you're too big for your britches."

"He told you that?"

"I checked your references. What Amos had to say about you won't qualify you for a Horatio Alger award, but it was more than enough to make me like you." Akin chuckled. "Some of us think Amos Poole's a bit too big for his britches. You're hired."

Akin was an open-faced, avuncular man in his late fifties who tended to treat Doug as if he were his son. Akin's brother-in-law, Ned McDevitt, was an architect and Hastings's most aggressive developer, then in the midst of planning two new subdivisions. Much to his satisfaction, Doug was hired primarily to design not only the street lighting in each of the subdivisions but also all interior wiring for the hundred-odd houses. McDevitt Homes were advertised to be state-of-the art: "Power pre-installed of sufficient voltage to accommodate all the promised conveniences of tomorrow—electric refrigerators, electric stoves, superheterodyne radios, floor lamps—and enough wall outlets (no more unsightly ceiling drops) to let you put them wherever you want them."

No less forward-looking than his brother-in-law, Mr. Akin saw a future in retailing. He expanded his shop, added a showroom, and began to sell ice refrigerators ("Make your Ice Box a Frigidaire"), electric irons, lamps and lamp bulbs, and extension cords. When Doug showed him his home-made crystal set, Akin immediately saw a market for a do-it-yourself construction kit. For several months thereafter Doug spent his evenings assembling and packaging kits, each complete with "never-fail" instructions of his own composition. Materials for each kit cost about two dollars, plus four dollars for a pair of Brandes earphones. Mr. Akin sold them for eleven dollars apiece and for each one sold he paid Doug a dollar and a half for building and demonstrating them. When they proved to be especially popular with teenage boys, Doug canvassed the dozen or more shop teachers in the area high schools and persuaded them, in exchange for free kits, to assign crystal-set assembly as homework. For the better part of a year, kit sales provided a modest addition to his salary. Maude was able to hire a part-time maid and for a while she allowed herself to feel secure and hopeful.

Radio had come to have an irresistible attraction for Doug, a virgin landscape that beckoned to be explored. He wrote his old professor at Tech asking for anything he might be able to tell him about the transmission of sound and the social and commercial implications of the nascent radio industry. In return he received a long bibliography that for weeks had him spending his lunch hours at the USC library. His face flushed with excitement and his body freshly energized, he reported to Maude after each venture into the literature, sometimes sounding as if he were quoting. "Imagine," he said, moved one day to summarize what he'd learned from his reading. "In only a few years every family in America will have a radio in the living room—not a crystal set but a set housed in a cabinet with a cone speaker, so everybody can listen at the same time. No more earphones. Think about it—we'll be able to hear the president speaking to Congress, and descriptions of big events, political conventions for instance, while they're happening, and news around the clock, and concerts and opera and lectures. There'll be the best medical advice and cooking schools and bedtime stories. There'll be broadcasts of plays and boxing matches and tennis at Wimbledon—all the things we can only read about after the fact. Radio is going to bring us all together, north and south and east and west, and we'll come to appreciate what we have in common and be better able to cope with our differences. I tell you, Maude, it's going to be wonderful, a whole new world, a new way of living."

Impressed by his eloquence, she did not risk disputing him. She did, however, think he might have overlooked a few things. "I don't want to throw water on your lovely fire," she said tentatively. "But darling, how do we get from here to there? How much is all this going to cost? Who's going to pay for it?"

His face relaxed in thought. "People will have to buy their own receivers, of course. Maybe we'll have to sell subscriptions for transmission and programming costs."

"And how do you propose to keep the people from listening who don't subscribe?"

"Well," he said, frowning. "If not subscribers, advertisers. The same people who advertise in magazines and newspapers. They'll pay for it." He slapped his knee, struck by a revelation. "You're right, Maude. The time has come to concentrate on the sending end."

A moment's reflection was enough to validate his insight.

The crystal set was already beginning to lose its appeal, many early purchasers of the kits having abandoned them when the novelty wore off. It was not always easy to bring in a distant station—and in 1921 distant stations were all there were. Reception was uncertain, static hard to control. Even the most curious listeners were tiring of time signals, irrelevant weather reports, and occasional bursts of band music.

But he believed with the faith of a prophet that with the invention of the vacuum tube radio was about to take off. "Reception is going to be easier and clearer," he predicted in a conversation over lunch with Strut. "The big question is, what'll be on the air that's worth receiving. We need a station right here in Hastings. Under local ownership, with local talent."

Two years before, recognizing that he had only a limited aptitude for engineering, Strut had entered USC law school, meaning to join an uncle in corporate practice. He was now a few months short of a degree and already looking for clients.

"Why don't you build one?" he suggested to Doug, not quite sure that he meant it. "A radio station, I mean. I could help you get incorporated, get a license, sell stock maybe—that sort of thing."

"Maude," he announced, shouting as he entered the house that evening. "We're going into business."

She came in from the kitchen, wiping her hands on her apron.

"We?"

"You, me, and Strut. We're going to start a radio station."

She took a deep breath. "Does this mean you'll be leaving Mr. Akin?"

"Maybe," he said.

Her heart sank.

Doug did leave his job with Akin, but the parting was amicable. Fortunately there was a bright young engineer on the staff prepared to replace him. Though reluctant to see him go, Mr. Akin raised no serious objections once assured that Doug could complete all pending assignments before he left. Moreover, he promised Doug he could have his job back, or one comparable, should the new venture not pan out. Doug tried to talk Akin into buying shares of stock in the company, which Strut figured had to be capitalized at thirty thousand dollars, but Akin shook his head. "I wish you well, Doug," he said, "but I'm overextended right now and my so-called discretionary income is running low."

"But you may be missing the opportunity of a lifetime, Mr. Akin."

"I don't think so, Douglas. If you want to know what I really think—radio is a marvelous invention but it has no commercial possibilities. Nobody has a clue how to make any money with it."

"How about with advertising? Why can't radio be used to sell things?"

"An absurd idea. Direct advertising on radio is a well-nigh impossibility."

"By direct advertising you mean what?"

"Specific sales messages—you know, something more than merely mentioning the name of a sponsor."

"Why not? Why can't that kind of advertising work on radio?"

"Because listeners won't stand for it," Akin said patiently. "Would you like to invite a bunch of pitch men into your living room—turn your home into a medicine show?"

"So you think radio has to be left to schools and nonprofits."

"And maybe a few big corporations—newspapers, appliance manufacturers, maybe Metropolitan Life and a few other insurance companies—outfits that would like to own a radio station for the publicity value and the name recognition."

"You really believe that, Mr. Akin?"

"If there's money to be made in radio," Akin said emphatically, "it'll be at the receiving end, where I am. When you get licensed and on the air, I expect to sell a lot of radio sets."

"Well," Doug said, rising to go, "I'd hoped you'd see it as I do and we might keep on working together."

Akin smiled; much as he liked Doug, he had hardly thought of him as a junior partner. "I'll miss you, too," he said, affectionately. "But I have to say, I think you've made a reckless decision. You're making a mistake." He caught a faint expression of condescension in Doug's eyes and it momentarily annoyed him. "Don't be a fool, Doug. There's nothing more foolish than a man who's too far ahead of his time."

And on that semi-sour note, Doug shook his hand and left.

Throughout the summer and fall of 1922, Doug busied himself with plans for WSC. Sometimes with Strut's help but more often alone, he worked late into the nights examining equipment catalogs and writing for bids from manufacturers, and drafting a prospectus that would satisfy the embryonic standards of the U. S. Department of Commerce. His days were spent mostly raising money; auditioning and tentatively recruiting future staff; interesting musicians, preachers, and teachers in going "on the air"; and generally promoting community support. He was by now an extraordinarily appealing salesman, with rare exceptions infecting his prospects with enthusiasm and dreams of wealth. He talked the owner of the Francis Marion Hotel, which happened to be the tallest building in three counties, into letting him build the transmission tower on the roof ("We'll put the hotel's name in lights on the tower. It'll become a town landmark!") and creating an acceptable studio out of a little-used storage room on the floor below. He sold an option for two thousand shares, at seven dollars and fifty cents a share, to the board of Carolina Power & Light and another option for fifteen hundred shares to Hastings's most prosperous automobile dealer, both collectible on the day the license was approved. Strut's uncle was down for four hundred shares and, in a touching act of faith, Maude transferred fifteen hundred dollars from her inheritance account and put it in escrow toward two hundred shares. When Ned McDevitt, who apparently did not share his brother-in-law's skepticism, volunteered to buy five hundred more, Doug was almost ecstatic in the certainty that he'd soon have more than enough in pledges to meet start-up costs.

During these months Maude viewed Doug's behavior with a pleasure edged with apprehension. Success, or the prospect of it, became him. She was glad to see him so happy, so absorbed, so sure of himself. But she could not escape the feeling that this was but a transient episode, that it was only a matter of time before the sky fell. For much of the time she also felt lonely; his mind seemed everywhere but on her and home.

Damon was now going on four and required a lot of attention, none of which Doug seemed to have the time or inclination to give. It was perhaps this that worried her most. Time after time she watched him at the dining table, concentrating on some numbers, while Damon hugged his daddy's knees, cooing to be noticed. Finally she could contain her irritation no longer.

One evening, Damon reached up and looked as if he was about to climb in Doug's lap, perhaps to pull at the document his father had on the table before him. Doug gave him a brush with the back of his hand. Damon dissolved into tears. Scooping the child up in her arms, Maude left the room.

When she returned a few minutes minute later, there was fury in her eyes.

"This is too much, Doug," she said heatedly. "You're not even aware of your own son."

He dropped his jaw, not quite comprehending.

"I don't care how important all this is," she told him bitterly. "—or how involved you are in this monomaniacal obsession of yours. You've got to cut it out. Don't you know what you're doing to us?"

"Doing to us? I'm not doing anything to us. I thought I was doing everything for us."

"The devil you are. You're so preoccupied with your—your pipe dream—you don't know what you're missing. And one of the things you're missing is Damon. If you keep this up he'll be grown and neither of you will have ever known the other. I can't stand it."

He rose and reached out to hug her.

"Don't you dare," she said.

His shoulders slumped. He looked genuinely contrite. "I'm sorry, Maude, but you do understand, don't you? This is my chance—"

"Your chance! To do what? You should have told me," she said, and instantly regretted saying it. "I didn't know I was marrying Tom Swift or one of the fun-loving Rover Boys."

She burst into tears, drained of her anger. He kissed her and held her close to his chest until the tension left her shoulders. "I'll go now," he said, "and introduce myself to Damon."

In September he put in the mail to Washington his prospectus for a 5000-watt, clear-channel station. Two weeks later he received a brief note of acknowledgment. After that, for six weeks or more, he heard nothing. Surprisingly, he maintained his high spirits, as Maude observed with concern, by a kind of categorical optimism and a manic show of energy. He was enormously buoyed by reaction of his shareholders to the prospectus. Ned McDevitt called it "the clearest, most convincing feasibility statement I've ever read," and comments from the others were only slightly less complimentary. Although he was living on his savings, he spent as if he thought the money would never run out. He bought himself a set of clubs and took up golf and paid the club pro two dollars a lesson. He played tennis three afternoons a week. Whenever Strut and Trudy were available to sit with Damon, he took Maude to the movies. There was a new young actor named Rudolf Valentino appearing as Armand in *Camille*. (Maude thought he was "gorgeous" and talked Trudy into going to a matinee showing so she could see him again.) All told, they saw eleven movies during September and October. To round out their calendar, on alternate Tuesday evenings they had three couples in for bridge. Doug volunteered to accompany Maude to Wednesday night prayer meeting, he washed dishes and polished the furniture, and he insisted that he be the one to bathe Damon every night before bedtime. He behaved as if any vacant hour would invite an intolerable anxiety.

The ax fell with the morning mail the Tuesday after Thanksgiving:

Dear Mr. Krueger:

I regret to inform you that we have had to reject your proposal. There is, as you know, limited air space for AM signals. Until we complete a comprehensive assignment plan, our agency considers it wise to restrict broadcasting to one station in each metropolitan area and to favor petitioners with established records in public education or communications.

Our compliments on a splendidly conceived proposal."

Sincerely,

D. G. Smith

U. S. Department of Commerce

He phoned Strut and read him the letter.

"I was just picking up the phone to call you," Strut said. "Have you seen the noon edition of today's *Courier*?"

"No. Why?"

"We had some heavy competition. That petitioner with a record in public communications is the *Daily Courier*."

For a moment Doug couldn't speak.

"Did you hear me, Doug? Are you there?"

Doug swallowed. "I'm here."

"It's all politics, Doug. In everything but name they're all a bunch of dirty Republicans."

"I guess it's over," Doug said softly. A moment later he had a second thought. "You think there might be a chance for us to get a management contract to build and run the thing?"

"Not a prayer," Strut said. "You know who the *Courier* lists as the general contractor?"

Doug held his breath.

Strut laughed sourly. "Amos Poole."

"Oh my God." Doug racked his brain to think of something to say that wouldn't sound paranoid. "Could we appeal?"

"I don't know," Strut replied patiently. "I don't think there's a provision for appeal. I don't think I'd advise it in any circumstance. We'd have to show evidence of fraud in the filing, and I think we'd have a hard time—meaning it might take a lot of money and a lot of time—even getting our hands on a copy of the *Courier*'s proposal and all the supporting documents, much less proving fraud. Besides, Doug, do you really want to take on City Hall and the Chamber of Commerce? Do you know how much power the *Courier* can swing in this town?"

Doug felt his body sag. "I never felt more defeated in my life."

Strut made a sound somewhere between a sigh and a chuckle. "Poor Doug. Poor good ol' Doug."

"You're laughing."

"Not really. I was just thinking. You know what your problem is? A man's got to do two things to get ahead and make good in this country. Work hard and kiss ass. You've never learned to kiss ass."

He had hardly put down the phone when it rang. It was Helen calling from Chesterton. "Papa's been hurt," she said between loud sobs. Dr. Pitts says he's dying and may not last the day."

His attention was diverted by Maude's appearance. She wanted to know whom he was talking to. "Helen," he told her, cupping his hand over the receiver. "Something's gone wrong with Papa. This, too—" and he handed her the letter from Washington.

"I'm sorry, Helen, what did you say?"

"I said Papa's dying. There was an accident and his heart's been damaged. Dr. Pitts says there's nothing to be done. He may die before morning."

Doug was having trouble concentrating.

"You say he's dying?"

"Doug, are you listening? I said he's had a fatal blow to the heart." Her words were almost lost in her sobs. "An accident."

"What kind of accident? How did it happen?"

"I don't know exactly," she said with annoyance. "He was helping James unload some new caskets. They fell off the truck and one of them—one of those heavy steel things—crushed him in the chest. His heart."

Doug rose shakily to his feet and tried to imagine the scene in Chesterton. "Where is he?"

"Memorial Hospital."

"Does Mother know?"

"Of course she knows. She's with him now."

Maude was tugging at his sleeve. "Just a minute, Helen." He turned to Maude. "Papa's dying."

Maude was still looking at the letter, shocked, appalled by its implications. In her distress, she could only partially take in what Doug was telling her now. It struck her that the two messages, coming as they did almost at the same time, constituted some sort of capricious joke by a merciless God. Despite herself, she gave a slight moan.

"If you want to see him before he dies," she heard Helen screaming into the phone, "you better get over here. Now!"

"I'll be there shortly after dark. Can you have Walt meet me at the station? "

She said she would. They hung up.

Maude moved to him and put her hand under his chin, pulling his head closer to hers. All the color had left his face. It was paler, more ashen, than she had ever seen it. His eyes registered something beyond physical pain, a despair beyond surrender. She put her arms around him and held him in a firm embrace. She had a strong impulse to let go and bawl, but she didn't, restrained intuitively by fear of the emotional torrent her tears might bring on and engulf them both. At that moment she felt that something youthful, something rich with hope and promise, was slipping away, that the buoyancy, the exuberance in him that had first endeared him to her and in large part sustained their marriage, was fast being lost. Standing awkwardly with her arms in his, she kissed him everywhere her lips could reach.

After a while he straightened himself and pulled his arms away. He looked at the Seth Thomas on the mantle. "If I hurry," he said with effort, "I can catch the noon express to Atlanta and be in Chesterton before eight tonight." His mind raced forward, speculating on what he would find when he got there. "I'll go in what I'm wearing, but I may be gone most of the week. I'll take the oxford gray suit. I should have five or six fresh collars, and some clean BVDs."

His love and appreciation of her suddenly overflowed. He pulled her back to him and held her tightly to his chest, hoping she couldn't see that his eyes were watering. "I'll phone you tonight," he said, swallowing hard. "Maybe you could call me a cab. Later, call Helen and remind her to have Walt meet me at the depot. And maybe you ought to call Trudy and see if you can leave Damon with her and Strut. You may have to join me tomorrow."

She nodded. "I'll help you pack."

His body took him to the depot by muscle memory. He felt numb, unfeeling, and tired to the point of exhaustion. He had already accepted his father's death. If Helen's account of the accident was accurate, it seemed inevitable. Doug, however, felt neither sorrow nor grief. If he mourned, it was for a father he never had, from some sense that he had been deprived of a birthright. His loss had occurred long ago, somewhere in his childhood. Now, to be honest, what he felt was an abiding resentment. That, plus an irritation that his father's death was coming at this particular time. There were consequences that he was not ready to face, awkward questions about their relationship that he could never answer and would pain him to only half-answer. The few days ahead were not going to be easy.

Chesterton, Georgia, was a proud little community but too much like most of the other towns created by acts of the state legislature and public auction to be called distinguished. There was a central square, in the middle of which stood the county court-house and a statue of a Confederate soldier facing north. Next in dominance was the old McIntosh Tavern, dating from 1828 and made of sixteen-foot hewn oak logs, now restored into an eight-room hostelry catering mostly to visitors on county business and to the Rotarians who met there for lunch every Tuesday. From its porch once could see the marquee of the Bijou ("Coming: Lon Chaney in *The Phantom of the Opera*") and surrounding the square was a series of low two-story buildings, a few faced with brick but most of pine siding. Most of the ground stories were occupied by merchants: Jenson's Drug Store ("The oldest family-owned pharmacy in Georgia"), a shoe repair shop, a hardware store, a dry goods store, a bakery, the Citizens' Bank, a dry cleaner, a stationery shop ("Books and gifts for people who care"), and—in the northeast corner—Krueger's Furniture and Funeral Arrangements. Over the hardware store was the local Masonic lodge and above the other shops were the offices of the county's two dentists, eight lawyers, and ten doctors. Feeding into the square were the town's four main streets, with residences that, as one approached the outskirts, went from shotgun cottages to mansions, three of them, like the Kruegers', designed by an architect who had a commendable but incomplete grasp of Greek Revival. Interspersed were a few warehouses, a small hospital, the Methodist, Baptist, and Presbyterian churches, two public schools, the campus of the A&M College, four car lots, the Andersen Cotton Mills, and the Peacock Gin. To the west, at the town limits, was Cabbagetown, where most of the town's Negroes lived. In 1923 there were no more than six hundred automobiles in Chesterton, although there were four automobile agencies; most of the roads were yet to be paved.

Doug's train was fifteen minutes ahead of schedule. It brought him to the Chesterton station at sunset, just as a windless, tranquil sky was fading from blue to dark. The air was fresh and cool. Oddly, now that he was here, he felt no urgency to see his father. Rather than phone Walt to say he'd arrived early, he decided to stand on the platform and wait. He had the platform to himself, for the few other passengers who'd left the train with him had scattered quickly. He leaned against a post, glad to be standing after sitting four hours in the cramped coach. He breathed deeply, lit a cigarette, and let his thoughts drift with the smoke.

The last time he'd been in Chesterton, other than for an overnight or weekend visit, was the summer between his freshman and sophomore years at Tech. It was the summer of 1914. He was seventeen. He realized now that those few months represented his last chance to take on the role his father had expected of him. There had been a series of confrontations, some trivial, some with serious and delayed consequences, but it was not until the end of that summer that both came to acknowledge that Doug was cut from a different cloth: Douglas Krueger was never meant to be an undertaker, even less a country squire. The following spring, the threads that held them together were broken once and for all. When the separation came, Doug felt released, relieved, but nevertheless insecure in his new freedom. What his father must have felt he could only guess. Anger, for sure. Disappointment? Failure? Rejection? Probably.

That was the summer Archduke Franz Ferdinand was assassinated and seventeen million men from eight European nations mobilized for war. For Doug, it was the summer he met Azalie. For its long-term consequence, the affair was all too short-lived. He met her in June; by the following February it was over.

Chester County, like most of west Georgia, was struck that summer by a mysterious infection that defied local diagnosis. With its chills and fevers, it resembled malaria, but the aches that accompanied it seemed to be more in muscles than bones and not quite so disabling. Though miserable for the month that it usually took to run its course, victims regained strength rather quickly once they survived the worst of it. In 1914 the medical profession was only beginning to understand bacterial infections and it would be years before it discovered viruses. In the absence of any other explanation, Dr. Pitts assumed that it was mosquito-borne and that there was nothing to do but keep patients quiet. His standard prescription was bed rest, plenty of water, aspirin four times a day. and hourly applications of ice on the forehead.

Doug was the first in his family to come down with it. For three weeks he was in and out of consciousness, alternately hot with fever and shaking with chills, and always weak from pain. For much of the time his mother was at his bedside, holding his right hand in hers and regularly wiping his face with a cold damp cloth.

One morning, however, as the fevers were beginning to subside, he awoke aware that she had been replaced by a stranger, a young woman whom he would forever associate with the smell of lemon, Ivory soap, and Jergen's lotion. He opened his eyes to a vision of incredible beauty.

Without thinking, he raised his arm and touched her cheek lightly with his fingers. She responded with twinkling eyes and a wide grin.

"I just wanted to be sure you're real," he said haltingly. He tried to raise himself on his elbow and failed.

"I'm real all right," she said, putting a cold towel on his forehead. "My name's Azalie."

"Spell it for me."

"A-Z-A-L-I-E."

"Azalie? I never met anybody named Azalie before."

"And you never will again," she said. "My mother meant to name me Azalea, but the birth certificate came back Azalie. They'd made a mistake at the vital statistics office. Mother liked the sound of Azalie and the name stuck."

She had a thermometer in her hand. "Lie back down and let me take your temperature."

He put his head on the pillow and opened his mouth. She inserted the thermometer under his tongue, putting her free hand on his forehead. Her touch sent a shiver through him.

"You're running maybe a degree of fever," she told him, reading the thermometer. "But Dr. Pitts says the worst is over for you."

"Are you a nurse?"

She gave an embarrassed laugh, "Not much of one, but my mama taught me how to care for sick people. Your father asked me to come help Bessie and take care of you while your mother is down. She's caught it too."

"Since when? Yesterday?"

She nodded. "I guess your father will be next." Her voice was soft and though she had an accent common to the region, her speech had none of the common stretching of syllables within words. He wondered where she might have grown up.

She had, in fact, grown up in Chesterton. Her father was Fred Taylor, a tall, broad-shouldered, exceptionally dignified Negro with smooth skin the color of a ripening banana, and short-cropped gray hair, the only hint that he might be more than fifty. He was the town barber—in fact, the only professional barber in the county; he had apprenticed at Herndon's in Atlanta. He operated two shops, one with three chairs on the square for white men, the other with two chairs in Cabbagetown. Sometimes, by appointment, he did simple cuts for women in their homes. Catherine, who thought highly of his work and knew him to be much smarter than he let on, called him "The Venerable Blade." Nobody knew how much money he earned. He and his family—his wife and Azalie, their only child—lived modestly and thriftily and he was careful to see that they did nothing to offend the ruling whites. His male patrons gossiped and argued heatedly about baseball and politics. Resolutely, he kept his opinions to himself, by and large limiting his conversations to harmless jokes, the weather, birth, deaths, and cotton. But underneath his friendly, non-committal manner lay a consuming hatred of segregation, and probably of all whites, and an equally burning ambition for Azalie. He worked and saved primarily for her full emancipation.

Although he had never gotten beyond the eighth grade, Taylor was by no means an uneducated man. Once he learned to read, he read hungrily and indiscriminately. He held to two ideas: education was the key to getting ahead, and if you were colored you had to be twice as competent as the nearest white to get anywhere at all. Determined to give Azalie every advantage he could during her years in Chesterton's one sub-standard school for blacks, he sent her with her mother to Atlanta twice a month for special tutoring. After his wife died, by which time his daughter was ready for high school, he arranged for Azalie to go to Philadelphia and enter a Quaker-run boarding school. She early outdistanced her peers in Chesterton; by the time she was seventeen there were few adults in town who could match her knowledge of the humanities and the physical sciences. As Fred Taylor had intended from the day of her birth, she was unprepared to spend her life in Chesterton.

"I'm here just for the summer," she told Doug, and then what came to him like a non sequitur: "My father's not very healthy."

"Fred Taylor? He's been cutting my hair, twice a month, from the first day I was able to sit in his chair. He looks great to me."

"Turn over and I'll give you a back rub."

He turned over with effort. She pulled down his pajama coat and splashed alcohol on his back. At the first touch of her fingers he got a hard on.

"Daddy's got a weak heart," she went on, massaging his shoulders. "He's always looked a lot younger than he is. He married late."

"Where're you going when you leave Chesterton? Back to Philadelphia?"

"No. I'm going to college, in Massachusetts. I'm a sophomore at Smith. On a scholarship."

"Where did you learn to do what you're doing?"

"At a community hospital near Bryn Mawr. I worked there last year part-time as a nurse's aide."

He gave a sound—half sigh, half moan—of approaching satisfaction. "I think you better quit," he said, "or we're both going to be embarrassed."

The next morning he woke up to find her sitting close to the bed, a sketchbook in her lap, drawing his face in deft, bold pencil strokes. He had leaned to his right on the pillow and his hair had fallen over his brow.

"Do you mind?" she asked. "You looked so sweet, so peaceful, so—" She searched for the right word. "So guileless."

He was flattered. "May I have it when you're done?"

"You really should be drawn in chalk. In color. I love your hair." She paused. "I love your voice, too."

"I love you," he said, he was hot and sweating.

She put the sketchbook aside and stood up. "Are you ready for breakfast? Sit yourself up, if you can. I won't be but a minute."

He had dried himself and brushed his hair by the time she returned. She poured him a cup of coffee and buttered his toast. "Would you like me to read to you while you eat?"

"Yes. Anything."

"Do you like poetry?

"It depends."

"Tell me if you like this." She reached into a pocket and pulled out a Little Blue Book edition of *The Rubaiyat.*

> Into this universe
> and why not knowing,
> like water willy-nilly flowing.

And out of it
as wind along the waste,
I know not whither,
willy-nilly blowing.

"Go on," he said.

Then to the lip of this poor earthen urn
I lean'd, the secret of my life to learn:
And lip to lip it murmured—"While you live,
Drink!—for, once dead, you never shall return."

"Wow!" he said sleepily. She read until his eyes grew heavy and he dozed off. She leaned over, kissed his forehead, and left the room quietly.

He became stronger and more alert. One morning she asked him to get up and sit in a chair while she made the bed. She leaned over to remove the bedsheets, exposing her cleavage, and the sight stirred him to an erection. He watched her with extraordinary interest as she replaced the bottom sheet. She was smoothing the corners when, in a state of urgent lubricity, he pushed her down on the bed.

My God, what was he doing? He pulled back, breathless, expecting her to slap his face or to break into tears. Instead, she received him playfully, and when they were done she smiled and said, "That was nice. We should try it again sometime."

Over the next three months they did it, he counted, eight times. They would have done it more but in 1914 in a small town in Georgia a young white boy and a young Negro woman were at grave risk even to be seen together. To carry off an affair undetected took ingenuity, a lot of energy, and more faith than sense. They managed it by lying artfully to their parents about their whereabouts and by meeting at dusk and going to places unvisited by Chesterton residents after dark—the small park that bordered the town cemetery, the far side of Chester Lake, the picnic grounds at the site of the Baptist Camp Meeting. They did it usually on a blanket over grass, in the cover of big oaks, or on the back seat of the Kruegers'

Model-T. It wasn't too bad in warm or cool weather, but when the rains came, beginning in late August, they found outdoor lovemaking messy and uncomfortable, no matter how many fantasies they brought to it.

Azalie seemed to regard sex as no more than a natural bodily function, something to be neither feared nor romanticized but enjoyed. Though no virgin, neither was she promiscuous; there had been only two boys before Doug. He had never known a girl like her, and he never would again. He was in awe of her.

She was easygoing and straightforward, conditioned to be respectful of everybody regardless of age but overly impressed by nobody. She moved with the beauty of a healthy cat; it gave him pleasure every time to see her pour herself into a chair. There was often a twinkle in her eyes, as if she alone could see the irony in some commonplace event. She read serious fiction, and she seemed to be reading at every otherwise unoccupied moment. In the time he knew her, she went through *Heart of Darkness*, *Pudd'n Head Wilson*, *Tess of the D'Urbervilles*, and *Huckleberry Finn* (twice). When they parted, she was half-way through *Madame Bovary*. In the months she was in and out of the Krueger house, first attending him, then his mother, he saw her reading only one work of nonfiction. It was *The Soul of Black Folk*.

"I never think of you as black," he told her.

She winced. "I'm not often allowed to forget it."

He looked for the name of the author. "I never heard of W. E. B. Dubois."

"You will," she said. And that was the only time she ever mentioned race in the whole time he knew her.

Somehow Azalie had escaped the crippling effects of the Protestant fundamentalism that passed for conventional wisdom in Chesterton. Her years with the Quakers in Philadelphia had produced in her a strong social commitment but had done nothing to increase her fidelity to the church or her belief in the supernatural. "If there is a God," she told Doug during one of their post-coital discussions, "he's got a lot to answer for." Like Margaret Fuller accepting the universe, she accepted the predatory order of nature but she had only contempt for whatever force had invented it.

"If I weren't such a coward, I'd be a vegetarian." She thought the human being inherently both good and evil. The purpose of civilization, she said, was to make it possible for people to be more good than bad; organized society was nothing more than a system of rewards and punishments. She felt obligated as one of the enlightened members of that society to do whatever she could to help bring out the best in people. That meant, among other things, working to relieve the poor, to conquer disease, to insure justice. It helped, too, to expose them regularly to love, truth, and beauty. Nothing you did was likely to make any difference, she said, returning to her usual air of cynicism. "But one has to try."

"Good grief!" Doug said, trying hard to absorb it all. "That mind of yours scares me to death. Here you are, with everything all figured out, and here I am just trying to get from here till Tuesday."

Whereupon she giggled, rolled over on her back, and sang, "Come on baby, let's have some fun. Put your hot dog in my bun."

In September, immediately after Labor Day, she went North for her sophomore year at Smith and he returned to Tech. Shortly before Thanksgiving her father died suddenly of cardiac arrest. When she came back to Chesterton for the funeral, he talked with her by phone, but they agreed he would be making himself too conspicuous were he to attend the service. (White boys were not expected to make a special effort to honor a black barber.) After his burial, she went promptly back to Northhampton.

He did not see her again until January, when she came South again to wrap up her father's estate. On her way back, he arranged for them to spend a weekend together in Atlanta. They spent it at the Imperial, a declining mid-town hotel whose chief virtues were that it was clean and reasonably quiet. To conceal her give-away hair, she wore a helmet-type hat when they registered. He signed them in as husband and wife and there were no questions asked.

They ventured out of their room only once, for Sunday dinner at the home of one of her friends near the Atlanta University campus.

Her mood was strangely somber when they got back to the room later that evening. They made love, but joylessly, and when they were finished she spoke with a sob in her throat.

"We have to stop seeing each other," she said.

Startled, he asked her to repeat herself.

"It's over, Doug," she said. "We've got to put an end to this."

"What in the world are you talking about?"

"Oh Doug," she said, in a tone of exasperation. "You should know, as well as I do. This can't continue. There's no way we can live together and be—" She faltered.

"Be what?"

"Be true to ourselves, I guess." She stroked his chest tenderly. "How do you think I feel, faking that I'm a white woman just for us to have some privacy? That's how it'll be from here on. Even in Philadelphia, or New York, or Chicago, there's no way we could live normal lives. We'd be shunned, pitied, constantly discriminated against. I don't want any of that."

He didn't know quite what to say. "But Azalie, I love you."

"That's the problem," she said. "I may love you, too. But love's not enough." She looked at him tearfully, apologetically. "I just can't, Doug. There are a lot of things I want to do with my life, and it's hard enough just being colored. I can't take on the additional burden of a mixed marriage. We have to call it quits before it goes any further."

He pled with her. She was adamant. He put her on the train the next morning. It would be twenty years before he saw her again.

"Mr. Doug?"

Doug roused himself. "That you, Walt? I didn't hear you drive up."

"It's your daddy's new Packard," Walt said, stooping to pick up Doug's suitcase. "It's quiet as a toaster."

He followed Walt off the station platform and onto the small parking lot. The only car in view was a black twelve-cylinder sedan, "Wow," Doug said. Walt laughed softly. "Ain't this somethin'? It's a Twin Six. Latest model. Your papa's pride and joy."

"I bet," Doug said, climbing into the passenger seat.

Walt turned on the ignition but paused for Doug to answer before pulling out of the lot.

"I suppose you want to go straight to the hospital."

"Please. Helen says he may go any minute."

The Packard moved forward and passed a street light. For a moment Doug could see Walt clearly. He was coal black and he had the features of an African prince. Except for the purity of his color, little about him was remindful of the friend Doug had known as a child.

"Anything I can do for you while you're here, Mr. Doug?" Walt was saying.

"Yeah. You can stop calling me Mr. Doug."

Walt returned the smile and spoke teasingly. "You changed your name?"

"Oh, come off it, Walt. We've known each other all our lives."

Walt grunted. "Not really. Maybe only for the first twelve years."

Walt was right, and at the memory Doug felt a flash of tribal shame. Until the coming of puberty and the response to some unstated racial code, he and Walt had napped together, eaten together, played together, shared secrets, wrestled and fought and made up like brothers. Doug remembered him as a cheerful, unusually bright young boy. He wondered how much of that sharp intelligence had been dulled and lost in the years since, under the suffocating effects of segregation. He sighed heavily. They rode in silence for several minutes.

"I'm sorry about your papa."

"Thanks."

"Your papa was—is—a fine man."

Doug turned in his seat to catch Walt's expression. What he saw was a blank page, a stoicism that must have taken years to develop.

"You know better than that. My father is a cheat—a goddam hypocrite and an incredibly clever one."

Walt grunted again. "I went to his office a couple of weeks ago."

"You went to see him on business?"

"I went to see him with a petition from the folks in Cabbagetown. We need a new classroom and some indoor privies. We could use a high school."

"What's wrong with the high school you've got?"

"You've been away too long. We ain't got no high school. The school board figures colored boys go—or ought to go—into the fields or one of the mills after grammar school. We don't need a high school."

"And what did Papa say to you?"

"He said he'd think about it."

After a long pause, "Maybe you could speak to your father."

"I'll speak to my mother."

Walt nodded, as if he understood. They continued in silence until they reached the access road to Memorial Hospital. Walt slowed the car and said, almost explosively. "You're a hero in Cabbagetown. Did you know that?"

"Me?"

"Because of what you did for Gus."

Doug didn't know what to say.

Walt said, "Don't think we don't know what that must have cost you."

Doug made no reply. He reached to the back seat for his bag. He opened the door and got out.

"Thanks, Walt. I'll see you back at the house." He leaned over to shake his hand.

"Yeah," Walt said. He shifted into first.

Doug kept his hand on the door.

"Walt?"

Walt regarded him expectantly.

"I'm no hero." He gave Walt a squeeze on the shoulder, "But I think you may be."

He picked up his bag and walked wearily up the steps to the door of the hospital. Helen greeted him with the news that his father had died less than an hour ago, apparently in no pain. "Mother was with him when he went. Dave took her home just a few minutes ago." They were waiting now for the ambulance to take Papa to the funeral home, his own, where James would embalm the body. "Do you want to see him?" she asked. Doug shook his head. "Then I think we may as well go home. I've phoned Luther Taggert, the preacher. He's coming over in about a half hour and help us plan the service."

At the house, Doug phoned Maude. She said she'd be over tomorrow afternoon, that Trudy and Strut would be pleased to take care of Damon. He then moved upstairs to speak to his mother.

Her bedroom door was ajar. For a moment he stood at the threshold, caught at the lovely sight of her. She was sitting in a rocker near the window, looking pensively at the garden below. She was wearing a coral colored robe that flared at the neck, revealing a bit of lace at the throat and the collar of the matching nightgown. The lamplight brought out the warmth of her beige skin and the highlights in her brown-gray hair, which she had let down for the night and now fell in waves to her shoulders. She sensed his presence and said, without turning. "Why don't you come in, dearest."

He moved toward her and kissed her on the cheek. "I was just struck how handsome a woman you are."

She gave him a wan smile. "This is no time for romance," she said. He relaxed and laughed with her.

"How are you managing, Mother?"

"Don't worry about me. It just came too suddenly. I'm in a bit of shock, I guess."

"Is there anything I can do?"

She sighed. "I've asked Helen to make all the arrangements. She's a capable girl. I'm just going to sit here awhile, till I feel sleepy."

She looked at him as if she were seeing him for the first time. "You look tired, dear. Maude wrote me how hard you've been working. Maybe you ought to let up for awhile." She paused. "You feel sad about your father, don't you?"

"A little. But not for the usual reasons."

"I can imagine," she said, cryptically. "Your father was a man of many parts. I've lost a husband and you've lost a father, and you'll miss parts of him I never knew."

"I'm sure."

"I don't know what I'll miss the most—his dumb two-line jokes or his addiction to buttermilk and ginger snaps." She shook her head, as if to correct herself. "No, what I think I'll miss most will be Sunday mornings.

He's brought me breakfast in bed every Sunday morning for the past forty years." She sighed. "Now, kiss me good-night, and let's both get some rest. Tomorrow's going to be a hard day."

Doug was hardly aware of the passage of the next few hours. Luther Taggart the preacher, a red-haired, middle-aged man who seemed to have been programmed for end-of-life duties, asked for the names of Papa Krueger's favorite hymns and Bible verses. He said he would be honored to do the eulogy but wondered if the family might like to have somebody else, a business associate perhaps, say a few words in remembrance. Doug was tempted to suggest that one of the sharecroppers be invited to speak, but held his tongue. His main contribution to the evening was to nod agreement every time Helen made a decision.

Next morning, Walt and James brought the body to the house and laid it out on a simple catafalque in the study. After breakfast, Doug went there, closed the door behind him, and stood, alone, looking down on his father's face.

James had done a good job. The cheeks were firmer and the fat under the eyes removed, and his father's lips had been shaped in his signature smile of false comfort. He seemed invulnerable, as he had in life, self-protected by a posture of aggressive innocence.

"You son of a bitch," Doug said under his breath.

From mid-morning till ten that night, friends, neighbors, business acquaintances, came to pay their respects, hundreds of them, some of them bringing flowers and covered dishes. His mother had sensibly decided to stay in her room, admitting only her closest and oldest friends. Doug, Helen, and Helen's two teen-age daughters received condolences for the family. Shortly before noon, they were joined by Aunt Sarah, Papa Krueger's younger and only sister, who had driven over from Edwardsville. They stood together in the foyer, hands outstretched to shake the hands being offered, mouthing "thank you" mindlessly in response to comments of dubious sincerity: "He was such a fine man." "He was a joy and a blessing." "It's not ours to question the ways of the Lord." "He'll be missed on Earth, but God must have had a reason to call him so early." Doug stood in the one spot for several hours. His body was stiff, his face fixed in an expression of solemn welcome, his intelligence forfeited to a round of cheerless clichés.

They took turns for lunch. Sarah and Doug went together. They sat across from each other in the kitchen at a small pine table loaded with plates of food brought by the neighbors—fried chicken, potato salad, bean casserole, apple pie.

Twelve years ago, when Doug had seen her last, Sarah had been busy as a cricket, friendly, quick to laugh, an open-hearted, appealing young woman—not pretty and with a regrettable tendency to quote too readily from the Gospels but nonetheless the kind of woman you wanted to hug. Today her face was drawn and colorless, her hair pulled back into an old lady's bun, her dress an unrelieved black sheath. She smelled of glycerine and rose water. She looked tired.

"I was sorry to miss your wedding, Douglas," she said. She grimaced. "Better I should have missed my own."

He was taken by her candor. "As I remember, at the time you were with your husband in Colorado."

"I was in Colorado. God knows where Josephus was."

"He'd left you?"

"Not exactly. He'd go and come. I often didn't know where he was."

"You know where he is now?"

"No, and I don't care to know." She gave a rueful smile. "It was not a happy marriage."

They ate silently for a while and when she spoke again it was to reflect on her brother's death.

"I suppose whenever somebody dies you have something to regret. I'd been meaning for months to get in touch with Jacob. We hardly ever saw each other. After Daddy died five years ago I'd thought he might invite me to visit him in Chesterton. He never did, and I'd about decided to invite myself. Somehow, I couldn't bring myself. Now I'm sorry."

"You and Papa were never close, were you?"

"Not really. He was six years older and he was restless to leave home, even in his teens. He hated farming."

"You came back to Edwardsville after your mother died?"

"And after Josephus left me one last time, with just enough money in the cookie jar for a ticket home. Daddy was getting on. He wasn't well and needed care."

"I take it Papa was of no help."

She took a bite of pie before answering. "One is not supposed to speak ill of the dead."

"So Papa was of no help. But he was doing well by then, wasn't he—with the store and the funeral parlor and all that real estate?"

"Jacob always did well." She paused. "If he couldn't help himself, he knew how to get whatever help he needed. Did you know that he got Daddy to lend him two thousand dollars to buy the furniture store?"

"I never knew how he managed to buy the store. Did he pay Grandpa back?"

"I don't know. I don't think so." Again, a pause. "But I shouldn't complain. Daddy left me the house and eighty acres of the best bottomland in Alabama."

Doug swallowed his coffee and pushed back his chair. "I guess we ought to get back to the receiving line."

"I guess." She started clearing the table, and then, reaching for comfort, she said, "The Lord giveth and the Lord taketh away."

The mild December day grew increasingly warm; God knows what it would have been like had Papa died in June. Doug was dressed in a dark wool suit, a white linen shirt, a starched collar, and a black-and-white rep tie. By two o'clock he was sweating heavily. He kept counting the minutes until four, when he could leave to meet Maude's train.

He drove to the station in his mother's Buick and had some difficulty getting the hang of it. The clutch was slow and the motor had a habit of hesitating on turns. The trip took him longer than he'd figured. By the time he'd cleared the square and gotten to the depot her train had come and gone. Maude was waiting for him on the platform.

He rarely had the chance to see her from a distance, without her knowing she was being watched, and he took a moment now to savor the image. She was waiting, patient and self-possessed, with no visible signs of anxiety. Her head was encased in a tight blue cloche. She was wearing a long pleated pink shirtwaist and a navy blue skirt that came just below her knees, commanding attention to her firm calves and long slender legs. At the sight of her he dropped his jaw and took in a deep breath.

Suddenly he was in a disorienting vertiginous descent, as if all the ego in him had been released and he was left deflated, miserably inadequate to do whatever was required of him. What the hell was happening to him? He tried to bring her back in focus and was seized with an impotence he had never experienced before. He was not the man for her. She needed somebody more stable, more responsible, somebody who wouldn't be victimized by mercurial enthusiasms, somebody who wasn't subject to paralysis from guilt, somebody whose competence was equal to his love. He didn't deserve her. She deserved better.

He opened the car window and sucked in the cool evening air. A moment later, he had recovered himself and was walking toward her, his arms poised for an embrace. "It must be dreadful for you, darling," she was saying as he opened the car door for her.

He didn't attempt an answer until he was behind the wheel and had turned the starter. "I guess," he said. "But I don't seem to be feeling much of anything. I feel like a sleepwalker."

"Maybe that's not so bad," she ventured. "It may help get you through these next awful days."

"How was Damon?"

"Precious. He asked where you were."

"And what did you tell him?"

"I tried to tell him that we both had to be away for several days, but that we'd be back real soon. And that we loved him and would miss him."

"You think he understands?"

"Probably more than we can possibly tell. How's Catherine taking it?'

"In stride." He thought for a moment. "She may have loved him. I find it hard to believe she liked him. But then Mother has always been good at hiding her feelings, putting up a brave front, that sort of thing. Anyway, I don't think we have to worry about her. She asked me to tell you that she'd be joining us for dinner."

"I hope it's soon. I'm a little hungry."

"Me, too," he said. "I ate lunch early. I didn't sleep last night, either. Maybe that's why I'm feeling so woozy."

"You'll sleep better tonight," she said. She sounded surprisingly maternal.

Bessie fashioned a modest banquet out of some of the food neighbors had brought—black bean soup, more fried chicken, an oyster casserole, potatoes au gratin, green beans in some sort of peanut sauce, cucumber and tomato salad, and pecan pie. He ate a full plate and began to feel somewhat sturdier. After dinner, he excused himself and relieved Helen in the receiving line, while Maude accompanied Catherine to her bedroom upstairs. The number of callers swelled during the first hour after supper, then diminished to a trickle. At nine-thirty or thereabouts he told Helen goodnight and went to the back porch for a last cigarette. He took a seat in a rocker and searched the sky for stars.

He ought to be able to think of something to thank Papa for aside from the seminal contribution to his birth. He was, however, at something of a loss. His father had kept him in material comfort, and for that he should be grateful, but otherwise what had his father done for him except to ignore him or to make his life miserable? He had taught him to swim, yes, but by taking him in a rowboat out to the middle of Chester Lake and tossing him overboard. He had taught him to ride, too—by hoisting him into the saddle, giving Jenny a whack on her rump, and telling him to hold on when the mare bolted for the barn. The experiences were enough to still give him occasional nightmares. He should be grateful?

A figure was moving out of the shadows into the moonlight on the porch steps. It was James, standing as a lifetime of obeisance to white men had taught him to stand—slightly stooped, chin up, cap in hand. His bald head glistened in the moonlight. His eyes were filled with anxiety.

"James? Is something the matter?"

"I need to talk with you, Mr. Doug."

"Here, come sit down."

"I'd rather stand if you don't mind, Mr. Doug."

Doug moved his rocker closer.

"What is it you want to tell me?"

James coughed to clear his throat.

"It wasn't no accident, Mr. Doug. I killed him."

Doug's blood turned to ice. "You what?"

"I killed him. I didn't mean to, but I killed him."

"You're saying you killed my father?"

"Yessuh. We were working that coffin off the truck, to take it into the showroom. Your daddy was on the ground, holding it one end. I was at the other end, in the truck, lifting it so we could slide it onto the dolly. The coffin was heavy and both of us was sweatin' and strainin' and your daddy got out of sorts. He kept fussing at me and calling me boy, until he called me boy once too often." He stopped.

"And then?"

"I dropped my end of the coffin and gave it a shove. It caught him in the chest and smashed him. I went to him soon's I knowed what I'd done. Nothin'—"

Doug's pulse quickened. He thought very fast. "Did anybody see you?"

"No, suh."

"Have you told anybody else?"

"No, suh."

"Don't."

"Shouldn't I tell Sheriff Knight?"

Doug took a deep breath and pointed to the rocker next to his. "Please sit down, James." James sat. He held himself stiffly and transferred the cap to his lap. "Now listen very carefully. No, James, do not tell the sheriff. Don't tell anybody. Do you hear me? Don't tell a living soul."

James nodded. He looked dubious.

"Believe me," Doug said, "there'll be nothing but grief for everybody if it's ever reported that my father died from anything but an accident. What you just told me will be our secret, something between you and me, and nobody else. I mean nobody else. Do you understand?"

James began to weep. "I didn't mean to do it."

"Of course you didn't."

"Somethin' flew all over me. I couldn't take it no more."

Doug reached over and put his right hand in James'. "Nobody who knows you could ever think you did it on purpose. It was an accident, James. Let's make sure to keep it that way."

"Your daddy was good to me, mostly."

Doug gave him a handkerchief. "If you think so," he said. "It may also comfort you to know, I think Papa provoked you, and not just this once. It's a wonder you didn't strike him—it's a wonder somebody didn't kill him—years ago."

James wiped his eyes. "You shouldn't talk about your papa that way."

"I have neither your grace nor your charity," Doug said.

When, shaken, he went upstairs to the bedroom, he found Maude standing in front of his old bookcase, apparently having interrupted herself in the process of undressing. She was leaning over, inspecting the framed pictures and certificates on the wall.

"You never told me you were the class valedictorian," she said, squinting at his high school diploma.

He tried to sound casual. "Or that I played in the school band," he said, pointing to a picture of himself—fourteen years old and skinny, sagging under the weight of a tuba.

"You were a manly little follow," she said.

He had moved into the center of the room under the ceiling light. What she saw in his face caused her to suck in her breath.

"What's happened to you, sweetheart? Are you sick?"

He sank heavily onto the bed. "I hope not. The day's just getting to me. I'm worn out."

"We both could use some rest," she said. "Let's hurry and get undressed."

"Not just yet." He rubbed his temples. "Where were we?"

She looked again at the photograph. "I was saying what a manly young fellow you were."

He managed a smile. "But not a very precocious one." He left the bed and pulled a book off the shelf. "You want to see the first book I ever read cover to cover?" He showed it to her. It was *Tom Swift in Captivity*. "Don't believe mother if she ever tells you it was *Pilgrim's Progress*."

She laughed. "I thought you were going to show me *The Brothers Karamazov*."

"God, Maude, I love you."

She brushed a lock of hair off his face and kissed him on the forehead. "I love you too, baby." Her eyes followed the line of pennants and stopped at another photograph. It showed him in a khaki uniform, leggings, and a combat helmet.

"There's so much about you I don't know," she said, thinking about his year in the army. "Sometimes I think, there was never a time when we weren't together, that nothing at all happened in my life till I met you, and then there are other times—like now—when I realize that there were years when you and I lived separate lives and I resent having been left out of your life, and I want to know everything there is to know about you before we met." She sighed. "The thing is, no matter how much time we have left, there'll always be things about you and your past I'll never get to know."

He began to feel uncomfortable. "It's probably just as well," he said. He began to undress. "You want to take a bath?"

"You go first," she told him, and gestured toward the photo albums, the scrapbooks, the arrowhead collection, the baseball cards, the model rail cars, and the other boyhood souvenirs on the shelves. "I'd like to enjoy the relics for a minute or two." When he returned in pajamas ten minutes later, she was returning his high school yearbook to the shelf. She eyed him sweetly, then picked a robe out of her bag and went down the hall to the bathroom. He turned off the overhead light, leaving the room in shadow. He lay on the bed and thought about James and his father. Lord, he asked himself, how many secrets can a man keep? He closed his eyes and sank into a swamp of sorrow and incertitude.

Stifling a cry, he roused himself and turned the light back on, his hands shaking and his right leg in a cramp. He put his head in his hands and thought to himself, "Dear God, what's happening to me?" He pulled himself upright and massaged the cramp out of his leg. Then he heard the door open and turned to see her come in, smiling.

She switched off the light and slipped off her robe.

They made love. He fell promptly asleep and slept soundly, dreamlessly, through the night.

IN 1923 THE POPULATION of Chesterton was about five thousand, of whom half were under the age of sixteen and nearly a thousand were Negroes. Of the two thousand adult whites, Doug figured that as many as fifteen hundred came to the First Methodist Church that morning for his father's funeral service. Dressed in their Sabbath best, they filled the main auditorium, stood in the aisles, packed themselves in the choir loft. Had he not entirely appreciated it before, it was impressed on him then that hardly a soul in town had escaped his father's reach. In every home in town there was some piece of furniture bought at Krueger's, some member of every family had been embalmed and buried by Krueger's, no businessman had prospered without a carry-over loan, and few lot owners had been able to finance their homes without a mortgage from the bank his father had helped organize. Apparently, no Sunday-Go-to-Church-Christian in the county had escaped his guileful benediction.

A dozen or more self-supporting wreaths and a forest of sprays—larkspur, lilies, iris, chrysanthemums, holly, carnations, roses—filled the chancel and lined the walls. Late morning light pierced the stained-glass windows and played off the evergreens and the blossoms. What Doug remembered as a simple, faintly Octagon-soap scented, Protestant church had been transformed into a perfumed, rainbow-hued alien temple. Miss Ruth at the organ played "How Firm a Foundation" and "Be Still My Soul" while the audience took their seats. Immediately afterward a male quartet, members of the Sunday School class his father had taught for eighteen years, sang "Jesus, Lover of My Soul," "Asleep in Jesus," and "It is Well Within My Soul." Sitting down front in the family pew, Doug was weak and half-sick with anger at the irony of the whole display. Though he appeared to be showing only appropriate grief; his eyes were watering and he was gripping Maude's arm so hard she was wincing.

"Jacob Zackarias Krueger was a kind friend, a loving husband, a righteous man of peace, and a servant of God," the Rev. Luther Taggart was saying from the pulpit, only his face, sweet and serious as he'd practiced it to be, showing above the floral offerings. "This town can claim no better citizen. Jacob Krueger was a man who had convictions and stood by them. He did not hesitate to let his position be known on matters that concerned his community, his county, and his state. He was a man of the highest type of character and one whom a benign providence had smiled upon through all the years he was permitted to live. The church, the Sunday School, the prayer meeting, all will miss him more than words can tell. For he was a faithful man and feared God above men."

At eleven the next morning the family assembled around a conference table in Tom Luck's office on the square for a reading of the will. Helen and Catherine were in black, Maude in mauve. Helen's husband Dave, who had been Jacob Krueger's deputy at the store and presumably would be his successor on the bank board, was wearing loose-fitting gray flannel and a small figured blue tie. He was a large, barrel-chested man with big strong hands, his palms reddened and calloused, and he looked miscast as the executive he hoped to be. He sat stiffly, expectantly, a bit too self-conscious in his presumptive role as favored son and heir. Doug eyed him without envy. He knew what was coming, at least partly what was coming, and he had long been resigned to it; the only hurt left was with the awkwardness that would come when Maude and the others learned of it. His father had worked it so that the only inference the family could draw was that Doug had rejected his inheritance, forfeiting a life of security and well-being, out of some inexplicable, capricious gesture of principle. How Doug wished that were true, for if he had done that he could have salvaged some measure of pride. As it was, he was left only with a killing sense of incompetence. At a critical moment, he had been able to summon neither the integrity nor the guts to reject his father, and for that failure he would live the rest of his life in self-contempt. He sat waiting, sick with apprehension, his hands clenched in his lap, his buttocks tight and his stomach touched with nausea, desperate for the morning to be behind him.

Tom Luck had been Papa Krueger's lawyer for as long as Doug could remember. He was the kind of lawyer, Papa once said of him, who was "to be prized more for his loyalty than his judgment," but he had served the family faithfully and Doug had nothing but good will for him. He remembered Luck most vividly, and most fondly, as his scoutmaster—then a friendly, reproachfully healthy man in his forties, with the physique of a mountain climber. He was now approaching sixty, graying, and showing the beginning of a pot, but he still moved gracefully and his eyes had not lost their alertness. He welcomed the group with a hearty smile only slightly subdued for the occasion and went immediately to business.

"Mr. Krueger revised his will only three weeks ago," he said, passing out carbon copies. "Unless I hear an objection, I'll skip the boilerplate and go immediately to the bequests." He proceeded to read:

"I direct that at the time of my death the sum of $5,000 be given and bequeathed to my daughter, Helen Krueger Nelson; $3,500 to my friend and employee, James Oliver Sims; $5,000 to the First Methodist Church of Chesterton; and $5,000 to the general operating fund of the West Georgia Academy. All of the rest, residue and remainder of my estate property, both real and personal, tangible and intangible, of whatsoever nature and wheresoever situate, I give, devise, and bequeath to my wife, Catherine Newcomb Krueger, if she is living at the time of my death. I further direct that upon her death, all my residual estate be given and bequeathed to my daughter, Helen Krueger Nelson."

Luck paused. "This next paragraph contains the revision Mr. Krueger instructed me to make on November 10." Doug closed his eyes; here it comes. "At his request, I bequeath no part of my estate to my son, Douglas Patrick Krueger, and direct that nothing of estate be bequeathed him by my successive heirs. I leave my son only my sorrowful affection." There was a gasp from Maude and an audible intake of breath from the others. "In his name, however," Luck continued, "I bequeath $15,000 to the Chester County School Authority to be used exclusively for the construction of a new building, or buildings, with all facilities necessary for the comfort, health, and education of Negro children in the elementary and high-school grades. I further direct that this new facility be named the Douglas Krueger School and that the name Douglas be prominently emphasized in every public reference."

Luck put down the will and focused on Catherine. "I am named executor, a function I'll be honored to carry out according to your wishes, Catherine."

Catherine nodded. She sat silent for a moment, her face expressionless, and when she spoke it was hardly above a whisper. "I must say, my husband was full of surprises."

Stunned or embarrassed, the others sat in silence. Dave, sitting across from Doug, raised an eyebrow. He opened his mouth and immediately closed it.

"Yes, Dave? You looked—"

"I was just wondering. I never knew you had an interest in Negro education."

"Apparently my father did," Doug answered weakly.

Helen was clearing her throat. "Mr. Luck, does this mean that I will get everything upon mother's death, and Doug nothing?"

"That's how your father wanted it. He insisted that it was done at Douglas's request."

"Is that true, Doug?" Helen asked him.

Whatever he said, he knew, would be clumsy and unconvincing.

He gave a shrug, trusting it to be dismissive, and lied. "I've already received more than my share of the estate, Helen."

She frowned. "How strange," she said. Helen turned back to Luck. "Do we know the value of the estate?"

Luck coughed. "We estimate it to be in excess of a million dollars. The auditors say they'll be able to give us an accurate figure in two weeks."

Maude could hardly face Doug. She was angry, hurt, and confused, and she did not want him to mistake or oversimplify her reaction as disappointment. If it were true that he had requested to be written out of his father's will, then he had sacrificed his and his son's heritage to some quixotic statement of honor, and she could never forgive him. But, as often as she had seen him show an impulse to take the moral high ground, she could not quite bring herself to believe that he would have done such a costly and irretrievable thing as this willingly. There was surely something else involved, something too painful, too personal for him to disclose. In any event, she decided that this was not the time for her to try to find out. So she said nothing. Instead, as if to reassure them both, she reached across the table and squeezed his hand. He responded with a rueful smile.

They were back on the street when he stopped and asked Maude and his mother to go on without him. "I think I left my hat," he told them. "I won't be but a minute. Wait for me in the car."

He found Luck at his desk signing letters.

"What can I do for you, Doug?"

"I'm sorry to trouble you, Mr. Luck, but did father have any other message for me?"

Luck looked at him sympathetically. He shook his head. "I asked," he said. "Your father said he'd already said everything he had to say to you."

"But is there anything you can tell me?" His voice shook. "Where is she? Is it a boy or a girl?"

Luck got up from his chair, came around the desk, and reached out hesitantly as if to console him." You know I can't answer that, Doug. I vowed to your father—"

"I know, I know," Doug said, in despair and frustration. And then he could restrain himself no longer. He let go and the tears flowed. "You have no idea what it's like, not knowing."

Tom Luck put out his arms and wrapped Doug in a giant hug. "Go ahead, boy, let it out. You only think I don't know."

He waited for Doug to stop heaving and handed him a handkerchief.

"I hate myself," Doug said, his voice cracking. "I've been such a coward."

"You're not a coward, son." Luck searched his mind for some final words of comfort. "You just tried to break a taboo. Our tribe hasn't learned yet to tolerate its taboo-breakers."

He cleared his throat and went on before Doug could say anything.

"I can tell you this much. She and your child are well provided for, and will be for the rest of their lives. Your father has seen to that."

He got back to the car in time to wave good-bye to Dave and Helen. It was about eleven when they returned to the house. His head was swimming. "If you don't mind," he said to Maude as they were hanging up their coats, "I'd like to lie down for a few minutes before lunch."

There were a lot of questions she wanted to ask him but one look at his pale face told her this was not the time. "Of course, darling," she said. She went with him to the upstairs bedroom and helped him out of his jacket and shoes. He lay down and closed his eyes. "I'll call you when lunch is ready," she said. She pulled down the shade and left him.

He was developing a headache. His mind was swarming with more images than it could accommodate. Then, like a spinning reel of film that stopped when it found the story it had been searching for, it brought vividly into focus the events of that awful afternoon.

IT WAS LATE IN THE SPRING QUARTER of his sophomore year at Tech. Her call caught him in his room at the Phi Delt house. It was on a Friday and he didn't sleep for the next three nights. His mouth was dry no matter how much water he drank. He felt weak and tremulous. Scotch didn't help. On Monday he called his father and told him he had to see him. "I'm booking you a room at the Kimball House. If you catch the four-thirty, you should be here by six. "

"Well, now," his father responded, no more moved than if he'd been asked for the loan of a nickel. "That'll be a little difficult, Douglas. I have a meeting with the mayor at—"

"Papa, I have to talk to you. I'm in trouble."

His father hesitated. Doug held his breath. Finally, "I'll be there."

"And Papa, don't tell Mother."

When he got to the hotel five minutes before seven, Doug found his father already in his room. He was sitting in an easy chair under a ceiling fan. He had removed his jacket and collar and was dabbing at his forehead with a bath cloth soaked in cold water. He was drinking iced tea.

"This better be worth the trip, Douglas," he said in greeting. "Have you heard the one about the doctor who—"

"Papa," Doug interrupted, "you know Azalie Taylor, don't you?

"The colored girl? Old Fred's daughter?"

Doug nodded. "She's pregnant."

"So?"

"By me."

His father put down his glass and reached into his coat pocket for a cigar. Neither said anything until he'd trimmed the cigar and lit it.

"Well, now, son, I guess you're not the first horny young man who's knocked up a whore."

Doug bit his lip. "She's not a whore, Papa."

"It's still not the end of the world," his father said, amazingly calm. He took a long swallow of tea. "You want me to arrange for an abortion?"

"She doesn't want an abortion. And neither do I, I guess."

His father looked at him in disbelief. "Then what do you want?"

The words came in a desperate burst. "I want to marry her. I love her."

"You can't be serious," his father said, trying hard to understand what he was hearing. "You can't love a nigger, much less marry one. It's one thing to go for a little nigger poontang, but to marry a nigger?"

"Why not?"

"Deuteronomy Seven Three," his father said in a tone of finality.

"Sir?"

"Deuteronomy Seven Three. Look it up."

A pause. His father blew out a cloud of cigar smoke. "Besides, I won't let you. It would break your mother's heart."

"Azalie and I—we could live in New York, or Chicago."

"Ridiculous. Even if you could—it would break your mother's heart."

"Papa, please. I'm in love with her."

"Well, you'll just have to get over it." His father spoke coldly and then relaxed into locker-room sympathy: "You think I don't know what it's like to lust after a piece of black pussy?"

"Please, Papa."

His father grunted. How could God have given him such a self-righteous ass for a son? He tried a new tack. "All right, I'll try not to offend your precious sensibilities. But we do have a problem, don't we? Who else knows?"

"Nobody."

"So the lady won't hold for an abortion. I won't speculate as to why, but let's just assume abortion is out of the question. She's going to have your baby and I'm going to be grandfather to a bastard pickaninny. You can't marry her. That's the other given. So what's the honorable thing to do, Doug?"

Doug shook his head, despairing.

"The honorable thing," his father said, with no emotion and in tones of a negotiating accountant, "the honorable thing is to see that she gets medical care and has the baby safely, and that the two of them are somehow guaranteed the means of support for the rest of their lives."

He waited for Doug to take this in. "Do you know where I'm headed, Douglas?"

Doug wasn't sure. He was terrified at what might be coming.

"That'll cost money. A considerable amount of money. Over years."

Doug nodded slowly. His father sucked audibly on his cigar and brushed ashes off his shirtfront before resuming.

"I can find the money, Doug. It may not come in ways that your refined conscience will approve of, but I can raise the money. And I can make sure she gets it and doesn't squander it."

Doug raised his head hopefully. "How?"

"I'll get Tom Luck to work out a spendthrift trust." His father took a long puff on his cigar and went on, his eyes betraying the satisfaction of a man who knew he had the upper hand. "There will, however, be some caveats."

"Yes, sir?"

"One, the money will come out of what otherwise you'd receive as your share of my estate when I die. I'll be writing you out of my will."

Doug gulped and nodded. "How will you explain this to mother and Helen?"

"I'll make it clear that you didn't want my money. I'll let them know—or ask Luck to tell them when the will is processed—that that's how you wanted it. You didn't want my tainted money. You requested that I leave you out."

"And you think they'll buy that?"

"Helen, I assure you, will be happy to hear it. Your mother may wonder and be a bit disappointed, but she's always been tolerant of your ten-cent idealism. She'll accept it."

Doug nodded glumly. "What are the other conditions?"

"One, you'll never say a word about any of this to your mother. She must never know."

Doug nodded again.

"And you must promise me that you'll never see this girl again. Never."

Doug shook his head. He began to tremble.

"I can't promise that. I won't."

His father shrugged. Doug rose in a sudden surge of rebellion and went to the door. "You can keep your money—and your conditions," he said recklessly. "I'm going."

His father laughed. "Don't be an idiot, Douglas. How old are you? Eighteen? If I disown you, how could you support this woman and a child? Do you want to add poverty to your litany of sins?"

Doug felt sick. He cracked the door, closed it again, and stepped back into the room, turning to face his father. Later, all he would remember of that moment was that somewhere down the hall a gramophone was playing "I'm Always Chasing Rainbows." The image of his father swam, spun, and dissolved before him. He began to retch. He fell to his knees and vomited. His father went to the bathroom and returned with a cold wet towel. "Get up," he commanded.

Doug rose unsteadily.

His father slapped him hard in the face.

"Go clean yourself. We have to talk about details."

The memory faded but he made no effort to get out of bed. He lay with his eyes open, his body rigid, his mind caught in a web of shame, frustration, and anger. Aware that Maude was at the bedside, he turned slightly in a gesture of recognition; his face remained expressionless.

"Here," she was saying, "I've brought you a cold wet towel. Rouse yourself. Bessie has lunch waiting for us."

He moved his legs to the side of the bed and took the towel from her. She kissed him. "Try to hurry, darling. I'll be downstairs with Catherine."

After she left the room, he got up and went to the bathroom. He splashed cold water in his eyes and rubbed his cheeks with the wet towel. He combed his hair. Back in the bedroom he raised the window and took several deep breaths of the December air. He began to feel more like himself. He put on his jacket and went downstairs.

They had a quick lunch of chicken salad, banana nut bread, and strong black coffee. Maude had explained to Catherine that the Montagues were leaving tomorrow for a week in Miami and that she and Doug would have to reclaim Damon before bedtime, which meant catching the 2:30 train to Hastings. With her usual efficiency, she had packed earlier that morning.

When Maude went upstairs to freshen up for the trip, Doug had a few minutes at the dining table alone with Catherine. Almost as if to avoid the questions he knew she must have in her head, he found himself urging her to spend the upcoming holidays with them. "This will be Damon's first Christmas, at least the first that he'll remember, and it would be a great joy to have you share it with us."

"Of course," she said readily. "That would be good for all of us." Her face had lost its accustomed expression of sardonic humor and her shoulders were drooping. She fixed her eyes on Doug's and spoke from her heart. "It isn't true, is it darling?" she asked, "that you asked to be cut out of the will?"

"No, mother," he said honestly. "It's more complicated than that."

Catherine sighed. "Maybe someday you'll tell me what went on between you and your father." She looked down at her empty plate. "Though I'm not sure that I want to know. Jacob could be a difficult man—and I'm afraid a mean one when crossed."

God, how much had this sweet, smart, generous, forgiving, deceived woman suppressed and denied all these years?

Despite himself, Doug began to weep.

"I think I must be overtired," he said, drying his eyes. They rose and embraced, exchanging an understanding beyond the ability of either to articulate.

4

Once settled in their seats on the Georgia Atlantic Express to Hastings, Maude figured the time had come. "Now, Doug—"

She was at the point of wondering if he would ever answer her when his voice reached her in a tone she'd never heard from him before. It was the lifeless voice of a man who had dropped all defenses and all pretenses, a man who could not tell what to make of himself and needed help of a sort he could not define. She shuddered, her mind suddenly struck by a half remembered line from Kierkegaard.

"I guess the first thing to say is that I did not ask Papa to write me out of his will. Perhaps I should have, because to take his money, knowing how he got it—well, it would be hard, living with the shame. But it was his idea to disown me, not mine. And the second thing I want you to understand is that it was not for charity, and not for any degree of affection for me, and certainly not for any concern for colored people, that he left the fifteen thousand dollars to build a Negro school. He did it all for spite. He hated me, probably as much as I hated him."

Momentarily shocked into silence, Maude told herself that surely she must have misunderstood him. "Speak up, darling," she said when she could find her voice. "You're not in a confessional, you know."

He smiled feebly and repeated what he had just told her. "My father was a hypocrite, a crook, a cheat, and a sham," he went on.

"How do you know?"

"The summer I was sixteen, I worked for him. I'd worked in the store on occasion before, in short spurts between times at camp and summer school, but it was always scut work, opening boxes and moving furniture, helping with window displays and helping lift coffins into the hearse, sweeping the floors, that sort of thing. But that summer—I guess he had the idea that I ought to start learning the business—he put me part-time in the office and part-time on the floor and part-time with Dave and James in the embalming room."

He gave a slight shudder. "I couldn't stand working with corpses. Papa insisted that Dave teach me, and I tried. I really did. But the whole procedure made me sick. First, you have to drain the blood vessels and the body cavity, and if you're lucky to have done that without running into clots, you inject a fluid—formaldehyde and alcohol mostly—usually with some dye added for the hands and face. From there on it's mostly cosmetic. All the families want the face to be lifelike and that takes a lot of skill, wiring the gums and fixing the eye caps." He shuddered again. "I never learned to do it very well and I could never get through it without getting nauseated. Daddy called me a sissy and took me off it and put me to work in the office instead. And it was there that I began to get an idea of what went on."

"What was going on?"

"One day a farmer came in to pay his bill. His child, a little boy, maybe five or six years old, had died a week or so before. The child had been buried in a plain pine coffin. I knew, because I had helped bury him. Well, I was in the store alone at the time and the bill the man showed me was for an expensive mahogany steel-lined coffin, top of the line. I told the man there'd been a mistake. I changed the price on the bill and charged him for the pine coffin, about three hundred dollars less. When Papa came in later that afternoon, I told him what I'd done and he went livid."

"What did he say?"

"He first said I was wrong, that the man had wanted the best available coffin for his little boy. I said then there must have been a mistake, and I got out the inventory records and showed him that we still had the mahogany coffin in stock. He shouted me down—how dare I dispute him—called me a self-righteous little prig and worse. He sat me down and gave me a lecture. 'We're not selling caskets and grave sites,' he said. 'We're selling peace of mind and an opportunity for next of kin to show love and respect for the deceased. The higher the price of the funeral, the more the respect.' He said that most of the fools want to pay as much as they can, not only to impress their neighbors but because they believe the higher the price the surer the ticket to heaven."

"What did you say?"

"Not much. I said I must have read the invoices wrong, and I was sorry. 'Sorry!' he yelled. 'You've lost us three hundred dollars.' I offered to go the farmer and say I'd been wrong, that his son had in fact been buried in the more expensive casket and try to collect from him. Papa looked for a moment as if he was considering it. Then he told me we should just forget it, say nothing more about it, he'd take the loss. Then I realized that I hadn't made a mistake at all."

"He'd done it on purpose?"

"Deliberately and habitually. He'd sell the bereaved a high-price casket, put the dead body in it for the viewing, then switch to a cheap wood casket just before the body was taken to the gravesite."

"But wouldn't the family know they were getting a cheaper coffin?"

"No. After the viewing, just before the funeral procession left for the cemetery, he'd drape the cheap casket in a blanket of flowers. 'My personal offering to the family,' he'd say, and they'd all thank him and tell him what a sweet man he was. Then he'd bury the blanket with the body, and they'd never know."

"My Lord," she said.

"After that he took me off accounts. Said he didn't want me doing paper work any more and assigned me to the furniture floor and body-preparation. But I still saw enough, heard enough, to understand how he was making his money." He stared through the train's soot-streaked window at the gray leafless landscape, as barren as his own wounded spirit.

"Go on."

"I'd overhear him on the phone negotiating with suppliers—he was very good at pitting competitors against each other and working out under-the-counter deals, usually at a salesman's expense—and bargaining with delinquent customers. With customers it was always with honey in his mouth. They couldn't meet a payment, or they were three months' delinquent? In lieu of cash, maybe he could settle for a piece of land. Did they have any land they could let him have? And usually they did—five acres, ten, fifteen—and in exchange, at prices way under market value, they'd get funeral expenses or furniture bills cleared. He always managed to make them feel grateful.

"He was obsessive about land. He must have owned half the land in Chester County. He bought thousands of acres at foreclosure sales and was absolutely uncanny figuring out where the population was going. What land he couldn't sell for a good profit he'd plant in cotton. He must have had contracts with as many as ten sharecroppers. Last year they brought in twenty-four hundred bales of cotton.

"Six years ago he got an inside tip that the state water authority was planning to turn Baker's Pond into a reservoir. He went out and secretly bought all the land around the perimeter, every square foot of it, an acre or so at a time. Two years later, when an Atlanta developer started planning home sites around the lake, he refused to sell. He held out instead for forty-five percent ownership of the development company. Lakeview Estates is now the county's fanciest neighborhood. Papa must have netted a thousand dollars a lot."

"I guess few people would see anything crooked about that," Maude ventured. "That just sounds like smart business."

"Everything he did was just good business, according to Papa. If he saw a farmer in distress, he'd offer to buy some of his furniture, furniture that might have been in the man's family for generations. Papa would buy it as used furniture, for a song, and ship it to an antique dealer in Atlanta, where it would go for at least ten times more than he paid for it. And he always made these people think he'd done them a favor."

He stopped long enough to light a cigarette.

"It was James who clued me to his treatment of the sharecroppers. You've heard of James. He's the 'faithful employee' Papa left the thirty-five hundred dollars to. James and I got to be good friends after Papa banished me to the furniture department. A big, powerful man, strong as an ox. James could read labels but not much more, and he could hardly write his name, but he was loaded with common sense and he was sweet-natured and cheerful, though I doubt if he had much to smile about. He was almost sixty when I got to know him, though he'd been working for Papa since he was in his teens. I never heard Papa call him anything but Boy. I was surprised that Papa knew enough or cared enough about him to be able to put his full name in the will."

He took a deep drag and let the smoke out slowly. "One slow afternoon while we were taking stock James reached into his overalls and pulled out a crumpled sheet of paper and handed it to me. It was a statement in Papa's handwriting, addressed to somebody named Sam Barry. James asked me to look at it. "Sam Barry's my cousin," he told me. "He's been sharecropping for your father maybe three, four years. Hard as he works, he never seems to be able to get by." James was nervous, maybe thinking he was about to overstep. "'This don't look just right to me, Mr. Doug,' he said.

"I sat down and studied the invoice. It showed how much cotton Barry had produced and how much each bale had brought at auction, and how much Barry was due from the sale—fifty percent, as I remember. But it also showed charges—for seed, for fertilizer, for paint, for repairs to a wagon, for a loan: principal seven hundred and fifty dollars, interest fifty dollars. 'Your share sale, two hundred bales cotton, four thousand five hundred dollars. Less advance, four thousand, five hundred sixty dollars and fifty cents. Please pay ten dollars and fifty cents.' The man had worked a year and ended up ten dollars and fifty cents in debt."

Doug sighed. He crushed out the cigarette and lit another.

"I told James it didn't look right to me either but I didn't know what could be done about it. I asked him to leave the statement with me anyway, I'd see what I could do."

"And could you do anything?"

"No. I thought hard before I said anything to Papa. I stepped on the statement, leaving a shoeprint, and crumpled it some more, then one morning when we were alone in the store I showed it to him, said I'd found it on the floor near the front door where somebody must have dropped it. I told him this was the first sharecropper account I'd ever seen and asked him if they were all more or less like this one. He said, 'More or less. You find something wrong with the addition?' I said no, but it looked to me as if this man Barry had worked hard all year for next to nothing. Papa said, 'He should have worked harder. And it's not true that he got next to nothing. He got a new plow and he got his house painted and his doctor bills paid.' I then made the mistake of asking him about interest on the loan. 'This figures at six percent,' I said. 'I thought the usual rate is two percent.' He looked at me as if he thought me hopeless and said, 'Lord Almighty, Douglas, you don't know the first rule of business. There's no such thing as usual. You charge as much as you can get, as much as the customer is willing to pay or as much as the competition will allow. Between you and a sharecropper there ain't no competition.' I asked him how much choice Barry had been given. He laughed. 'No choice at all. That's why sharecropping has been such a good thing for us.'

"I didn't say anything more, but he knew I was bothered. 'What's the matter, boy? You don't approve of that?' I told him it didn't look right to me. I said it looked like a new form of slavery. 'So?' he asked, and he laughed again. 'You don't believe in slavery?' 'You should never have taught me the Golden Rule if you didn't mean for me to try to follow it,' I told him, trying to control myself. 'Or shown me the Declaration of Independence if you hadn't wanted me to believe it.' I'll never forget how he looked at me then. He had an expression that was half pity, half scorn, as if I were some sick animal he was going to put out of its misery. 'Oh come now, boy,' he said. 'It's time you came out of the nursery. Let me tell you something.' And he laughed again, the same laugh he gave whenever he was about to tell a joke. 'Christianity and democracy? They're very useful fictions—nothing but artful inventions to keep people like me in power.'"

For a moment they both were stunned into silence. When Maude found her voice, she spoke haltingly. "Did he really say that, Doug?"

"Word for word. How could I forget it?"

"Is there more?" She saw him reach into a coat pocket for his cigarettes. "Please, don't light another one. I'm getting a headache."

"There's more." He laced his fingers together tightly and put his hands in his lap. "The spring of 1918, I came home from Monmouth on a week's leave—" He stopped, looked out the window, and saw that houses and city streets had replaced the open fields. The train was slowing. "We're almost in Atlanta," he said, reaching for his pocket watch. "Time to change trains."

With some effort, he got their bags down from the overhead luggage rack. He helped Maude with her coat, and the two of them made their way down the aisle, off the coach and onto the main concourse. "Go on over to Track Nine," he told her. "I'll meet you there in five minutes. I've got to pee."

He found an empty stall in the men's room. Alone, he removed a flask from his inside coat pocket and took a long drink. There was indeed more to say about his father and himself. He could not yet bring himself to tell Maude everything, but having gone this far he felt committed to tell her more, whatever the risk. The prospect unnerved him.

The connecting train to Hastings was on time. It took only a few minutes to find their seats. Once settled, he took a deep breath and picked up where he'd left off.

"In the spring of 1918, we were expecting to ship out any day. I was able to get a got a week's leave before the orders were cut. I came home and found the town about to snap. Everybody looked either scared or angry or wary. People who'd been together all their lives were looking at each other as if they didn't know who they were. It was spooky. Something had happened, and I got the feeling that people were afraid the same thing was going to happen again—some of them, they seemed to want it to happen again. Well, I learned there'd been a lynching, a week before I got there. A Negro farmhand had shot and killed an overseer who'd raped his wife—at least that was the story in Cabbagetown, and I'm inclined to believe it. The landlord formed a posse of Klan members. They came riding onto the farm, all dressed in sheets and hoods. They caught the hand, forced him up a tree and out on a limb, gave him a noose and told him to tie it to the tree trunk and put his neck in it and jump. He did. As he died, James says they pumped him with more than a hundred rounds of shot."

Maude gasped. "And nobody was arrested?"

"Arrest the Klan?" His tone was sour and despairing. "Now follow me carefully. One effect of the lynching was to quiet the Negroes in town. They hardly said anything—even Bessie, who used to greet me with secret hugs and volunteer stories about Walt and her other her children, stopped talking and moved around the house like a ghost. The Negroes just seemed to pull into themselves. They no longer lingered after work but went straight home, as if they wanted to make sure nothing had happened while they were away and everything was still safe. Even the sound of the town had changed. It was all whispers and rumors, except when some good ol' boy raised his voice to swear. The general opinion seemed to be that 'niggers in the county had gotten too uppity,' and more and more often you'd hear somebody say that another lynching might be a good thing.

"A lot of the rumors were fed by the coming of a stranger. He'd come to town while I was away, had been there maybe as long as six months. He was James's nephew, a man about thirty or so, and he'd come down from Pittsburgh, James says, to do research at the college—something to do with public health facilities for Negroes and Negro migration to the North after the Civil War. He was a teacher, a sociologist, working toward a Ph. D. He was light-skinned and freckled. His hair, which was kinky enough, was almost red. He wore suits and sometimes a Panama hat and he spoke in this Yankee accent and all his sentences parsed. The white people in town looked on him with suspicion. They couldn't understand what he was doing here, and they didn't believe what they were told. One story was that he was an organizer for the AFL, sent down to organize the cotton mill; there'd been a lot of worry about the possibility of an AFL move on the Anderson Mill ever since the strikes in Atlanta and Macon a couple of years back, and I guess the arrival of any stranger would have made them worry more. There was another rumor—that he was working for the Republican party. Negroes were banned from voting in the Democratic primary, you know, and there was, I think, some effort by the few Republicans in the county to get Negroes to switch parties and vote Republican in the general election. Anyway, James's nephew—his name was Gus—was not in an easy spot. He'd already been getting anonymous messages to go back where he came from, or else, and there'd been at least one cross burning in the front yard at James's place, where Gus was staying. Well, one night there was a fire in the cotton gin. It almost burned down, and the sheriff investigated and said it was arson, and the rumor spread that Gus was the one who'd set the fire, and next thing a mob, the Klan in front, was on its way to lynch him."

"I don't think I want to hear it," Maude said, interrupting him.

"It's all right," he said, quickly reassuring her. "They didn't get him."

"Why not?"

He dropped his voice so low that she had to strain to hear him. "I was on the square, just coming out of Johnson's drug store, when word came that some white men were arming and getting ready to ride. I drove immediately to James's house where I found a line of Klansman forming at the steps to the front porch. Gus was inside. They kept shouting to him, calling him a coward and ordering him to come out. And then, just as he opened the screen door, I found myself on the porch between him and the mob. I was in my uniform and I guess I confused them. Somebody yelled, asking what the hell I was doing there, and then everybody seemed to be shouting, telling me it was none of my godamned business and to get out of the way. I held up my hand and stood as straight and as tall as I could and tried to speak in the voice of command they'd tried to teach me in basic training, and somehow I got them to shut up.

"'Turn around and go home,' I told them. 'You've got the wrong man.'

"'The hell you say. How come you know we got the wrong man?'

"And I said, 'Because this man, Gus, was with me the night the gin caught fire.'

"'You're lying,' they screamed. 'What were you doin' with a nigger after dark.' 'Where were you?'

"And I told them. I said, 'Sadie's Chapel. Gus and I were playing black jack at Sadie's Chapel.'"

Maude was puzzled. "Sadie's Chapel?"

"Chesterton's original and only den of iniquity. A whore house."

"You were in a whore house?"

"A Negro whore house. And sort of a poor man's casino—craps, blackjack, poker, betting on the numbers, simple-minded gambling. I told them Gus and I were together at Sadie's."

"And they believed you?"

"They said how could I prove it. I told them to ask Sadie."

"Then what?"

"This Klansman in the front spoke up, a high-pitched voice, not his natural voice, but distinct and loud enough to be heard. He said 'May as well break it up, boys. A Krueger don't lie. We got the wrong man.' And there was this general murmur, and then the Klansmen turned in their saddles and rode off back where they came from."

"My God," Maude said. "You could have been killed." Her eyes formed a question and she bit her lower lip. "You weren't at a whore house—a Negro whore house—were you? You made all that up, didn't you?"

"I was telling the truth. Gus and I were together at Sadie's the time the gin burned down." He looked hurt. "Now you'll hate me."

"No," she said slowly. "But I don't think I can ever again think about you quite the same way."

"I shouldn't have told you. I was a fool to have told you."

"Well, you've done more foolish things," she said. She thought about her two brothers and wondered how many indiscretions and whore-house visits they might have kept to themselves. Impulsively, she leaned over and kissed him on the cheek. "I just said I'll think of you differently from now on. I may love you all the more."

He was squirming in his seat. "I don't feel very lovable."

"I bet Gus loves you, for one," she said. "What ever became of him, and did somebody actually set the fire?"

"Gus went back to Pittsburgh, practically on the next train out of Chesterton. I think James keeps in touch with him. And no, the fire was not set. The insurance company sent down an investigator and found a short circuit, some sort of bad wire."

"Did you father know about all this?"

"I'm sure. You know the man, the Klansman, who spoke up and said I was telling the truth? I recognized his eyes and his shoes. One leg was longer than the other and one shoe was built up."

"You knew him?"

"It was Papa. It was my father."

"Oh my Lord. Did he say anything to you later?"

"Oh yes. He said I should leave town, get back to the Army, and not come home again for a long time."

It was after dark by the time they got to Hastings and well after ten by the time they found a jitney and got home. Hurriedly, they left their bags on the porch and went across the street to the Montagues to pick up Damon. Trudy had given him his bath, put him in his nightshirt, and laid him on the living-room sofa, half asleep, to wait for his mother and daddy. Though he had been told they were on the way, he had not been able to stay awake. He yawned when they kissed him, murmured something sweet but unintelligible, and fell again into sleep. Doug picked him up the warm little body, brought it close to his chest, and walked with it the few hundred feet to the house. He breathed in the smell of Pear's soap and talcum powder. He felt the steady beat of a tiny heart under the thin baby blanket. He was touched with a poignance so intense it caused him to suck in his breath.

Maude followed them into the nursery. Rather than risk awakening Damon, she left the room in semi-darkness, the only light through the window from a distant street lamp. She took Damon from Doug, placed him in his crib, covering him with a thin flannel sheet, and put his head on a small embroidered pillow, a gift from Catherine. She and Doug stood together for a moment, hand in hand, gazing in awe at this pure abstraction of innocence and vulnerability. The street light went off suddenly, casting the room in shadow, and Doug felt the quiver of a premonition. "Oh God," he prayed, his eyes closed. "Please, don't let me fail this child. Don't let me ever fail my boy."

5

In the weeks that followed, Doug forced himself to write thank-you letters to the thirteen pledged shareholders, telling them what they probably already knew, that the license had been denied. He then wrote the secretary of state to report that the WSC Corporation was being dissolved. In a mood to put the whole failed project behind him, he threw away the rejected application and its supporting documents. Maude immediately scooped them out of the waste basket. "Don't do that," she said sharply. "There may come a time, sooner than you think, when this town will have use for a second radio station, or there may be some other town—"

"I haven't the heart, Maude."

"You will, dearest," she said. "You will. Anyway, you're not going to throw all this away." She left him, carrying the files with her.

She worried. Several weeks went by. Doug made no effort to go back to work. Except for the four thousand dollars from her father's legacy that she had put in bonds, they were nearly out of money. He was drinking and smoking too much. He moved listlessly, he had little to say, and his eyes too often had the expression of a man who knew he'd lost something but couldn't remember what. He wasn't suffering from grief; of that she was sure. Something else, a near bankruptcy of the spirit, had occurred that could not be explained entirely by failure of the radio project. Nothing she did or said seemed to restore or comfort him. She came to feel increasingly helpless and alone. There was nobody she could confide in. Her parents and brothers were gone. She could not bring herself to talk about Doug's condition to his mother. She could only hope that when Catherine came for Christmas she would see for herself.

Close to desperation, she turned to Strut. She never knew what he said to Doug, or what finally moved Doug to shed his lethargy, but whatever it was—embarrassment to reveal a psychic weakness to a male peer, or what—Doug left the house one morning saying he was going to ask Mr. Akin for his old job back.

His manner remained subdued. He did, however, get to work on time and do his job creditably and, most encouragingly, his hours with Damon seemed to energize him like a tonic. One day he observed that Damon would soon be outgrowing his crib, whereupon he went out to the lumber yard, came back with maple and poplar boards in assorted sizes, went to his old workshop in the basement, and proceeded to build the frame for a child's bed. When she heard him whistling, for the first time since their return from Chesterton, she began to think he might soon be his old self.

Christmas was an unqualified joy. Doug made whistles and spinning tops and a handsome hinged toy box for Damon. He put up the tree without complaint and, although Maude trusted no hands but hers to trim it, he seemed to watch with pleasure as she dipped into a storage carton, pulled out an ornament, pondered where to put it, hung it, changed her mind, and hung it somewhere else. A lot of the ornaments had been her parents', many of them imported from Germany before the war—mouth-blown glass angels suspended in gauze, silver birds in swinging cages, artificial fruit and globes in all colors and sizes, beautifully crafted stars of polished wood, tiny wreaths of dried vines, papier-mâché figures of Santa Claus and flying reindeer, yards of red and green garland, and, the biggest prize of all, an exquisite crèche, complete with meticulous small sculptures of Mary and Joseph, barnyard animals, and the three wise men, carved from cherry and walnut.

The week before, Maude had busied herself in the kitchen. She made fruit cake, date nut cake, banana nut bread, Bourbon balls, butter mints, mincemeat tarts, and enough cookies to feed a regiment. Catherine proved to be a relaxing presence and an eminently satisfactory house guest. Her black ensembles, each of a notably understated cut, were the only reference to the recent death of her husband. She smiled readily, laughed appropriately, and personified seasonal good cheer. She made clear her approval and affection for Maude the moment Doug delivered her from the station and ushered her into the living room. Breathing in the smells of sugar and spices that wafted from the kitchen, she rolled back on her heels in a mock faint. “My Lord,” she said to Maude, greeting her with a kiss, “I’ve realized the dream of my life. I’m living in a candy store!” After sampling a Bourbon ball and a cookie, she was ecstatic. “Maude darling, you ought to be in business,” an idea she repeated often during her stay. She helped with the laundry, washed the dishes, polished the silver, made her own bed, dusted the furniture, and otherwise made herself useful without fuss, like a woman accustomed to doing her own housework, which she was not. She was marvelous with Damon, romping with him, teaching him games, and reading to him at bedtime. Before her visit was over, his vocabulary had increased by at least twenty-five words, among them “adowable,” “preshus,” and “God Awmighty,” and there was noticeable improvement in his diction. One afternoon Maude had an informal tea to introduce her to Trudy and a few other friends. They were all enchanted by her. “You’re kidding,” Evelyn Ames whispered to Maude as she was leaving. “She’s your mother-in-law?”

Her Christmas presents were thoughtful and perhaps a bit excessive. She gave Damon several picture books, a Teddy bear (his first), a sailor suit, and a five-dollar gold piece. She gave Maude a mohair coat and a gold ring set with a giant opal. (“It was my mother’s. I’ve enjoyed it for years but the time’s come for it to be passed on to a woman with young hands.”) Her gift to Doug was a check for five hundred dollars, which troubled Maude a trifle. How often before at sinking moments in Doug’s life had his mother brought him up with a check?

In any event, Doug showed his mother no signs of a wounded spirit. He said and did nothing that Christmas to suggest anything other than that all was going well with him in every department of his life. Maude was apprehensive after Catherine’s departure, preparing herself for what she had come to identify as a predictable swing in his mood. None came. The only change she detected in him was a tendency to restrain his enthusiasms. He was doing well at work. Mr. Akin gave him a raise in June and promoted him three months later, leaving him in charge when he and Mrs. Akin took off on a month-long holiday.

He got the raise as a reward for creating a new market for Akin & Company's fledgling industrial services department.

From reading the professional journals, Doug had grown excited by the potential of air-conditioning, an invention still so new that the *New York Times* put it in quotation marks. Some twenty years earlier an engineer named Carrier had invented a system for cooling the air and regulating the humidity in an overheated printing plant. Before the war, his system had been introduced successfully in a number of textile mills, in a Minneapolis mansion, and in at least two movie theaters, one in Chicago, the other in Montgomery, Alabama. Its development had been halted with the country's entry into the war, but now, in 1923, Doug reasoned that air-conditioning was about to emerge as a major industry. So convinced, he called on Joseph Pellisier, owner of the Majestic Theater.

Pelissier's office was located on the top floor over the projection booth. It was the only finished room on the floor, the rest of the space being occupied by the furnace, fading broadsides and posters, theater seats waiting for repair, dusty seasonal decorations, and two rows of wooden file cabinets, their contents known only to God and Pelissier. There were also various props salvaged from past promotions with the expectation that they would be used again—a billboard featuring John Barrymore as *Dr. Jekyll and Mr. Hyde*; horseshoes and wagon wheels mounted on a piece of split-rail fence; several Confederate uniforms; a *papier-mâché* frigate; a small facsimile of "The Iron Horse"; replicas of Charlie Chaplin's cane and derby; furled flags and rolls of bunting.

To reach Pelissier's office, Doug had to climb three flights of stairs. It was unusually warm for March and the temperature seemed to rise with every step. By the time he got there he was panting and out of breath.

Joseph Pelissier was a slight man with the pale complexion of someone who spent most of life in the dark. He wore round wire-rimmed glasses. He had a friendly face and his eyes customarily expressed the delight of a child awaiting a surprise for good behavior. To him, movies were life, blood, and a high art form. He thought of the Majestic as an opera house and he did everything he could to encourage patrons to come to his theater as if it were an occasion, say the opening night of *Rigoletto* or *La Boheme*. The Majestic's decor was appropriately grand—carpeted floors, an enormous crystal chandelier overhanging the central auditorium, papered walls, polished brass in the rest rooms, reproductions of fine European art in the lobby. If the Hollywood product was something less splendid, he was only momentarily disappointed. Next week, there would be Lillian Gish or Douglas Fairbanks, Mary Pickford, or William S. Hart (his favorite) and what was on the screen would be commensurate with the setting he gave it. The show would be worth dressing up for.

Conscious of his role as chief monitor of the arts and good taste in Hastings, Pelissier dressed well and was rarely seen without coat and tie. On this warm March afternoon, however, Doug found him at his desk in shirt sleeves and with his collar unbuttoned.

"Please excuse my appearance," he said in greeting. "It gets hot up here in the afternoon."

Doug sat down. He pulled out his handkerchief and wiped his brow.

"How much business do you lose during the summer?" he asked.

"Oh my. Sometimes it hardly pays to open the doors. I give 'em fans and free lemonade with ice, and still everybody sweats. Even with Rudolph Valentino I'm doing half a business."

"Suppose I told you I could lower the temperature in the Majestic by at least ten degrees?"

"I'd say you were lying."

"Want to bet?"

Doug showed him his schematics. "It's largely a matter of piping in water-cooled air. You pipe in hot air during the winter, don't you? It's the same principle."

"How do I know it'll work?"

"It's working in Chicago. Also in Montgomery. I'll make it work for you here."

Pellisier was not convinced.

"Tell you what I'll do," Doug said. "I'll air-condition your office free. If the temperature goes down ten degrees, you agree to let me do the entire theater. The main dislocation will be building the duct and putting in ceiling vents. But we won't start the installation until your last show. I have a two-man crew. We'll work through the night. You'll never have to close the theater, not even an hour."

"How much?"

"Cost plus."

"Plus what?"

Doug took a deep breath. "Thirty percent."

Pelissier's mind began to tick. Escape from the heat of a summer's day in Hastings should increase patronage by at least sixty percent.

"You could add a nickel at least to the ticket price." Doug said.

Pelissier put down his pencil and gave Doug a smile. "When can you start?"

Doug started the first week in April. Pelisser's office was only sixteen by thirty-two and Doug figured it wouldn't take much to cool it. He rigged up a system that consisted essentially of an electric motor, a fan with revolving blades, a small spray chamber with a refrigerated coil, and a couple of vertical baffles. From this he ran a duct, three inches in diameter, through the office wall into a perforated vent at ceiling height. When he turned the machine on, Mr. Pelisser's office filled slowly with saturated air. Within an hour the temperature had gone down seven degrees. In another half hour, it had gone down ten.

"You're a magician," said Pelissier, elated. "Do you think we can have the whole theater ready by June?"

"How about June 21, the first day of summer?"

DESPITE HIS SHOW of confidence, Doug felt considerable unease at the prospect of cooling the auditorium. It was one thing to do a small room. To extract moisture from air by forcing it over refrigerated coils and then to pump the air evenly into a large space was a bigger challenge. The main problem was to design a safe and effective chiller. A piston-driven reciprocating-compressor might do for a small space, but the refrigerant he used, ammonia bring its main ingredient, could be flammable and toxic. He sensed disaster at the thought of using it in a system with the capacity to cool an entire building. He went back to the professional journals seeking a solution.

He found it in the newest invention by Willis Carrier—a refrigeration machine that worked on a centrifugal-compressor similar to the centrifugal turning blades of a water pump. No more ammonia. The centrifugal chiller was the first practical method of air conditioning large spaces safely and it was ready for purchase from the Carrier Engineering Corporation. With only passing thought to its cost, Doug ordered one, with delivery promised in eight days. He breathed easier.

The duct installation went smoothly. By June 15 everything seemed to be in place and in good working order. But on June 19, when he turned on the motor to test the system, his heart sank. Noise from the motor was deafening, It roared throughout the system and was loud enough to distract even the most enthralled moviegoer from action on the screen. "Oh my God," he said, despairing.

"Well, son," said Pelissier with commendable patience. "What can we do to fix that?"

Doug's shoulders sagged. "I don't know," he said, honestly. "I need time to think."

There wasn't much time—certainly not enough to build insulated housing for a forty-horsepower motor. What the hell could he do? He went to the window in Pelisser's office and looked blankly at the street below. Noonday traffic was flowing. He heard a cop shouting at some driver to move along. He heard a number of automobile horns and, from a distance, the sound of a motor starting up.

It was then that he remembered. "Quiet as a toaster," Walt had said. He picked up the phone on Pelissier's desk and called the Packard dealer.

"I need a motor from a Packard Twin Six," he said and proceeded to tell why.

"You mean you'll be using it to power an air-conditioning machine?"

"Precisely. And I need it now."

"Hang on," said the dealer. In a minute he was back.

"You're in luck, Mr. Krueger. Some idiot crashed a Twin Six yesterday afternoon. About the only thing worth salvaging is the engine. You can have it for a hundred and seventy-five dollars, plus the cost of hauling it away."

Doug restrained his impulse to shout. Instead, he said, "Suppose I give Packard Motors credit on opening night and in every public reference about the system thereafter. Would you let me have it for a hundred and twenty-five?"

Pause.

"Sorry, I had to consult my partner."

Pause. Doug held his breath.

"You can have the motor for a hundred and thirty."

"I'll arrange to pick it up before three o'clock." Doug put down the phone and turned to Pelissier. "Don't worry," he said, beaming. "By tonight I'll have that system so quiet you'll think you're in church."

Joseph Pelissier introduced the system with all the to-do of a Hollywood premier. At one evening show two weeks before June 21 he surprised his patrons by standing in the lobby and personally passing out free tickets to the first two hundred to enter, inviting them to enjoy "an evening of comfort in South Carolina's first air-conditioned movie palace." He ran a full page ad in *The Courier*: "Come, Celebrate the First Day of Summer in the Cool of the Majestic. Bring a Sweater." He hung blue-and-white pennants in the shape of icicles from the marquee and decorated the roof with cut-outs of polar bears and Eskimos holding an enormous sign reading "COOL."

On the twenty-first, Doug turned on the machine at five o'clock. There was a barely audible hum of the motor. An hour before start of the ceremony the theater was an invigorating seventy-four degrees; the outside temperature was ninety-six. Pelissier opened the doors at seven to a mob of sweating patrons. They filed by a sign reading:

Air-Cooling by Akin and Company
Douglas Krueger, Chief Engineer
Powered by a Packard Motor

They took their seats, wiped their foreheads, felt their flesh dry, and gave a collective "aah." From the orchestra pit, loud and upbeat, came foot-stomping tunes by the Columbia Hotshots: "Runnin' Wild," "Toot Toot Tootsie, Goodbye," "Barney Google," "Way Down Yonder in New Orleans," and "Carolina in the Morning," the last of which stirred the audience into a sing-a-long. Promptly at seven-thirty, Pelissier stepped into a spotlight on the stage apron, lifted his hand to silence the band, and spoke winningly in his best barker's voice. "Ladeez and gentlemen. Welcome and thank you from the management of the Majestic—this incomparable, beautiful, one-and-only motion-picture palace—on this historic occasion." He went on to introduce Mayor Sam Wallace, who said a few words in praise of Joe Pelissier and the businessmen of Hastings who were creating "a cultural mecca in the heartland of Dixie." That done, Pelissier waved Doug on stage and said, "And here is the brilliant young man who designed and installed the system that we enjoy tonight. Let's show him our appreciation with a big round of applause." The audience responded thunderously. Doug blushed and gave a slight bow. "And now," said Pelissier, gesturing to his projectionist, "a brand-new motion picture, brought to you a month before its national release, an epic saga of the American west that will make tonight even more memorable. Ladeez and gentlemen—*The Covered Wagon*."

For weeks thereafter Doug basked in unaccustomed celebrity. Friends phoned, strangers recognized him on the street, notes and letters came from collegial engineers, some of them asking for technical advice. Mr. Akin was beside himself with pride and dreams of expansion. A day after giving Doug a raise and an additional commission of ten percent on every appliance sale, he gave him a new title, Chief Operating Officer. He also took him to his luncheon club and introduced him to the powers and shakers of Hastings. A few days later he was invited to join the Civitan Club, "where young business leaders meet for the civic good."

Doug tried to maintain a posture of modesty but he was plainly moved by the attention. Noting the new assuredness in his voice and stride, Maude told herself that all he needed had been one sure success and now that he'd achieved it everything was going to be all right. She felt a security she had not known since the first year of their marriage.

Contracts did not roll in; a cooling system was not inexpensive. But the commissions did come, and at a pace that Doug could handle them comfortably. After the Majestic, he and the Akin crew signed up to do the Lewis & Wright Department Store, the Richmond County court house, the Central Carolina Bank, St. Paul's Memorial Hospital, the dining and game rooms at the country club, and an office building scheduled to begin construction the next spring.

Akin returned from the mountains in good spirits. But he had celebrated his seventy-third birthday while away and Doug thought he was beginning to show his age. He tired more easily and often seemed distracted. One day Doug found him napping at his desk. It occurred to him that it would surely be only a matter of time before his boss would be selling out and retiring. In which event, what?

One morning he asked Akin for a half hour of his time. On arriving he spread out the new contracts and pointed out the sum that each would yield in profits. Akin smiled sleepily. "That's very impressive, Douglas," he said. "What can I do for you?" Given his opening, Doug went immediately to the point. "I'm thinking about my future," he said, and added quickly. "And also the future of the firm."

Akin smiled appreciatively. "You want another raise?"

"No sir. I want to buy the company."

Startled, Akin raised his eyebrows. "You want to do what?"

"Not now, sir. But eventually. When you retire. I'd like first option to buy."

"Oh my." Akin took out his handkerchief and wiped his face. "Well now, Douglas. I'm not quite ready to retire."

"I know, sir. But maybe, in five years or so."

"Don't push me, Douglas. This business has been my life. What in the world would I do in retirement?"

"You could work here, as a consultant, as long as you liked and as much as you liked."

"You make it sound very attractive. But do you know how much the firm is worth? How much it might cost you?"

"No sir. Do you?"

"I'd have to ask the accountant," Akin said. "The last time I had us appraised, when I borrowed to build this place eight years ago, the bank figured a quarter of a million. Do you think you could raise that much?"

"I'd like the chance to try."

Akin reached for a pencil and pad. "Thanks in good part to you, we're worth more now—I suspect a lot more." He was not a man to deny credit where it was due. "Let's see. How much do you think we may have in inventory? A hundred thousand? And in accounts receivable—let's say twenty thousand. Property and equipment, another hundred thousand. Pending job contracts, a hundred and twenty-five thousand. Fixed customer accounts, fifty thousand." He paused. "And the most important of all, in goodwill and intangible assets. How much would you guess?"

Doug had no idea. Akin began to add. "Let's forget about good will for the time being. Everything else comes to four hundred thousand." He put down his pencil and regarded Doug skeptically. "Do you really think you could raise that amount?"

"I don't know. But I have a good credit rating and a little bit of cash and the bank should accept inventory and accounts receivable as collateral. If I need more, I could probably borrow it from mother—that is, so long as the mill stays solvent and her Coca-Cola stock holds."

Akin sighed, thinking as much about his weakening lungs as he was about Doug's proposal.

"Sir?"

"Well, Douglas, it can't hurt to give you first option to buy. When I decide to sell."

"Then it's a deal?" Doug held out his hand.

"It's a deal," Akin said, accepting the handshake. "You can count on it."

Elated, Doug was at the door when Akin spoke again.

"Oh yes, Douglas." He smiled broadly. "I'll be sure to give you a discount for good will."

Flush with prosperity and happy with his prospects, Doug bought Maude a lavaliere with an emerald in the pendant. He practically redid the kitchen, installing a Frigidaire and a gas stove with two ovens. He bought himself a white Panama suit and a new straw boater. Every two weeks he gave Maude an extra twenty dollars over the amount for house expenses, which she put in savings, and he began to invest regularly in the stock market. Maude demurred slightly when he told her he was buying stock, for her father, despite his proclivity for risk-taking, had always equated speculation with gambling and Wall Street with evil. But as the value of their stocks rose, she voiced her misgivings less and less and even began to share some of Doug's excitement. "The trick," he told her, a bit patronizingly, sounding as if he were passing on something he'd learned from his Civitan brothers, "is to keep a balanced portfolio. You know, a little in oil, a little in steel, a little in railroads, a little in banking, that sort of thing. That way, we can't lose." She nodded, as if she believed he knew what he was talking about.

6

For the next four years they lived like one of the upwardly mobile couples who smiled and danced and played and consumed in the *Saturday Evening Post* ads. Maude joined the League of Women Voters and organized a monthly book club. Doug took up golf. They bought a Victrola and built a good collection of dance records. They had friends in for a party at least once a month, and went to parties at the club more often than they went to church. Almost too fast, Damon grew out of his babyhood. He seemed to add inches in height between bedtime and breakfast. To Maude's regret, he had her sallow complexion but, to her great satisfaction, Doug's nose and hair. He was a happy and loving child, fascinated by balls, books, birds, butterflies, music, and mud.

In 1925 Maude became pregnant again but miscarried in her third month. She developed a pain in her colon that wouldn't go away. Her doctor, unable to determine the cause, ordered exploratory surgery, whereupon she was found to have an endometrial tumor. The surgeon removed six inches of her lower intestine and then did a complete hysterectomy. "To avoid the risk of a malignancy," he said. She was thirty-two.

Maude was more than a month recovering physically. She never fully recovered from the radical assault on her identity. Despite her great will and her consummate good sense, she could not escape the feeling that she was now less than a complete woman. She brooded for weeks after returning from the hospital. Doug was awakened and rendered helpless by sounds of her sobbing into her pillow at night. She came to treasure Damon in a way that she agreed might not be healthy; it was only with conscious effort that she didn't crush him with solicitude for his safety.

Though happy at the prospect of a second child, Doug had not considered it a vital event, and he was more concerned with the effect of the loss on Maude than with his own disappointment. His words of comfort were clumsy and often irritably rejected. He soon abandoned attempts at sympathy, acknowledging, as she was inclined to insist in her frustration, that it was a woman thing no man could possibly understand. This was a point that Trudy and Catherine tacitly impressed on him as well. Catherine came over from Chesterton to spend a week with Maude, and Trudy was in almost daily attendance. When they were in the house, Doug felt shut out, as if sentenced to life for being a male. To compensate, he tried, in many small ways, to reassure her of his love and to dissuade her from the notion, which her doctor had warned him she might have, that her inability to bear more children was in some sense a failure to him. He arranged for Wilma, who had been coming only two days a week, to start full-time and take care of Damon during the day when he was at work. He also found a woman to clean the house once a week. He fixed and brought Maude breakfast in bed every morning. He never failed to phone her during his morning break and again during his lunch hour. He kept the bedroom fragrant with flowers.

In October Catherine invited Maude to accompany her to New York for a week of playgoing. Doug encouraged her to go. "It'll do you worlds of good to be away for awhile," he said. "Damon will be perfectly all right with me and Wilma, and I'll phone you every night."

It was the first time he'd been in the house without her since their marriage. He missed her, but for the first few days of her absence he felt a curious sense of freedom. He went unshaven over the weekend, skipped church, and spent most of Sunday in his pajamas. He left work early to pick up Damon after school. Every afternoon, after a frolic on the playground, on the way home they stopped at Hawk's for ice cream cones, something that Maude reserved for celebrations of exceptionally good behavior. "This will be our dirty little secret," he told Damon, chuckling. He could feel the parental bond tightening and it gave him pleasure beyond description.

Wilma fixed supper each night and stayed to wash dishes. After she left, he read Damon to sleep and then went to bed. He had no difficulty falling asleep, but he slept restlessly, disturbed by recurrent dreams, occasionally by nightmares, and by two o'clock in the morning he would be wide awake. For more than an hour thereafter he would be alone with his thoughts, none of them of a kind to cheer him, and when he dozed off again it was always to return to visions of his times with Azalie.

He forced himself awake when Damon came into his room asking for breakfast. As quickly as he could, he went to the kitchen and prepared a bowl of cornflakes with milk and a warm cinnamon roll. Watching the little boy's delight as he spooned the cereal in his mouth, the milk dripping down his chin, he felt an acute ache in his heart, a yearning for the other child he'd never seen. He made up his mind. It had been long enough.

Mid-morning at the office, he rang James at the store in Chesterton.

"James, I have a favor to ask of you and it's important that nobody else know."

"Anything, Mr. Doug."

"Find out where Azalie Taylor is and how I can get in touch with her."

"Azalie Taylor?"

"You remember Azalie. Fred Taylor's daughter."

"Fred Taylor is dead."

"I know, James, but there must be somebody in Chesterton who knows where she is. She left town sometime in 1917. She may have been back, I don't know, maybe to see about her father's property after he died. Ask around for me. I need her address and phone number."

"I'll try, Mr. Doug."

"And James—"

"Yes suh?"

"This is just between you and me."

"I'll be careful, Mr. Doug."

Two days later James phoned. "She's in Chicago."

At home that evening, he got a Chicago operator and asked for the number James had given him. He lit a cigarette and took a long drag.

There was a ring, and then another. He was breathing fast and his tongue felt swollen. He closed his eyes and prayed.

She picked up on the fourth ring.

"Hello."

For a moment he could not bring himself to speak.

"Yes?"

He found his voice just as she was about to hang up.

"Azalie?"

"This is Azalie Taylor." Friendly, but very professional. "What can I do for you?"

"This is Doug."

"Doug? Doug Krueger?"

"I couldn't help it, Azalie. There've been times, all these years, when I've been practically out of mind not knowing where or how you were."

There was a long pause, then: "Aren't you afraid your father will find out?"

"Papa's dead."

"Should I say I'm sorry?"

"He was a bastard."

"Not entirely," she said thoughtfully. "Anyway, I guess he can't hurt us any more."

"Or anybody else." His mind was spinning. "Azalie, I have so many questions. Please, are you all right?"

"I'm fine. Doing well."

He breathed heavily.

"And the baby?"

"A boy. He's eight. But I guess you knew that. He's in the third grade."

"Does he look like you?"

"He's got my hair, your eyes."

"Oh God. What's his name?"

"Frederick Douglas. We call him Fred."

"What's he like?"

"He's smart. And sensitive. Like you."

"I'm sorry to hear that."

"He's a cat lover."

"That's a good sign. What have you told him about me?"

"That you're dead. That you were in France during the war. You died in 1918, in the flu epidemic."

"Would you like to have a picture of me in uniform? You know, to show him?"

"He'd like that."

His eyes were misting. There was a catch in his throat and he could hardly speak.

"I can't hear you, Doug."

"I'm sorry. I'm just so overcome by the sound of you. Tell me about yourself. How are you wearing your hair? Have you changed—I mean, your looks."

"A trifle heavier. How about you?"

"I'm up to 150 or so." He rushed on nervously. "Are you working?"

"At the University of Chicago. I got a degree two years ago. In library science. I'm in the reference department at the main campus library."

"I want to know how to think of you. What were you doing when I called?"

"I was reading *The Great Gatsby*. For the second time."

"I gather you like it."

"It may be the great American novel."

"You used to say *Huckleberry Finn* was the great American novel."

"I changed my mind."

"Are you married?"

"I expect to be, not soon but maybe next year. To a lawyer."

"Is he—?"

"Yes. His family came from Jamaica."

"You say a lawyer? What kind of lawyer?"

"A good one. He's thirty-two, in practice with one of the big firms here. Mostly family law. But he's also interested in race, civil rights, that sort of thing. I met him at the university when he came out to give a lecture on Plessy versus Ferguson."

"Could I send you a wedding present?"

"That would not be a good idea." She laughed lightly.

"I'd like to write you now and again."

"But not too often. You're dead, remember?"

"Could you send me a picture of the boy?"

"If you like. Where are you? I heard you'd married, but are you in Chesterton?"

"No. Maude and I live in Hastings. That's in South Carolina."

"I know." He gave her his office address.

"Any children?" she asked.

"One. Also a boy. He'll be six in November."

The conversation was not going as he'd hoped. She sounded cool, remote, excessively self-controlled.

"Azalie?

"Yes?"

"Are you sorry I called?"

Another pause. "Maybe. I'm just not sure how to handle it. Good Lord, Doug. It's been almost nine years. Maybe we should just let it be."

"I can't."

"Well, you should try harder. This thing between you and me. I may have loved you once. It wasn't easy, getting over you, even after I'd convinced myself it could never work."

He remembered.

"I can't tell you how sorry I've been," he said. "I've hated myself, still do. I'll never forgive myself. I should never have given in to Papa. We should have left Chesterton together and gone somewhere—"

"Somewhere else? Where else, Doug?" She was almost shrill now, no longer dispassionate. "Don't be stupid. Do you seriously think, just because we'd be some place that permitted miscegenation we could ever be happy? Your father did us a great favor. I never intended to live a life of open wounds, always on guard, submitting to insults morning, noon, and night. A marriage between us could have ended only in one way. We'd have wound up hating each other."

He gulped and said nothing.

"Doug? Are you still there?"

"Barely."

"Listen, Doug. It's not all your fault. I didn't have to go to bed with you. I was the one who chose to have the baby, you know." Her voice grew softer. "If it's of any comfort to you, I think you did the right thing, taking your father's offer—at whatever sacrifice to your glorified manhood."

Sacrifice? She didn't know. He'd never tell her.

"Have you been getting the checks regularly?"

"Like clockwork."

He crushed out his cigarette and lit another.

"Azalie."

"Yes?

"Are you happy?"

"As happy as I ever expect to be. And you?"

"Sometimes." A catch came into his throat. "Is there a chance I might see my son some day?"

Silence.

"Azalie?"

"I heard you." She was considering an answer, but when it came he couldn't tell quite what she meant, or if she meant to be anything more than sad and regretful. "Some day, Doug. Maybe some day."

"I'll always love you, Azalie."

There was a long pause. "This is not good, Doug." He heard a sigh and then "Good-bye." There was one last sound—perhaps a sob. And she was gone.

7

Maude and Catherine had left for New York as mother and daughter in-law. They came back more like sisters. Doug met them at the depot, five-year-old Damon at his side, and watched as they stepped from the passenger car, each easy in the company of the other. Throughout the trip, Catherine had shown such critical sensibility, such independence of spirit that Maude was embarrassed to remember that only recently she had thought of her as an obligingly dependent, passively accepting Southern lady. Similarly, Catherine had discovered in Maude a compatibility of likes, dislikes, interests, and biases that she'd not known since her college days at Agnes Scott.

Catherine rejected their invitation to spend the night before going on to Chesterton. The four of them, with Damon nodding in Doug's lap, sat together in the overheated waiting room for half an hour before the connecting train arrived. During that time, like two excited school girls, the two women reported on what they had seen and done.

"Catherine is a late sleeper, did you know that?" Maude said, rushing her words. "But it didn't matter because we had adjoining rooms and while she was sleeping in the morning I'd take a long walk—up and down Madison and Fifth and Park avenues—and I'd stop on my way back at an automat for coffee and a bagel. I never had a bagel or been into an automat before, and Doug dearest New York in October is just as you said it would be. I loved the clean cool air and the way light and shade played off the buildings on the cross-town streets, and the way my skin felt when I came into the warmth of the sun. It made me feel like writing a poem."

"I think you just did," he said.

"I was so afraid Maude would be one of those ruthless up-and-at-'em morning types," Catherine said. "And she may be, for all I know, but we agreed at the start to spend our mornings apart in quiet time, and while Maude was taking her walks I'd be pulling myself together over a second cup of coffee. We'd meet for early lunch, and then go on from there till midnight. And it was wonderful, learning how much we had in common."

"Like what?" Doug wanted to know.

"Like hot fudge sundaes and Greta Garbo and Milton Sills."

"And wanting to see as many sights as we could and at the same time wanting to spend hours at every one of them."

"It could be frustrating—but we spent almost a day at the Metropolitan Museum and we saw the Statue of Liberty and the Bowery and Wall Street and we took a boat ride around the island—"

"And we went on the Hudson River Day Line to Peekskill and back."

"We didn't quarrel once about what to do," Maude said. "And we usually had the same reaction to the plays we saw."

"Not always," Catherine corrected her. "I thought the Marx Brothers were hilarious. And you thought they were silly."

"But we both had misgivings about *Craig's Wife*."

Doug didn't know about *Craig's Wife*.

"It's about this compulsive woman," Maude explained. "She kept everything obsessively in order and it wrecked her marriage."

"It was marvelously done," Catherine added, and laughed. "but it made us uneasy. We couldn't help thinking it was saying something ugly about women."

"Women like us," Maude said, giggling.

"But we loved the Garrick Gaities," Catherine said.

"Yes, and what didn't make us laugh made us think. There's this new play called *Processional*—all about class warfare. The things they can do and get away with in New York!"

Catherine's train came. They went with her to her compartment and said good-bye with kisses and tears. Later, they had a light supper and, after cleaning up and putting Damon to bed, went to their bedroom. He was pulling on his pajama bottom when she touched him gently in the crotch and said, "Voulez vous couchez a moi, soldier?"

She was going to be all right.

IN 1926, BOBBY JONES won the British Open, Gene Tunney beat Jack Dempsey to become the world heavyweight boxing champion, and Gertrude Ederle became the first woman to swim the English Channel. But to Maude and Doug the most memorable event of the year was Damon's enrollment in the first grade at Hill Street Elementary School.

Little Alice, a few months younger than Damon, would also be starting school that September. Maude and Trudy planned to escort the two to the registration desk. Doug wanted to go along but Maude dissuaded him, arguing that his presence might embarrass Damon during a ritual that traditionally was performed only by mothers. Doug deferred, but on the morning of the great day, after Maude and Trudy and the two children had taken off on the three-block walk, he drove around the block and parked out of their view but within sight of the school entrance. From there he watched Damon and Alice, their mothers a foot behind them, go the last block together, swinging their lunch boxes and finding courage in the hand of the other. It was a sweet vision of hope and promise that he would keep stored in some private and shamelessly sentimental corner of his mind for the rest of his life.

Damon soon became the most popular boy in the first grade, largely because of the quality of his lunch box. Maude never failed to include a half dozen cookies or candies for Damon to share with his friends. Once Jimmy Adams, the class bully, tried to grab the cookies and run with them. Damon caught him and gave him an uppercut to the jaw that sent him sprawling. After that, Damon was regarded, especially by the girls who had long tired of Jimmy's teasing, as something of a hero.

One mild May afternoon, Doug phoned Maude from the office and told her to put her bonnet on, he was going to take her for a ride.

She greeted him with a wan smile. "Are we going anywhere special?"

"You'll see," he told her, trying to look mysterious.

He drove to an undeveloped wooded area just within the eastern city limits, parked the car off the road, and helped her out. "Hold onto my arm," he directed. "And walk carefully. We're going only about a hundred yards, but I want you to see something at the bottom of the hill."

He guided her down natural paths of pine needles around sweet shrubs, wild azaleas, feathery ferns, and tangles of wisteria. As they walked he called her attention to trees he'd learned to recognize years before on Boy Scout hikes—loblolly pines, hickories, maples, poplars, black walnuts, a few elms, and an abundance of oaks, some of them eighty or ninety feet tall. When they came to a small clearing, he put his hands over her eyes and told her to listen. She heard a bird call, then the sound of flowing water. He removed his hands and she saw a rushing creek. It took her breath away. "Now turn around," he said. "Look up there. How'd you like to live on that hill?"

"Are you teasing me?"

"I was hardly ever more serious in my life. The city is extending the sewer line next year and Ned McDevitt—you know, Akin's brother-in-law—has bought up most of the land for development. You're at the foot of a three-acre lot, complete with stream. McDevitt will let me have it for twelve hundred dollars."

"Have we got twelve hundred dollars?"

"More," he said proudly. "Not only that, McDevitt is giving Strut an option to buy the lot next to ours. Wouldn't that be great, to have the Montagues as next-door neighbors the rest of our lives? Now, let's go to the car. I've got something else to show you."

Back at the road, he asked her to stand by the car, facing the lot. He reached under the driver's seat, pulled out a roll of drafting paper, and spread it out over the hood. On the top sheet was a penciled sketch of a house and a floor plan.

Maude squealed with delight. "Dearest! That's Daddy's old house on Woodrow Street."

"Not quite," he said, relishing the rise of goose bumps. "It won't have the dependencies, it'll have only three bedrooms, and it'll have simple oak steps to the second floor instead of the grand walnut staircase. But it will have the four Doric columns and the Palladian windows and otherwise it'll be just like the house you grew up in."

She kissed him but she felt obliged to signal a reservation. "How can we afford it, sweetheart? A house like this could cost as much as ten thousand dollars."

She had never seen him look happier or more full of himself. "Are you forgetting?" he said. "You're looking at the future owner of Krueger and Akin."

She was struck with a familiar shudder of apprehension.

During the summer months Doug spent every weekend, and at least two afternoons a week, at the lot. With Damon's help, he hacked away at the honeysuckle, cleared out all the dead wood, shoveled out a path to the creek and topped it with gravel. He edged the creek with ferns, hostas, and wild flowers. In an area shaded by the giant oaks near the creek site he created a small open park, planting it in Bermuda grass. From the office of the county agent he got pamphlets on the care of pools, ponds, and brooks and stocked the creek with oxygen-generating vegetation, fish (mostly small perch), mosquito-eating frogs, and other water life. His energy seemed inexhaustible. He built a picnic table and a half dozen lawn chairs. Regularly, on late Sunday afternoons Maude would prepare a light supper, inviting Strut, Judy, and Alice to join them for a picnic of sandwiches, potato salad, and iced tea. Doug's pleasure, his generally relaxed behavior, and his certainty of a future that would fulfill his dream, awed her. "In a year or so, this will be home," he told her, hugging her. "Meanwhile, it'll be our retreat." She was tempted to ask, "Retreat from what?" but he looked so happy and so absorbed that she held her tongue.

"If things keep going right," he said, "we can break ground next February and be in the house before Christmas." She noticed that he kept tinkering with the house plans, adding a library and a flagstone terrace in the rear. Where the money was coming from she no longer asked.

The next several years passed with no noteworthy reverses. Commerce Secretary Herbert Hoover reported that the United States had achieved the highest standard of living in its history; unemployment, he said, was virtually nonexistent. Encouraged by what was generally believed to be a perpetual state of national well-being, Doug invested more and more in the stock market although, in Maude's opinion, he tended to defer to his broker too readily and uncritically. On his broker's advice, he decided not to pay cash for the building lot but to take out a loan instead. He then put his savings of $1200 in shares of common stock, which his broker assured him would bring a higher rate of return than the cost of interest on the mortgage. Although eager to break ground, he also decided to delay the start of construction and to live as thriftily as possible until Akin's retirement, when he would know how much it would cost him to buy the company. It looked realistically as if the time would be soon. Akin was now thin, stooped, almost white-haired, and unsteady, sometimes trembling with a palsy that looked like the onset of Parkinsonism. He was rarely at his desk before ten. He had fewer and fewer business lunches, preferring to go home for a noon meal and a long nap. He had trouble remembering what was told him and he frequently forgot to take his medicine. His voice had become quivery and he often stuttered. He repeated himself, sometimes more than once during the same conversation.

A letter from Catherine:

Dear Ones,

Surprise! I've bought a house in Atlanta, a one-story Cape Cod within walking distance of Emory, It was built about ten years ago by a professor who's retiring and going back where he came from—Boston, I think.

Also, I'm going back to school. I'll be sixty-three next March and I figure I've still got ten good years in me. Frankly, I'm tired of playing the not-so-merry widow and I'm more than a little tired of Chesterton. I've decided to do what I've wanted to do for forty years—go back to Agnes Scott and get my degree. As you may know, I quit after my sophomore year to marry Jacob, which may have been a mistake on more than one count. Now I want to learn the European history I missed (we hardly got beyond the Crusades) and to know something about the Far East, which has always been presented to me as a no man's land. I'd like to try a little writing and, who knows?, try out for the Emory Players (Did you know I'm secretly a ham?). If Emory accepts me in its graduate program, I may go on and get a Master's, maybe in social work. It's high time I stopped being the pampered one and started helping somebody else.

I'm keeping title to the house here but will be turning it over to Helen and Dave in August, when I'll be moving to Atlanta. Thank goodness, Bessie is coming with me. She didn't need much persuading. The move will bring her closer to her daughter, who works in the tea room at Rich's, and also her older sister, whose husband is a Baptist preacher with a church on Auburn Avenue. I've arranged to have the back porch enclosed and converted into a small apartment for her, with a private bath and a private entrance. She seems to be thrilled to death.

The house has three bedrooms and two baths. I want you to be my first house guests. Be happy for me.

Much love,

C-"

IN NOVEMBER THEY DROVE to Atlanta for Thanksgiving with Catherine. Doug thought he had never seen her so happy. She obviously loved the house in a way that she had not loved the big Greek Revival in Chesterton. In this simple, unadorned Cape Cod, with its plain white clapboard siding, she felt at home as she never had before. "It's me, children," she said when she walked Maude and Doug through it. "It's mine and it's me."

She had a bedroom large enough to hold a *chaise longue*, a small French secretary with a companion ladder-back chair, and two bookcases that also served as night stands, one on each side of an oversized bed. "Think of me in this room," she said. "This is where I do most of my studying and all my correspondence. And look out the window." She pointed to an English garden. "That professor I told you about—the garden was his wife's. Isn't it perfection?" She gave a satisfying sigh and laughed. "I never, ever thought I'd come to this in my old age."

She had made one bedroom over into a sitting room. A wood-burning fireplace was at one end and a console radio and a phonograph at the other. Shelves on two walls held books and records. Two overstuffed chairs, upholstered in chintz, separated by a mahogany Sheraton table, were fixed at angles to catch both the warmth of the fire and the sound of the radio. "This is where Bessie and I come in the evenings to hear the news and listen to 'Cities Service Concerts' or the 'Atwater Kent Hour.' Sometimes, though, we just come in here to read and enjoy each other's company."

Doug's eyes went to the rows of photographs on top of the book shelves. There were a lot of pictures of him—one in his Army uniform, one in a gown and mortar board at the Tech graduation ceremony, one of him with Maude cutting the wedding cake. There were several of Maude, one in her wedding dress and another as a young mother with three-months-old Damon in her arms. There were snapshots of Helen and Dave and their twin daughters Sue and Flo. There was a touching shot of Catherine in a swing with Damon when he was about four years old. There were no photographs of Jacob.

"The place is just right for me and Bessie," Catherine was saying as they gathered around the dining table on Thanksgiving eve. "It's not so big that we can't handle all the cleaning ourselves. And Bessie, it turns out, has a green thumb. She and I work the garden together. If we need help there's a wonderful old colored man just a block away who'll come on a moment's notice."

"Where is Bessie?" Doug asked.

"At her brother-in-law's church for Wednesday night prayer meeting. She's looking forward to seeing you at breakfast. Meanwhile, she made this marvelous oyster stew for our supper."

Doug asked Catherine what she was studying at Agnes Scott. "Sociology 101, abnormal psychology, history of the Far East. I've been accepted into the graduate program at Emory. Next term, beginning in February, I'm taking Garland Smith's course in Shakespeare."

"My," Maude said. "That's a pretty big load."

"I love it," Catherine said. "And you know what? At mid-term I got two A's and a B."

Doug looked at her beaming face. "I'll never worry about you again," he said.

Catherine picked up her soup spoon. "This is one of Bessie's specials. Enjoy."

A moment later she put down her spoon and became pensive.

"It's odd," she said "I don't miss Jacob at all."

8

There was never any question of Doug's love for his mother or of hers for him. But during the visit with her in Atlanta he came to see her for the first time as a strong woman with a remarkably penetrating mind. To his love for her was added heightened respect. Somehow, being with her also made him more aware of his good fortune to have a wife like Maude and a son like Damon.

He had never imagined family life could be so gratifying. As he prospered, he sought to enrich it with as many amenities as his budget would permit. When the Ford Motor Company announced that it was closing down production of the Model T for a year, preparatory to introducing a revolutionary improvement, he cut down on restaurant lunches and clothing purchases and began putting a few dollars aside every week. When Ford's Model A came on the market in 1927 he was among the first in town to have one. It cost him six hundred dollars.

His work was going well. He continued to draw the plans for the wiring of McDevitt's houses, which were now going up with such regularity and in such numbers as to provide the Akin company with a basic income and Doug the equivalent of a retainer. The number of homeowners in the county was increasing markedly, sparking a spiraling demand for household appliances. By methodically cultivating manufacturers and suppliers, Doug was able to stock new products earlier than competitors. He also proved to be a very good salesman. He brought a technical knowledge to his sales pitches that were remarkably effective, perhaps because it flattered his customers' intelligence as much as it informed them. Moreover, his fantasy life was enhanced with the news that a machine to transmit images by wireless had been demonstrated successfully at a meeting of the Royal Institution in London; its inventor, a Scotsman named John Baird, called it "television." Intrigued, Doug wrote Baird for details and was rewarded with an answer that led him to write a paper, "What next after radio?" which the *Courier* abridged and ran as a Sunday feature. Among Hastings's elite, he was becoming recognized as a young man to watch.

The bubble burst on a warm and cloudless day in April, 1928. Arriving at work that morning, Doug found on his desk a typewritten notice:

"TO: All Employees

"We will close for business a half hour earlier this afternoon. Please come to the main showroom no later than 4:30 PM to hear an important announcement about our future.

John Akin"

Doug was curious, mainly because Akin customarily told him before calling a staff meeting and often asked him as Operations Officer to preside. But it didn't worry him, even after he'd talked with Akin's secretary and learned that Akin didn't plan to appear until just before the afternoon meeting. Akin frequently used such meetings to introduce a new product line or a new distributor, and Doug figured that his failure to tell his deputy in advance was probably nothing more significant than his growing forgetfulness. Doug was hardly prepared for the shock when it came.

The meeting was short and the message brief. Akin cleared his throat, asked for quiet, and raised his voice. "I will be re-re-tiring as of June 30, at the end of our fis-fiscal year," he said. "The company is being sold to Amos Poole & Company, which will for-formally take control on July 1. Your jobs will be unaffected. All of you can count on uninterrupted employment. Needless to say, I am grateful to every one of you. I will miss-miss you all." He turned his back and limped slowly out the showroom's rear door and down the corridor into his private quarters.

Doug knew then what it must be like to be kicked by a mule. His stomach knotted. He felt sick and dizzy. He thought he might vomit. It was a minute before he could open his eyes and collect himself. When he did, he was aware that virtually everybody in the room was looking at him. He responded with a weak smile and a shrug.

He went to his office and sat at his desk, his head in his hands, trying to control the rush of emotion and to make sense of what he'd heard. To calm himself, he took several deep breaths. He then got up and walked to Akin's office, pausing at the cooler for a long drink of water.

He found Akin alone, standing in the half light at the window, brooding. Akin turned when he heard his door open.

"I thought it might be you," he said.

Doug wasted no time. "I thought it best I give you my notice now. I'd like to leave as soon as possible without embarrassment to you and with as much dignity as I can."

"I wish you wouldn't," Akin said, almost pleading.

"How could I not? We had an agreement. You promised me first option to buy."

Akin made no protest. "I broke my promise." He sighed and sat down behind his desk. "I feel terrible."

"You feel terrible!" Doug's voice was rising. "I feel betrayed."

"I can't blame you, Douglas, but I really had no choice. Poole made me an offer. I'll never again get another one like it, and it was one you couldn't possibly match."

"But you could have given me the chance. Or you could at least have discussed it with me beforehand—told me why you felt you had to renege on me. I trusted you like—" He caught himself. He had started to say "like a father."

"There was no-no-no beforehand," Akin said falteringly. "At least not much. Poole has an inside tr-tr-track for the electrical contract for the new municipal stadium, but to get it he has to show a crew almost twice as large as the one he's got. The best way for him to get it is to merge with me and to do that he's will-willing to pay a premium. The deadline for filing is next Mon-Monday. He insists on moving fast and secretly. He doesn't want it to look like something cooked up at the last minute in order to qualify."

"Of course he's got the inside track," Doug said contemptuously. "It probably cost him a mint, but there's no doubt he'll be the preferred bidder."

Akin spoke placatingly but without conviction. "I told him I would sell only on the condition that he keeps you as chief operations officer."

"Good Lord, John!" Doug was surprised to hear himself call Akin by his first name. It was the first time in their six years together. "Do you really think I could work with Poole, knowing what I know about him? Do you really think he could tolerate me for long on the same premises, knowing that I know?"

Akin struggled to defend himself. "He's not all that bad, Douglas. Whatever he's been doing he's been very successful at it. You could go far with him if you could just bring your mind around."

"Go far with him! More likely, go to jail with him! My God, the man's a crook. He's been paying bribes and giving kickbacks for years, and one of these days the whole story's going to come out and he'll be in the middle of the biggest scandal since Teapot Dome. When that time comes, believe me, I don't want to be anywhere near him."

"Well," Akin said, looking as if he might cry, and beginning to stutter again. "I'd app-appreciate it if you would stay on these next thirty days. I'll see that you get a decent sev-severance check."

"Good-bye, John," Doug said quietly. He had turned and was moving toward the door when Akin called him back.

"I don't have much t-t-time left, Douglas. I owed it to Jane and the g-g-girls." He slumped in his chair and he suddenly looked ten years older. "I'm not well."

Maude was furious.

"How could he do that?" she wanted to know. "You had a contract."

"We shook hands on it."

She gave him a puzzled look. "You mean you had nothing in writing?"

He nodded.

"Good Lord," she said, in full voice. "How naive can you be! And what else have you got to tell me—that you've quit?"

He nodded again, his head drooping.

"Doug, I could kill you!" She was shrill with anger. "Who exactly do you think you're punishing by quitting? Certainly not Mr. Akin. You're punishing me and Damon, that's who. Me and Damon, and also yourself. My God, Doug, won't you ever learn?"

"Maude—"

"Whatever else you've got to say, I don't want to hear it." They were sitting in the living room. She got up to leave, probably to retreat to the kitchen.

"Maude," he yelled after her. "Akin has sold out to Amos Poole. I'd be working for Amos Poole."

She turned and saw the anguish in his eyes. Her anger diminished in a rush of sympathy. "Oh," she said. "How awful."

He closed his eyes and began to sway but caught himself on the back of a chair before he fell. Alarmed, she ran to him and put her arms around him.

"Are you all right?"

"I feel a little queasy," he said weakly. "I could use a drink."

He drank increasingly over the weeks that followed, always in the late afternoon when his spirits seem to fall with the coming darkness under an oppressive, threatening sense of failure. He was sick at heart. He tried to fulfill his last obligation to Akin & Company, but after two days back in the office he asked his old boss to drop him and record his last month on the job as sick leave. Akin's attitude toward him was now a mixture of embarrassment and contrition; he readily agreed.

Doug slept fitfully at night and needed a nap after breakfast before facing the day. Late morning was the best time for him; after lunch he grew drowsy and listless. More and more he caught himself speaking irritably to Maude and Damon. Asked what he wanted to drink with his dinner, he would say "tea." When she brought him tea he would say testily, "I asked for coffee." Damon had a habit of removing the dust jacket while reading a book and neglecting to replace it. This angered Doug irrationally. "You can start putting the jackets back on," he roared at him one evening, "or I'll make sure you never read another book. How'd you like that, young man? Will you do what I say, or would you prefer to be illiterate all your life?" Scared, Damon broke into tears and fled the room.

Invariably, Doug followed such outbursts with pitiful attempts at apology, but the outbursts only became more frequent.

At Maude's insistence he saw his doctor, who found nothing wrong. "You're just worrying yourself sick," the doctor said dismissively. "Get more sleep and exercise, and lay off the booze for awhile." Ambition had deserted him. He lost interest in sex almost to the point of impotence. He wanted nothing so much as to be let alone. He knew that he had to make up his mind about what to do when his terminal pay ran out, but he could not bring himself to concentrate. He got a call from Ned McDevitt, who said he'd be pleased to have Doug continue to plan and spec wiring for his housing developments. Other than that, he got no job offers, and he didn't have the will to send out resumes.

Strut was his usual anchoring presence but, to Doug's disappointment, he expressed neither surprise nor indignation over Akin's behavior. "What did you expect?" he asked Doug with impatience. "Money is like a stiff prick. It's got no conscience."

To be constructive, Strut suggested with some enthusiasm that Doug go into business for himself. "Some people," he said, "aren't cut out to work for a boss. You may be one of them."

Maude too thought it a good idea. "You've built up quite a nice record," she told him encouragingly. "You brought Akin a lot of customers, and they all like you. I think you could do very well for yourself. Krueger and Company. I like the sound of that."

Although Doug found it hard to warm to any prospect, he decided that setting up shop for himself was perhaps the best of the few options he could think of. He would need capital, however—maybe not much, but enough to rent and furnish an office, establish a basic inventory, and hire a clerk, a salesman, and at least one technician. For a starter, he figured he wouldn't feel comfortable for less than six thousand, and to get that amount of money he'd have to sell some stock.

So one morning in May of 1928 he summoned enough heart to make an appointment with Possum Trott, his bright-eyed, aggressively upbeat broker. And Possum was appalled at what Doug was suggesting. "My God, Doug," he protested, practically at the top of his voice. "Are you crazy? Now's no time to sell. Now's the time to buy! The market's down, temporarily. Prices per share are lower than they've been in two years, and they may never be lower. Sell? I won't let you. In fact, I want you to sign a letter authorizing me to buy on margin for your account whenever I think the time's right, with no time lost asking your okay. Trust me."

"On margin? What's a margin?"

Possum gave him a pitying look he normally reserved for the mentally defective.

"A margin account enables you to borrow from your broker—me—to finance part of a stock purchase," he explained. "You can borrow up to half the cost of the transaction. You deposit cash or securities to fund your half. You pay interest, but usually at less than market rates. You repay the loan from the profits earned as the value of the stock increases."

"If it increases," Doug said.

"It will," Possum assured him. "You want a hundred more shares of Radio? It's down this morning twenty-three points. General Motors is down. So's Montgomery Ward. But in a month they'll be up again, higher than ever. You want profits? For God's sake, buy now! You want to cash in? Wait a year. At least wait till after the election. My bet is that, whether it's Hoover or Smith, the market will take off again and go out of sight."

Possum's certitude was overwhelming. Doug left his office after signing a letter authorizing purchases on margin of common stock up to the market value of his portfolio, currently about $8,000. Better now, he thought, to postpone any venture into self-employment. He was half persuaded that within a year he'd be so rich he might never have to work again at all.

When Doug was about eight, his father's sister, Aunt Sarah, came for a visit of several weeks while his mother was off at Lake Junaluska attending a leadership camp for Methodist women. One Sunday morning after the eleven o'clock service, as the two of them were standing in the shade of the church waiting for his father to pick them up and drive them home, a strange man appeared and walked to the curb below. He was unlike any man Doug had ever seen before. He was tall and slender and his cheeks looked not merely shaven but sanded. His skin was soft and pink, as if it had never been exposed to the sun. It was summer and the time for seersucker, but he was dressed in flannel with a gray waistcoat and a starched collar higher than any collar Doug had ever seen, with a tightly knotted necktie in red and back stripes that seemed similarly alien. His shirt sleeves fell two inches below the sleeves of his coat and the cuffs were linked by jewels of some sort. Doug could not keep his eyes off him.

Aunt Sarah was poking him in the side with her elbow. "See that man?" she whispered in a strong tone of disapproval. "He's from New York. He plays the stock market."

A week later while he and Aunt Sarah were walking home from the drug store, they paused at an intersection. Aunt Sarah pointed discreetly across the street to a deranged old man, stooped and lame and drooling. In the same warning tone she had used to call Doug's attention to the man from Wall Street, a tone that said plainly "Let this be a lesson to you," she said, "see that man? He plays with himself."

From that time on, well into his adolescence, Doug had thought of the stock market as something obscene, shameful, forbidden, and unhealthy. When he grew older he came to accept it as a barometer of the American economy but he never quite understood how it worked, and he wasn't satisfied that anybody else did either. He drew a moral distinction between investing and speculating. Investing was what his mother and father did when, in the spirit of a civic obligation as natural as supporting the local sheriff, they bought shares in the Chesterton Village Bank; in the gin and textile mill that served the county's farmers; and in a new company organized to manufacture and sell a soft drink from a formula invented by a popular pharmacist in a neighboring town. Investments like these were good, he assured himself, for they provided the capital for useful enterprises and they represented the enduring loyalty of owners who behaved like stewards. But speculation was something else. It was an exercise in self-aggrandizement, a mysterious game that treated human institutions like abstractions and played by rules that seemed to change with the wind. By the ethic Doug had inherited, profits were supposed to come from the production of something necessary or desirable, something a person could feel, taste, wear, inhabit, use, or enjoy. It did not seem fitting that a person should profit merely from a talent for following and manipulating numbers. Speculators may not be altogether evil, but to Doug they were a race apart who spoke the language of a continent he didn't care to explore, participants in a tacit conspiracy to direct the common wealth into their own pockets. With the self-righteousness drawn like breath from the egalitarian wing of his Protestant culture, he shunned and deplored them.

But in the second decade of the twentieth century white middle-class Americans were infected by a raging speculative fever and Doug was not immune.

Beginning as early as 1921, the country was afflicted by an epidemic that spread to raging proportions, fed by a bull market that seemed to rise and expand by the day and by a romantic conviction that affluence was one of the natural rights of man. By 1925 it had become a mass movement. Doctors, lawyers, clerks, teachers, small-town storekeepers, Western cattlemen—most of whose investment experience had been confined to the purchase of Liberty Bonds—had acquired brokers and subscribed to the *Wall Street Journal*, and were discussing market shares with the familiarity of baseball statistics. Like addicted casino gamblers, otherwise reasonably sane citizens were buying and selling shares in companies suddenly imbued with the glamour of movie stars—General Motors, U. S. Steel, the Pennsylvania Railroad, the Radio Corporation of America, Chrysler, International Harvester, Montgomery Ward, Sears Roebuck. Their frenzy was fed by two Republican presidents who, in speeches from the White House embodying boundless optimism and a near deification of business, exhorted them to follow the ticker tape into the promised land. Despite the devastation of the boll weevil and an agricultural depression in the Northwest and Middle West, Washington talked only of surging markets and increasing material abundance.

Caught up in the prosperity of the Coolidge years and the contagion of the get-rich-quick psychology, Doug had invested modestly in radio and automobile stocks as early as 1924. He had done so, however, largely on the advice of his friends at Civitan and with more of a desire not to be left out than with any passion for the market. ("Everybody else is doing it," he said to Maude, "Why shouldn't we?") Having hired Possum

Trott on recommendation of a Civitan friend, he was content to let the broker call the shots, satisfied to count the profits. Once, after reporting to Maude that one day's activity on Wall Street had netted them three hundred dollars, he confessed to a discomfort he could define only as a residual mark of his Methodist upbringing. "I don't feel that we earned it. I don't think we did anything to deserve it. I can just hear Aunt Sarah telling me I'm gonna roast in Hell."

Though never entirely shed of the nagging sense that he might be thriving at the cost of personal integrity, Doug soon came to follow his ticker earnings with the intensity of a zealot. No longer was he immobilized with lassitude. The prospect that he might soon have the capital to start Krueger and Company brought a noticeable lift in mood; his metabolism seemed to change with the value of his securities. On the day of his meeting with Possum, Radio had dropped twenty-three points, but Possum's advice to buy 50 more shares on margin at the low of 176.5 proved to be sound. By November it was selling at 400.

"Shouldn't we cash in now?" He asked Possum.

"God no," Possum answered. "In another year Radio will break 500. How many times do I have to tell you—never give up your position in a good stock!"

Doug sat tight and watched Radio drop 72 points over the next thirty days but then start a dizzying ascent. Within nine months it climbed almost 200 points. In September 1929 it closed at 500.

The fast rise made Doug nervous.

"Now?" he asked Possum.

"Not yet," Possum said.

So Doug held on.

9

Maude agreed with Doug that it wasn't smart to venture into a new business until you had ample start-up money. Yet she sometimes wondered if he hadn't overestimated the amount of capital he needed. She was uneasy that he was getting distracted—no, intoxicated—by the higher and higher flight of the stock market. She also developed an intense dislike for Possum, whom she hardly knew, sensing that his advice was self-serving. "He's nothing but a pencil-sharpening sorcerer," she said once to Doug in a fit of annoyance. "To leave to a man like that a decision that could have everything to say about the future and welfare of this family is madness. It's like forfeiting fate to the turn of a roulette wheel." In any event, she thought it counter-productive for Doug to do nothing until the money was in hand. She told him so often, and with increasing vehemence. "There are plenty of things you could be doing now," she said. "To get ready. Like planning the store—you do mean to sell appliances, don't you?—and finding the place for it, and lining up suppliers. Things like that."

Chastened, he turned the guest room into a small office and went to work. For a desk, he brought the old harvest table up from the dining room, where it had been used for little more than decoration. On one side of it he put his drafting board and on the other a small typing table. He bought an oak swivel chair and a typewriter, both second-hand, for a total of twenty-five dollars. He installed a ceiling droplight and had the phone company put in a second line. So equipped, he began to feel that he was already in business.

Once at it, concentrating on layouts and inventories and staff organization and budgets, he found his old enthusiasm returning. Planning was something he had always done well. List-making gave him a peculiar satisfaction, and his lists of to-do and to-get grew longer every day. More and more often, Maude caught him whistling and humming. Few things pleased her more than to see him with Damon at his elbow, cheerfully explaining some detail on a floor plan, or describing, with more earnestness than clarity, what an electrical contractor did.

Damon's questions, in fact, inspired him to draft a statement of purpose for distribution to prospective customers. The company would provide goods and services for "The New and Abundant Age of Electricity"—system designs for industry, state-of-the-art wiring for new homes and expert upgrading of the wiring in old ones, air-conditioning for large buildings, lighting equipment, and the most modern home appliances, each to be sold with a guarantee of free repairs for a year after purchase. The company would be staffed by two sales personnel and three technicians, two of them with degrees in electrical engineering. Its headquarters would provide space for a show room, offices and warehousing. Emergency service would be available around the clock. Two vehicles—a pick-up truck and a Chevrolet sedan—would insure customers of quick delivery. Suspecting that he may be doing more dreaming than planning, Doug revised as he went and worked out a reasonably realistic schedule for development in phases, based on increments in quarterly profits. He added another five thousand dollars to his initial budget estimate.

From the town clerk he obtained population figures that confirmed his sense that the town was moving north. He got records of appliance sales, and some insight into consumer preference, from the Chamber of Commerce. He went searching for office space on the north side. When he found nothing where he wanted it, he decided to buy and remodel a vacant nineteenth century dwelling less than two miles from the building lot in Honeysuckle Hills. To insure its availability, he gave the owner three hundred dollars in earnest money.

He also kept busy researching the newest makes of appliances and cultivating the suppliers he'd dealt with while employed at Akin's. He solicited bids for phonographs, console radios, lamps and lighting fixtures, washing machines, electric stoves, vacuum cleaners, and refrigerators.

In a month's time he had put together a paper inventory he was sure no competitor could match.

His sense of well-being during this period was enhanced by the time he spent with Damon, now an exploratory eight going on nine. He was pleased when Damon asked him to review his homework (arithmetic was not Damon's long suit) and Doug did it patiently. Two afternoons a week they went to the Y together for a swim and every Saturday morning, weather permitting, they went to the club for tennis, after which they changed clothes and went to work at the lot together.

Aware that his terminal pay from Akin would soon be exhausted, Doug earned additional income by taking on assignments from McDevitt and working from time to time as a commissioned salesman for General Electric, a job that had him calling on customers in most of the towns within a fifty-mile radius of Hastings. He traveled at least once a week throughout the summer of 1928 and he often took Damon with him. Damon would bring along his favorite books—he was going through Don Sturdy, the Rover Boys, and most of the other juveniles that kept pouring out of Grossett and Dunlap—and he was content to read alone in the car while his father was in a store making a sales pitch. Some days Maude would pack them a lunch—sandwiches and fruit and lemonade and always a dessert made from a recipe in the Charleston or New Orleans cookbook. Doug would pull the car off the road and they would sit and eat in the shade of a tree or, if they were lucky, near a cool stream, not talking much but feeling a companionship beyond description. On other days, they would have lunch in a boarding house, which for Damon constituted an experience as exciting as a trip to a circus. Doug couldn't tell what delighted Damon more, the conversation among the guests at the table or the variety of dishes. It was at one of these boarding houses that he got his first sight of a Mormon missionary and his first taste of beer-battered catfish and sweet potato soufflé. Years later, whenever he thought about these rare and sweet months with his father, the taste of boarding-house food would come to his mouth, as strong as the memory of the dust in his nostrils from the dirt roads they traveled.

They talked about whatever came to mind. When Damon expressed an interest in his grandparents and his great grandparents, Doug told him everything he could remember about the family, including their experiences during the Civil War. Damon knew about the War, for he had seen the Confederate Memorial Day parade every spring of his childhood, but he was beginning to have questions about it that went beyond ritual and sentiment. How had it started? Why? "Miss Bolton says we shouldn't call it the Civil War," he told Doug, referring to his home-room teacher. "She says it should be called The War Against Northern Aggression. Why, Daddy?" A discussion of the War occupied them for all of one day-long trip and sent Damon to the library looking in vain for a for a history he could understand. When he announced at supper that the war made no sense to him, that he didn't think it should have been fought at all, neither Maude nor Doug knew quite what to say. How could you explain slavery and state's rights to a nine-year-old? "Just keep asking questions, darling," Maude said, trying to put a positive close to the conversation, "and maybe some day you'll understand, though it may never make sense." Later that night, she and Doug agreed that their son was showing signs of a scary precocity and they'd better get prepared.

That summer was bonding time for Doug and Damon. Never again would they be so close. Nor would Doug ever again feel quite so acutely his role, and his inadequacies, as a father. Once, out of the blue, Damon asked him. "Daddy, when are you gonna take me hunting?"

Doug sensed that in his son's eyes he may be about to flunk a rite of passage. "You're too young to start hunting," he said feebly. "Why do you ask?"

"Jim Jennings is only eight, and his dad takes him hunting."

"Do you want to kill birds and squirrels and rabbits and things?"

"I don't think so. But seems like you're expected to go hunting sooner or later."

"Well, maybe later." Doug breathed more easily. "Tell you what we'll do. When you get to be twelve or so we'll buy 22s and go skeet shooting."

"Skeet shooting? What's a skeet?"

"It's kind of a clay target. Like a clay bird. It takes just as much skill to bring one down, and nothing gets hurt."

"You promise?"

"I promise."

Doug knew about peer influence but it had never before occurred to him that he might have to contend with the author of the Bobbsey Twins. One afternoon, on the way back from Somerville, Damon talked about the book he'd just finished. "There was this brother and sister and they were colored and they'd just come to this town where the Bobbsey Twins lived. The Bobbsey Twins made friends with them and then their other school friends stopped speaking to them because they'd taken up with niggers. They called the Bobbsey Twins bad names and accused the colored boy and girl of lying and cheating and stealing and all kinds of things."

"How did it end?" Doug asked.

"Oh, it ended all right. It turned out that the new friends weren't niggers after all. They were Indians."

"We don't say nigger, Damon," he said. "We say colored, or Negro. Were these American Indians, or real Indians from India?"

"That wasn't clear," Damon said, frowning. "Does it matter?"

"It shouldn't. What did you think of the book?"

"I didn't like it. It was a real dumb story. Why should it have been all right for the Bobbsey Twins to have Indians as friends but not colored people?"

"Exactly," said Doug. He turned in his seat and gave Damon a hug.

In June of that year the Republicans nominated Herbert Hoover for president, as predicted, and the Democrats nominated Al Smith, a former three-time governor of New York. Hoover was bland and Smith was spirited. Hoover ran on his record as the country's cheer-leader for prosperity. Smith ran as an equally strong business advocate but also as an unapologetic anti-prohibitionist. The campaign was divisive, largely because Smith was a Roman Catholic.

The campaign re-ignited Doug's dormant interest in politics. He signed up with the Smith partisans and agreed to go door-to-door in Precinct Seven recruiting voters to the Democratic cause. Damon asked if he could go along and somewhat hesitantly Doug said yes. He welcomed Damon's interest, but he had misgivings. The issues in this campaign weren't for the innocent; more than his sense that Damon was too young to understand them was the feeling that he, the father who was supposed to know everything, may lack the competence to describe them. When he confessed his insecurity to Maude, she showed him an article in *Ladies Home Journal*: "Take your cue from the child. Don't bring up a complicated subject; wait for the child to ask, and don't make the mistake of telling him more than he cares to know." That was some comfort, but not much; Damon was not an average child and his curiosity could be formidable."Why are we for Mr. Smith, Daddy?" Damon asked him on the first day they were making their rounds. "Bob Miller's daddy says if Mr. Smith's elected it'll be like having the Pope in the White House. Who's the Pope?"

Here it comes, Doug said to himself. He took a deep breath. "Well, in our country, Damon, we don't think religion and government should mix. It's something called the separation of state and church." He sounded pompous and pedantic. Try as he might, he couldn't do better. "We believe that everybody ought to be judged as an individual, not because of who he knows, or where he comes from, or what church he goes to. So this election is kind of a test. Mr. Smith had a good record as governor of New York and there's no evidence that he ever did anything because he was a Catholic or because he wanted to give Catholics an unfair advantage. In fact, he may have leaned over backward just so people wouldn't think he would. Your mother and I believe he'd make the best president. And we also believe that people who say he should be defeated because he's a Catholic are the ones who're bringing religion into politics. They're the ones who threaten the principle of separation of church and state. We have to fight them and their ideas. Do you understand what I'm saying?"

Damon nodded politely. "I guess. But Daddy—what's a Catholic?"

They had come to the next house and Doug was glad.

A week or so later, he and Maude took Damon with them to a candidates' forum in the town hall sponsored by the League of Women Voters. Doug had been asked to make the case for Al Smith. Maude thought he was eloquent, and apparently so did many others in the audience. Leaving the auditorium in a flurry of approval, he was gratified to see that the supply of pro-Smith flyers at the registration table was almost exhausted.

Then, on second glance, he noted that so too was the pro-Hoover pile.

On their way home Damon started giggling. He had a silly satisfied expression on his face and he was obviously expecting his parents to be proud of him. "See what I did?" he said. He reached under his shirt and pulled out a bundle of Hoover flyers. There must have been a hundred or more.

"What in the world, Damon!" Maude said.

Doug stopped the car, turned around, and headed back to the town hall.

"Take those back where you got them, son," he said, trying not to sound too scolding. "And hurry, before everybody leaves."

"But why, Daddy?" Damon looked confused and about to cry. "I thought we didn't like Mr. Hoover."

"We don't, darling," Maude told him. "But Republicans have just as much right to pass out folders for Mr. Hoover as we Democrats do to pass out folders for Mr. Smith."

"And we don't take their folders and throw them away," Doug added. "That's not playing fair."

"Mr. Miller says all's fair in love and politics."

"That's just what people say. Mr. Miller is wrong."

"But how can we be sure that the Republicans are playing fair too?"

Doug sighed. "We have to be alert and keep our eyes open," he said. They were back at the town hall. He pulled the car to a stop.

"There are some people still in the auditorium. Now get out and hurry and put those flyers back where you got them."

Damon was silent for a few minutes after he returned. When he spoke it was to ask more questions:

"What's Prohibition?"

"What's Prosperity?"

Al Smith lost to Herbert Hoover and bigotry. Doug felt let down but he was surprised only by the size of Hoover's victory—more than twenty-one million votes to Smith's fifteen million—and by the fact that anti-Catholic feeling had proved strong and wide enough to split the Solid South. He had halfway expected Florida and Texas to go Republican, but North

Carolina and Virginia? He made a note never again to underestimate the power of ignorance.

The election over, he returned to his piecework and to anxieties about the future. With Damon back in school, he was traveling by himself and there were days when he felt acutely alone. He had not realized how much he would miss his child's company.

So far Damon was the promise of everything Doug could wish for in a son—healthy, reasonably athletic, emotionally secure, inquisitive, and caring. With one exception. To Doug's disappointment, Damon showed no aptitude for carpentry. On his seventh birthday, Doug had given him a Junior Woodworking Kit—a hammer, a small saw, a square, a brace-and-bit, a screwdriver and an assortment of nails and wood screws. With reluctance and uncharacteristic petulance, Damon had used the tools once, following instructions included in the kit for building a hinged handkerchief box. ("It'll be a nice gift for Alice," Maude said encouragingly.) Damon spent hours at it, but try as he might he could never get the sides even or the lid on straight. He refused Doug's help. He sulked and pouted and fussed and finally, in tears, threw both his lopsided box and all the little tools into the garbage.

"This won't do, Damon," Doug told him severely, whereupon Damon rolled his little fingers into fists and proceeded to pound Doug in the chest with all his strength. Angry, Doug slapped him. "Go to your room, Damon," he said. "We'll talk later." But he was already reproaching himself and when, a half hour later, he went to Damon's room he was still wondering what to say.

Damon had his head in his pillow and he was sobbing as if his heart would break. Doug got on his knees and, reaching over, gave the boy an awkward hug. Damon rolled over. His face was full of confusion, hurt, and frustration. He spoke first.

"I'm sorry, Daddy. I tried. Really I did."

Damon gulped. "I know. I'm sorry I got mad at you. I shouldn't have done that, expecting you to do something, and like doing it, just because I wanted you to."

Damon started crying again.

Doug sat on the side of the bed and took him in his arms.

"Please don't, Damon. It's all right. We can't all be good with a saw and a hammer, and you certainly don't have to be. There'll be other things and you'll be very good at them."

Damon choked back the tears. Doug had trouble hearing him, but it sounded like "Daddy, I love you."

He never slapped him again.

Two years later Damon discovered that one of the things he was very good at was the trombone. Music appreciation had been introduced into the sixth-grade curriculum that fall and once a week a man appeared to demonstrate the instruments of the orchestra. His name was Dan Parker. He had been bandmaster for the Sims-Kroto Circus until its sudden bankruptcy the year before and he had been stranded, along with all the other circus hands, in nearby Columbia. He was going on sixty when that happened, he was tired of the road, and he was happy for the chance to settle down when it came in the form of an offer from the Hastings School Board. Although what he knew about an orchestra was seriously deficient when it came to the string section, the board hired him anyway, largely because he was such a hearty and obliging soul and because his only competition for the job was a humorless woman of Wagnerian girth who played the violin well but whose unfortunate lisp greatly diminished her ability to teach it. Over the course of a semester Parker brought to class trumpets, cornets, tubas, trombones, french horns, and sousaphones. His pupils, especially the boys, were enchanted. When he let it be known that he would be available to give private lessons and could offer beginners' instruments at a discount, the response was enough to strain the budget of every family in the school district. Doug chose to take trombone lessons with the understanding that trombone players were in short supply and that after a year of lessons and practice he'd be qualified to join the junior-high marching band.

"Better the trombone than drums," Maude said when Damon first brought the instrument home. Happily, most of what she and Doug had to endure had the suggestion of melody, for his teacher had moved Damon quickly through scales and exercises before releasing him to practice by himself. One afternoon, about a month after Damon's first lesson, Doug was at his desk trying to add up a column of figures, half-listening to Damon blowing away in his room on the floor above. Gradually, there came the halting notes of a familiar song. Red-letter day!

"Maude," he called out excitedly. "Do you hear what I hear?"

She came to the door of his office and cupped her hands to her ears. "Oh my God," she said. "He's playing 'In Your Sweet Little Alice Blue Gown.'"

"For Alice," Doug said, as if Maude didn't know.

She smiled, nodding. "We won't say a word," she said.

Damon developed other interests that fall, each of which distanced him a bit farther from his father. He joined the neighborhood troop of cub scouts, which met early every Saturday morning, recessing in time for the members to go to morning matinees at the Majestic. The matinees were held exclusively for children under twelve. Admission was ten cents and the bill always included a western and a one-reel comedy, sometimes a cartoon to boot. Quite often, the movie let out so late that Doug had to cancel the weekly tennis game with Damon, and he came to resent it unreasonably. It sometimes seemed that he was gradually losing Damon to his music teacher, the cub scoutmaster, and the movies. It was Mr. Parker said this and Mr. Adams that, and if it wasn't Mr. Parker or Mr. Adams it was Tom Mix, Tim McCoy, Hoot Gibson, Ken Maynard, Buck Jones, or Jack Hoxie. Doug felt excluded and admitted to an infantile jealousy.

In February of 1929 the stock market experienced a brief collapse, then almost immediately righted itself. A month later it dropped again. It sank even lower in May before resuming a steady advance in June. By mid-summer prices were soaring and most investors, as many as a million of them trading on margin, were convinced that they were back on the route to Easy Street. ("Two steps up, one step down, two steps up again—that's how the market goes . . . I tell you, in a year some of these prices will look ridiculously low.") In September the market peaked; RCA, which had split its common stock the year before, was selling at an adjusted price of 505, having effectively staged an increase of nearly 400 points in fifteen months. Among the prospering majority, the conventional wisdom was that America had arrived at an era of perpetual growth; the Big Bull Market had no end.

Possum Trott was certainly of this opinion. Doug tended to agree, for so far Possum had given no cause to question his judgment. Maude, however, was made increasingly nervous by the market's performance, an apprehension that her distaste for Possum only intensified. She had seen the broker several times since their introduction the year before. With each new encounter what had begun as a simple dislike grew more and more into active distrust. "Those tiny beady eyes behind those pretentious gold-rimmed glasses!" she complained to Doug. "Those tight thin lips and the whiny way he talks and those small mincing steps when he walks—he gives me the creeps. And he scares me, if you want to know. God knows where he's taking us, but you can bet your last dollar, which well you may, it's not to the Promised Land."

Doug knew better than to laugh off Maude's anxieties but he considered them baseless and, on the evidence, unfair to Possum. Nevertheless, he had learned to respect, if not fear, her intuition. Gradually, his resolve weakened under her repeated and fervent entreaties. She kept pushing him to get out of the market—to take the winnings and use part of them to finance a construction loan and the rest toward start-up expenses for Krueger & Company. "You keep waiting, just because you're afraid you may lose a dollar or two if you pull out—before long it'll be too late." Finally, he struck a bargain with her. Let him hang on till November, then, no matter what the market was doing, he'd order Possum to sell. "Just a few more months, darling," he beseeched her. "I promise you, if the weather holds, we'll break ground in January."

Not altogether reassured, she agreed and said nothing more.

10

Early in October posters went up all over town announcing the coming of Jack Hoxie:

The famous cowboy star of the silver screen
IN PERSON
See Jack film a rootin'-tootin' scene
for his next movie!
ONE PERFORMANCE ONLY
Thursday, October 24
8 PM
MAIN EXHIBIT HALL, COUNTY FAIRGOUNDS
A special presentation of Davis Brothers Circus

Doug was afraid Damon might pee in his pants. "Jack Hoxie, Daddy! Can we go? Please, Daddy! Can we go?"

"Don't beg, Damon," Doug said, chuckling. "Of course we'll go. Would you like to take Alice with us?"

"Alice doesn't like cowboys," Damon said.

"All right, it'll be just you and me. Okay?"

"I'd like that," Damon said, barely able to contain himself. Touched, Doug gave him a giant hug.

"I've never seen him so excited," Maude said, pleased. "Are we raising our son to be a cowboy? Who's Jack Hoxie?"

"A sort of second-string western star. That is, he was. The talkies have not been kind to him. He's probably already made his last picture."

Doug remembered the runaway happiness in Damon's eyes. "I never quite appreciated this before," he said, "—how little it takes to give him pleasure, and how scary and satisfying it is to know you've got the power to give it or not. I just hope Damon's not disappointed."

She looked puzzled. "You mean with you, or Jack Hoxie?"

He frowned. "Maybe both," he said.

On the night before the big day, Maude had to give Damon two cups of warm milk and an aspirin before he could fall asleep. He went to school the next morning with nothing on his mind but Jack Hoxie and came home in such a state of anticipation that Maude feared he might be having a fever.

Doug was not at home to greet him. Earlier that day he had received a distress call from a customer in Lexington. The cords were missing in a shipment of seventy-five electric irons and the customer had to have them before quitting time in order to put them on display for a sale he'd advertised to begin the next morning. There was nothing else for Doug to do but to drive to the warehouse in Columbia, pick up enough cords to replace the seventy-five missing, and deliver them to the customer. In all, it was a trip of about sixty miles.

He made good time. The customer was grateful and asked Doug to have a drink with him before he hit the road again. Watching the clock, Doug agreed. At four-thirty he telephoned and asked Maude to reassure Damon that he'd be home in plenty of time for the show. He thanked his customer, excused himself, and started the return trip.

The road was dry and the sky clear. He pushed the Model A up to fifty. Relaxed, happy, and a bit light-headed from the booze, he began to sing—new songs like "Betty Coed," "I Got Rhythm," "Walkin' My Baby Back Home"; and some old ones—"Bye Bye Blackbird," "It Had to Be You," "Casey Jones," and "Show Me the Way to Go Home." His song repertoire exhausted, he started on all the verses he could remember: "Trees," "Ode on a Grecian Urn," "I Wandered Lonely as a Cloud—"

He was approaching the line, "I saw a crowd, a host, of daffodils," when out of the thick shrubs bordering the right berm came a dog, running full speed as if being chased. Doug slammed on his brakes and swerved to the left. He was too late. The right front tire caught the dog on his left leg. He went down and lay bleeding.

Doug stopped the car and ran to him. It was a magnificent animal, of mixed breed, more German shepherd perhaps than anything else. Thank God he was still breathing.

Doug looked at his watch. It was nearly seven o'clock, little more than an hour before he and Damon were due at the fairgrounds. Mindlessly, he began to cry—from shock, from compassion, from frustration, from anger. But he didn't hesitate. Using all his strength, he picked up the dog, carried him to the car, and put him on the front seat. The dog looked at him vacantly but somehow comfortingly. It was almost as if he were saying, "I know you didn't mean to do it," and it broke Doug's heart.

It was dusk now and Doug was afraid to drive fast. It took him at least a half hour to reach Lexington and another fifteen minutes to find and rouse a veterinarian.

The veterinarian, a soft-spoken, kindly man of about fifty-five, carried the dog gently to an examination table. Doug waited anxiously in silence. After a few minutes, the doctor smiled and said confidently, "There don't seem to be any internal injuries. Fortunately, you gave him only a glancing blow, just enough to break the femur and to take the wind out of him. He's going to be all right. I'll give him a mild sedative. I can mend the break, although he'll have to be in a splint for a while."

The dog was wearing a collar. His name was "Rinty" and he belonged to a farm family in the adjacent county. There was no phone number.

Doug looked at his watch again. It was now seven-thirty. There was no way he could make it home in time. He slumped in a chair in the vet's office, his head in his hands, despairing.

"Try not to feel too bad," said the vet. "It happens. It could happen to anybody."

"It's not just the accident," Doug said. He went on to explain.

"You go on home," said the veterinarian. "Let me take care of it. I'll locate the family and return Rinty. We have a very good humane society here and if I have any problems, I'll get one of their folks to help."

He gave the veterinarian his name, address, and phone number. When he offered him twenty dollars, the vet declined. "I do a certain amount of work pro bono," he said. "You've done more than your share." Doug took his card and made a mental note to remember him at Christmas.

He borrowed a phone and called Maude. He knew she must be wild with worry by this time and he tried not to upset her further. "I feel awful," he said. "It could have been a lot worse if I hadn't found such a good vet, but it'll take me another hour to get home. I'll never make Damon understand."

"Oh yes, you will," she said. "You underestimate your son."

"Maude, you'll have to take him to the fairgrounds."

"How can I, dearest? You've got the car. And have you forgotten? Trudy's taking me to the League meeting tonight. I'm leading the discussion. I don't see how I can get out of it."

"You've got a half hour. Find somebody who'll take him. Maybe Strut. The tickets are on top of my dresser. Damon will never forgive me if he misses Jack Hoxie."

She took the time to correct him. "What you mean, Doug, is that you'll never forgive yourself."

He swallowed hard. "Please, Maude."

"I'll see what I can do."

When he got home, he found only the hall light on. Neither Maude nor Damon was there. Maude had left him no note, but he assumed that she'd found somebody to take Damon to the show; the tickets were missing from his dresser. There was, however, a penciled note from Wilma: "3 PM. Mr. Trott. Urgent you call him." Urgent? It would have to wait till morning.

He was terribly tired. An almost impossibly heavy weight was descending on his shoulders. His stomach was churning. Slowly, and with effort, he made his way to the kitchen. He poured himself a stiff drink and took it into the living room, where he sat in the half dark and waited for Maude and Damon to return.

He must have dozed, for the next thing he heard was the sound of female voices on the porch and the opening of the front door. A moment later he was aware that Maude had turned up the lamp and was leaning over to give him a kiss.

"Trudy said to tell you how sorry she is about the dog."

He forced a weak smile. "I gather you found somebody to take Damon."

She took off her hat and coat, threw them over the back of the sofa, and sat down in the chair across from him. "Dan Parker."

"I'm glad," he managed to say. But he wasn't glad. He felt estranged.

"He was the first one I thought to call. He said he'd been thinking of going anyway—an old mate of his was in the circus band. He came right away." Damon got up to pour himself another drink. "I'll find a way to thank him," he said.

When he got back to his chair, he remembered to ask Maude how the League meeting had gone. She proceeded to tell him but his mind was elsewhere, confused by a fast choreography of disparate images drawn from the day's events, and he understood little of what she was saying. She sensed his detachment and stopped.

"We'll talk later," she said, giving him a pat on the shoulder. "You're tired. Damon should be here any minute now and we can go to bed."

He heard a car pulling into the driveway, and then the sound of a door slamming, followed by Damon's young voice and the soft tread of his Keds scurrying up the porch steps. A moment later Damon was in the room, his eyes sparkling and his face flushed. He jumped onto the arm of the chair and gave Doug a wet kiss.

"Oh Daddy," he said breathily. "You don't know what you missed! Mr. Hoxie came galloping in and he had Beauty—that's his horse—bow and roll over and play dead, and he did rope tricks and killed a man—not really killed, but you know—in a gunfight, and he knocked a cigar out of a man's mouth with a whip, and he shot bulls eyes with a bow and arrow. And there was this movie camera and he showed us how it worked. It was so much better than seeing him in the movies."

Doug hugged him to his chest. "I'm so sorry I couldn't have been there with you," he said. "Did mother tell you what happened?"

"Yes, sir," Damon said, momentarily chastened. "I'm glad the doggie will be all right."

"I would have been with you if I could."

"Don't feel bad, Daddy." His face was bright and alive again. "Mr. Parker knew this man in the band and the man introduced us to Mr. Hoxie, and Mr. Parker took our picture—me with Mr. Hoxie. And Mr. Hoxie gave me his address and said that if I'd send him the picture he'd autograph it for me. I bet I'll be the only boy in Hastings with an autographed picture of Mr. Hoxie! Mr. Parker—"

Maude saw the anguish in Doug's face. "That's enough for now, Damon," she said softly. "Daddy's had a very bad day, and we all need sleep. Come with me and I'll give you a glass of milk."

11

Doug woke up sluggish and with a mild headache. Maude was already up, fixing breakfast and getting Damon off to school. After taking an aspirin and splashing his face with cold water, he joined them in the kitchen and poured himself a cup of black coffee. Still glowing from the handshake with Mr. Hoxie, Damon kept asking how long he'd have to wait for Mr. Parker to get the picture developed. About the only response Doug could muster was, "Not long." Damon said he'd want more than one picture—maybe as many as three. "I want to send one to Grandma and give one to Alice." "Of course," Doug said, trying to summon the enthusiasm Damon expected of him. "And after Mr. Hoxie has autographed one, we'll get it framed. I'll make a special frame for you." Damon's eyes flashed with delight. "Oh, Daddy, will you? Will you, please?"

"I promise," Doug said.

After Damon had left for school and Maude was in the kitchen, Doug went to his desk and phoned Possum's office.

"I'm sorry, Mr. Krueger," Possum's secretary told him. "Mr. Trott can't take calls for a while. He's on the other line trying to get through to New York."

Puzzled, Doug turned to the *Courier*'s financial page. At first sight of the headlines his mouth went dry and his heart began to quiver.

WALL STREET CRASHES

Thousands of Accounts Wiped Out

The most disastrous decline in the biggest and broadest stock market of history rocked New York's financial district yesterday. The break carried down speculators big and little, in every part of the country, wiping out thousands of accounts. Total losses cannot be accurately calculated,

> but they were staggering, running into billions of dollars. Thousands of prosperous brokerage and bank accounts sound and healthy a week ago, were completely wrecked in the debacle.

Doug turned on WSC. "... the most demoralizing downslide in history. 'Sell! Sell at the market' was the cry heard yesterday on Wall Street and in board rooms all over the country. The ticker system was absolutely overwhelmed by the deluge. The ticker was running forty-eight minutes late before noon yesterday, meaning that its quotations were completely worthless. Stocks may have lost twenty or thirty points in the interval. Prices shot down in a devastating free fall and numerous stocks have been unable to find buyers at any price. It is estimated that before trading stopped the staggering sum of twelve billion dollars in market value had simply disappeared.

"Banker Thomas Lamont, of J.P. Morgan and Company, acknowledges that, in his words, there has been 'some distress selling,' but, encouragingly, Mr. Lamont goes on to say that he finds 'no houses in difficulty' and that 'reports from brokerage houses indicate margin position is satisfactory.'

"According to Mr. Lamont, the situation that arose on the floor late Wednesday afternoon was caused by technical rather than fundamental considerations. The foundation of the market is sound, he says, and too many sound stocks are selling too low."

Doug was sweating. He tried to reach Possum again. The secretary said he was still on the phone with New York.

"Give Mr. Trott a message for me," he told her. "I'm leaving immediately for his office. I'll expect him to see me in half an hour."

Upon Doug's entrance, Possum smiled, left his desk, and put out his hand. His palm was wet but he showed no other sign of nervousness. "What's the matter, Doug?" he asked indulgently. "Have the headlines got to you?"

"I want you to unload my portfolio. I want to get out."

Possum gestured Doug into a chair and returned to his desk.

"I never thought you were a summer soldier or a sunshine trader, Doug. Just because there's been some disturbance doesn't mean the market has collapsed."

"Then what has happened? Why were you trying to reach me yesterday?"

Possum looked as if he were being asked for uncalled-for sympathy. "Because I believe in being prepared. I thought we might get to the point where we might need to shore up your account."

"Shore up my account?"

"With additional margin—say a few thousand more, just enough to cover your losses."

"I thought I was covered."

"In fact you are covered. For now."

"So what are you saying, that you expect the slide to continue?"

"On the contrary," Possum said hastily. "I'm expecting the market to rally tomorrow."

"Then why do I need more margin?"

"Because I'm figuring the contingencies. And we have to be prepared for the worst. We have to contain the risks."Doug slumped. "I haven't got 'a few thousand more' to give you."

"We may not need it. We've nothing to worry about, unless we panic. There's nothing basically wrong with the market. What's happened has more to do with technical factors than with fundamental conditions. It just requires a little readjustment."

"I've heard that," Doug said sourly. "What does it mean?"

Possum ignored him. "It would be a very foolish thing for you to do, to sell out now. If anything, now's the time to buy. It's always time to buy when things look blackest. Prices are bound to go up again. Have I ever let you down?"

"So you think I should just sit tight. To keep the portfolio intact."

"Exactly," said Possum. "Let's see what happens Monday."

On his way out Doug passed through the customers' room, where perhaps as many as a dozen men, their bodies stiff with tension, were gathered around the ticker. Doug paused. RCA, which only a month before was selling for $110 a share, had dropped to $30.

He gave a shiver and went home—to wait for Monday.

Did Maude know? Of course she knew.

"How bad is it, darling?"

"Bad."

"You want to talk about it?"

"Later."

First, there was the weekend to get through.

Friday afternoon he raked leaves and chopped firewood, hoping to tire himself out. After supper he read himself to sleep with *The Bridge of San Luis Rey*. Awake at three, he got up and wrote a long-overdue letter to Catherine then went back to bed and tossed restlessly until seven. After a cup of coffee, he took Damon and Alice to the church's annual pancake breakfast. After dropping the children off at the Majestic for the Saturday morning western, he returned to the church and joined a group of male volunteers repainting the walls of the Sunday School room. Thereafter he moved on adrenalin and psychic energy. He played two sets of tennis with Strut, beating him 6-3 and 6-4, and three with Damon. Saturday evening he and Maude went to the club for the weekly dinner dance.

Sunday was a crisp and clear autumn day. After the eleven-o'clock service and a heavy lunch, he took Damon and Maude on a nature walk, starting from the lot on Huckleberry Lane. His wife and son were worn out and cross before they got back. He was invigorated. He raked more leaves until supper. He helped Maude wash up, then insisted on an hour of "family time" playing anagrams. When his wife and boy went off to bed, he picked up *Anna Karenina*. It didn't work. His sleep was broken with dreams of flight, failure, poverty, and impotence.

Irritable and in a mood of concentrated anxiety, he spent Monday trying to follow the reports from Wall Street. Possum's anticipated rally on Saturday had been followed by a rout. U. S. Steel was down 17.5 points, General Electric 47.5, Westinghouse 34. The bankers' earlier efforts to steady the leading stocks had failed.

The call came sometime after eleven Tuesday morning.

"Mr. Krueger? Please hold for Mr. Trott."

He waited five minutes. Finally:

"You better get on down here," Possum said.

"What's happening?"

"And bring your checkbook."

AN HOUR LATER Doug was out of Possum's office. He had made it back to the car and was sitting now behind the wheel, limp and weak, his heart skipping. He was hesitant to turn on the ignition for fear that he might faint before he could get home. He felt as if an invisible swarm of blood-sucking insects had invaded every orifice of his body and vacuumed the life out of him.

The session with Possum had been brief and, considering the circumstance, remarkably civil. Doug was so angry he didn't trust himself to speak, and whether from embarrassment or exhaustion Possum said little more than necessary. He offered no apology but went quickly to the point. The exchange was having its busiest day in history, the expectation being that more than sixteen million shares would have been traded before the final gong. Prices were perilously low and for some stocks there were few buyers at any price. The New York bankers ("the bastards)" were calling in brokers' loans, and brokers like him had no choice but to place calls for more margin. With an average loss per share of 40 percent, the market value of Doug's portfolio was now exactly $125.79 less than the $10,000 or more he'd been lent on margin, including interest at 6 percent. In addition, of course, there would be a modest brokerage fee. So, a check for $386.79 please. Possum had buyers on hold for a half hour. If he worked fast, he should be able to liquidate Doug's portfolio before dark. Trust him.

Stunned, Doug wrote the check, noting that it reduced his balance to $18.

Possum took the check and said nothing more except "the bastards," He kept repeating it under his breath like a satanic mantra.

Doug let his head fall on the steering wheel, closed his eyes to stem the tears, and considered where things stood. Five years of work and savings, down the drain. Investments a year ago worth $22,000, irretrievably lost.

Job prospects—dubious.

He figured that he and Maude had less than $650 in cash on hand, counting the $500 or so in their joint savings account and the three dollars and sixty-five cents he had in his pocket. For immediate income, he could count on only commissions from future appliance sales and system-design fees from Ned McDevit, both dependent on the purchasing power of families whose solvency was now surely in jeopardy. And what of his hopes for Krueger and Company? Where could he possibly find the capital now?

Liabilities? The biggest one was the outstanding loan for the three-acre lot where he and Maude were going to build a down-sized facsimile of her father's mansion. How hard from here on would it be to make the seventy-five dollar monthly payment? And there was rent to pay, and groceries and gasoline to buy, and clothes, and the tithe to the church, and club dues, and God knows what else.

He sat in silence for perhaps as long as a half hour. Finally, he sighed, took a deep breath, turned on the motor, and headed home to face Maude.

Maude had been listening to the radio off and on all morning. The news had gotten progressively worse. "At least ten thousand forlorn men and women have crowded into New York's financial district, including those long since wiped out, to follow the figures on the ticker. A *New York Times* reporter describes the scene as a street of shattered hopes and of curiously silent apprehension. Bankers and brokers alike agree that no such scenes will ever again be witnessed by this generation."

She switched the dial: "Estimates of margined accounts that will have failed before the close of business range as high as 70 percent." Disaster, she knew, was on its way. Indeed, it looked as if only a few among the insiders and the crafty—Joseph Kennedy, Bernard Baruch, the Rockefellers and the Fisher Brothers, if you could believe the financial pages—would escape it. For the gullible rest, the money loss was inevitable. How many other kinds of losses would there be—the loss of faith, the loss of trust, most importantly perhaps the loss of nerve?

She felt a shiver in her shoulders. She shook it off, wiped her hands on her apron, and walked out to the porch to wait for Doug.

She could hate him now for his naiveté and his vulnerability, the very things that she had always found so maddeningly endearing in him. She felt also like hating herself—for her ability neither to keep him from being victimized by his enthusiasms nor to save him from the lethal attacks of guilt that followed his failures. She swallowed hard. No matter what, she was not going to say I told you so.

"All right, let's get it over with," he was saying as he came up the steps. "Say it. You told me so."

She looked up from where she sat in the porch rocker. His cheeks had no color and his eyes were dull, but there was an unnatural smile, an almost desperate smile, around his lips. She rose and gave him a kiss.

"Are you trying to be funny?"

His body sagged. "I figured the best defense would be a strong offense."

"You are trying to be funny." She looked at him soberly and took his elbow. "Come on in the house. I've fixed you an egg-salad sandwich. You can tell me about it while you eat."

At the kitchen table where, it occurred to her, they seemed to transact all the important business of the family, she plopped down a bowl of tomato soup and his sandwich, and sat down in the Coca-Cola chair across from him. "Okay," she said. "How did it go? Where are we?"

He told her. When he finished, she sat in silence, expressionless. She didn't think of anything to say. Finally, she reached over and patted him affectionately on his wrist. She got up and went to the sink with the dirty dishes, turning her back to him. She didn't want him to see that her eyes were misting.

"You want to know how I feel?" Doug asked her.

"You don't have to say a word, Doug. I know how you feel." She ran a towel across her brow and, dry-eyed, turned to face him. "The question is, what do we do now?"

"I don't know where to start."

She returned to the table. "Oh yes you do. We start with the money. Or the lack of it."

"I feel awful. All I want to do is go to bed."

Her temples grew taut. She snapped. Her fists clenched and it took all her self control not to shake them in his face. "I can't bear it!" She heard herself shouting. "I can't bear it if you go into one of your blue funks. I'll never speak to you again!"

She saw the alarm, the fright, in his eyes. Instantly, she was horrified at what she'd said. "I'm sorry. I didn't mean that."

His chin had fallen to his chest and he was staring vacantly at the table cloth. "You're sorry. I'm the one who should be sorry." He raised his head and looked at her pleadingly. "I really don't know what to do. And I can't think. I'm so terribly tired. My legs feel like dumplings."

"Will you forgive me?" she asked.

"For what? I'm not worth your patience, much less your love."

"Oh shut up," she said.

They sat not speaking for a moment. Then Maude took a deep breath and said, reflectively and with quiet conviction: "Look, Doug. I didn't expect it to be all sunshine and fruit cake when I married you. I meant it, the business about sickness and health. I love you deeply. It's just that I can't stand it when you start flagellating yourself. I want you to appreciate yourself for the things I appreciate in you. Why can't you see that?"

"Because I think there's a terrible flaw in me. I keep making the same sort of mistake, over and over again. It's as though my instincts are all wrong. I should have known enough to be wary of Possum Trott. Why did I let him lead me on that way?"

She had no immediate answer for that. "Put Possum Trott behind you," she said, realizing that she was not being very helpful. "The thing is, we've got tomorrow to think about, and all the years ahead of us. And though it may be putting a cruel burden on you, we can't afford for you to be unemployed."

"It may be too much for me."

"Oh shit!"

He had never heard her use that word before and it shook him.

"What must I say to you?" she asked him sternly. "You're smart. You're handsome. You're talented. You've got friends. You've got a wife and a child who dote on you. You're still a young man. Finding another job can't be all that hard. Wallowing in water over the dam is like drowning in self-pity. You've got to get busy. Do you hear me, Doug? Get busy!"

The front door slammed. A moment later Damon had bounced into the kitchen.

"Look, Daddy," he said, holding out his hand. "Look what I found!"

It was an Indian arrowhead.

Damon looked at his father, his eyes full of innocence and faith and tacit devotion.

"That's wonderful," Doug said. "I want to hear all about it—where and how you found it. But now—" he rose and gave Damon a kiss on the top of his curly head—"Daddy's got to excuse himself."

He went to his desk and began drafting a letter to Professor Hunter asking if he knew of any available jobs.

MAUDE SAID THAT WITH THE MARKET CRASH America would never be the same again. She was right. An era had ended; the country was set for radical change. But the change did not come immediately and it took almost a year for it to become pervasive. Later, historians would describe the decade from 1920 to 1929 as a period of unprecedented prosperity, and indeed by many measures it was. The domestic market for automobiles was almost saturated during the decade; by the beginning of 1929 one out of every six Americans owned a car. During the same period power consumption increased at the rate of fifteen percent a year. Before World War I radio had been wholly unknown to most Americans; by the mid-twenties there was hardly a living room in the country without a receiver. True, some unlikely types—shoeshine boys, barbers, caddies, waitresses—had profited handsomely from market tips picked up from overheard conversations among affluent customers. But the bull market that would be remembered as the most visible expression of this mythical runaway prosperity was largely of benefit, and virtually confined to the country's elite. Many members of the great white middle-class, among them the Kruegers, the Montagues, and their country-club friends, had subscribed eagerly and cheerfully to the Glorious Illusion perpetrated by this elite. The vast majority of Americans, however, were non-participants; in a population of 110 million, most did not own even one share of common stock. Unaffected, if not disinterested, in the wane of fortunes among the players, most Americans were preoccupied as always with getting from one payday till the next, or, if farmers, from one crop season to the next. Cotton and wheat prices were approaching all-time lows. Appeals to Washington for relief were either dismissed by Congress or, on the one occasion they were embodied in remedial legislation, vetoed by a president who thought them inspired by Communists. The average weekly wage for factory workers was less than twenty-five dollars. Organized labor was savagely resisted and strikes were futile. In Gastonia, North Carolina, in 1928, a woman organizer for textile workers was murdered; the grand jury refused to indict her nine alleged killers "for lack of evidence." A few economists and political analysts, most of them viewed by editorial writers as Cassandras, pointed out that all may not be skittles and beer: the country was now a creditor nation, inventories were dangerously high, and the Labor Department estimated that four million Americans were unemployed. President Coolidge and after him President Hoover were nevertheless sanguine and programmatically reassuring. A month before leaving office, Mr. Coolidge spoke of the stability and "the permanent prosperity" achieved under his administration. On the day of his inaugural, Mr. Hoover said: "We have reached a higher degree of comfort and security than ever existed before in the history of the world . . . I have no fears for the future of our country."

Probably the hardest hit immediately after the crash were the nation's banks, more than a thousand of them failing between October 1929 and December 1930. Though the press tended to exaggerate their number, there were also enough suicides among brokers and investors to generate a new genre of sick jokes. Early on the morning of November 14, 1929, eight hours after the ticker reported stocks at an all-time low, W. D. "Possum" Trott—he of the iron will for whom "hold on" had been the first commandment—was found dead in his office of a pistol shot through the heart.

It was, however, well into 1930 before what came to be known as the Great Depression began to seriously affect the day's business. Stores continued to open at eight-thirty and close at five. In the cities and small towns there was little shortage of leisure time nor of the wherewithal to fill it. Miniature golf was fast replacing Mah Jong as a national craze. Movie houses flourished; more and more theaters were installing sound and patrons were flocking to hear Garbo call for a whiskey ("And don't be stingy, buster.") New York City reported a rise in unemployment as early as December 1929, but it was spring before jobs in industry and retailing were showing signs of declining elsewhere.

Doug and Maude had decided not to tell Catherine of their loss. They did not want to solicit her sympathy or to tell her anything to suggest they could use her help. When they visited her in Atlanta for Thanksgiving they skirted the subject, talking rather in general terms about prospects for the new year. Catherine said she worried about the stability of the Chesterton bank, for it was obvious that the board had authorized too many loans with insufficient collateral—"something your father would never have permitted." And there were rumors, she said, that Atlantic Ice and Coal, where she was a major shareholder, might not be able to make its regularly quarterly dividend. "We got badly overextended last year when we built that annex." Doug considered her remarks noteworthy mainly because it was the first time he had ever heard her express any qualms about money at all. They had discussed their situation with Strut and Trudy, not in morbid detail but sufficiently to make the Montagues understand that there would be no ground-breaking this year and that Doug would have to defer, if not abandon, his plans for Krueger and Associates. Strut too had lost in the debacle of Black Thursday. Wisely, however, he had sold his GM stock in September, just before it began its precipitous decline, so he had not been hurt beyond redemption. In fact, he offered to lend Doug some money if he needed it. "Maybe you ought to go ahead with Krueger and Associates in any event," he said. It was a tempting thought, but Doug said no. "I hardly think the time is ripe."

Doug continued to travel for General Electric. It made him more than a bit uneasy, however, that orders for big-ticket items—refrigerators, stoves, washing machines—were becoming fewer and fewer. What he took to be an even more forbidding omen was that one week in December, when sales normally increased with the coming of Christmas, orders were down so much that it took only one day on the road to fill them. Still, he did not feel immediately imperiled. He had three new assignments from McDevitt, which would bring in more than enough money to carry the family through the holidays. He also found comfort in the fact that he would no longer be having to make making monthly payments on the building lot. Maude had taken a look at how much interest her $3,000 inheritance was earning and compared it with the interest they were being charged for the bank loan, which after two years had been reduced to $2,100. It was clear that now they'd be better off to get clear title to the lot, so she urged him to let her pay off the bank. "If it's important to your ego," she said, teasing him, "you can consider it a flirtation loan." He opened his mouth to say, "I don't have enough ego left to worry you." Instead, he gave her a kiss and said "thank you."

Shortly before Thanksgiving he got a reply from Professor Hunter.

Dear Douglas.

What rotten luck!

I wish I could help, and I'll try. The job situation, however, is murky. The utilities are hiring only at the entry level and they've all but stopped active recruiting. Like most corporations I'm familiar with, they're in a waiting posture, hoping for better times but meanwhile cutting back. The prevailing policy seems to be to reduce the work force by attrition. Experienced supervisors and executives are rarely fired, although in many companies they're being encouraged to take early retirement. Vacancies, when they occur, aren't being filled.

I'll keep you in mind should anything turn up worthy of you. Try not to be too discouraged. I don't think anybody truly understands how our economy works, but one thing for sure: it can't function at all if it lets men of your ability stay idle for long.

Keep in touch.

Fondly,

Abe Hunter

During the first two weeks after the market failure, Doug had sent out a dozen resumés to businesses and small manufacturers in and around Hastings. To some he got polite rejections; from two he got suggestions that he try again after New Year's; the others might as well have been addressed to the dead letter office. By the end of November he was getting jittery. With home building at a halt, he was getting no new assignments from McDevitt, and in December General Electric informed him that new orders for home appliances were being put on ice pending reorganization of the production and marketing departments.

At the critical moment, however, he got an offer.

"Mr. Krueger? This is Jim Rogers. We've met, I think, at Civitan. I'm the station manager at WSC. We've just lost our chief engineer—rather unexpectedly, I'm afraid. Are you available? Joe Pelissier tells me you're the best electrical engineer in the state."

Bless Joe Pelissier's heart! "When do you want me?"

Doug heard a cough. Presumably, Mr. Rogers was having trouble collecting his thoughts. "I guess I should tell you," Doug heard him say after a moment's pause. "We had to fire our chief engineer this morning. He was caught making obscene phone calls. Last night, on company time, from the office phone. Apparently he'd been making a habit of it. Could you start at four this afternoon?"

So Doug swallowed his pride and went to work as a technician at the radio station that had killed his dream.

From Joe Pelissier, who now sat on the WSC board, he learned more about the event that brought him the opportunity. Adam Green was one of two engineers on the staff. He was an unprepossessing man, about fifty years old, a widower and childless, a quiet diffident type, not unfriendly but also not of a mind to speak unless spoken to. He'd been at the station from the day it opened and was thought to have done his job faithfully and well.

The two engineers were supposed to alternate day and night shifts and were doing so until a month or so ago when, surprisingly. Green said he'd prefer to work nights only. His colleague, being a family man who'd rather spend his nights at home, welcomed the new arrangement and thought nothing of Green's request other than that it seemed a bit eccentric.

"Now we know," Pelissier said. "From nine till sign-off at midnight, nobody's on duty at the studio except the engineer and an intern who does the station breaks, so Green pretty much had the place to himself. He had this thing—he got his kicks out of calling young girls and talking dirty. I guess some of the girls liked it. But a few of them obviously didn't and they told their parents and the parents got the phone company to trace the calls. They were some agitated, I must say, when they found that the calls were coming from WSC. Anyway, they've had Green arrested and they're threatening to sue the station."

"Had he been drinking?"

"Not that we know."

"And he hasn't denied it?"

"No." Pelissier gave an ambiguous grimace, as if he didn't know whether to show pity or distaste. "All he's said—he told Rogers he got lonely, especially at night. He said nobody loved him. Nobody even liked him."

Pelissier's words struck a nerve in Doug with the force of a premonition. It was not a long stretch to identify with Adam Green. The poor, sick bastard.

12

His starting salary with WSC was $225 a month, only twenty-five dollars more than he'd been earning in 1922 when he'd quit his job with Amos Poole. He and Maude were back on their newlyweds' budget. Rent had gone up by $15 a month, living expenses generally were higher, and they had to watch their pennies. Still, Doug counted himself lucky. He was promised a raise in January, assuming satisfactory performance, and he felt secure for the first time since his break with Akin. The feeling, he told himself, was not altogether justified, for economic forecasts were mixed and talk among his Civitan friends had lost its canonized optimism. The image of a former California millionaire named Fred Bell, reproduced in newspapers all over the country, had emerged as a symbol of the times: along with thousands of others, Mr. Bell had been reduced to selling apples on street corners.

Doug shared a desk and a control panel with an amiable forty-year-old Clemson graduate named Harry Ashmead, whom he saw every day but only long enough to exchange greetings and transfer the log when the shifts changed. Doug began on the evening shift, from four to midnight. Two weeks later he went on the morning shift, from eight till four, and thereafter alternated shifts with Harry every fourteen days. The work was largely routine, although it was understood that his main value to the company was that he would be on hand and would know what to do in case of a power failure or some act of God that threatened transmission. Once he had learned the switching schedules, the work was relatively free of stress. It actually gave him, especially on the night shift, an unconscionable amount of free time, most of which he spent reading the *New York Times*, three copies of which the station received every morning by air courier. He told himself that, considering the fragile nature of his spirit, it was probably exactly the kind of job he needed at the time. The only disadvantages, in fact, were the hours. To get to the station by eight, he had to get up an hour earlier than he'd been accustomed to rising, which meant that he was out of the house before Damon was off for school, and he missed the time with him around the breakfast table. When he was on the night shift he barely saw Damon at all. Because Christmas fell during his turn to work nights, Maude and Damon went to the club's Christmas party without him, gifts were exchanged at breakfast instead of on Christmas Eve, and Christmas dinner was hurried.

The job had little to challenge him. Once he'd picked his way through the day's *Times*, boredom set in. Worse, his mind tended to wander and to dredge up unpleasant events from his past—gaucheries from his childhood and adolescence, mistakes in judgment long beyond remedy, good intentions gone bad, wrongs he had committed and wrongs that had been committed against him. Some time before, into a secret compartment of his wallet, he had tucked the picture Azalie had sent him of young Douglas. Days, weeks, months had gone by when he had failed to look at it, indeed almost forgotten that he had it, but now, in the hours that he was alone at the station, he found himself pulling it out as almost an act of ritual, caressing it, looking at it hypnotically, wondering how his boy was faring and if there would ever come a circumstance when he could see him. It was a painful thing to do, and why he invited the pain he did not know except that he was moved by some dark punishing compulsion. The snapshot had been taken when Douglas—dare he think of him as Douglas Junior?—was ten. It was of an attractive young boy with black hair, deep-set, somewhat brooding eyes that were either deep brown or black, a strong nose, full lips, and a rather wistful expression. The photograph was in black and white and Doug could not tell the color of the boy's skin; he imagined it to be the color of a pecan shell, like his mother's. Clearly, he took his good looks from his mother. Doug was glad that he did, for somehow he wanted to keep him distanced from Damon. It was not the picture of a carefree or uncritical child. There was a wry smile on his face that suggested an intelligence, an awareness of the real world, too sharp and clear for sustained happiness. For that, Doug blamed himself.

Douglas would be fourteen now, a sophomore in high school undoubtedly. What was it like to be a Negro and fourteen in Chicago? Doug's imagination failed him. After their telephone reunion, he and Azalie had agreed to be in touch only to let each other know of a change in address and only in emergencies, and God help there be few of these. From two short notes received over the past three years, he had learned that, though in a committed relationship with the same Jamaican lawyer, she was still unmarried. She and young Douglas were living in an apartment in Oak Park. When asked, she apparently presented herself as a widow; Doug Jr. was known as Douglas Krueger. She had obtained her degree in library science and was working at the University of Chicago.

Alone for so much of the time, Doug slipped into a numbing lethargy that extended into the weeks when he was working a normal daylight shift. He began to feel tired all the time. He was either getting too much sleep or not enough. Driving to work every day was increasingly troublesome; he developed a tendency to pull to the left and he was afraid he might swerve into an oncoming car. Scared, aware of the change in him, and determined not to fall into what Maude had called "another blue funk," he fought back. He joined a calisthenics class at the Y. He met with male friends for lunch at least twice a week. In the afternoons he drove out to the lot with Maude and tried to wear himself out planting dogwoods. Before breakfast on the mornings he didn't have to go to work he pressed her into making love. The forced activity brought him little satisfaction. Sex was joyless; his orgasms came like an exercise in therapy and he was sure Maude sensed it.

One night early in February the young intern failed to show up. For a minute or more, WSC went dead. As fast as he could, Doug made it to the turntable and, without looking at the label, put on the first record he could put his hands on. Fortunately, it was "Sleepy Time Down South," which gave him a theme. He picked up the microphone. "All right folks." The words came unsolicited, from some alert prompter in his subconscious. "Lie back, close your eyes, and relax for some easy bedtime listening." His voice suddenly became honeyed. As he spoke, ("This is your friendly old sandman—") his hand pawed frantically through the stack of records for soft ballads and waltzes ("No Dixieland tonight, folks, and no marches. Just some waltzes and a few lullabies. It's sleepy time in Hastings"). He spent the rest of the evening until sign-off spinning records, improvising as necessary to cover the pauses when he changed them. Every half hour, he interrupted the music to make a station break. He had barely closed out with the Star Spangled Banner when the phone rang.

"Who was that scrumptious voice tonight?" Some girl, obviously a young one, wanted to know. He said he didn't know and hung up. A second later, the phone rang again. Another voice, same question.

The third call was from Jim Rogers.

"Was that you on sign-off, Doug?"

Doug gulped and told him it was.

"What happened to the kid?"

"I don't know. He didn't show. I thought I better fill in."

"Thanks. My wife's fallen in love with your voice. She says we ought to have you doing the news."

Doug forced an embarrassed laugh. "I might like that if it meant I could get off the night shift."

"Perhaps we can talk tomorrow," Rogers said sleepily.

Rogers was true to his word. He asked Doug to come to the studio the next afternoon for an audition.

Doug ran through an AP news report and two commercials. Rogers sat in his adjacent office studio and listened. With him were the station's program director, the sales and promotion managers, and his secretary. When Doug was done, Rogers called him into his office and offered him a new job.

"We've been getting complaints about our news man," Rogers said, "He's gotten careless. Slurs his words. Has been insulting to a couple of sponsors. We think he has a drinking problem. The four of us who heard you this morning"—he turned to his secretary and smiled—"including Miss Hagerty, whose taste is impeccable, like what we heard."

Doug, who was feeling vaguely disoriented, didn't speak.

"We'd like to give you a try—put you on the air doing the news round-ups, fifteen minutes, three times a day. You'd be on probation, say, for a month. After that, if all goes well, as I expect it will, you'd have a contract and a raise. How about it?" Doug swallowed hard and tried to smile. "Would I write my own scripts?"

"You could, of course. It would be a matter of pulling items off the AP ticker and editing pieces from the *Courier* and patching in the weather reports, government handouts, announcements from local organizations, that sort of thing. It shouldn't be difficult, three times a day."

"When would I start?"

"As soon as we can find another engineer—and another intern, preferably one with a happy love life. You know what happened last night, don't you? Thomas had a fight with his girlfriend and went off on a bat."

Two weeks later Doug was off the night shift and on the air every day at eight, noon, and five. Rogers had decided to make no announcement of the change in newsmen until the change was permanent. The response from listeners, however, was so enthusiastic that a columnist for the *Courier* gave Doug a long mention. "What a relief to hear somebody give us the news without sounding as if there's a crisis around every corner. Doug Krueger comes to us like our next-door neighbor and he credits us with an average amount of common sense. He speaks clearly and in a voice that's pleasant to hear. He's as friendly and as believable as your favorite uncle." Doug was overwhelmed with phone calls and notes of congratulation, most of them from strangers. He had never before realized the strength of radio's appeal and he was awed by it. "Just don't let it go to your head," Maude warned him.

Maude need not have worried. Acknowledging his inexperience and sensitive to the tacit responsibility that came with radio's power to influence, he sought advice from the veteran managing editor of the *Courier*. Much of what the editor said was obvious: "You're in a new medium and we're only beginning to understand how to use it. It's a more informal medium than print. Few readers remember our by-lines, but listeners can feel absurdly personal about radio reporters and I think they may be quicker to believe what they hear than what they read." Doug took to heart some of the editor's advice: "Keep it low-key and intimate. I think

Graham McNamee and that early bunch had it all wrong; they sounded like evangelists at a revival meeting and that can soon become be a very tiresome sound. Keep your sentences short and your style conversational. And by all means keep your opinions to yourself. Objectivity should be the standard for reporting in any medium. Besides—you editorialize too much and people are going to turn you off, believe me."

The news Doug was given to report during the spring and summer of 1930 was of a kind neither to inspire the community to loosen the hatches nor to lift his own spirits. The French pulled their last troops out of Germany's Rhineland. Jack Sharkey threw a low blow and lost the heavyweight championship to Max Schmeling on a foul. Gang warfare was renewed in Chicago. Drought reduced U.S. corn production by more than 690 million bushels. Adolf Hitler's Nazis went from twelve seats in the old Reichstag to a hundred and seven in the new to become the second largest party in Germany.

Doug leavened his dreary summaries with as many stories about animals and babies and sports figures as the wire services provided. Twice a week he devoted five minutes of the evening broadcast to an interview with some local personality, starting with Joe Pelissier, whose candid and oblique views about the movie business were received like sherbet after spinach. ("There's a new production head at Warner Brothers. His name is Darryl Zanuck and he's determined to bring reality to the screen. No more tea-cup dialogue. Watch for films drawn from the headlines, featuring gangsters and their molls, starring a new breed of actors from Broadway who know how to talk.") When the mail brought in requests for more, he made Joe a regular guest every fourth Friday of the month. His interviews with Hastings's civic leaders and local heroes proved to be almost as popular, especially after he introduced "The Citizen of the Month" award. The feature was so popular that Rogers extended the six o'clock news show on Fridays to thirty minutes and gave Doug another raise.

To help him find guests, Doug organized an advisory board—the president of Rotary, the executive director of the Chamber of Commerce, the head of the League of Women Voters, the dean of students at Hastings

Junior College. The board didn't produce as many interesting guests as Doug would have liked, but its existence was extraordinarily good public relations for WSC. Techniques for measuring audience size were primitive in those days (It would be years before A. C. Neilsen invented the first scientific rating system) but the volume of mail and the increased sales of his sponsors' products were clear evidence that more and more people were listening to WSC News and liking it. Jim Rogers was delighted; he was almost as pleased with Doug as he was with himself for having hired him. After a year on the air Doug was established as a local celebrity, a status confirmed when his picture was displayed in four colors and in billboard size on the panels of the *Courier*'s delivery trucks. He was asked so often to speak at schools and luncheon clubs that he had to prepare a form letter explaining apologetically that his duties in the news department didn't permit personal appearances. The station assigned a secretary full time to help him handle his mail.

Curiously, it was at this time in his life, when he was prospering and his work was being widely respected and appreciated, that his depression returned. Absorbed in his job and exhilarated by the opportunities to apply himself creatively, he had been emotionally well, on occasion almost euphoric, for more than a year. Now, inexplicably, he was revisited by his old fears and anxieties.

The illness moved gradually from moderate to severe and it was marked by a diurnal shift in mood. Regularly, right after supper, and often before supper was over, an enormous weight began to settle on his shoulders and back. He felt himself being pulled down. The lights were dimming. He had to take deep breaths for fear of suffocating. The symptoms grew worse as the evening wore on, when he became increasingly contrary. ("Try not to be so perverse, dear," Maude told him once, "You're acting like a precocious two-year old. Either that, or a cranky old man, and there may not be much difference.") He was impatient when friends called, ridiculously bothered every time the phone rang and resentful of the need to make conversation. Getting dressed and going to a party or to the theater was an intolerable burden. When he went to bed for the night, he fell asleep promptly, but he habitually woke up at two or three in the morning and rolled and tossed sometimes for as long as an hour before managing to go back to sleep. He had bad dreams, two of them recurrent. In one, he was walking in a panic, seemingly forever, between rows of automobiles in a strange parking lot, looking for his own car and never finding it. In the other, Maude had fallen and was lying helplessly with a broken hip and he was unable to help her, either because he was too weak to lift her or because somebody had tied his arms and legs and he was immobilized. Sometimes it was not Maude who had fallen but Azalie.

Invariably, when he woke up after such dreams he was quivering and his pajamas were soaking in sweat. Trying not to awaken Maude, he would let himself out of bed as quietly as he could and shuffle into the guest room, where he would lie on his back in the darkness, his eyes shut, his body numb. An oppressive sorrow would descend upon him. He would begin to weep soundlessly, fearful that he might never stop. It was usually then that the thought would come to him like a rifle shot: this was the way it was going to be for him the rest of his life. He was struck with terror. He wished to die.

Miraculously, when daylight came his mood would reverse itself. Climbing back into bed with Maude, he felt oddly dry and cool, the way he remembered feeling as a child after a summer attack of malaria. Tired, he would fall into a deep and healing sleep, awaking only on Maude's third summons to breakfast.

During the daylight cycle his demons left him. His mind was clear. He did his job competently and occasionally invested it with brilliance of invention. His manner was more subdued, his speech more deliberate, but otherwise the WSC staff noticed little change in him. The approach of dusk, however, brought a renewal of suffering that grew into terror as the night wore on. He hated to go to bed, knowing that rest would elude him and that what sleep he managed would be accompanied by nightmares laden with guilt and self-loathing.

About ten one morning, as he was beginning to pull together his noon newscast, Miss Wren, his secretary, brought Doug a special delivery letter. "Sorry to interrupt you," she said, "but I thought you might want to see this. It's from Chicago."

His mouth went dry. He was trembling as he opened the envelope. A news clipping fell out.

> VALEDICTORIAN DIES OF MENINIGNITIS
>
> Douglas Krueger, class valedictorian and winner of this year's Spencer Medal for Athletic Achievement at Walt Whitman High School, died yesterday morning from spinal meningitis, a few days short of his seventeenth birthday.
>
> Doctors at Roosevelt Hospital said his illness had been sudden and—.

An enormous hammer hit Doug in the pit of his stomach. He lowered his head to hide the turmoil in his face. How could it be?

"Mr. Krueger?"

He looked at his secretary but didn't recognize her.

"Are you all right, Mr. Krueger?"

He spoke with great effort. "I'd like to be alone for a while," he said, his voice barely audible. "I'll be all right."

Miss Wren looked at him uncertainly and left his office, closing the door behind her.

A note in longhand was attached to the clipping. "I'm notifying Mr. Luck. Phone me when you can. Love. A."

He picked up the phone and asked the operator to get him Azalie in Chicago. No answer. He tried again. Still no answer.

Dazed and agitated, he rose, put the envelope and its contents in the inside pocket of his jacket, slipped on the jacket, and walked unsteadily out of the station without saying a word to anybody. He made it to the parking lot, oblivious to the soft October rain that had begun to fall. He held the tears until he was in the privacy of the parking lot. Once behind the steering wheel he began to cry in great convulsive sobs. Hardly conscious of what he was doing, he pulled out into the downtown traffic and drove north until he picked up the macadam road to Columbia. Crying and cursing, he pressed the accelerator to the floorboard and sped recklessly into open country.

13

About eleven that morning Maude got a call from Miss Wren. "I don't mean to alarm you, Mrs. Krueger, but it's only a half hour or so before air time and we can't locate Doug. Is he with you?"

"No. I don't expect to see him till suppertime."

"It's probably nothing to worry about," Miss Wren said. "Except it's not like him. He just left the office about an hour ago without telling a soul where he was going."

Maude had to know. "Did anything out of the ordinary happen this morning?"

"He got a letter. A special delivery letter, from Chicago, I think. He said he wanted to be alone for a while. Next thing I knew he was gone."

"He probably just wanted some quiet time," Maude said, trying hard to believe it. "Let me know when he shows up."

She hung up the phone and fell into a chair. Her mind was racing. What should she do? Where was Doug? What ever had possessed him? For him to have left the studio in mid-morning and told no one where he was going, he must have had a panic attack or otherwise been taken sick without warning. But what had in God's name had moved him to drop his work and hurry away to God knows where?

At a loss, she called Strut's office. "Mr. Montague is in conference," the receptionist informed her. "Would you like to leave a message?"

Maude's voice was shaking. "This is an emergency. Please—" A moment later Strut was saying, "Maude? What's up?"

"Doug's missing," she said, trying hard not to sound alarmist. "I think he may have had some sort of seizure. I need your help."

The phone was muffled. She heard him give somebody an apology and perhaps a last-minute instruction.

Then, "Are you at home? I'll be right there. I'll pick up Trudy."

She opened the front door, saw that it was drizzling, and came back to the hall for a raincoat. She went out on the porch and sat in a rocker to wait for Strut and Trudy. By the time they arrived she had eliminated all but one on her short list of places where Doug might possibly be.

She rose when the Montagues drove up. She climbed into the back seat of the Chevrolet before Strut had time to open the door for her. She wanted to hug them both but the best she could do from her position was to give each a kiss on the tops of their heads. "What would I do without you?" she said, barely able to contain the tears.

"Where do we start?" Strut wanted to know.

"He's either just driving around, not caring where he is and not going anywhere," she said, "or maybe gone out to the lot. The lot has always meant refuge for him somehow. If he's not there—" She shuddered. "If he's not at the lot, I'll begin to think he's been in an accident. But I don't want to start calling the police or the hospitals until we've had a look. Let's try the lot."

The four-mile trip to Honeysuckle Hills was agony for her. The drizzle had turned into a light steady rain and the sky was the color of charcoal. As they approached the piney woods that occupied most of the land on their still undeveloped lot, fog rolled in. The landscape was suddenly unfamiliar and unfriendly. She rolled down the window and stuck her head out for a clearer view. At the entrance to their lot, fifteen or so feet off the road, she spotted their A-model Ford.

"Stop," she told Strut, opening the car door and stepping out as she spoke. "If you don't mind, let me go to him. If I need you, I'll yell."

As fast as her legs could carry her, she ran down the makeshift path that led to the clearing by the side of the creek, her feet slipping on the wet pine needles and her nose full of the sour smell of damp decaying leaves. She moved in and out of shadows and had to squint to see ahead of her. Several times she had to stop to disentangle her skirt from briars and thorns. At the edge of the clearing, she tripped on a fallen log and came close to falling.

When she straightened up she saw Doug on the ground before her.

He was lying face down on a bed of wet weeds and mud, his body moving in spasms. His hair was matted. His jacket was awry, his collar open, and his chin and shirt crusted with vomit. She ran to him. She kneeled and cradled his head in her arms. "My God, Doug," she sobbed. "What happened, baby?"

He opened his eyes and the expression on his face was like that of a figure in some Old Testament illustration of the damned. In the high, cracking voice of a very old man, he said: "Help me."

She yelled at the top of her voice. "Strut! Trudy!"

She found Kleenex in her coat pocket, dampened it with rain water, and wiped his face and chin. She spoke to him but she wasn't sure that he heard her, for his head had fallen back, his eyes were shut and he appeared to have lost consciousness. She tried to lift him to a sitting position but his body was a dead weight and she could not move him. Strut arrived on the run, followed by Trudy, panting heavily, a few seconds later. Strut bent down and put his forefingers on Doug's carotid arteries. "He's got a strong pulse," he said reassuringly. "Let's see if we can get him to the car." He put his hands under Doug's armpits and pulled him forward. "Doug, it's Strut. Can you hear me? Try to put your arms around my neck."

When Doug made no response, Strut sat on his heels, put his hands under the limp and helpless form and, with strength he didn't know he had, lifted Doug and drooped him over his right shoulder in a fireman's carry. "Let's go," he said and began to trot, almost unmindful of the weight of Doug's body, with Maude and Trudy behind him struggling to keep up. He had gone only about twenty feet when Doug stirred and mumbled.

"I think he's trying to say put him down and let him walk," Trudy said.

Maude spoke into Doug's left ear. "Is that what you mean, dearest? Do you think you can walk to the car?"

Doug nodded but said nothing. Strut lowered him gently to the ground and held onto him until he got his balance. Slowly, supported by Strut on one side and Maude on he other, Doug took a step forward, paused, and then another. Slowly, the four of them made it back to the road.

Assuming command, Strut gave Trudy the keys to the Chevrolet and told her to drive to the nearest phone. "Call Dr. Wolfe and tell him to get to Doug's house as soon as he can—immediately." His words were clipped and he was moving as he spoke. He would drive the Ford, he said, with Doug in the back seat with Maude. They would meet at the Kruegers'. "Don't waste any time, but drive carefully. It's raining harder."

Maude sat with Doug's head in her lap all the way home. She comforted him as best she could, murmuring wordless messages of confidence that she prayed time would justify. He was silent throughout the trip.

As they neared their house he roused himself and, again with Strut's help, made it up the steps, onto the porch, and from there up to the bedroom on the second floor. Once he fell into the bed he passed out again. With some difficulty, Maude removed his jacket and took off his muddy shoes.

"Let him lie like that till Wolfe comes," Strut said. "Whatever's wrong with him, sleep can't do anything but help."

Trudy joined them. She sat in the room's one chair, Strut on the window seat, Maude at the foot of the bed. The three of them waited nervously for the doctor, taking warmth from one another's company and what satisfaction they could from the fact that Doug was breathing regularly.

Stan Wolfe arrived a half hour later. He was almost seventy years old and had been practicing common-sense medicine for almost forty-five years. He took Doug's pulse and blood pressure, put a stethoscope to his chest and lungs, looked at his eyes and tongue, and checked his reflexes. "Except for that ugly wound on his forehead—he must have fallen, hit his head on a log perhaps—I see nothing abnormal at all." He dressed the wound, then fumbled around in his bag and pulled out a vial. "If he has trouble sleeping tonight, give him one of these."

He closed his bag and gave Maude a fatherly hug. "You never can tell—maybe there's something internal. I need to give him a complete physical. Bring him to the office tomorrow." He felt into a coat pocket for his appointment book. "Say about eleven."

He saw the mist in Maude's eyes and gave her another hug. "I won't tell you not to worry," he said. "But I will say I'll do everything I can." She kissed him.

After the doctor had gone, Strut wanted to know if there was something he and Trudy might do. "Would you like us to stay awhile?"

"I don't think so," Maude told him. "This has already cost you too much time. And the truth is, I think I'd rather just be alone with him. I'll call if something comes up."

"We understand," Trudy said, rising to go. "But Damon will be home from school before long. Why don't you send him over to be with me and Alice? I'll fix milk and cookies."

Maude went with them downstairs to the front door. She was having trouble finding the right words. "Oh God how I love you two," she said clumsily. She watched them go down the porch steps and cross the street to their own house. She waited until Strut had gotten into the Chevrolet and was headed back to his office and until Trudy had closed the door and gone inside. Then she burst into tears.

Back upstairs, she washed her face and looked in on Doug. He was still lying motionless. When Damon came in a bit later, she told him that Aunt Trudy had called and invited him over to have cookies with Alice. He looked surprised but pleased and left obediently. She went back to the bedroom.

She pushed a chair close to the side of the bed and sat for some time watching Doug and trying to bring her thoughts together. He was asleep on his back, an uncustomary position for him, his head sunk in a pillow, his arms folded on his chest. He was drooling slightly. Every now and again his body would give a twitch and his head a fleeting jerk, as if in reaction to a bad dream. Otherwise his posture was one of incorrigible innocence.

What he evoked in her now was a mixture of undiluted love, a fear that he might be suffering a disease beyond diagnosis, and an anxiety about the future for which she could see no relief. Doug would be thirty-five in September. He had lost none of his good looks. He might have gained ten pounds since their wedding but he still had the body of an athlete. His cheeks and neck were firm, his hair still the color of champagne, his stomach as flat as a long-distance runner's. But what turbulence lay under that handsome skull? What crazy sirens were singing from his seething brain? She leaned over and patted her husband on the shoulder. Her friend, her child—this beautiful flawed man!

She rose, went to the bathroom, and returned with a basin of warm water, a wash cloth, and a towel. She took off his socks, unbuckled his belt and pulled off his trousers, and unbuttoned his shirt. "I can't get your shirt off, baby, unless you sit up. I want to give you a sponge bath and get you into some pajamas." Without a word, he rolled over on his left elbow and sat up. She helped him out of his shirt and rolled down his BVDs. "Now, lie back down and turn on your side. I'll do your back first." He did as he was told and as she rubbed him with the warm wet cloth he dozed off again. A moment later he was murmuring softly and sighing, whether in protest or from pleasure she couldn't tell. She thought she heard him giggling. Then, distinctly: "That's enough, Azalie."

She stopped. "Doug?"

"Uh-huh."

"Were you giggling?"

He opened his eyes, turned on his side, and gave her a questioning look.

"I was giggling?"

"Who is Azalie?"

Oh my God! "Azalie?" He swallowed hard and tried to look as if he was having trouble remembering.

"You were talking to somebody named Azalie. It sounded like Azalie."

"Oh, Azalie," he said convincingly. "She was a nurse I had—that summer when I had malaria or something, when I was seventeen."

With the help of the chloral hydrate that Dr. Wolfe had left for him, Doug got through the night with less disturbance than usual. Shortly after daybreak, he felt a spurt of energy and an easing of mind and he remained calm and relatively lucid until first dusk.

Over a late breakfast, Maude told him that Jim Rogers had called.

"He wanted to know how you are and to ask if there was anything he could do to help. He said to tell you to take as long as necessary to get well. Not to worry. He asked what you wanted the station to say about your absence. I gather they've been getting a lot of calls from listeners."

Doug grunted. "Tell him to say I had a stroke."

"You don't mean that."

"Or I've had a heart attack."

"That won't do either, Doug."

He frowned and became very serious. "Tell him to announce that I was stricken suddenly and that the cause is yet to be diagnosed. Tell him to say I hope to be back on the air soon. Meanwhile I'm on indefinite sick leave."

She wrote it down.

"Don't you also want to thank the people who've phoned to ask about you?"

"Of course."

She went to the phone and read Rogers Doug's statement. When she returned, she poured herself another cup of coffee. "They're issuing a news release," she said. "There seems to be a lot of interest in what happened to you." She raised the cup to her lips, took a long swallow, and looked at him with an expression of sympathy edged with mild reproach, wondering why he hadn't volunteered what she was about to ask him.

"So, Doug, what did happen?"

"I panicked."

"I know. But why?"

"I can't remember."

"Miss Wren says that just before you left the studio you got a Special Delivery from Chicago."

"I did?"

"Who was it from?

"I don't know."

"What did you do with the letter? Do you remember that?"

He shook his head.

"And you don't remember what it said."

"No."

Doug was not good at dissembling. She knew he was lying.

But now was not the time to press. She sighed and began clearing the table. "We're due at Dr. Wolfe's at eleven. We better get dressed."

Doug went without protest. He submitted uncomplainingly to being probed and prodded. He gave blood and urine specimens and was x-rayed in every body part that the somewhat primitive machine could reach. Wolfe then sat him down and talked with him like an old and caring friend, soliciting a detailed account of Doug's symptoms. He dismissed him about one o'clock, saying he'd phone with the test results in a day or so.

The next day his nurse called the house and asked to speak with Mrs Krueger. "This is Mrs. Krueger," Maude said, suspecting bad news. A second later, Wolfe was on the phone.

"Maude?" She said yes, tremulously. "Can we speak in private?"

"Yes," she answered. "Doug's in bed and Damon is in school. There's nobody here but me and Wilma."

"I've changed my mind," he said abruptly. "Maybe we should talk in the office. Can you manage to get down here this afternoon alone, without letting Doug know?"

"You've found something awful, haven't you?"

"No," he said quickly. "That's the problem. I've found nothing at all organically wrong with Doug. I want to talk with you before I see him again."

SHE WAITED FORTY-FIVE MINUTES in Wolfe's anteroom before his nurse ushered her into his office. "There was a hospital emergency. He just phoned. He's on his way back."

He arrived hurriedly five minutes later, winded. "Sorry, dear." He sat down at his desk and caught his breath. "Let me get to the point. Do you think we can persuade Doug to see a psychiatrist?"

He didn't wait for an answer. "From what Doug told me yesterday, I think he has all the symptoms of clinical depression. It's been coming on a long time. He needs help, and depression is beyond my competence."

She felt her body grow tense. She found it hard to talk. He gave her a glass of water.

"You asked if we could persuade Doug to see a psychiatrist," she said after a sip. "You expect him to resist?"

"Most people do," he said. "There's a stigma, you know. The popular idea is that if you've got a mental illness you're weak, you've got no guts, you're unreliable. You've got a bad character, or worse."

"Doug's not most people," she said. "Neither am I."

"Good. But it won't be easy, Maude—not for him, not for you. It may take a long time." He paused, as if considering how much to say. "We're in something of a no-man's land. We don't truly know what causes depression. The medical literature is scant. There's been little significant research since Freud published *Morning and Melancholia* and that was thirteen years ago. If you've read that—" Maude nodded to indicate that she had—"you know as much about depression as the average doctor and maybe more."

"How serious is it with Doug?" she asked.

He spoke reflectively. "It's not mild. It's severe enough. He needs immediate attention." He hesitated. "It can get worse."

"How much worse?"

"It can get unbearable. From the experiential record, such as it is, about fifteen percent of the cases end in suicide."

She gasped.

"But then—" he rushed to reassure her—"and we don't now why, in time most patients recover on their own. In most cases the disease is self-limiting."

"And a psychiatrist can help?"

"If anybody," he said. "At the moment we don't know any more about the causes of depression than our ancestors knew about the origins of the plague three hundred years ago. What we're doing doesn't qualify as research. It's almost pure speculation." He saw the questioning look in Maude's eyes and rushed on to explain. "It's generally assumed that depression is an emotional phenomenon. It's believed to come as a reaction to intolerable grief or to a series of disappointments or failures—to what psychologists call environmental circumstances. That's undoubtedly true, but it may be only half true. I have an idea that depression may be a genetic disorder, that some people are simply born with a predisposition to it. Who knows, maybe twenty, thirty years from now we'll discover that depression is more the result of some chemical or hormonal imbalance, like diabetes or thyroid deficiency. Someday we may have a pill for it. But right now the most effective treatment we know is psychotherapy."

"So whatever treatment Doug gets—" she was fighting despair—"will be experimental."

"Not entirely. The one thing we do know about treatment is that it helps the patient to talk. If a psychiatrist can't help with a cure he can at least slow its progress until the patient cures himself."

"Do you have a psychiatrist to recommend?"

Dr. Wolfe sighed. "There are no psychiatrists in Hastings. Doug will have to go to Columbia or Atlanta. I'd recommend Atlanta."

"You mean move to Atlanta?"

"Maude, dear, you're in for a long haul. Yes, Doug will have to be in Atlanta. And for him to get the kind of loving support he needs—you may have to be in Atlanta with him."

"For how long?"

"Who knows? A year. Maybe five years." Maude bit her lower lip and held back the tears. "We have no choice, do we? Can you get us an appointment with a psychiatrist in Atlanta?"

"I have a good friend there—a younger man, a student of mine when I was teaching at the College of Charleston. He's been a practicing internist for the past twenty years, but a few years ago decided to go into psychiatry. His name is Ned MacMillan. I'll ask him to recommend somebody. I should have a name for you within the week."

She got up to go. He rose with her and followed her to the door. "I know I don't have to tell you this, Maude," he said in parting, "but one of the few things we know for certain is that nothing is more important to a victim of depression—nothing is more likely to hasten his recovery—than the constant assurance from somebody who loves him that it's not hopeless, that he's going to get well."

14

After Maude left, as soon as he heard the sound of the Ford leaving the driveway, Doug struggled out of bed and, having established that Wilma was downstairs and out of earshot, made his way to the room that two years before he'd converted into a office. He phoned Azalie. This time he got her, on the fourth ring.

"I called as soon as I could," he said.

"It's all right," she said, in a voice that had lost all trace of a Georgia accent. "I just thought we ought to talk."

He didn't quite know how to begin. "I don't know what to say. Ever since I read the obit I've felt so—so helpless, so desperately alone. Like a castaway." "I can imagine." There was a catch in her throat. "I've been devastated. It happened so fast."

"What did happen?"

"About two weeks ago he started having headaches, for no particular reason. They got worse and then, along with the headaches, he developed a stiff neck. He was nauseated, began to run a fever, and started vomiting, couldn't stop. We were late, I think, getting him to a doctor." She took a deep breath. "Almost before we knew it, he was gone."

He couldn't speak for a moment. "I'm so sorry," he said when he got his voice back." It must have been terrible for you."

"Paul was wonderful. Without him, I think I might have cracked up."

"I take it Douglas and Paul had grown close."

"Very." She paused. "Funny. I kept wishing for you and at the same time glad you were being spared. If there'd been time, I would have phoned you before he died but I don't know why. After we knew it was meningitis and that he was in real danger, I kept telling him to be brave, like his father."

"Oh Azalie." He started to weep but caught himself and asked haltingly. "He still thought I'd died in the war? You never told him differently?"

"I never told him the truth."

"How's Paul taking it?"

"I don't know exactly. I think he feels so strongly that his job has been to comfort me—"

"He sounds like a strong man."

"And a good one," she said. "I wish you could know him."

"I've glad you've got him."

"The party's urging him to run for the state assembly."

"The party?"

"The Democrats. He's been precinct chairman going on four years. The governor would like to see him elected to some state office—I think by way of placating colored voters, who haven't always been too happy with him."

"Do you think Paul will run?"

"I'll let you know."

Azalie changed the subject. "How've you been, Doug?"

"Not well." How much to tell her? "I've had a seizure. Passed out. They don't know yet what may be wrong."

"Have you been working too hard?"

"Maybe."

"Doug?"

"Yes?"

"Have you ever told Maude—that's her name, isn't it—about you and me?"

"No. Daddy made me promise—"

"Your father's irrelevant. Have you thought it might help to tell her?"

"How could it possibly help?"

"For one thing, I think silence about something like this can be an impossible burden. I think you may need somebody you can talk to."

"I don't know how Maude might take it. Telling her might be too much of a risk."

"A risk of what? You think you might lose her if you told her?"

"I couldn't bear it if she stopped loving me."

"Oh cut it out, Doug. From everything you've told me, your wife is anything but magnolias and moonlight. I can't see her as one of those swooning ladies Southern gentlemen are suppose to die protecting. Has it occurred to you that you may be insulting her, thinking she may not have the smarts or the compassion to understand?"

He was feeling light headed. "I guess I don't know what to think."

"Well," she said, and paused. "Let me ask you this, Doug?"

"Yes?"

"Would you think differently—do you think she'd react differently—if I were white?"

The question unnerved him. For moment he couldn't think what to say.

"I'll think about it."

"Do." There was a coolness in her voice now, as if his response had disappointed her. "Think hard. Sometimes suppression can be a dangerous thing. It can make you sick."

To their joint conference two days later, Stan Wolfe brought the wisdom of long experience with pain and human diversity, together with the empathy and realistic optimism he was born with. He gave Maude and Doug coffee and after pouring himself a cup left his desk and sat with them around a small table, a vase of roses at its center. "Well," he said, smiling inoffensively, and proceeded to give Doug his diagnosis in some detail. "You're in good company," he said when he finished. "It will give you no comfort, but the fact is, Abraham Lincoln, Woodrow Wilson, Hart Crane, Tschaivoksy, Shakespeare—or whoever wrote *Hamlet*—literally thousands of other creative types—all suffered from depression and did some of their greatest work under its influence. I can imagine how painful it is for you, but only a fool would say he really understands what you're going through. All I can say in honesty is that although you may get worse before you get better you will get better. Believe me."

Doug said almost nothing while Wolfe talked. His eyes were glazed and his body rigid. Maude wasn't even sure that he was listening. But when Wolfe said that he would like to refer him to a psychiatrist, Doug seemed to relax, as if relieved. "You understand, Doug—a psychiatrist will help you get to the roots of what's bothering you. In many cases that's half the battle. If psychotherapy works, there'll be no fundamental change in your personality, but you'll be better prepared to deal with the things that could cause a recurrence."

"You mean I'll be easier to live with," Doug said.

Wolfe corrected him. "It'll be easier for you to live with yourself."

Doug gave a wan smile. "I'd like that. Thanks very much."

It was agreed, then, that Doug would go to Atlanta for what Wolfe called "a flirtation interview" with a Dr. Isaiah Orenstein, whom Wolfe's friend Ned Macmillan had described as "the best Emory has to offer," a brilliant, relatively young specialist in depressive disorders. If the interview established a promising relationship, Doug would see him regularly thereafter, initially as many as three times a week. Maude and Damon would join him in Atlanta later.

"I've got a problem, Mother," Doug said when they called Catherine that evening to report. "I'm not well. We need your help. I'm going to ask Maude to tell you about it."

He turned the phone over to Maude and left for the bedroom to lie down; his palms were sweating, his heart was racing, the furies were back upon him. Glad at least that she could talk in private, Maude explained as best she could, describing Doug's behavior of yesterday and paraphrasing everything she could remember of what Stan Wolfe had told her. At first stunned and disbelieving, Catherine rallied true to form.

"When is the appointment with this Dr. Orenstein?" she asked.

"Sometime next week, I presume. Dr. Wolfe said we'd be hearing from Orenstein's office, maybe as early as tomorrow."

"I'll have the guest room ready. You'll be coming with Doug, won't you?"

"I thought I'd drive over with him, not only to be of what comfort I could, but to be on hand in case Orenstein wants to talk with me."

"What'll you do with Damon?"

"He'll be all right without us for a day or two. He's almost eleven now and Wilma will be here."

What to tell Damon?

"Your father hasn't been himself for some time, darling."

Damon looked as if he knew that only too well.

"He's quite ill. He's going to have to go to Atlanta to see a special doctor—a specialist. I'm going with him, and we'll have to leave you here with Wilma for a few days."

"Why can't I go with you? Couldn't I be excused from school for a day or two?"

"Perhaps darling," Maude said, "but we don't really know how long we may be have to be there and suppose your class starts algebra or something while we're gone?"

"We've already started algebra," Damon said, pouting.

"Don't sulk, Damon. It's not at all attractive." She forced a smile and kissed him on the forehead. "Daddy's going to be all right. It will just take time."

"But I don't want to stay here with Wilma. She's no fun. And she hums all the time."

Maude heard her voice rising. "Stop it, Damon."

"But she does. And when she's not humming she's singing—'Bringing in the Sheaves' and 'Love Lifted Me' for gosh sakes."

"I thought you loved Wilma."

"I do, but she drives me crazy,"

She bit her lower lip in an effort to control her impatience. "Maybe you ought to try accompanying her on your trombone. She'd like that, I bet."

"Mother!"

"Don't make it harder for me, Damon. Like it or not, you'll have to stay here with Wilma."

"But why, Mother?"

"Because I say so!" She pulled back her right arm and opened her hand, meaning to slap him. She caught herself, pulled back, and embraced him instead. She shivered, feeling the wind of a close call. She closed her eyes and took a deep breath.

"Of course you can go with us, darling. You can help me help your daddy."

Isaiah Orenstein's office was in a small medical center converted from a 1915 Neel Read house on Oakdale Road near the Emory campus. Its facade unchanged, from the outside it looked like any one of the other handsome Druid Hills residences. Orenstein shared the building with another psychiatrist, a psychologist, a pediatrician. and a physical therapist. The common rooms showed the hand of an interior decorator—oriental throw rugs on a beige carpet, sofas and chairs upholstered in leather, library tables with an indiscriminate assortment of current magazines, and a large reproduction of Rembrandt's "The Lesson" on the far wall of the communal waiting room. The individual offices, however, had been left to the taste of their occupants. Orenstein's was eclectic. His desk was a drawerless nineteenth-century hunt table. There were two straightback Shaker chairs, surprisingly comfortable, an overstuffed arm chair with an Ottoman and an end table, a walnut bookcase, and, of course, the indispensable couch. Three Monet prints hung in the wall over the desk.

Maude waited in the anteroom while the receptionist ushered Doug into the office. "Make yourself at home," she said pleasantly. "The doctor will only be a minute."

"I just bet," he thought to himself.

She left, closing the door behind her.

Doug began to have misgivings. There was a small brass menorah on the top of the bookcase. Under the sheet of glass that covered the top of the desk were family photos, a set of post-card size Rembrandt self-portraits, and a quotation in large script, like a page from an illuminated manuscript. It read:

"But the liberal deviseth liberal things;

and by liberal things shall he stand."

—Isaiah, 32:8.

Isaiah Orenstein! Weren't their any good psychiatrists named Smith or Brown or Jones? Why in the hell had Stanley Wolfe assigned him to a Semite from the garlic-scented streets of New York? Orenstein could not possibly know what it was like to have been born and raised in the suffocating confines of a small town in Georgia. How could a New York Jew, undoubtedly a scholar and a sophisticate, be expected to understand the crippling effects of institutionalized racism, or the ball-crushing consequences of an arrogant Protestantism? How much good could a man like that do a man like him? For a moment he considered turning on his heels and walking out.

But a minute later he was ashamed of himself. Orenstein came in, arm extended for a handshake, smiling and apologetic. "I'm terribly sorry," he was saying. "But my son had a solo in this morning's Assembly."

"You have a son?"

"Bill. I couldn't bear to saddle him with Isaiah. He's ten and he's learning cello."

"My boy is ten—no, almost eleven. He plays the trombone."

"Really?" Isaiah Orenstein looked genuinely interested. "Would he consider switching to French horn? Bill's ensemble could use a horn player."

Orenstein sat down at his desk. "Now," he said. "What do your friends call you, Mr. Krueger?"

"Doug."

"Well, Doug, call me Izzy. I don't like it, but I'm used to it. "

From there, the interview moved along to a state of trust and compatibility. The more Orenstein talked the more Doug liked him. He could imagine Orenstein twenty, twenty-five, years from now with long hair and a black beard looking like the prophet his mother had named him for; he had thick black brows and there was the intensity of a true believer in his eyes. But now, at forty or forty-five (he couldn't be older than forty-five) he looked more like a character in a Booth Tarkington story. Doug guessed him to be about five feet seven. He was lean, hardly an ounce of fat on him, and his flesh was firm and tightly stretched over his bones. His hair was cut short, almost in a crew cut, and its texture suggested that if he didn't brush faithfully every morning it would get away from him, turn curly, and go off in all directions.

He was not a New Yorker. He was born in Philadelphia, where his father was a boilermaker. He had done his undergraduate work at the University of Pennsylvania, then gone to Johns Hopkins for a medical degree. He had come to Emory straight from Baltimore. He preferred checkers to chess; if he couldn't have both Mozart and Brahms, he would rather have Brahms; and he thought Herbert Hoover was a sad case whom history had miscast. "He would have made a brilliant company clerk."

In answer to his questions, Doug gave him a brief account of his own life and preferences. "I've had a lot of jobs," he told him, "but I don't seem to have stuck with any one of them for very long."

"That could be a problem," Orenstein said. "Some people have more talent than they can contain."

"I think you're being charitable if you mean me."

"We'll see." Orenstein laughed lightly. "Now—are you ready to commit to therapy, or do you want time to think about it?"

"I'm ready," Doug answered.

Orenstein consulted his appointment book. "I have an hour open—two o'clock on Tuesday, Wednesday, and Friday afternoons. Can you make it?"

"That's my best hour," Doug said. "Nights are terrible for me. By noon I'm in my right mind, more or less, and I can function fairly well."

"And you stay in reasonably good spirits till sundown, when the willies get you. Is that the pattern?"

"Usually. Unless something awful happens during the day."

"Like what?"

"Like the death of a son."

"Oh." Orenstein paused. "Shall we start next Tuesday, then? You won't have any trouble getting off? Who's your employer?"

"Nobody. I haven't worked since the last episode two weeks ago."

"Do you need to work? Well, we all need to work. What I mean is, do you need to work for money?"

"I will shortly. We have some savings I can draw on for a while."

"This is not a good time to be looking for a job." Orenstein wrote himself a note. "And we ought to try to find you something part-time, something not too stressful, half days, mornings."

"We?"

Orenstein smiled. "I have contacts, here and there, mostly at the university. I'll put out some feelers. You never know."

Doug couldn't help himself. It was a moment or two before he could speak without choking up. "I didn't know there were people like you," he said finally.

Orenstein looked embarrassed. "We'll see," he said again. He rose, the interview over, and walked with Doug to the door. "One more thing," he said, his hand on the doorknob. "It would be a good thing if you stopped drinking."

"Sir?"

"Whiskey can be a comforting thing. But it can be treacherous, too. We think of it as a stimulant. It's actually a depressive. You do drink, don't you?"

"Yes."

"Try to stop. It may be hard for a while. But before long you won't miss it at all."

"That's hard to believe."

"Believe me," Orenstein said, with his light little laugh. "I know."

Doug sighed. "I can give up liquor," he said. "It's not as if you're asking me to quit cigarettes."

Orenstein smiled. "For now," he said, looking as if he might be making a mental note.

As he opened the door wider he saw an attractive young woman seated in the vestibule. She wore a simple cotton dress, dark blue with white piping, and over it an unornamented cloth coat, unbuttoned now to receive the room's warmth. At the sound of the door opening, she turned in her chair and faced him. She looked worried. Her eyes showed signs of tears and hours without sleep. She rose and stepped toward him. He fought a strong impulse to take her in his arms.

"You must be Mrs. Krueger," he said.

"I'm Maude."

"And I'm Izzy. Call me Izzy." He offered her his hand, and a smile that invited confidence.

Her shoulders relaxed. She returned the handshake and the smile. Doug came to her and gave her a hug meant to be reassuring.

Maude wanted to hear from Orenstein. "What are the prospects, doctor?" She corrected herself. "—Izzy. What can you tell us?"

His smile broadened. "Only that I think we're off to a very good start."

"HE SEEMS LIKE a good man," Maude said once they were in the car and headed for Catherine's. "I just hope he's as good a psychiatrist. How did you and he get along?"

It was early twilight and Doug was feeling the onset of his usual late afternoon anxiety. He didn't want to talk. His temples were beginning to throb and to rub them he took his right hand off the steering wheel. It seemed like a long minute before he answered. "Very well, I think. I'm to see him three times a week, beginning Tuesday. Did you like him?"

"Instantly," Maude said without hesitation. "I think I could come to like him very much."

Doug peered through the windshield at the fading sky. "I hate this time of day," he said. "Why can't it just go ahead and get dark!"

Abruptly, he turned the car to the curb and pulled to a full stop. "Would you mind taking over from here?" he asked, his voice quavering, as he stepped out. "I don't trust myself."

They exchanged seats in silence. They had gone several blocks down Clifton Road before she spoke. "I'm sorry, darling."

Doug lowered his head to his chest, his eyes closed. He was trying hard to control a tremor in his hands. "Why, Maude?" said, gulping. "Why is this happening to me now? I should be relieved. And hopeful. Instead, I'm thinking I'll never get well. I feel like disaster's waiting for me at the corner."

At a loss, she said, feebly, "Maybe it's been just too stressful a day."

He struggled to speak. "It's as if some enormous weight has come down on me, without warning. I feel wrapped in darkness." His voice caught and he could not continue.

Maude patted him on his knee. "You're not in pain—I mean physical pain—are you?"

He gulped again. "I can't describe it."

"Don't try to talk any more, baby. I'll be quiet. We'll be at Catherine's in a minute or two and you can lie down."

"I don't want mother to see my like this," he said weakly. "Pull over as soon as you can and let's sit awhile until it passes."

She did as he asked. They sat in silence, perhaps for as long as half an hour, until he took a deep breath, straightened his back, and told her to go on. "I can manage now." By that time the street lights were on.

15

Doug settled in at Catherine's, occupying the guest room upstairs next to Bessie's at the far end of the hall. Maude and Damon returned to Hastings in the Ford. The plan was for the two of them to stay in Hastings until Damon's school year ended and the lease on the house ran out in June. That would give Maude three months to sell or give away what furniture that would be too expensive to move, to find a buyer for the lot, and to pack. Meanwhile Doug, with Catherine's help, would look for a suitable house for the three of them.

Doug had sessions with Orenstein three afternoons a week. The sessions passed quickly and were usually over before he'd talked himself out. True to his word, Orenstein had found him a part-time job in Emory's office of development, a euphemism for fund-raising. The job required little more than a regard for accuracy, consisting mostly of record-keeping and filing. He worked three mornings a week in a basement office in the administration building. The only other staff members were a harassed middle-aged accountant who planned and conducted semi-annual direct-mail campaigns, and two young girls who did most of the typing and filing. Doug's most challenging task was to prepare a monthly report—how many pledges, how many delinquencies, how much received in cash donations—for President Harvey Cox. As the Depression wore on, he had less and less to do.

By late April Doug had found two rental houses to show Maude. She came back to inspect them over a weekend. Both were in Atlanta's near Northside. The one Maude preferred was on Penn Avenue, within walking distance of St. Mark Methodist Church and O'Keefe Junior

High School, which Damon would be entering that fall. It was a leafy neighborhood of well mannered middle-class families, most of whom had been conditioned to accept Protestantism, white supremacy, the food chain, the justice of the Confederate cause, and the primacy of Bourbon over Scotch as self-evident truths. The house, sited to face north, was a single story bungalow of beige-pink brick trimmed in cedar. It looked smaller than its twenty-two-hundred square feet. Immediately east of the front porch was a sizable screened loggia with a terra-cotta floor of ceramic tile. The front door opened into a living room large enough for two bridge foursomes. Beyond that was a dining room with space for a sideboard, separated from the adjacent kitchen by a breakfast nook with a rectangular table for four and two banquettes. A doorway on the south wall of the dining room led to the central hallway, just big enough for a linen closet, a broom closet, a telephone table, and a chair. The walls in this hallway were almost fully taken with five doors, one of which concealed a stairway to the cellar that housed the hot-air furnace and a coal bin. Behind the others were the only bath and three bedrooms. The largest bedroom was to the east, with two large windows that caught the morning sun. The other two, smaller but adequate, were side by side at the rear and overlooked a scraggly yard dominated by an old but still productive apple tree; a child's swing, its seat worn and split, hung from the lowest limb. In the front yard Bermuda grass was being overtaken by crab grass and clover, and the two boxwoods, one on each side of the front steps, were dying. The house was blessed with finished carpentry, including waist-high wainscoting in the dining room and oak molding throughout, but none of it appeared to have been cared for. There were dark water stains on the hardwood floors, paint peeling from the walls and ceilings, a stopped-up commode, and loose or broken hinges on the pantry door and kitchen cabinets.

"It needs work," Doug said ruefully.

"But Doug dear. As is, the rent is only thirty dollars a month."

"And I could do all the fixing. Is that what you're thinking?"

She giggled and kissed him on the cheek.

They took the house on a three-year lease. When Maude went back to

Hastings to arrange for the move, Doug busied himself with the repairs, working as fast as he could during the daylight hours when he was freest of his furies and his energy level was highest. Except for the two days when Catherine and Bessie came to scrub the porch and bathroom floors and to clean the kitchen fixtures, he worked alone with only a small radio to keep him company. Anticipating the onset of despair that settled on him regularly at first dark, he knocked off at sundown and made it back to Catherine's before he was too disabled and demoralized to move.

While working he tried to concentrate fully on the task before him, but the radio proved to be an indispensable crutch. The nature of the work was so monotonous that without the radio his thoughts might have fixed on the losses, failures, and misjudgments in his past, fragmentary memories of which swarmed at the doors of his consciousness. The news as reported by WSB was hardly of a kind to cheer him. The unemployment rate was rising to 15 percent, the highest ever recorded. Four national banks had gone into bankruptcy after their chief executives had been found guilty of conspiring to defraud their depositors of sixteen million dollars. The deficit on the national budget was forcing Treasury to sell eight hundred million dollars in bonds. Overseas, inflation was putting Germany in such peril that its foreign minister was begging President Hoover to declare a moratorium on its war debt, a petition that the president was inclined to grant had he not feared its effect on the U. S. stock market. In Austria, the Credit Anstalt was about to fail, precipitating a panic throughout western Europe. A panel of experts assembled in Washington to consider the prospects for recovery dissolved in frustration, its members admitting a lack of confidence to explain either the Depression's causes or its effects. President Hoover, heretofore inclined to be optimistic and reassuring, was urging Americans to "stand steadfast through this Valley Forge of Darkness."

Closer home, in Scottsboro, Alabama, the conviction on dubious evidence of five young black boys for the rape of two white women was working its way through an appeals court. Doug felt in his guts that all five were innocent. Interviewed on the air, the prosecutors and some of the jurors sounded like the good ol' boys he'd known in Chesterton.

"Alabama justice," a county solicitor said, "cannot be bought and sold with Jew money from New York" and for several nights thereafter Doug had bad dreams of his father in Klan regalia. Impelled to do something, he went to the Emory hospital, where he'd heard Type O was in short supply, sold a pint of blood for $25, and sent a check in that amount to the NAACP.

There were times during these weeks when his spirits sank amd he wanted nothing more than to find the nearest bootlegger and get drunk. Each time, however, he rallied by convincing himself that he could not afford the consequences; that one drink would only lead to another and that more than one, as Orenstein had warned him, would only intensify his depression. As if to compensate, he talked himself into believing that cigarettes were good for him; almost without realizing it, he developed a two-pack-a-day habit. When, at fifteen cents a pack, it became too expensive to buy ready-made brands, he bought Bugle's tobacco and rolled his own.

He sanded and refinished the oak floors, rehung the pantry doors, steamed off wall paper, patched plaster, and repainted the walls throughout. The floor stains gave him the biggest problem. One spot, about five inches in diameter, in the center of the dining room resisted repeated sandings and everything else he tried, including bleach, which he allowed to stand all one night. Finally. he cursed it, christened it Lady Macbeth, and gave up. For years thereafter, almost every time he sat down for a meal, he was conscious that the damn spot was defiantly there under his feet, like a relentless symbol of failure, a reminder that there were some problems in this world that you simply had to learn to live with.

Early in the afternoon on an extraordinarily hot Saturday as he was putting the last coat of enamel on the pantry shelves, there was a knock at the front door loud enough to be heard over the sound of "Aida" on Metropolitan Opera. He answered it to find a man with a pitcher of iced tea in one hand and a plate of cookies in the other.

"Hello," the stranger greeted him, smiling broadly. "I'm Jethro Moneypenny, your next-door neighbor. Call me Jet. Please."

Doug returned the smile. He wiped his hands on the seat of his pants and extended a hand. "I'm Doug Krueger. Did you say Moneypenny7?"

The man smiled even more broadly. "Honest to God." He stepped in and looked around for a place to set the pitcher and plate.

"Sorry," Doug said, taking the pitcher from him. "I can only offer you this old stool. It'll be another week before I have the place ready for furniture." He took a swallow of tea and downed a cookie in one gulp. "God, that was good. How nice of you."

Jet Moneypenny sat down, his thick bottom spilling over the stool. "My wife," he said. "She's been spying on you. She figured it was time you had a break."

"Do thank her for me."

Doug eased himself to the floor and sat with his back on the wall. He had another swallow of tea and another oatmeal cookie and took a good look at his visitor. Jethro Moneypenny looked to be in his mid-thirties. He was no more than five feet eight. His legs were too short and his torso too long. He was wearing a collarless shirt with rolled-up sleeves, exposing a thick neck and forearms almost as large as Doug's thighs. His hands were huge, his fingers disproportionately slender. His left eye appeared to be slightly cocked, the bridge of his nose was thin, and his upper lip was fat. Altogether, he looked as if the creator had assembled him from mismatched body parts. Nevertheless, there was something almost irresistibly attractive about him. His hair was black, thick, curly, and cut close to the scalp. His dark brown eyes were set deep, curtained by long lashes. They were alive with curiosity. His face was fixed in an expression of gratuitous good will, as if he'd never known rejection or hostility.

"Hortense." Moneypenny was saying. "That's my wife. She'll be delighted and I dare say relieved when I tell her what you're doing to the place. And that you look like a neighborly soul."

"You sound as if the previous tenant wasn't."

"Nichols? He lived here three years. I hardly saw him more than a dozen times. He was gone every night and slept during the day. The story was that he was a bootlegger, and I could have used a friendly neighborhood bootlegger. But friendly he was not. On the few occasions I spoke to him he looked as if he was about to pull out a gun. And he had this sick, sour expression on his face, like he had just had a dose of calomel. He was a mastigophorer."

"A what?"

Moneypenny gave a soft laugh. "A mastigophorer. That's what my mother would have called him. It's what she'd call me when she'd thought I deserved a whipping."

He saw the bewilderment in Doug's eyes. "Archaic English," he said. "Elizabethan English. We lived in north Georgia, in the hills—almost pure Anglo-Saxon. Mother was full of words like that."

"Well," Doug said, "Gopherer or not, he certainly left this place in a mess."

"He left in a hurry. I think the feds may have been after him."

"Was there a Mrs. Nichols?"

Moneypenny nodded. "And a son. A boy about sixteen. He had polio and was at Warm Springs. His wife was a recluse. We'd see her every now and again, usually in the backyard hanging out clothes, but she withdrew as soon as you started talking to her. She was in and out of sanitariums. Somebody told me she had some sort of serious mental illness—paranoia or dementia praecox or clinical depression. Whatever it was. she wasn't expected to recover, but then I guess nobody ever does from something like that."

Doug felt a chill. "Maybe," he said.

Jet Moneypeny returned the next afternoon, bright-eyed, in overalls and with a paint brush. "I thought you might use some help."

His help was welcome and may have been indispensable. That afternoon the two of them painted the woodwork throughout the house. They also replaced the fake Victorian chandelier in the dining room with a recessed ceiling fixture, something Doug could have managed alone only at risk of dropping the chandelier and splintering the newly varnished floor with glass. Jet also proved to be good company. He talked freely, and in the course of the afternoon Doug learned that he'd been born in Hiawasee, a poor town in mountain country, the seat of Towns County, where moonshining and the home production of carpets and chenille bedspreads were the principal industries and subsistence farming the common occupation. His father was the county sheriff and his mother one of the three public school teachers. Largely through the influence of his father, he won a scholarship to nearby Young Harris College. Three years later he went to Atlanta, enrolling in the Southern College of Dentistry. "My best friend was George Ezell, Jr., the smart but lazy son of an extraordinarily successful Atlanta surgeon and a member of the Emory board of trustees. His father had wanted George to go into medicine but his grades as an undergraduate, as well as his attitude, made it clear that he'd never make it, so his father pushed him into dental school. Dr. Ezell, I gather, regarded dentistry as a second-class but respectable form of medicine. Anyway, George Jr. enjoyed all the privileges of the upperclass. He was a Chi Phi at Emory and his family was a member of the Piedmont Driving Club and two country clubs, so he got invited to all the fraternity dances and debutante parties and he was very popular. One of the clubs had tea dances every Wednesday afternoon. One day after our clinic tour he asked me if I'd like to go with him. I did. Later He taught me the box step and introduced me to a girl, a tall, broad-shouldered girl whose size intimidated most of the boys. We became friendly, just friendly, and next thing I knew she'd come to think of me as her reliable escort and I was on the list of boys to get invitations to all the club dances—usually as her assigned date. It was at one of those dances that I met Hortense. Her father was the founder of Cherokee Life." Jet paused and chuckled. "I married above me."

Jet talked fast, almost without stopping, like a man who spent his days by himself, as indeed he did. "When times are bad," he said, sighing, "the first thing people let go is their teeth. These past few months—I'm lucky to have two patients a day. Some days it's only me and the telephone, and whenever it rings, unless it's Hortense telling me to bring home a loaf of bread or something, it'll be to break an appointment. My hygienist left to go back to the farm with her husband. I was relieved. Otherwise I would have had to fire her."

Jet paused long enough to wipe up some spilt paint before it dried, then continued. "I may have made a mistake setting up practice where I did. George had wanted me to share a suite with him out north Peachtree, where the money is, but—I dunno—I had this notion that I'd rather help people like those I'd grown up with, in an area where dentists are in short supply. So I've been working on South Whitehall, in an office over a used furniture store. Most of my patients are poor whites, mill hands (Doug noted that Jet did not say "lintheads"), but I have a chair for Negroes, in a separate room of course, and I guess you could describe my practice as poor, faithful, and appreciative." "Are you thinking about moving your office, say to Buckhead?"

"Maybe, but not yet. I've got enough in the bank to hold me for a while, assuming the bank doesn't go under. And Hortense is bringing in enough to keep us afloat till things break."

"Hortense works?"

Jet smiled, somewhat sheepishly. "She's Polly Peachtree."

"Excuse me. She's what?"

"She's Polly Peachtree. You know, the column in the *Journal*. On the society page. She writes Peachtree Promenade."

Doug had read Peachtree Promenade on occasion. It carried trivial but flattering items about the families who populated Atlanta's clubs. It was the sort of thing an economist might credit for help in perpetuating the class consciousness that supported real estate values on the Northside.

"Sometimes she writes under her maiden name, Hortense Murphy," Jet said. He stopped, as if expecting Doug to register disapproval. "It's harmless stuff," he went on defensively. "The editors wanted a former debutante who could spell, and Hortense qualified."

"I'm looking forward to meeting her," Doug said, with unforced sincerity.

"How about tonight? How about joining us for a light supper?"

Doug was tempted to tell him why that was out of the question, for Jet Moneypenny had a manner that invited confidences. Instead. he said, "Not tonight. I'm having dinner with my mother."

"Some other time, then," Jet said. He put down his brush and left the room to take a leak. When he returned, he spoke a bit apologetically. "I've been babbling away about myself," he said. "How about you? What brought you to Atlanta?"

Doug told him that he was an unemployed electrical engineer, that he'd lost all but his shirttail in the market crash, and that he had come to Atlanta thinking the prospects for work might be better. He considered himself blessed to have a wife like Maude and a young son and, yes, he and Maude played bridge.

"I don't know what to expect," Jet volunteered wanly, "Except that things are gonna get worse before they get better."

"You think so?"

"I can't get a handle on it," Jet said. "Being so long alone in the office, I've done more reading, more brooding, than ever before in my life. What I really think is that—"

His mind shifted gears. "At first I just read anything at hand—mostly old magazines. Then I figured that if I was going to have this no-end of quiet time I ought to make the most of it, so I asked myself, what was it I ought to know? Have you ever asked yourself that question? The answer can be damn humbling, believe me. So I went to the library and asked for a reading list of books about politics, economics, and history. I've spent most of my daylight hours this past year plowing my way through it."

"Such as?"

"Oh, Plato's *Republic*, *The Wealth of Nations*, *Das Kapital*, *The Theory of the Leisure Class*, *The Autobiography of Benjamin Franklin*. Also a few novels, like *War and Peace* and *The Red and the Black*. And the New Testament, sort of at random."

"Don't you find that pretty heavy going?"

"I cheat a little. I'll read a Sherlock Holmes every now and again. Or a Zane Grey western. And I try to keep acquainted with the best-seller list. Right now I'm half way through *The Good Earth*. Fascinating."

"My Lord,"Doug said. "What are you in training for—a Ph. D.?"

"Only if they're offering one for ignorance and indecision."

"Why indecision?"

"Well, the more I read the more I discover how dumb I am and how much more there is to know and the more uncertain I am about anything."

"For instance?"

"For one thing, whether or not the market crash was the cause of the Depression we're in."

"I didn't think there was any doubt about that."

"There were basic weaknesses in the system, beginning a long time before the crash," Jet said, sounding a bit professorial. "We didn't notice them, that is those of us in the get-fat middle class, because we were all too happy to be partners in a national con game. The crash, I believe, just exposed the weaknesses and greased the decline. Ask some of my poor friends from the mills. Ask a sharecropper."

Doug didn't like where he thought Jet might be heading. "You don't like capitalism?"

"No," Jet answered with conviction. "The problem is, I can't think of anything better."

"How about a dash of socialism??"

"Inevitably," Jet said. He did not sound at all happy.

When he spoke again, it was in a lower and minor key. "My trouble," he said with great seriousness, "is that I'm with Margaret Fuller. I accept the universe only because I have to."

"I don't understand," Doug said.

"It's not just the economic system," Jet said. "It's the whole Goddam predatory world. If there is a God, and if he's so loving and all powerful, how come he invented the food chain?"

"Maybe he didn't," Doug said. "Maybe that was an invention of the devil."

"I know," Jet said, "if you're going to believe in God, you'd better by a damn sight also believe in the devil. Maybe that's my problem. I don't believe in the devil. And on that happy note—" He scraped some excess paint back into the can and looked at his wristwatch. "I'll clean the brush, and then I'll have to go. Maybe you should too. You look tired." He laughed. "No need to get quanked."

"Another word your mother taught you?" Doug laughed with him. "I must say, besides saving me a day's labor you've—"

"Don't thank me," Jet said. He dipped his brush in turpentine and wiped it almost dry. "I should be thanking you. What I needed today was a good listener. Maybe I'll see you tomorrow."

At the door, Jet paused and spoke soberly. "What I do know, in my gut, is that nothing's going to improve until we're rid of Hoover and until somebody takes his place who knows how to use the government."

"You have anybody in mind?"

"A Democrat."

"Al Smith?"

"No, not Smith. Not again." His eyes brightened and he sounded almost cheerful. "Keep your eye on the governor of New York."

IT WAS NOW THE LAST WEEK IN MAY. Doug had only to wax the floors, clean and paint the shelves of the linen closet, and touch up the exterior trim. Another five afternoons, at most, and he should be done. But something was telling him it would take longer, for he wasn't working well and he no longer seemed to get things right the first time; before he was satisfied, he had scraped, resanded, and repainted the sills in the dining room three times. At the start, he'd seen the move into the Penn Avenue house as a prospective return to normalcy and a new life. He had fought his way each morning through a quagmire of anxieties, the residue of his restless nights. With a quiet desperation that would have awed Thoreau, he forced himself to do whatever that particular day demanded of him, winding up on Penn Avenue for three, four hours of manual labor. And there had been some gratification in the work accomplished. But now, when he paused and looked at the newly papered walls and the varnished floors and the smoothly plastered ceilings, he no longer felt the promise of a reunited family and a fresh beginning. What he felt was the aching loss of the dream of the big house he'd planned with Maude in Honeysuckle Hills, with its Doric columns and Palladin windows and the stream that broke and spread to form a natural pond at the rear and the informal grove of dogwoods and sweetgums and tulip poplars and sugar maples he had planted and shaped with such studied abandon over so many spring mornings. To have had this realistic dream, a house of his own design, with elements remindful of Maude's childhood and subtle expressions of her impeccable taste and of compromises made as acts of love, a house unlike any other house in the world—and to be reduced to this tacky little bungalow, like every other tacky little bungalow on the block! It was not merely the loss of a dream house. It was the loss of an identity. It was castration.

His life seemed to have been diminished to so many hours in a doctor's office, so many in prescribed exercises, so many at a job better left to some mentally deficient student intern for which he was being paid thirty-five cents an hour, and time spent between soap-opera episodes. (What sane man would have let himself become addicted to "Ma Perkins" and "My Gal Sunday"?) He did not, could not, like himself. He saw nothing in himself to be proud of. Here he was, forty years old, and it was time he faced it: his life was worthless. He had failed Maude, failed fatherhood, failed himself. And why? What was it? Did he have some character deficiency that caused him to compound defeat? Had his behavior been governed by heedless, groundless self-confidence? Why his incorrigible inability do deal with authority? Was he never to profit, to learn, from experience? Why did he persist in investing uncritical trust in people, in relying so stupidly on the fraudulent good will of strangers? He thought of his boyhood in Chesterton. He thought of his father. He thought of his months at Fort Monmouth. He thought of his undergraduate days at Georgia Tech, of his engineering degree and how he had wasted it. He thought of Azalie with almost unbearable sorrow. It was not only the poignant loss of a first love. It was his unforgivable abandonment of her, his surrender to Papa and to the ball-crushing power of conventional morality. Somehow, he had missed a crucial passage in his coming-of-age and he did not know how to find it.

And so it was his fault. He had lost the house, he had lost Azalie, he had lost his manhood, because of his incompetence, his hubris, his cowardice. No matter what Izzy Orenstein maintained, it had been his fault. He was to blame, and how to get over it was his problem and his alone.

"I'm not going to quarrel with you," Izzy said. "What or who's to blame doesn't really matter. We should talk about what's caused it. To dwell on blame or fault is to indulge in self-pity, and you know what self-pity is."

Doug raised his eyebrows.

"Self-pity," said Izzy, "is the eighth deadly sin."

"You made that up."

"Okay, but in my book it's a whole lot deadlier than gluttony. What's important is that you come to understand the origins of your depression. Once you know and manage to tolerate the memory of the events that brought it on—that's half the cure. At least half the cure."

"Now you're saying that to understand a problem is to resolve it. Not too long ago you were telling me that my kind of depression may be a matter of bad chemistry, a brain disorder, not some errant psychological response. What am I suppose to believe?"

Izzy sighed. "I've been telling you it could be one or the other, or a little bit of both. We don't know."

"Whatever the cause, you still think it's self-limiting? I'm going to get well?"

"Count on it."

"But when? How much longer can we expect this to go on?"

Izzy shrugged, not dismissively but in a gesture of honest doubt. "It's unpredictable. What I can tell you with certainty is that your recovery will be slow and gradual, and it will come quietly. But if it goes the normal route—if anything about this business can be considered normal—your improvement will accelerate as you approach the end. You'll be discouraged—there'll be setbacks—and you'll get more and more impatient with the course of your therapy, with me. I can tell you too, not to expect an epiphany, or some high drama like Paul on the road to Damascus. But you will get better. In fact, you're already better."

"How can you say that?"

"For one thing, you're no longer reporting nightmares."

"Well, that's true—not as often, or as paralyzing." "And every now and again you even have a good dream?"

"That's true, I do."

"And it shows. You look like an entirely different man from the one who walked in here three months ago."

Doug was not comforted. "But I can't live like this. I don't want to live like this. I can get through the day, most days, although I get no pleasure from anything. But come nightfall I feel as if I'm dropping into a swamp, a deep black swamp. I try to write Maude every night, but some nights I can hardly get off a short note before I get this pain in my temples. It can get to be excruciating before the chloral hydrate sets in. Before long I'm practically immobilized. All I want to do is go to bed and lie there. If somebody even speaks to me, I want to scream."

"I understand," said Izzy, and he spoke as if he really did. He referred to his notebook for a moment and, apparently prompted by what he found there, said. "I have two recommendations for you."

Doug sagged. "Oh no."

"I want you to cut the dose of chloral hydrate in half. And I want you to step up the exercise."

"But I'm already doing a half hour every morning."

"I mean exercise with a partner, or with a group, something competitive, preferably in the afternoon."

"Like tennis?"

"Like tennis. Hard—three sets, at least three times a week. Preferably singles, with somebody you like."

"Tennis will be good for me?"

"Almost any strenuous exercise will be good for you. We don't know why yet, but exercise releases something in the system that helps counter depression."

"Why didn't you tell me this before?":

Izzy sighed again. "I didn't know it before. We're learning something new—or think we do—about depression every day."

Closing his notebook, he leaned back and gave Doug an encouraging smile. "Last session you wanted to talk about Azalie. Now, about Azalie—"

16

It had rained during the night but by noon the sun had dried the streets and warmed the air to an invigorating seventy-two. A mild breeze brought an indefinite smell of budding flowers and new green growth. Altogether, it was a perfect day to be painting outside, and Doug hoped to make the most of it.

He was just putting the last stroke of the first coat to the frame of the rear bedroom window when he felt something brush against his pants leg. He stooped to give it a swipe and then caught himself. An enormous orange cat was at his feet, sitting upright with great dignity, his big golden eyes looking into Doug's with loving familiarity. Doug felt slightly faint. A long sealed cell in his subconscious opened just enough to let rise a single word: "Butterscotch."

Though the cat didn't recognize the name, he obviously thought Doug meant well. He walked between Doug's legs and rubbed against his calves, purring loudly. Doug breathed deeply to recover himself. He put the paintbrush down, squatted, and began to stroke the cat, first on top of his head, then under his chin. This went on for at least five minutes, the cat twisting and purring and acting as if he'd just found a lost friend. With some effort, for the cat must have weighed twenty pounds, Doug picked him up, one hand under the chest, the other under the rump, and brought him close. He seemed to be in good health and, except for one smudge at the back of his neck where neither his tongue nor paw could reach, immaculately groomed.

"Are you hungry, baby?" The cat answered with a soft mew and the pat of a paw on Doug's cheek. Doug put him down and went back into the house to fetch the chicken salad sandwich Catherine had fixed for a late afternoon snack. Returning, he found the cat pacing at the door and scolding him for being so slow.

He unwrapped the sandwich, opened it to expose the chicken salad, put it on the grass, and stepped back. The cat went at it in polite little bites and licks, something that Doug found curiously endearing, thinking how a dog in similar hunger would have gobbled up the food in one swallow. He was standing, looking down on the cat, smiling foolishly, when he was aware of another presence.

"Oh, I think you've found Roger." A tall and striking young woman was practically at his elbow. She sounded like Margaret Sullavan with a Savannah accent. "Or maybe it's Roger who's found you."

"God," Doug said. "You look like a fashion model."

"Well thanks," said the young woman, embarrassedly. "I don't usually dress like this. I'm in my working clothes. I've been covering a Junior League luncheon. I'm Hortense Moneypenny. "

Doug blushed. "Forgive me. I've been talking to myself too much." He wiped his hands on the seat of his trousers and put out his right hand to meet hers. "But you do look great."

She was dressed in a suit of raw silk, black except for a bit of gold embroidery at the neck and cuffs. Her rich sorrel hair was cut loosely—much less severely than most women had worn it last year—and curled at the back of her head. Her fair complexion and her carefully shaped eyebrows accentuated the green in her eyes. Except for lipstick, applied sparingly, she wore no make-up.

"How's it going?" she was asking.

"I'm almost done," he said. "But I think I'm slowing down."

She bent down to pet the cat she'd called Roger. "Jet has told me what a marvelous bit of rehabilitation you're doing."

"Jet was a great help Sunday."

"He enjoyed it. Both of us are looking forward to having you and the family for neighbors." She stood up. "I think Roger may still be hungry."

"You know him, I take it."

"Ever since he was a kitten."

"And how old is he now?"

"About eight, I'd say. He belonged to Mac Todd, the old man who lived the other side of us. Mac died last week and Roger disappeared two days ago. Mac's son—he lives somewhere in Ohio, I think Toledo—was down for final arrangements and had promised his father to take Roger, but he didn't spend much time looking for him and said he couldn't wait for him to come back. He's not a very nice man."

"So what'll we do with Roger?"

"Jet and I could take him in until we can find a good home for him. He's a darling animal. I'd like to keep him, but we have a collie who doesn't get along well with cats. Roger would be miserable."

Roger had licked up the last of the chicken salad and was looking for more. Hortense Moneypennny picked him up with a grunt. "Meanwhile," she said, "I'll take him home and find something more for him to eat. Thanks for feeding him."

"My pleasure," Doug told her. He watched her move away, unsteady in her high heels in the dormant grass. She had transferred the cat to her left shoulder and his head now lay against her neck. Doug was feeling wistful. He wondered if Maude would like to have a cat.

Hortense stopped and turned back toward him. "I almost forgot," she said. "I'm fixing a cheese soufflé for supper. It's one of Jet's favorites. It would be nice to have you with us."

"I'm sorry," he said, meaning it more poignantly than she could ever imagine. "Another time?"

On his way the next afternoon he stopped at a nearby A&P and bought a fifteen-cent can of salmon. He would have bought a quarter pound of ground beef but as yet there was no refrigerator in the house and he was afraid that fresh meat might spoil before Roger could finish it.

He had hardly emerged from the back door, paint and brush in hand, when Roger appeared galloping. A moment later he was sitting at Doug's ankles mewing expectantly. He purred loudly all the time he ate. When he finished he wrapped himself around Doug's legs in a gesture of thanks, curled himself in a ball on the grass, and went to sleep instantly in the afternoon sun. He was in that same position when three hours later Doug knelt and gave him a good-bye pat before leaving for supper with Catherine. Roger visited him the next afternoon and on three successive days after that, each time at one-fifteen or only a few minutes later. It was odd how quickly Doug came to take the visits as a habit. Every afternoon he arrived confident that he'd find the cat either waiting or on his way, and every evening he left with the comforting murmur of Roger's purr in his ear.

On the night of the sixth day, Doug had a nightmare, his first in a month. In his sleep bad dreams usually appeared as vividly as events in a newsreel, but when he awoke, disturbed and in a state of foreboding, he could remember few, if any, details. This time, however, the dream endured long after he'd come into consciousness, and with remarkable clarity. In reconstruction, it emerged slowly but proceeded—sometimes rapidly, at other times, agonizingly, in slow motion—through a series of sharp images that recurred with developing intensity to a pitch of terror: a small yellow-haired boy in rompers; an enormous, grossly fat man, half naked, in a red executioner's mask; a big and muscular orange cat (Butterscotch!). The boy first looked to be smiling happily. Then came the sound of a slap followed by the picture of an ugly purple bruise; then a furious Butterscotch, teeth out and claws unfurled, hurling himself at the masked man. Blood. Fat red hands like a vise around the cat's neck, and the sound of the cat being thrown savagely against a wall. Finally, the cat's broken, lifeless body and the sound of a child weeping, weeping, weeping.

Doug came to in a sweat, dry-mouthed, breathing hard. The moon was still out. It was barely five, but further sleep was impossible. He got up, made it to the bathroom, threw up, took a cold shower, dressed, and went downstairs to wait for breakfast with Catherine. He had coffee percolating, bread in the toaster, eggs ready for scrambling, and their places set by the time she joined him. Seeing what he'd done, and noting the dread in his eyes, she said immediately, "Something's the matter. What is it, precious?"

"If I can keep it down," Doug said, "I think I'd like to eat something first."

Catherine gave him a worried look and turned on the stove. "Sit down. This won't take a minute."

They ate in silence. When they were done Doug took a false start. "I had a bad dream. I was a child and—" He interrupted himself and started over, swallowing hard. "Did we ever have a cat named Butterscotch?"

Catherine blanched. "A handsome orange tabby," she said. "When you were three."

"What happened to it?"

"It was lovely to see, that cat's attachment to you. Don't ever let anybody tell you cats don't love." She looked down and plucked at a loose thread in the tablecloth.

"What became of it?"

"Butterscotch couldn't stand your father. He'd growl and make all kinds of threatening sounds any time Jacob came close to him. A couple of times Jacob tried to pick him up and both times Butterscotch bit or scratched him."

"You loved Butterscotch, and Papa didn't?"

"Your father—" Catherine appeared to be having difficulty with the word—"hated him."

"Again, Mother. What happened to Butterscotch?"

Catherine buried her face in her hands. "I can't bear to think about it."

"Mother?"

"Your—" She paused. "Jacob killed him."

Depression came early for him that day and did not lift. His body was numb, his eyes heavy, his mind adrift. He drove inattentively to the house on Penn Avenue. He had finished the outside work. Only the insides of the linen closet in the center hall were left for him to do.

He parked the car in the driveway and went through the house to the rear door. As yet no sign of Roger. He removed the adjustable shelves and stacked them on the dining-room floor, where later he would wash them and perhaps give them fresh paper. From the utility closet next to the pantry, he got out a canvas drop cloth and carried it back to the center hall, where he spread it neatly on the closet floor. He went back for the paint and brushes. He thinned the paint with turpentine and was about to apply the first coast to the closet walls when he changed his mind. He walked to the rear bedroom and opened the windows. He turned the radio off and left it off. He wanted to be sure Roger could make himself heard when he came.

By three-fifteen Roger still had not shown up. By now Doug's disappointment had turned to worry. Suppose the cat had been hit by a car and was lying helpless on the side of the road somewhere?

Doug dried his hands and left the house. For the next half hour he drove north and south on Penn Avenue, up and down Fifth and Sixth streets, and west to Boulevard. When he found no dead body he didn't know to be relieved, or sorry not to have found the cat alive. Oh well. Roger must know how to take care of himself. This was surely not the first time he'd been missing.

Early dusk came and Roger still had not shown up. Before he left for the drive to Catherine's, Doug put out a saucer of canned salmon.

The plate was there, untouched, when he got to the house the next afternoon. His heart sank. Listlessly, he took the plate to the sink and washed it.

That done, he started on the rear wall of the linen closet.

Curiously, unlike the other walls in the house, it was made not of plaster but of wood, some sort of cheap paneling. At his waist's height he noticed a dark horizontal seam, too straight to be a natural crack. He gave it a push. A hinged board fell toward him, exposing two concealed shelves, each about twelve by fourteen by thirty-six—wide enough and deep enough and high enough to hold God knows how many bottles of what? Doug reached in and ran a hand the length of each shelf. At the rear of the top shelf, in the right corner, he felt a bottle. He pulled out a fifth of Johnny Walker Black Label.

So Jet had been right. Nichols had indeed been a bootlegger. What else might the man have secreted from the law and left behind? A more careful look through the linen closet disclosed nothing more, but wasn't this enough? How lucky can you get? A fifth of Black Label! Obviously, Nichols catered to the carriage trade. Doug made a mental note to search the premises thoroughly before Maude came, especially the crawl space and the storage wall in the garage.

He was surprised to find himself trembling. He felt like a teen-age boy trying to duck a cigarette before his mother caught him. At that moment he wanted nothing more than a long drink of Scotch. The desire was overpowering. He didn't take the time to go to the kitchen for a glass. He twisted the stopper, meaning to drink straight from the bottle. But suddenly he heard the unmistakable sound of a cat's cry. He put down the bottle, almost dropping it in his haste, and ran to the back door.

Roger was sitting on his haunches looking the worse for wear.

"Damon!"

Damon? His mind was playing tricks. He shook his head to clear it. "Butterscotch!" he said, correcting himself. He stepped through the door onto the porch.

Confused, the cat pulled back. "I meant Roger," Doug said, as if the cat could understand him. "Of course I meant Roger." He bent over and scooped him into his arms. "Where've you been, baby? You had me scared."

Roger responded with a loud purr and a soft paw to Doug's cheek.

"Here, let me get a good look at you."

Doug held the cat at arm's length. For the first time he noticed a long tear in the left ear and a rip above the right eye. Blood had matted the cat's whiskers. There was a circle of dried blood, the size of a silver dollar, at the back of his neck. In spots his fur had been torn out, revealing patches of flesh discolored by more blood.

The sight of it set made Doug dizzy and caused his eyes to blink. For a second or two, he relived the horror of the dream he'd had two nights before. Rocking on his heels, his head swimming, he put Roger down as gently as he could and leaned heavily against the door jamb. It was at least a minute before he got his breath back.

"First, I guess we ought to clean you up a bit," he said. He went to the kitchen and came back with a wet cloth. But Roger would have none of it. When Doug touched a wound on his lip, he hissed menacingly and unsheathed his claws.

"That hurt, baby? All right, no more. I'll get you something to eat."

Roger ate ravenously. No wonder, Doug thought; most likely the cat hadn't had a bite to eat for two days. Doug sat on the porch steps beside him and observed him closely while he licked his plate. "You know what I think? I think you may look worse than you feel." Roger gave him a scolding eye as if he didn't know what all the fuss was about. "I know, I know," Doug said. "I should see the other fellow." He picked Roger up and turned him on his back. "Here, let's have a look."

Just as he'd thought, Roger was an intact tom. "We'll have to do something about that. I mean, soon."

Roger squirmed and jumped out of his arms. He sat on his haunches and regarded Doug tolerantly. Doug laughed lightly. "You want more? Okay, you may have more. Then I'm going to have to leave you for a few minutes."

He went back into the house, his body relaxed, aware that the intense desire for a drink had left him. He returned to the porch a moment later with a fresh plate of salmon in one hand and the bottle of Scotch in the other. "You stay here and gorge yourself. I won't be but a few minutes."

Hortense met him at the front door. She was wearing a plain cotton dress with a flowered apron, slightly food stained. She still looked lovely. "Jet's still at work?"

She sighed. "Well, he's still at the office. Habit. He hasn't had a patient in two days."

"Give him this for me." Doug handed her the Scotch. Hortense looked startled. "Tell him it's a going-away present from his not-so friendly neighborhood bootlegger."

"Really? You mean Nichols?"

"I found it in on a secret shelf in the linen closet."

"But you should keep it. It's yours."

"I can't drink anymore. Doctor's orders."

She opened the door. "I was forgetting my manners. Won't you come in?"

"I'm sorely tempted, but Roger's been in a cat fight. I'm taking him to a vet before he gets infected."

"Not again."

"Since for the time being we have joint custody, I guess I should ask you. Is it all right with you if while he's there I have him neutered?"

"Oh my yes. It will probably save his life. We'll share the vet bill with you."

Doug felt like skipping. The mysterious weight in his temples had lifted. For the first time since he couldn't remember when, a smile came naturally to his face. He pivoted lightly and began to run back to Roger. "See you later."

"Jet will be glad for the booze," she called.

He stopped and turned to face her. "I can't tell you how glad I am to be able to give it to him."

EXHAUSTED AND SURFEITED, Roger was fast asleep on the back porch by the time Doug got to the house. He left the cat undisturbed while he cleaned the brush and put away the paint. Then, moving as noiselessly as he could, he picked up Roger, carried him to the car, and placed him tenderly on the passenger's seat. Roger protested only with a quiet meow. Thank God, he continued to doze as Doug turned on the ignition and started the drive to Four Paws Animal Hospital.

Next morning, he went to the Emory Hospital and sold another pint of blood, this time to pay the vet. After that, it was time for him to get off a long report to Maude.

MEANWHILE MAUDE, having found a tenant for the Hastings house, was busy freeing themselves of all but essentials. The bed Doug had made for them, and the crib he'd made for Damon, she kept, along with the oriental rugs, the hunt table, and the late eighteenth-century dining suite inherited from her mother. Everything else she sold through want-ads in the *Courier*, or gave to the Salvation Army. At Doug's urging, she threw out most of his files, including all the early drafts of proposals for what would have been Hastings's first radio station. She could not bring herself to junk his blueprints for the house planned for Honeysuckle Hills. Finding no takers for the lot at her asking price of $2500 after advertising for a month, she withdrew it from the market and regarded its failure to sell as an omen. She packed the drawings in the same box with the prospectus for Krueger Associates. She labeled the box, "Still Possibles."

When the time came, Catherine and Doug drove to Hastings in Catherine's Oldsmobile. With help from Strut and Trudy, they loaded both cars, roped mattresses to the roof of the Ford and beds to the roof of the Oldsmobile. They shipped everything else by Railway Express. They held back the tears until they were on the highway to Atlanta.

17

In 1932 the economy dropped into the cellar. On average, wage earners fortunate enough to be still working were being paid fifty percent less than in 1929. Business as a whole lost between five and six billion dollars. More than a million Americans, many of them teenage boys and girls, were on the roads or in boxcars, hoping to find in flight the security that had deserted them at home. Wheat was selling below fifty cents, cotton below five. Since the 1929 panic, when the stock market was assumed to have gone as low as Wall Street's law of gravity permitted, shares in most U.S. corporations had in fact continued down, down, down. U.S. Steel, which only two years before sold at 261, was going for 21. On the rims of the big cities, homeless families huddled in "Hoovervilles," makeshift villages fashioned from packing crates, lumber scraps, cardboard, tin and anything else that could be pulled from town dumps to keep out the rain and snow. At the back doors of restaurants ravenous men waited for barrels of garbage to be brought out and fought one another for scraps of food.

The Depression was pandemic and it defied explanation. In London the governor of the Bank of England told the press that "the difficulties are so vast, the forces so unlimited, so novel, and precedents are so lacking, that I approach the whole subject not only in ignorance but in humility." A New York banker echoed him: "As for the cause of the Depression, or the way out, you know as much as I do."

Advocates of aggressive action by the federal government were met by a president who wavered between hesitation and petulance. Trapped in an ideology that had lost its sustaining power of myth, Herbert Hoover responded with a statement that defined succinctly the conservative fault in the nation's political divide: "Federal handouts lead to waste and corruption. Prosperity cannot be restored by raids on the public treasury." His critics were quick to point out that, though a well-intentioned man and on occasion a demonstrably compassionate one, Mr. Hoover could not possibly understand what it was like to be broke: he still had four million pre-inflation dollars from his engineering company.

The Kruegers survived the year by drawing prudently on savings. Most of the proceeds from sale of the household furniture in Hastings had gone for the purchase of kitchen appliances. Doug's cash earnings from his part-time job at Emory were enough to pay only about a third of Izzy's fee. To help out, Damon became a Curtis Junior Salesman, going door to door with a canvas bag over his shoulders selling copies of *The Saturday Evening Post*, *Country Gentleman*, and *Ladies' Home Journal*. He also became a substitute carrier for the evening *Atlanta Journal*. Some weeks he brought home as much as three dollars.

Catherine had the family for dinner at least once a week. Every now and again she gave Doug a small check ("For being a good boy"), but with the bank in Chesterton in bankruptcy and the decline in quarterly dividends from the stock bequeathed her by Jacob, her own income was unstable and she no longer had the means to contribute significantly. At the end of the year the family's total reserve had been reduced to what was left of Maude's inheritance, a sum of about $3,500 for which, mysteriously, interest at two percent remained steady.

Everything about Doug's situation called for him to find full-time work. That, however, depended not only on his finding a job when jobs were few and most of them demeaning but also on his ability to get by on fewer sessions with Izzy amd on his getting well enough to go reliably from nine to five every day. He ventured the possibility to Maude. She put her foot down. "Absolutely not," she said vehemently. "Your time with Izzy is the best thing we've got going for us."

"I think I ought to try," he said.

"I don't think so," she said, in a tone that entertained no contradiction. "You've made remarkable progress this past year. I can tell even if you can't. We'll live on tomato soup and leftover rice before you give up Izzy."

PERHAPS THE BEST THING about the move to Penn Avenue was the friendship that developed with the Moneypennys next door. Maude and Hortense bonded like sisters, Doug and Jet like two infantrymen in the trenches. Damon quickly came to think of Jet and Hortense as uncle and aunt. The families shared potluck meals and went on late afternoon picnics at Soap Creek. They had a mutual passion for tennis and, except for one or two miserably cold days in December, played doubles every Saturday morning. Some evenings, when Doug felt able, they played bridge or gathered after supper to listen to "Amos 'n Andy," the "Rudy Vallee Show," or the "Voice of Firestone." Of significant comfort to Doug, when the Moneypennys learned he was afflicted with bouts of depression, sometimes disabling and on better days merely bothersome, they took it sympathetically but made no attempt to press or push him and accommodated themselves without complaint to his changes of mood. However disappointed they might feel when he was too down to be good company, they let him be. It was a gift that Doug never found a way to repay.

After only a short time of testing, during which each progressed from tentatively voiced opinions to unequivocal statements of conviction, they found to their mutual gratification that they shared a serious interest in politics. In Georgia in the nineteen-thirties, this alone was enough to establish them as distinct minority, for the politics of that time was little more than popular entertainment. It played out every two years as a communal melodrama, staged at outdoor barbecues, in which gubernatorial candidates played the leads, speaking in the pulse-rousing, mind-deadening cadences of born-again evangelists to the accompaniment of fiddles and banjos. Campaigns were financed by the urban rich and addressed almost exclusively to the rural poor; the white middle-class was as effectively disfranchised by formula as the Negro population was by law. But whereas the scenario called for middle-class whites to suffer only the indignity of being ignored, Negroes were relentlessly attacked or ridiculed, the script casting them unfailingly as villains or feebleminded comics.

The system was cruel and it tolerated no dissenters. To hold that there might be important issues of health and welfare and education; to maintain the right of labor to organize; to advocate equal women's rights; to challenge the sophistry of the equal-but-separate doctrine; to maintain that Negroes had souls or, worse, to be seen shaking hands with one in public, was to position yourself in the cold margins of a closed and sick society. It was a lonely place to be and sometimes dangerous.

Alienated from their natural families, the scattered occupants of these margins reached out to one another and formed a surrogate family of nurturing deviants. In Atlanta as many as three dozen of them—all males—organized a club they christened the Copernicus Society, a name that satisfactorily masked their radical intent. The psychiatrist among them, in a mood of self-deprecation and noting the membership's common aversion to publicity, described the group as "a bunch of revolutionaries who can't stand the sight of blood." Maybe. What was more obvious was that they simply had the not uncommon obligation of some well-born to help those less fortunate. Raised in privilege, each Copernican had had some experience that shocked him into empathy, an affliction that embarrassed his parents, who were inclined to see it as a congenital defect or as evidence that he'd disobeyed orders and crossed the plantation boundaries. Now in adulthood most of them bore scars of guilt like birthmarks.

The club came together, without notes of reminder, on the fourth Friday of each month, usually in a member's home but occasionally at the meeting place of the local Society of Friends, it being the only church in town hospitable to racially mixed groups. Among its organizers was a Charleston-born, Harvard-educated pediatrician; a designer and manufacturer of ladies' undergarments; a sociology professor at Agnes Scott who also served as research director of the Commission on Interracial Cooperation; and a Catholic lawyer known for his pro bono defense of the poor. Its members included two Jews—a young rabbi only recently arrived from Boston, and the Atlanta director of the Anti-Defamation League. There were no Negroes in the membership, although prominent Negro professionals—the editor of the *Atlanta Daily World*, for instance, or the dean of men at Morris Brown College—were frequently invited to read papers and participate in the discussions. For informal liaison with Atlanta's black community, it relied chiefly on an elderly lawyer who headed the Georgia branch of the National Association for the Advancement of

Colored People. In a deliberate effort to round out a liberal constituency, the club also recruited the dean of Emory's bible school and the regional organizer for the AFL.

In a culture ruled by identifiable alliances between special interests, country clubs, and secret societies, the Copernicus Society functioned as perhaps the most elite, the most exclusive, club in town. It kept no minutes and no financial records. Most members rarely saw one another apart from the monthly meetings, and all of them were devoutly discreet in their references to its business.

Its business was the cultivation of democracy. Essentially, the club developed the strategy for political reform in Georgia and, with a reluctant concession to the pragmatic, set the priorities for action: first, repeal the poll tax; then push for an anti-lynching law; then sue in the federal courts for an end to the white primary; then turn to the courts again for abolition of the county unit system. All the while educate, educate, educate. The actions it prescribed, however, were always taken in the name of one or more of its individual members, or by the organizations they headed, never in the name of the Copernicans. That it did all its good works in anonymity and operated almost as clandestinely as the Klan, never struck members as at all ironic. It was simply a necessity of life. The thirty-six male mavericks constituted a movement of good-humored insurgents, who put their faith in the dubious powers of education and persuasion. Aching with conscience and confronted daily with simple choices of moral behavior in an immoral culture, they lived uneasily with the knowledge that one more public stand on principle, one more noisy peep of objection to the status quo, might cost them not only the comforts of their white heritage but their livelihoods. Sometime early in January of 1932 Jet suggested that he sponsor Doug for membership.

"The thing is," he said, somewhat hesitantly, "we meet for a light supper at seven-thirty. Somebody then reads a paper and we discuss it, maybe for an hour or more, depending on the issue. We usually don't break before ten-thirty or eleven. You think you might manage it?"

The invitation both flattered and depressed Doug. He looked earnestly in Jet's eyes. What he saw there encouraged him.

"I'd like to try," he said after a long pause.

Several old acquaintances from his years at Tech greeted him on his arrival at that first meeting. Their warmth eased the tension that had been rising in him; he felt as if something was pulling him into the safety of a cocoon. And when from his left he heard a familiar voice with a Yankee accent he was additionally reassured. He turned to find Izzy Orenstein at his elbow, holding an outstretched hand. "Glad to see you."

But it was too much to expect the evening to pass without pain. After supper, he went to the bathroom. While there he heard voices in the hall outside, from two men waiting at the door. The voices were muffled at first, then, as the men moved closer, they became quite clear. With a shock, Doug realized that they were talking about him.

". . . in Hastings," one of them was saying. "I was in Hastings off and on last year, helping a cousin get over a messy divorce, and I used to hear him do the evening news. He had this great voice."

"I guess I wasn't paying much attention tonight," Doug heard the other man say. "He didn't talk much."

"He's been through a rather bad time, I understand. People in Hastings loved him. He gave the news straight, and when he had somebody on to interview he always asked the kind of questions you'd like to ask yourself. He really was superb. Much better than anybody here on WSB."

"What happened to him?"

"I don't know. They say he had some sort of breakdown. One story is that he had a drinking problem, but I don't believe it. Nobody with a drinking problem could have been as sharp as he was on the air."

"When he cracked up, was he on the air?"

"I don't think so. They say he just left the studio abruptly one afternoon. A few hours later his wife found him somewhere in the woods, lying unconscious in the mud, out of his mind."

"How awful!"

"A shame, really. My cousin said—"

Doug didn't want to hear any more. He flushed the toilet, took a deep breath, and opened the door. Passing the two men, he forced a smile and said, "Sorry I was so long."

He was trembling when he rejoined Jet for the drive home. He said very little, grateful that Jet was too absorbed in his own review of the evening's discussion to notice. On his tongue was the bitter taste of failure, the dregs of a time that could never be retrieved. An important part of his life was over. Another was about to begin. He could neither welcome nor resist it.

MAUDE AND HORTENSE WERE ACTIVE, principally through the League of Women Voters, in campaigns to increase voter registration and to reform the municipal government. Hortense was editor of the League's monthly newsletter and Maude her most dependable contributor. For years Atlanta had been governed by a mayor and a bicameral council, with aldermen and councilmen elected on a ward basis rather than citywide. The ward system made it difficult to get any kind of ordinance passed of benefit to the city as a whole, for to a man council members were indifferent to any proposal that didn't affect their own wards. Maude spent much of her energy lobbying for abolition of the ward system and for legislation that would reduce the mayor to ceremonial status, transferring his powers to a city manager, whom conventional wisdom held to be less corruptible. Though they had right and logic on their side, Maude and her earnest colleagues failed repeatedly, largely because the trade unions, whose members constituted nearly half the city's registered voters, feared that any change would reduce working-class influence in municipal affairs. (Since the county unit system virtually barred them from involvement in state politics, influence at the ward level was about the only influence they had, and they had no intention of losing it under pressure from a bunch of perfumed ladies from Buckhead.) The effort served to acquaint Maude with an aspect of the class struggle that her liberal education hadn't prepared her for.

Much more productive was her participation in a project to bring attention to the deficiencies in public services. The project was initiated by a woman of majestic carriage and striking good looks—soft brown hair, eyes that were equally soft and brown, an unblemished complexion, a full bosom, and long, long legs. Her name was Arabella Perdue and her credentials were intimidating: her grandfather, a Confederate general, had served with Lee in the Wilderness campaign, and an uncle had been the first senator from Georgia to be elected after Reconstruction. A maiden lady of impressive dignity, she was the self-emancipated daughter of a prosperous manufacturer of denim work clothes ("Perdue Pants will never let you down") and her inheritance included prompt access to every power broker in the state. She had almost as much sex appeal as she had intelligence and almost as much intelligence as she had money, and she did not hesitate to use all three, discreetly, for worthy causes—provided the beneficiaries kept a respectable distance.

For the League's fact-finding project Arabella budgeted thirty thousand dollars, which she intended to raise by canvassing fifteen Georgia corporations headquartered in Atlanta. Maude's first job with her was to help schedule appointments, acknowledge in writing each donation as it came in, and keep records of expenditures. Only once did Arabella invite Maude to accompany her on a call, and without being offensively explicit she made it understood that Maude was to be quiet and keep her place.

Maude watched in awe as Arabella went into action. She arrived at the company's office exactly five minutes early. "I have a ten o'clock appointment with Mr. Adams," she announced to the receptionist in a tone of voice accustomed to making requests of chambermaids. "Please tell him that Miss Perdue is waiting."

Once in the man's office, she introduced Maude, gesturing her into a chair to her right, just behind hers. She straightened the jacket of her Bergdorf-Goodman suit, made a slight adjustment to her hair (done only the day before by Antoine), lifted her skirt slightly, and crossed her long, long legs.

The effect on plump, myopic Mr. Adams, as it would be on every no-nonsense business type she visited, was instant. He blinked his eyes, gasped, and let himself go in a seizure of mid-morning lust.

"As you know, Mr. Adams," Arabella was saying, precisely as she'd rehearsed it, "the League of Women Voters is scrupulously nonpartisan. We believe, however, that the deplorable situation in the country is such that regardless of who's elected president this fall the federal government will have to intervene. This means that money will be flowing from Washington to the states, in varying amounts according to the needs of each state. What I want to talk with you about this morning is a project we're launching to document Georgia's needs—to make sure we get our fair share when the dollars start rolling."

"Admirable," said Mr. Adams.

"Georgia needs help, Mr. Adams. Did you know that the annual per capita income is less than two hundred and fifty dollars?"

The fact was lost on Mr. Adams. Maude, repressing a smile, saw his eyes glaze over. He was blushing, aware that he had been concentrating on Arabella's bosom.

Arabella went on: "Did you know that at least fifty thousand people in this state are out of work and can't find jobs? That Georgia ranks forty-third in literacy? That almost ten percent of the population over the age of ten can't even sign their names?"

Mr. Adams gave an odd jerk and settled more deeply into his chair.

"What we plan to do, Mr. Adams, is to commission a series of papers on the condition of our public services. We'll have papers on education, health care, the criminal justice system, economic development, taxation and revenues, agriculture, welfare, and so on—all told, more than a dozen, each done by an authority in these fields. We'll publish the papers as pamphlets—as study guides—and distribute them to schools and civic clubs and use them as a platform for a statewide discussion program. We hope this way to start a real reform movement."

Arabella paused, expecting Mr. Adams to comment. When no comment came, she went on: "We need about thirty thousand dollars to pull this off. Every cent will go for printing and distribution. All the research, all the writing and editorial work, will be done by volunteers. Philip Saxon has volunteered to direct the research and John Maxwell has agreed to write the first paper."

Mr. Adams sighed and shifted his gaze to the view of the three magnolias outside his office window.

"Mr. Adams! Are you listening to me?"

Mr. Adams shook his head and suspended his fantasy, swallowing hard. “Oh yes I was,” he said, protestingly. “A splendid idea. Our company would like to support you any way we can.”

Arabella gave him a dazzling smile.

“How about two hundred and fifty dollars?” he said.

Arabella frowned.

“Or five hundred. We might be able to manage five hundred.”

“We were counting on a thousand.”

Arabella leaned forward to the edge of the desk. Mr. Adams caught a faint scent of Je Reviens. “Well, now, a thousand dollars—” He gulped. “I suppose we can find a thousand dollars.”

Arabella smiled, rose to her feet, and shook his hand. He got up from his desk to say good-bye—somewhat awkwardly, for he had a hard on. He gave a self-conscious cough.

“And of course, my dear, my personal best wishes. Come back to see me. I like to talk politics with you any time.”

18

For Damon, having the Moneypennys next door was like an extra helping of familial affection. Unaccustomed to the company of teenagers, the Moneypennys treated him as a peer, which sometimes stretched him to behave beyond his years. Better that, though, than to be talked down to or patronized, and the fact that they not only invited his opinions but considered them was very good for his young ego.

Damon's friendship with Jet began late one afternoon in June when he went looking for Roger. He found the cat in the Moneypennys' backyard lying in a bed of ivy on a low terrace that edged the garden. The master of all he could survey, Roger was grooming himself beyond all prerequisites for godliness, pausing occasionally to give Jet a monitoring eye. Jet, wearing what looked like the coat to an old pair of blue pajamas and khaki pants ready for the laundry, was busy fertilizing the roses. He was humming "Life Is Just a Bowl of Cherries." He stopped amd looked up when he heard the sound of Damon's Keds on the gravel path.

"Hello," he said cheerily.

"I was looking for Roger."

"My foreman?" Jet went over to the terrace and scratched Roger under the chin. "I've been trying to teach him to be nicer to the birds."

"I've never seen Roger go after a bird," Damon said, feeling vaguely defensive.

"It's not his fault," Jet said. "Blame Mother Nature."

Damon sat on the wall and stroked the cat's back. Roger rolled over to make it clear that he'd rather be scratched on the stomach. Damon complied.

"And you're teaching him not to?"

"Well, let's just say that by now he understands I don't want him going after the birds."

"What do you do, scare him?"

"Oh no. I just talked to him."

"You think he understands English?"

"Roger understands more than we'll ever know. You better believe it."

"I'd like to believe it." Damon said, smiling.

Jet turned back to his work. "I better get on with it," he said. "I want to finish before dark. But stay, keep me company."

"Could I help?" Damon asked.

"Why yes, maybe you could." Jet gestured toward a shed at the side of the lot. "Look in there and see if you can locate another trowel. And a bucket."

When Damon returned, Jet filled the bucket half with 10-30-20 and half with chicken manure. "A patient of mine has chickens and saves me the manure," he explained. "Mix it with a little nitrogen and you get the best kind of rose food. We do this now, just as the roses are budding, and again in about a month, when they're in bloom."

He showed Damon how to dig a shallow trench around each bush under the farthermost branches and to fill the trench with an even spread of the fertilizer. "Now when the rain comes the food will go into the soil. And that's all there is to it."

He led Damon to the last of the three rows of roses ("They're all Cherokees. Did you now the Cherokee is Georgia's state flower?") and left him to it. He watched Damon silently for a while before he went back to where he'd left off on the first row. It was easy work, but the sun was still bright in the sky. When they were done both were sweating.

"Hortense is off covering a garden party," Jet told Damon, "but she made me some tea before she left. Come, sit here on the terrace and I'll fetch a glass and some ice."

Waiting in the sun, smelling the fresh earth, the fertilizer, and the warm perspiration on his body, Damon felt lazily at ease. Roger crossed over and jumped in his lap, asking to be scratched between his shoulder blades. "You're a good cat and you get more than enough to eat," Damon said to him, "so why do you have to kill the birds?"

Roger gave him a sour look as if to say the question wasn't worth answering.

"I've been trying to talk to Roger like you," he said when Jet came with the tea. "I don't think he believes I have anything worth saying."

"Roger is like a lot of people I know," Jet said. "He can't stand criticism."

As if he'd heard and would tolerate no more, Roger jumped off the terrace and ran off to look for a butterfly. Damon and Jet laughed together.

They sat in silence for a while, sipping the sweet tea and watching the sun drop. A breeze came. Their flesh began to dry and cool. They felt pleasantly tired.

Damon spoke first.

"Dr. Moneypenny?"

"Yes, Damon."

"Why is the world the way it is?"

"I'm sorry, what did you say?"

"Why are things the way they are? I mean, why do cats eat birds and birds eat worms and lions eat deer, and people—we're the worst of all—kill everything. Why must everything feed on everything else? Why do we have wars and why are some people rich and other people poor? Please don't laugh, and please don't tell me I'll understand one day, when I grow up."

Jet saw the thoughtful expression on Damon's face. He felt at a loss to answer.

"No," he said solemnly. "I won't tell you you'll understand some day because I'm grown up, more or less, and I don't understand. I don't think anybody understands except God. And God doesn't like questions."

"But if God is good and if he's so all powerful, why does he allow so much suffering and so much cruelty?"

"Oh my!" Jet said despairingly. "Who knows? Preachers and poets and philosophers have built careers thinking about that one."

"You mean I shouldn't worry about it?"

"No. I didn't say that. Some of us just can't help worrying, and wondering. All I mean is, you'll be happier if you don't think about it."

"But how do you stop thinking?"

Jet chuckled. "Oh my, Damon, you are cursed. Most people haven't even begun to think."

"But what do you think?"

"I think it happened when God wasn't looking."

A look of bewilderment came into Damon's eyes. Jet realized that he was making too light of a subject that, to his credit, Damon was taking very seriously.

"I didn't mean that," he told the boy earnestly. "The truth is, Christians have been trying to figure that out ever since they decided there was only one God."

"And nobody has?"

"A lot of people think they have. There are about as many explanations as there are Baptists."

"I don't see how that could be."

Jet searched his mind for a graceful way to get off this track. Obviously, Damon was not a kid who could be satisfied with platitudes or inspired by sounding brass.

"There must be more than one book on the subject," Jet said, hoping to be helpful. "If you like, I'll take you to the Carnegie library downtown and we'll look one up."

"I'd like that," Damon said. "You mean something in plain English? Something easier than *Paradise Lost*?"

"Something written in this century," Jet assured him. "Something no harder than a Sunday School lesson."

Jet tried to remember what he'd been like thirty years ago when he was entering puberty. Had he, like Damon now, been concerned with God and meaning? He didn't think so.

"How old are you, Damon?"

"Twelve. I was twelve in January."

"You know what day of the week you were born on?"

"Mother told me. A Wednesday."

"I'm relieved."

"Relieved?"

Jet smiled. "I thought you might be a Friday's child."

Again, Damon looked puzzled. He didn't know what to make of this man.

"Why?"

"A Friday's child is full of woe."

"And a Wednesday's child?"

"Loving and giving."

"I'm loving and giving?"

"That's what my grandfather would have called you. He taught me a verse. 'Monday's child is fair of face. Tuesday's child is full of grace. Wednesday's child'—that's you—'is loving and giving. Thursday's child works hard for a living. Friday's child is full of woe.' And so on."

"And what day's child are you, Dr. Moneypenny?"

Jet chuckled. "I was born on a Saturday. I have far to go."

Damon laughed with him. "Go where?

Jet turned to get the sun out of his eyes. "I wish I knew." He sounded serious. His tone stopped any further questions. "Enough of this heavy stuff," he said. "What do you do for fun, Damon?"

"For fun?" Damon had to think. He hadn't had much fun lately. "I like movies. Westerns, especially. And back in Hastings I played baseball. Third base. I like swimming and tennis, and I like to read."

"Books? What sort of books?"

"Well, I've finished *Tom Sawyer*. And I'm starting on *Hans Brinker*. Grandmother Krueger gave me *Hans Brinker* for Christmas."

"Have you read *Huckleberry Finn*?"

"Not yet."

"I'll lend you a copy."

"I've read all the Rover Boys. And most of Tom Swift."

"Well," said Jet, grimacing. "The important thing is, you keep reading."

They lapsed into silence again, enjoying the sun and the breeze and each other's company. Damon caught the smell of Dr. Moneypenny beside him. It was the special smell of an adult male, a mix of musk and sweat and aftershave, and it reminded him of his father, except that his father would also have smelled faintly of tobacco.

"Dr. Moneypenny?"

"Yes, Damon."

"You don't smoke, do you?

"No, Damon. Smoking is bad for your teeth and I try to be a good role model."

"What's a role model?"

"Let's just say I try to set a good example for my patients."

A moment later: "Dr. Moneypenny?"

"Yes?"

"Do you think my daddy will get well?"

"Of course," Jet said promptly, with forced confidence. "It's only a matter of time."

"I miss him."

Jet patted Damon on the shoulder. "I'm sure your father misses you, too." He bit his tongue. He had started to say, "And probably misses himself."

Damon raised his eyes and gazed at the neatly cultivated garden before him—the eight furrows of weedless red clay planted in rose bushes, each two feet apart in mounds of pine mulch, and beyond them a row of climbing vines wrapping themselves around white stakes, and at least five rows of young sprouts and shoots and bursts of leaves, early promises of lettuce and beans and cucumbers and sweet onions. And finally, at the rear of the deep and fertile lot, a lush arbor of wisteria, the blossoms faded and dying with the coming of June.

Damon breathed deeply. "Daddy used to have a garden," he told Jet. "Well, not exactly a garden. He and mother had bought this big lot meaning to build us a house on it, and for a year or so while they were making plans, Daddy would go out in the afternoons, once or twice a week, and sometimes he'd take me with him, and we'd plant trees and shrubs—all kinds of hostas—and wild flowers. There was a stream at the back, and Daddy cleared maybe as much as an acre near it. Mother would join us there some afternoons and we'd have picnics by the creek."

"That must have been a lovely place," Jet said. "And time."

"Mother says we may go back there some day. But I don't think we ever will."

"Hortense and I were lucky," said Jet, "to have bought this property when we did. There were two building lots available, back to back. The space we have in garden was supposed to be a house lot, too, with the house facing Myrtle Street. The builder got in trouble and needed some quick cash, so he sold it to us for almost half what it was worth."

"I wish we could have a garden," Damon said. "But our back yard is so small and the apple tree takes up so much room it's all shade."

"Would you really like a garden?" Jet asked him. "If you do, we could lay out a small plot for you, back there just before the wisteria, and you could plant carrots and radishes and lettuce, and maybe a few flowers. Would you like that?"

Damon was surprised and pleased. "Could I?" But then he considered the work and the hours such a commitment would require and his face sobered. "I really would like to, but—"

"Well," Jet said, lifting himself out of his chair. "Just let me know. It could be fun."

Damon got up too. "Mother will be wondering where I am. I guess I better find Roger and get home."

"I've enjoyed our visit," Jet said. He wanted to say more, for he felt strangely affected; vague desires of his youth stirred in the vacuum of his unfulfilled fatherhood. He said merely, "I hope you'll come back."

Damon smiled and nodded. "You asked what I did for fun. I forgot to say music. I play the trombone."

Jet was struck with pleasure. "I'll be triggered!"

"Sir?"

"Sorry," Jet said, laughing. "Every now and again I lapse into my native tongue."

Damon looked bewildered. "I don't understand."

"Where I come from, we'd say 'triggered' when we were surprised and pleased."

"You're pleased?"

"Oh my yes, Damon. Did you know that I play piano? Jazz piano, sort of. Maybe we could team up, form a duo. What sort of music do you play?"

"Mostly marches and things like 'Stouthearted Men' and 'The Bells of St. Mary's.' I was in the school orchestra."

"You think you could learn Dixieland?"

"I've been playing for three years now. Daddy says I'm pretty good."

"And I bet you are. Now, let's see." Jet thought about his week's schedule. "Why don't we make a date? Say next Friday afternoon when Hortense has a meeting with her editor and we can have the house to ourselves? I'll get out some sheet music. Can you transpose?"

"Well enough."

"This'll be great," Jet said, grinning. "It's a date then."

They parted. Damon found Roger waiting at the back door and his mother at the kitchen sink. "Mother," he asked, "what day of the week was Daddy born on?"

THE ATTACHMENT FORMED by Jet and Damon was not easy to define. Although Jet took care never to act like a surrogate father, he clearly thought of Damon as the son he should have had. Damon early came to regard Jet as an older brother, all the more to be appreciated for the thirty years' difference in their ages. Still, having been taught since birth to show respect for anybody over twenty-one, he could not bring himself to call him Jet. Hortense's affection for Damon was equally warm but more demonstrable. Sometimes she took him by surprise by reaching out, pulling him to her, and giving him a hug and a kiss. There were times, too, when her eyes watered as she looked at him. What was she thinking?

Maude knew. Not too long after they met, Hortense confided in Maude that seven years ago she and Jet had left little Tom, one week after his first birthday, in the care of Jet's mother while they went to a church supper. When they returned they bent over to kiss him good-night and found him still and cold, a victim of crib death.

"How do these things happen? How long the child had been on his stomach we can only guess. He'd apparently turned over in his sleep. Julia—my mother-in-law, there's never been a more loving, more conscientious woman in the world—nodded off just long enough."

"Oh how dreadful."

"It was terrible," Hortense said, stricken. "For all of us. Maybe more for Jet than for me. Maybe most of all for Julia. She didn't know, and we didn't know, that she'd been suffering from narcolepsy and having small strokes. She died within a year."

"From a stroke?"

"I think more likely from grief and guilt."

"How do you ever get over a thing like that?" Maude asked, not expecting an answer. "Are you thinking of trying again?"

Hortense sighed despairingly. "Jet says he can't bear to run the risk."

"But isn't that foolish of him? The odds must be a million to one."

"I know," Hortense said. "And Jet knows, too. After all, he's something of a scientist, the most rational man you'll ever know. Still—"

Maude could think of nothing comforting to say. "Maybe in time."

"Maybe," said Hortense.

All during the summer of 1931, regularly every Friday afternoon, Damon took his trombone over to Jet's. The Moneypennys had made an all-purpose room out of what had been intended as a third bedroom. Bookshelves lined two of the walls, overloaded with scientific texts, the Harvard classics, and leatherbound volumes of James Fenimore Cooper and Mark Twain, done by a publisher who liked them both and had the notion that a common format might reconcile the authors. A massive rolltop desk, salvaged from the office of a bankrupt accountant, dominated the third wall. Against the fourth was a relatively new upright piano made of pine and walnut veneer. Distributed on the walls were framed diplomas and sepia photographs of what Damon assumed were family members. The furnishings were complete with an enormous Atwater Kent radio and a music stand.

"I wanted to call this the den," Jet said the first time he welcomed Damon into it, "but Hortense hates the word—thinks it's pretentious. So we just call it the music room, which I think may be even more pretentious. But then I prefer to quarrel about more important things." He chuckled. "Like fried or scrambled eggs for breakfast."

Jet could read music but he relied more on ear, which occasionally led to improvisations that challenged Damon to follow. From the beginning, however, they were remarkably together, intuitively responsive to the other's flourishes and riffs. Jet's tastes ranged from ragtime to the sentimental—folk songs and pop ballads—and Dixieland. "We'll take it slow at first," he said on that first visit after Damon had unpacked his horn and taken his place behind the piano bench. So first they tried "After the Ball" ("Great," Jet said encouragingly. "Your phrasing is great.") Then Jet led them through "When the Saints Come Marching In," "Bill Bailey, Won't You Please Come Home," "Darktown Strutter's Ball," and "Alexander's Ragtime Band." ("Faster now," Jet would say, "Let's pick it up," and he would increase the tempo till Damon's slide arm was aching and they broke up laughing with pleasure.)

Hortense came home early one afternoon and stood in the living room while they went through their repertoire. "They're good," she said to herself. "Really good."

She thought them so good, in fact, that she insisted they appear with her in the annual talent show of the Atlanta Variety Club. She gave Damon a bowler hat and Jet a boater, found a linen jacket for each (one with red stripes and the other with blue), and fashioned red garters on Jet's sleeves. She then worked up a ten-minute routine in which she figured center stage.

The talent show was held in October, when Franklin Roosevelt's candidacy was clearly ascendant, and the audience brought to the municipal auditorium a mood of pre-election expectancy. Jet and Damon opened with a funereal version of "Happy Days Are Here Again" that gradually became spirited and ended as a rallying march. After an even more rousing "Bill Bailey," the stage went dark. Then Hortense emerged in a lone spotlight wearing a red wig and dressed in castoffs from the PTA Thrift

Shop. A purple feather boa dangled from her shoulders to her knees. She stood quiet and motionless for a moment, until Damon's trombone greeted her with a plaintive vamp and Jet gave her her cue. The applause started before she opened her mouth to sing the verse of "Rose of Washington Square." After the second chorus she gave a toss of the boa, turned, and went into a sassy little dance. When she was done the audience gave her a standing ovation. Jet and Damon closed with a reprise of "Happy Days Are Here Again" that set the crowd clapping and stomping.

Maude and Doug sat on the first row. In spirit, however, Doug was far removed. Earlier, despite the onset of a migraine, he had summoned the will to dress and to drive the three of them downtown to the auditorium. With great effort he'd given Damon a hug of encouragement when they let him out at the stage door. Half blind with pain, he made it to his seat only with Maude's help. Thereafter, he sat in a slump, short of breath, his chin on his chest, his eyes half closed, his mind adrift. The music came to him only in discordant bursts, he was unaware of the lights and costumes, and Hortense's little dance was completely lost on him. Unable to share his son's triumph, he felt once again the crushing weight of failure.

19

The fall of 1932 was noteworthy for several other events. Doug got a part-time job with a sanitary engineering firm and managed to keep it four months. It ended with a call to the owner's office. The owner, a tubby little man with round dark eyes that flickered nervously behind rimless glasses, was not at ease saying what he felt he had to say. "My wife was waiting with our boy to see the pediatrician the other day," he said after twice clearing his throat. "She saw you coming out of a Dr. Orenstein's office." Disconcerted that Doug said nothing, he went on even more awkwardly. "She assumed that you're getting psychiatric care. Is that true?" Doug said yes, nothing more. "Well, I hope you understand. We can't afford to have a mental patient on the crew. The risk, you know. We can't accept the liability."

Doug's old job at Emory had been abolished; fund-raising had been all but discontinued. He remained unemployed until late spring of 1933, when from time to time his old Tech professor, who ran a discreet consulting firm on the side, would find him piecework at seventy-five cents an hour. The economic depression was at its worst. Men who years before had fought to escape the suffocating places of their births now felt betrayed, the promised benisons of the city unrealized, their faith shattered by mysterious forces they could not describe but which some historians were prone to see as serious flaws in the capitalist system and unintended consequences of the industrial revolution. Hard-put middle-class families whose rural kin could be persuaded to take them in began to return to the country, moved by a myth that life closer to soil would not only be less expensive but cleansing and renewing. A month before the presidential election, the movement was enough to cause a slight drop in the urban population and to make a theology of rural values.

In Atlanta the unemployment rate across the city was thirty percent; in black districts it ran as high as seventy percent. Jobless men and women walked the streets begging for nickels to buy cups of coffee; that year, a dime would buy you a pound of bacon. The municipal auditorium was converted into a relief center. The Salvation Army, the Traveler's Aid Society, and most of the churches set up soup kitchens. Once a day, men, women, and children would pass down the lines, collecting their dinners in small tin buckets—soup made of potatoes, large chunks of meat, onions, celery, and carrots; black coffee; day-old bread contributed by local bakeries.

Near bankruptcy, the City of Atlanta had to pay its employees, most of them school teachers, with scrip. Scrip was awkward, as Rich's Department Store was the only business in town that would honor it. Job competition between white and black workers turned ugly with organization of the American Order of Fascisti, the "Black Shirts," which intimidated many employers into firing their Negro workers and replacing them with whites. At one point in their campaign, The Biltmore was the only hotel in town not to have dismissed its black bellhops and given the jobs to white men. In June the county commissioners cut relief appropriations by a third to offset a projected budget deficit. The emergency relief center nearly closed for lack of funds. On the defensive, one commissioner said that community elders had been misled "about the huge army of gaunt, suffering people in our city." He challenged anyone with "evidence of widespread hunger" to come forward. In angry response, more than a thousand hungry Atlantans, blacks and whites in rare solidarity, marched on the courthouse. The commissioners said the protest was Communist-inspired but nevertheless restored six thousand dollars to the relief fund.

What went on in the poor and black enclaves of Atlanta was largely unreported in the three daily newspapers, which were commonly edited like house publications for a Presbyterian God.

The lawyers, doctors, merchants, bankers, insurance agents, realtors, and other white-collar types who populated northside Atlanta were not unaware or unaffected by the Depression. All had lost income and were practicing a fretful austerity. Many were having to help a suddenly needy relative, postponing the purchase of a new car, and canceling the family vacation. But none were going hungry. They managed to meet the mortgage payments, keep the maid (at five dollars a week) and, if they were members of a club, pay their monthly dues.

It was during this time that Jet decided to accept his old classmate's offer and open up a dental practice in Buckhead. He had little choice, for the hard-pressed mill workers he'd served for so long out of his office on Whitehall were coming to him now only if in extreme pain. He was earning in fees barely enough to pay the rent on his office. Reluctantly, he notified all his patients for whom he had addresses, assuring them that he would be available if they needed him; he would keep the Whitehall office open one day a week until his lease ran out. In Buckhead, where families were solvent and proud of their teeth, he quickly established himself for competence and relatively pain-free care. His practice grew and his income swelled. But he was not entirely happy serving the rich; as an act of conscience he reserved every Tuesday afternoon for duty at the public clinic run by the Atlanta-Southern Dental School. Moreover, his hours no longer permitted the frequent jazz sessions with Damon, and he felt their loss. He'd never appreciated how much being with the boy had meant to him.

Doug, meanwhile, was virtually unemployed. His chances for a regular job would have been better had his ability to work not been diminished by his illness and the hours of his availability reduced by his need to see Izzy three afternoons a week. He recognized, too, that once it became known to a prospective employer, his inconstant job history could hardly constitute a recommendation for reliability. Acknowledging his circumstance, he remembered what Strut had once said of him: "You're not the kind to take orders. Some people were just cut out to be self-employed and you're one of them. If you make it, you're going to have to make it on your own." He began seriously to consider what kind of business he might create in which he would be his own boss and accountable to nobody but himself.

Until he could work it out he took a part-time job on commission as a furniture salesman at Rich's. It was not an unpleasant job, except for the wool dust that filled his nose every time a customer asked to be shown carpet samples, but he was able to earn little more from it than he'd earned keeping gift records at Emory. As the year wore on he felt more and more insecure.

Fortuitously, in the spring of 1933, Maude's friendship with Hortense brought a modest but helpful increase in the family income.

One mid-morning in April, Maude was in the kitchen whipping up a fresh bowl of mayonnaise when Hortense came rushing in, not bothering to knock, her face flushed and her voice striking hysterically in the upper register.

"I need help," she said in a tone that commanded sympathy. "If she weren't so good and faithful I'd kill her."

"Who, Hortense? Kill who?"

"Jenny. Her little boy just ran over to tell me she's got the flu and can't make it today."

Maude wiped her hands on a towel and thrust out a kitchen chair. "Sit down, and take a deep breath before you blow."

Hortense flopped into the chair. "I've got fifteen of Atlanta's chartered snobs coming over at two for bridge. I was depending on Jenny to do the refreshments. Now what'll I do?"

Maude considered the possibilities. "Well, what are they expecting? Pheasant under glass?"

"Don't joke, Maude. These women are my golden sources and they have to be kept well fed and watered."

"Sources?"

"Where do think I learned Joe Burdge was going to marry Skirt McLean? Or that Joan Curry was taking a Caribbean cruise to forget a married man? Or—"

"I understand just how valuable they are," Maude interrupted. She looked at the clock. "Do you break to serve or do you just give them something to nibble on as they play?"

"We break for refreshments, usually after two or three rubbers."

"And what time would that be? Three? Three-thirty?"

"No earlier than three."

Maude looked at the clock next to the sink. "That gives us five hours at least. My Lord, Hortense, stop fretting. We could fix enough for a Baptist picnic in five hours."

Hortense gave her a look of undying devotion. "Could we, Maude? I mean, could you?"

"What sort of stuff do your club ladies usually serve?"

"Finger food. Watercress sandwiches. Something fancy. At least one dessert."

"Um," Maude murmured. "I've got half a leftover chicken, roasted. And yesterday was my baking day. We're half there. I can give you sweet potato biscuits and a Creole beauty cake."

"I never heard of Creole beauty cake."

"It's from a New Orleans cookbook. It's loaded with cherries and almonds. Very rich."

"That sounds exotic enough. I tell you, Maude, these are not peanut butter and jelly types. The club meets every other week and the girls make a big thing of the refreshments."

"Do I know any of these ladies?"

"Maybe one. Arabella Perdue."

"You're kidding."

"No, I'm not. Bridge may be Arabella's only indulgence. Besides, I think she works the ladies for contributions to her causes."

"And she'll be here this afternoon?"

"You can count on it."

Maude pulled out a writing tablet from a kitchen drawer and began to plan. "I'll need a few things," she said. "Can you go to the A&P while I get started?"

"I'll be off like a rabbit."

"Take this down. A jar of sweet pickles, the tinier the better. A bottle of stuffed olives. Celery. A half pound of cream cheese and a half pound of Roquefort. Two good-sized cucumbers. And at least a pound of roasted, unsalted almonds. I can perform miracles with almonds."

"Is that all?"

"And two loaves of thin—the thinnest—white bread."

"You think that'll do it?"

"I will not disgrace you, Hortense. What'll you give 'em to drink? Coffee and Coca-Cola?"

"And iced tea if anybody wants it."

"Can you handle the drinks?"

"Of course."

"Okay, get going. Here, take the cake and the sweet potato biscuits home with you now. And for good measure, here's a tin of my buttered mints. If you can get back with the stuff in an hour, I'll have everything ready and at your kitchen door by ten minutes of three."

The chauffeured Cadillacs, Lincolns, and Packards started coming at one forty-five. By two the card tables were full and Hortense and her sources, fifteen of Atlanta's richest and most idle young matrons, were in earnest competition. At five minutes of three Hortense excused herself to meet Maude at the back door.

In two quick trips, Maude brought a platter of celery stuffed with a mix of cream and Roquefort cheese and her own mayonnaise; a plate of sesame seed crackers spread with cream cheese and ginger; and three trays of sandwiches—one an egg spread flavored with a touch of sweet pickles and olives; one of cucumbers crisped in vinegar and seasoned slightly with onion salt; and one of chicken salad with almonds—all on thin, crust-free white bread. Hortense arranged it all on the buffet, where she'd already spread out slices of the Creole Beauty Cake. She'd put the mints in two small crystal bowls somewhat removed, hoping her guests would eat them last. In the center of the display were a dozen of Jet's snowy Festiva Maxima peonies.

Barely a second after departure of the last limousine, still in her party dress and high heels, Hortense rushed to report to Maude. The expression on her face was all victory.

"I take it all went well," Maude said.

"Maude, it was fabulous." Hortense threw her arms around her and kissed her on the cheek. "They just raved about the food."

"Did they like the beauty cake?"

"They looked absolutely deprived when they saw it was all gone. And the mints, and the—"

"Did they ask for your recipes?"

Hortense giggled. "They knew better than that. They know that without Jenny I'd be good only for cheese crackers, peanuts, and Coke, and since I told 'em Jenny was sick, they didn't know what to think or who to thank." She giggled again. "They kept asking me for the name of my caterer."

"Did you tell them?"

"No. But at least a half dozen of them asked me to have you phone them. Including Arabella. She's got some sort of fund-raising affair coming up."

"And she'd like me to cater it?"

"No doubt about it." Hortense turned serious. "Maude?"

"I'm listening."

"Have you ever thought about going into business?"

The Atlanta Journal, Friday, May 19, 1933

Peachtree Promenade

By Polly Peachtree

Have you ever tasted Creole Beauty Cake? I hadn't either, until earlier this week when I was having the girls in for bridge and Jenny came down with flu, leaving the refreshments unmade and my guests at my mercy, which is to say in peril of peanuts and potato chips. Happily, my next-door neighbor (May she sleep on rose petals and breakfast on champagne all the days of her life) came to my rescue. Not only did she bring over platters of luscious little sandwiches made with her own mayonnaise—but a platter of sweet potato biscuits (about which more later, maybe) and this superb cake.

For those who've asked for the name of my "caterer," she's my very good friend, Maude Krueger, a pathologically modest lady, who may be the best cook in town.

Maude studied with chefs in Charleston and New Orleans and she could teach Mrs. Rombauer a thing or two. She's hid her bright light under a bushel for years, but now I'm trying to coax her to go public.

> She says she may soon do just that, but only with finger food and cake, and only for friends. We should all be her friends.
>
> If you think I'm out of my mind from sugar poisoning, just try her Creole Beauty Cake. She'll be happy to give you the recipe.
>
> Unlike some other cooks I know, Maude feels no need to protect her recipes. No matter how good your beauty cake turns out, hers will be better, for she has magic in her hands. Next time company's coming, or you simply want to give the family a treat, give her a ring. And tell her you're a friend of Polly's.

THE PHONE CALLS STARTED coming before the afternoon *Journal* hit the porch. The first was from Arabella Perdue.

"I never knew you were an artist," she said in her usual clipped, businesslike voice.

"An artist?"

"In the kitchen, darling. I was at Hortense's last week. Why didn't you phone me?"

"Was I supposed to phone you?"

"Never mind. Look dear, I've got twenty-five businessmen coming to a meeting and I want you to help me seduce them."

Maude laughed. "You don't need my help, Arabella."

"I'm serious. I've booked the Pine Room at the Driving Club for four o'clock Saturday afternoon on June third. That's two weeks from tomorrow."

"What's the occasion, Arabella?"

"We need five thousand dollars more before we can start our fact-finding project. I've asked these men—bankers, executives of one kind or another, all the civic club presidents—to come and hear Dan Warren. You know, he used to be chancellor of the university system—to hear him talk about what we know and don't know about health, education, and welfare in Georgia. After he's done I'll explain our project and ask for donations. I've told them to bring their wives, thinking most of them will probably be going to the Club's usual Saturday buffet afterward. So, all told, I'm expecting about fifty and I thought they might be in a more generous mood if they had a drink and some of your incredible canapés before Warren speaks. You can do it, can't you?"

Maude demurred. "I don't know. I've never prepared food for as many as fifty people."

"But you could. You know you could. Just give them what you gave us at Hortense's. Except for the beauty cake. That might spoil their dinner."

Maude did a few quick calculations. "I could manage guacamole on crackers, pickled okra, cheese straws, and maybe little chicken-salad sandwiches."

"Perfect!" Arabella cooed.

"But I'd have to ask you to pay for the ingredients."

"Of course, darling," Arabella said impatiently. "I wouldn't think of asking you to do this pro bono. I'll also pay you for time and labor and talent."

"I'm embarrassed to ask you, but could you pay for the ingredients in advance?"

"Just tell me how much."

Maude was silent, trying to figure what it would take to fix and deliver hors d'oeuvres for fifty.

"Maude?

"I'm here. I was just trying to decide if I'm sure I can do it."

"Of course you can do it. You know what a difference our project can make. Please say yes."

Maude took a deep breath.

"Yes."

She was hardly off the phone when it rang again. There were four more calls during the next hour. Each was from a woman who wanted to place an order for party food "like the things I read about in Peachtree Promenade." Maude took down the names and told them she'd call back. With something of a shock, she realized that while she was prepared to cook, she wasn't prepared to go into business.

Doug came home an hour or so later, looking livelier and brighter than she'd seen him in a year. He had a copy of the *Journal* in his right hand, turned to the society page.

"Have you seen this, baby?" he asked, giving her a rough kiss. "Hortense has given you a rave."

Maude took the paper from him. "Good Lord. She shouldn't have said I'd studied with chefs in Charleston and New Orleans. I never 'studied' with anybody. I grew up in Henri's kitchen. He was my mother's cook. I've told you about Henri. As a boy in New Orleans he had a job in the kitchen at Arnaud's. As he chopped and peeled and sliced he'd watch the chefs and he learned a lot and he passed some of it on to me. He had a fondness for appetizers."

Doug grabbed her at the waist and thrust her into a chair at the breakfast table. He sat across from her, his face full of pride.

"Is that all you have to say, Maude?" He laughed, lovingly. "Do you know what Hortense has done? She's put you in the catering business and given you a captive market."

"Don't be absurd, Doug. Pleasing a bunch of bored, over-privileged women is one thing. Running a catering business for profit is quite another. I don't know how to buy wholesale, how much to buy of what and how to store it, or how the food should be packaged once I got it fixed, or how to schedule deliveries. I don't have the slightest idea of what to charge."

"That shouldn't be too hard to figure out," Doug said reassuringly. "I'll help. I could be your business manager." He thought he detected a quick sour look. Correcting himself, he said, "We could handle the business part together."

She got up and kissed the top of his head. "I know," she said. "We'll try."

Doug did, in fact, serve as Maude's business manager, and a gratifyingly efficient one. He asked Maude to do a dry run of the menu for Arabella's cocktail party, doing one item at a time, and clocked her from the time she got out the mixing bowl until it was done and on a tray ready for delivery. For each he assigned a value for her time in minutes (at the rate of a dollar an hour) and added the cost of ingredients, which gave him the item's unit cost. To that he added overhead at an arbitrary fifty percent and profit at five percent. It was not the most scientific method, but it gave them a realistic and no-risk price list. To see if the prices he came up with were competitive, he compared them with those for comparable items in Atlanta's upscale delicatessens. Considering the quality built into everything turned out in Maude's kitchen, he was satisfied that, in fact, Maude would have no competition.

Over the next several weeks he applied himself with something close to his old energy and enthusiasm. He visited every wholesale grocer listed in the telephone book, made notes of what each offered at what prices, and compiled a directory of suppliers rated for quality of product, dependability of service, and ability to deliver on short notice, as determined through a canvass of their customers. To give Maude more work space, he added a twelve-inch hinged shelf to the kitchen counter. He built a counter-height stool so she wouldn't have to stand the whole time she was mixing, and he almost doubled the storage room for canned and bottled goods by installing shelves in the narrow space between the stove and the refrigerator. He was equally creative in the design of various advertising and promotion pieces. With Maude's approval, he drew a logo: the words "Maude's Morsels" inscribed in script on two overlapping arches with a plate of sandwiches and tea cakes at their feet. He had a line engraving done of the logo and took it to the Tech print shop, where he ran it off in blue ink on two thousand white cocktail napkins, feeding the small hand press himself. He produced order forms, invoices, and several grades of business stationery on the same press, in a quantity that Maude figured would take several years to exhaust.

Thinking through the things needed to be done for Arabella's party, she worried first about how to bake, chop, mix, spread, and package enough food for fifty people and manage to have it all still fresh by the time it was served. She could roast the chicken and pull the butter mints the day before, but to keep the other ingredients fresh and moist she decided to delay work until after supper and continue as long as necessary into the night. It was fortunate that she tried to do the two chickens earlier, because it enabled her to face her first problem in time to fix it. Five minutes after she put the chickens in the oven, the gas flame went out and defeated her every effort to restart it. She had no option but to take the chickens next door and use Hortense's stove.

"Before we take any more orders for something I have to cook," she told Doug, "we're going to have to get a new stove."

He grinned. "And that's not all," he said. "Will tomorrow be soon enough?"

She looked at him curiously, wondering where his good humor was coming from and hoping it wasn't groundless.

Her usual apprehension came with sundown. As the two of them cleared and washed the supper dishes, she watched Doug's face for signs of progressive suffering and immobilizing lassitude. Astonishingly, his spirits remained high and his energy undiminished. So she gave him the two chickens and showed him how to debone them without waste and how to dice the meat finely. Damon, who had also volunteered to help, she put to work sharpening the bread knife and cutting the crust off eight loaves of white bread. As the night wore on she began to experience a joy she had not felt in years. She began to sing, "Someone's in the kitchen with Dinah—" The others chimed in. They sang merrily until the celery and apples were chopped and the eggs hard-boiled, ready to be mixed with mayonnaise and chicken into salad. "I'll wait till morning to do the sandwiches," Maude said. She washed and dried her hands at the sink before giving Doug and Damon each a kiss. They were all smiling, as if they'd each just come in first at the fair. "Now, sit down, and I'll get us some ice cream."

When they were done, she turned off the lights and they went upstairs, Damon off to his room and she and Doug to theirs. Doug fell into bed and lay on his back, waiting for Maude to come out of the bathroom. He was in no pain. He felt relaxed, nerveless, and calm. He breathed deeply. Could it be?

"Darling," he said when he heard Maude entering.

"Yes?"

"Kiss me."

She did.

His eyes misted. He couldn't believe it.

"Dare we hope?"

A letter from Strut:

You'll be pleased to learn that Amos Poole is under indictment for bribery and fraud. Some newcomer in the attorney general's office uncovered the liaison between Poole and the Office of Public Works and didn't know enough to keep quiet. The evidence is solid and irrefutable. The kickbacks and phony bids have been going on for years. The governor would like nothing better than to bury the kid who started it, but the *Courier* isn't about to let it drop, and it's beginning to look as if Poole is going to get his just desserts at last. I'll keep you posted.

The big news with me—and I say me rather than us because Trudy couldn't care less—is that I'm about to become the proud owner of a 1931 Ford Model A Deluxe Roadster. You may remember, I've lusted after this car ever since Ford announced it, even before it hit the showroom, but have never been able to afford one. Well, it so happens that one of my law partners is handling the estate sale for a client who died last month and this beautiful, miracle of an automobile is on the list. I can have it for less than $400. Can you believe it? It's got less than 10,000 miles on it. The guy kept it in prime condition. There's not a dent on it. You can put the top up or down depending on the weather. It has spoke wheels and a four-cylinder engine and leather upholstery and a rumble seat. I hope to pick it up Tuesday. If all goes well I'll drive over soon with Trudy and Alice for a visit. It's been too long. Love to Maude."

20

Now thirteen, Damon had reached the age of self-absorption, preoccupied with what was happening to his body under hormonal onslaught and the need to deal with an overflow of energy. For much of the time he felt confused, driven by something he couldn't describe to somewhere he didn't know. As the summer progressed and he faced the start of school, he withdrew into himself. He had made few friends since coming to Atlanta, none of them close. He saw almost nobody on his paper route and nobody his own age when he delivered the weekly *Saturday Evening Post*. Troop Nine had all but disbanded for the summer, most of its members away at Camp Hiawasee to earn more merit badges. He was lonesome. That fall he would enter O'Keefe Junior High. He wondered what it would be like going to a strange school where everybody else had known one another since the first grade and he was the odd boy out.

At one time he had thought that he too might go to Camp Hiawasee for a few weeks. For a while it had looked as if Maude's catering business might bring in enough money that the six-dollar weekly fee might be manageable. But summer was not a time for partying and orders for Maude's finger foods decreased sharply beginning in mid-June. Worse, after going to the expense of installing a new stove and a Frigidaire, they got a message from the landlord that he was putting the house up for sale. Unprotected by a lease, Maude and Doug faced the choice of buying the house or finding another and moving within thirty days.

Shocked and angry, they decided to buy. With Strut's help, they sold the lot in Hastings at a loss (Maude wept for two days) and with the proceeds made a cash payment of two thousand dollars. Luckily, they found a banker who would lend them the rest. The house cost a total of five thousand dollars; mortgage payments ran forty-five dollars a month, ten dollars a month more than they had been paying for rent.

Late one hot August afternoon, Damon was walking dispiritedly down Piedmont Avenue on his way home after delivering the last copy of the week's *Saturday Evening Post*. He was jolted to a halt by the noise of a racing motor and the sound of a car lurching to the curb just behind him. He jumped. The car crossed the curb and came to a stop at the edge of the sidewalk.

Damon hurried to the passenger side and stuck his head through the open window. For a moment he saw nothing. Then, as his eyes became accustomed to the shadowy light, he made out a slight figure slumped over the steering wheel, his right arm stretched and his fingers scratching at the dashboard. He was wheezing and gasping for breath.

"Please," he said between gasps, his voice hardly audible. "In there." He gestured toward the door of the glove compartment.

Damon opened the compartment. His fingers closed around a box the size of a cigarette package.

"These?"

The boy nodded and handed Damon a match.

The label on the box read: "Dr. Kaigler's Medicated Cigarettes. For relief from the symptoms of asthma." As quickly as he could make his fingers move, Damon took out a paper cylinder that seemed to be packed with menthol and small beads of dried grass. He lit it and put the tip between the boy's lips. The boy inhaled deeply and let out a small cloud of smoke. He coughed several times and took another long drag. Finally, he relaxed and turned in his seat to face Damon.

"Thanks," he said, clutching Damon's wrist. "I'll be all right now,"

He had shifted to an upright position but still could hardly see over the steering wheel. He must not be much over five feet, Damon thought, and he was as skinny as a matchstick. He had a small but nicely shaped head, black hair, and eyes that didn't quite seem of a pair, one being deep green, the other an off-shade of gray. It was a boy whom Damon reckoned to be a year or so older than himself, and he had the scrubbed appearance and confident expression of most Northside boys that made him seem familiar. He was by no means physically unattractive; the girls thought him cute. The fact that he was old enough to drive, had his own car, and was happy to play chauffeur to his younger friends made him all the more attractive. Damon had seen him in the neighborhood once or twice before, a conspicuous runt of a boy behind the wheel of a large touring car, the Lincoln he was driving now.

"You're Ben Aycock," Damon said, shaking his hand. "I've seen you around, I think at St. Mark last Sunday. I'm Damon Krueger."

Ben Aycock nodded and gave Damon a winning smile. "Hop in," he said. "I'll take you wherever you were going."

"I was going home," Damon said, moving onto the passenger seat. "On Penn Avenue, a couple of blocks from here."

Ben looked at his wristwatch. "I guess it's too late to go for a swim." He looked almost apologetic. "There's a pool not far from our house. We live on Westminster Avenue."

"I better get on home," Damon said. "Mother will be wondering where I've been."

Ben Aycock took another long drag from Dr. Kaigler's magic cigarette and snubbed out the butt in the ashtray.

Damon sniffed. "What's that smell? What are these things made of?"

Ben turned on the ignition. "I don't know. All I know is it makes me able to breathe again. I have these asthma attacks and the awful thing is, I can't always tell when they're coming."

"It smells like—"

"It does, doesn't it? I guess I've gotten used to it."

"You don't know what's in these cigarettes?"

"Not really," Ben said, pressing on the accelerator. "I asked the pharmacist once. He said he thought it was from the cannabis plant. Some sort of hemp."

BESIDES MEETING BEN AYCOCK, the only good thing about that summer for Damon was that it freed him and Doug to be together for tennis two or three afternoons a week. The occasions were not without anxiety. They came after Doug's session with Izzy and Damon was never quite sure what sort of mood he'd find his father in. Sometimes Doug had very little to say; sometimes he talked his head off. Sometimes he looked angry, as if he were involved in some intense unfinished argument; sometimes he looked almost cheerful, as if he'd finally resolved a prolonged and vexing problem. Whatever Doug's mood, Damon remained passive and accepting. He never asked his father how he felt. He sensed that to do so would be to commit a gross invasion of privacy. His father, in an exercise of great control, never allowed his mood to interfere with the game. Tennis was part of his therapy. He played hard. He taught Damon to take it seriously. By August Damon's footwork and his talent for retrieving were making up for a less than impressive service and he was turning into an opponent to be respected.

They usually played three sets. While drying off, they sat on a bench in the shade of an oak and talked. One afternoon, Damon was moved to express his foreboding about the coming of school. Doug looked at him thoughtfully, with sympathy. It did not take much of a stretch to understand what Damon was going through.

"You know what I think you should do?"

"Don't tell me not to worry, Daddy."

"I think you should go out for things."

"Go out for things?"

"Join things. That's the best way to make friends. Just see the friends you make after you've been in the orchestra for a while."

"I didn't make many friends in the orchestra in Hastings."

"Well, try the drama club or the debate team or the school paper. Try out for track or something. There are any number of things you'd be good at. In no time at all you'd find a lot of classmates happy to call you a friend."

"You think so?"

Doug brushed a stray lock off Damon's brow and gave him a kiss on the forehead. "I know so."

O'Keefe Junior High School was an imposing granite structure, with a scalloped cornice that gave it the look of an aborted cathedral. It had been built in the affluent twenties and was perhaps the best equipped and most competently staffed public school in town. With the onset of the Depression in 1929, it came also to claim an unusually mixed student body. Adolescents from Techwood and the mill villages were predominant, but they barely outnumbered boys and girls from Ansley Park and the near Northside who in more prosperous times would have been sent to private schools. It was an exercise in democratization that Damon would not experience again until he volunteered for the Army in World War II.

Differences did not go unnoticed. The boys from Peachtree had spending money, those from Techwood almost none; the girls from the so-called better families were driven to school and wore cashmere sweaters whereas the girls whose fathers worked in the factories walked to school and wore hand-me-down dresses, some of them made from flour sacks. But class consciousness in Atlanta did not begin until high school and by and large the poor and well-to-do at O'Keefe got along well and to their mutual profit. In fact, the Northside boys undoubtedly got more from the relationship than they brought—for one thing, an earthier attitude about sex, about which the mill boys seemed to be enviably less inhibited; for another, a knowledge of tools and machinery, which was especially useful when they were paired as benchmates in wood and metal-working shops. Those Northside girls who'd been taught to think of themselves as superior were soon deflated. That first semester in 1929, the daughter of a waitress was the only freshman to get straight A's, the daughter of a cleaning woman won the blue ribbon in debate, and the son of a teamster won the American Legion medal for the best essay on patriotism. Whatever rivalry they exhibited in the classroom was lost during public competitions. When a Techwood boy won the hundred-yard dash in the state track meet, and when a boy from Peachtree won the state spelling bee, the pride was universal.

The Atlanta schools opened for the fall term on the Monday after Labor Day. By the first week in October Damon had been welcomed as the first and only trombonist in the O'Keefe orchestra. The school budget had almost no money for art or music. It was necessary for the pupils to furnish their own instruments, and that, plus the school administration's insistence that no volunteer be denied a chance to play made for an uneven ensemble. There were twelve violins, only one viola, and no cello but, curiously, an exotic three-quarter bass violin. The brass and woodwind sections were fairly well balanced but for percussion there were only three snares, a triangle, and a cymbal. It was not until the spring of Damon's sophomore year, and only after a successful drive to sell three hundred gross of Skyland Bakery's packaged sugar cookies, that the orchestra had enough money to order a Sears Junior Champion Bass Drum.

By Thanksgiving Damon was spending almost as much time in extra-curricular activities as he was in the classroom. He was class reporter for the O'Keefe Log, a member of the John C. Calhoun Debate Club, and a survivor of the second round in the school tennis tournament. When the annual declamation contest was announced, he memorized "Invictus" and practiced at home until Maude and Doug were as familiar with its opening lines as he was: "Out of the night that covers me/black as the pit from pole to pole/I thank whatever gods may be/For my unconquerable soul." He won. He was rewarded with a gold medal and his picture on the school page of the *Journal*.

By this time he was enjoying the recognition and seeking it. It somehow compensated for the fact that the Peachtree boys had quarters in their pockets whereas he was lucky to have a nickel. As he approached his fourteenth birthday there also came a perceptible change in his appearance and manner. His hair turned darker, almost auburn. He shot up to five feet eight. He put on at least five pounds, and his forearms became taut and muscular. His voice dropped to an uncertain baritone. He adopted a fixed expression of confidence and self-satisfaction. Except that he was habitually quiet and polite, he could have been thought arrogant.

He discovered girls at about the same time they discovered him.

The first was Anna Frietag. It was Anna who owned and played the three-quarter bass violin. Slender and delicately boned, she was only a few inches taller than her instrument. She wore her black hair in bangs and she had dark, mischievous eyes under thick lashes. Her breasts were barely discernible. She looked fragile but she was anything but. The scaled-down double bass weighed forty-five pounds. She handled it as if it were no heavier than a book bag. Twice a week, on Mondays and Thursdays, she carried it, together with an overloaded tapestry utility bag, to and from orchestra rehearsal, walking it each way the three blocks to the car stop from her home and lifting it with no apparent effort on and off the street car. Damon asked her once why she didn't store it overnight in the instrument room. "Oh no," she explained. "It's my treasure. My grandfather made it and I wouldn't dare risk it being damaged by the cleaning people. Or stolen. It's the only valuable thing I own." She gave him a wry smile. "It's a family hair loon." He assumed she was making a joke.

When she was burdened with the bass was about the only time she was ever seen walking, for she usually skipped or moved in a rhythmic trot. She was blessed with a seemingly inexhaustible reservoir of energy. She never failed to make the Honor Roll. In her freshman year she came in first and won five dollars in the city-wide Latin competition. Things at home could not have been easy for her. She put in about three hours every day after school helping her mother keep house and caring for a baby sister before settling down with her home work. Her optimism was both inexplicable and irresistible.

Damon met her on the first day of rehearsal. Mr. Layton, the director, had positioned her next to him on the back row and he had to squeeze between her and the wall to get to his chair. "Sorry," he said as he brushed against her. Her response was to give him a teasing smile and a few strokes of her bow across the bridge. It sounded like "hello there."

"It can talk?" he asked.

Her smile broadened. From the bass came the refrain, "It Had To Be You."

He picked up his trombone and played the first five notes of "Somebody Loves Me."

She laughed, a bird's trill. Damon's spine tingled. "Don't do that again," he said, trying to return her smile. He had a powerful urge to pull her to him and give her a kiss. He was grateful that at that moment Mr. Layton raised his baton.

Although Damon and Anna were in the same grade they were in

different home rooms and had separate class schedules. They saw each other regularly only at orchestra rehearsal, which occurred during the second period, that is from eleven to twelve, each Tuesday and Thursday morning. After that it was their custom to go together into the cafeteria where each bought a half pint of milk for a nickel, sat together at a table with two or three classmates, and shared desserts from the lunch boxes their mothers had prepared. Anna always insisted that she got the better part of the deal, for to unwrap a treat from Damon's lunch box was almost like opening a Christmas gift. Damon on the other hand felt it was a better than even exchange; through Anna's little tin box, enameled in green and decorated with pink and white rosettes, he was introduced to German pastries.

There were other boys taken with Anna. Damon met two of them at lunch on a Tuesday. They were sitting at the table when he returned from the dispenser with two half-pint bottles of milk. "Meet Mutt," Anna said, gesturing to a lean, peroxide-headed boy in patched cotton pants too big for him. "And Jeff," a short, plump, brown-haired boy, conspicuous for his blue eyes and dirty fingernails. "They live near me, on the next block, on Techwood Drive." Damon gave them a weak smile.

"I know you," said Mutt. "You're the boy with the unconquerable soul." He sniggered. Jeff laughed. Anna looked uncomfortable.

"Well," said Damon, "at least I've got a soul."

Mutt stiffened and worked his face into a belligerent scowl.

"What'd you mean by that?"

Damon tried to laugh it off. For a moment he thought Mutt was going to hit him. "Nothing," he said. "I was just trying to be friendly."

Mutt seemed to relax. "Well, try again."

Damon opened his lunch box.

"What you got there?" Jeff wanted to know.

"My lunch."

"Those little bars in the wax paper. What are they?"

"Brownies. Mother fixes me a surprise for dessert every day."

Mutt mocked him. "'Mother fixes me a surprise for dessert every day.' Well, la-de-da. Lemme see." He reached over and put his hand in the lunch box. Reflexively, Damon stood up, pushed his chair back, and hit Mutt soundly on the wrist. Mutt gave Damon a push, which sent him back on his bottom to the floor. Lunch boxes clattered. Milk spilled.

"Stop it," Anna screamed, and the next thing either boy knew Mr. Layton was there, pulling Damon to his feet with one hand and holding Mutt by the collar with the other.

"Now take a deep breath, both of you," he commanded. "And count to ten." They did as he directed, sheepishly. "You two know better than to do any rough stuff in the cafeteria. Now shake hands and behave like white men."

Damon had lost his poise. He reached down and touched Anna gently on her shoulder. She pulled away. She was crying.

"I'm sorry, Anna," he said. She sniffled and turned her head.

Mutt and Jeff sat down and resumed their lunch. Damon noticed that Mutt was eating a sandwich of fat back and white bread. Jeff had a cold biscuit and sorghum.

On Wednesday night he asked his mother if she could put in one or two extra sweets in the next day's lunch. She smiled, thinking he'd found a girl friend.

At noon on Thursday he found Mutt and Jeff sitting several tables away from his usual place with Anna. Uneasy, he asked them to join him and Anna. Hesitantly, they agreed. "Mother made us a few special treats today," Damon said. He opened his lunch box and gave each of them a date bar and an apple turnover. Mutt and Jeff gobbled them down and when they looked to Damon as if they were still hungry he gave them the brownies his mother had meant for him. Embarrassed, the two boys from Techwood muttered their thanks and left.

Anna took Damon's hand. Her eyes went wide. As long as he lived, he would remember the affection in her voice.

"That was the kindest, the sweetest thing I've ever seen anybody do."

21

Then he met Agnes Caroline Spalding. Mr. Spalding was the executive vice president of the Sentinel Pines Life Insurance Company, a position that produced a gratifying income untouched by the Depression. He was additionally privileged by having been born into one of Atlanta's founding families and to a father who was one of the first shareholders in the Coca-Cola Company. Agnes lived with her parents and two siblings, a ten-year-old brother and a sister two years younger, in Ansley Park, in a big Greek Revival mansion. Her mother had wanted her to go to North Avenue Presbyterian School for Girls, where the best families of Atlanta traditionally sent their pubescent daughters, but Agnes preferred to be with her friends at O'Keefe and her mother gave in.

Damon had never expected to see the house. It sat at the rear of a three-acre lot shielded by loblolly pines and white oaks. Only the gable could be seen from Peachtree Circle. To reach the wide recessed entrance, one drove or walked through wrought-iron gates, rarely closed but nonetheless forbidding, down a macadam driveway lined at random with azaleas and rhododendrons. Damon had passed the house many times on his bike but it had never occurred to him that one of its occupants was the tall, smart, attractively self-possessed girl who sat in front of him in civics class.

So it was something of a surprise when a handwritten note in an expensive pink envelope arrived one day inviting him to

CELEBRATE THANKSGIVING
WITH MISS AGNES CAROLINE SPALDING
AT HER HOME, 2 PEACHTREE CIRCLE,
ON THURSDAY, NOVEMBER 22, 1934.

EIGHT PM TO MIDNIGHT.
INFORMAL RSVP.

Hortense was having coffee with Maude in the kitchen when Damon brought in the afternoon mail. "Well!" she said, her dark eyes twinkling, when he showed them the invitation. "You've passed inspection."

Maude raised an eyebrow. "Whose?"

"Hallie Spalding's. You've got to be pedigreed and certified before Hallie Spaulding'll let you through her front door."

"I wonder how she'd know—about us, I mean." Maude turned to Damon. "I've never heard you speak of a Spalding girl."

"I hardly know her," Damon said. "She's in the accelerated class. I only see her in civics. She's nice."

"They say she gets her looks from Hallie and her disposition from her father," Hortense said. She paused and gave a soft sigh. "Fortunately."

"Fortunately?"

"It's another one of those things," Hortense said. "Love him, can't stand her. Alan Spalding is Old Money and comfortable as a cotton flannel sheet. Hallie's a self-made snob."

"What do they do at parties like this?" Damon asked, somewhat plaintively.

Hortense laughed. "Play games. Eat. Dance."

Damon sucked in his breath, dismayed. "Dance? I don't know how to dance."

"We'll teach you," Maude assured him. "It's time you were learning anyway."

So for the next three weeks, almost every evening after supper, Maude cleared a small space in the living room, cranked up the Victrola, and guided him through the fox trot. "You'll get by if you can do the box step and just remember to look soulful when they start to play 'Stardust.' The trick is to listen to the music and move your feet with the beat. Hold your partner like this, keep your back straight, your left arm like so, and don't let your shoulders sway." He was not the quick study she expected him to be, but after repeated instruction he got the hang of it.

Maude bought him a pair of black silk socks, shined his black oxfords, washed the less worn of his two white shirts, and pressed his blue serge suit. Jet lent him a striped white-and Yale-blue foulard tie. He got a haircut. He cleaned and filed his nails, showered with Lifebuoy, and splashed his cheeks with Doug's aftershave. His overcoat was threadbare and too small for him; he decided not to wear it, hoping Indian summer would continue through the night.

Ben Aycock had also been invited to Agnes's party and was glad to take Damon with him, partly because it made him less nervous if he had company whenever he was around Agnes's mother; Hallie Spalding had a way of looking at him that could send him into an asthma attack. Before entering the house, he asked Doug to wait while he had one of Dr. Kaigler's magic cigarettes.

They were among the first guests to arrive. The door opened onto a grand hall with a high ceiling that ran without interruption to a rear wall of french windows. A wide staircase with low risers was at the right, a step or two beyond a doorway, now only half-closed, through which could be seen a row of floor-to-ceiling shelves and a library ladder. The stairs ended on a balcony, cantilevered from the wall of the second floor, which Damon guessed was where the bedrooms were.

Except for several sofas and straight chairs, placed there temporarily for the comfort of non-dancers, the hall floor was bare. The room smelled of wax and polish and, faintly, of chrysanthemums. On the balcony now was a quintet from Kirk de Vore's orchestra. When Damon and Ben came in it was playing "Sweet Georgia Brown."

They were greeted by a stocky Negro man of indeterminate age in a white coat and black bow tie who took Ben's coat and then directed them to the room on the left. "Miss Agnes," he said cheerfully, in a pronunciation so precise it must have been cultivated, "asks that you join the family by the fire."

Agnes was five feet eight and still growing. Her biggest fear was that she would soon tower over every datable male in Atlanta. The first thing she looked for in a boy was his height. Now, seeing Damon's head over the cluster of teen-agers around the punch bowl, she rose and gave him a smile of such radiance it could have been taken for love.

She was standing with her knees bent under a full ankle-length dress and her shoulders slightly stooped, under the mistaken notion that thus deformed she would appear to be an inch or two shorter. The dress was ecru, very plain except for the embroidered collar, designed especially for this occasion by her mother's dressmaker. She wore a choker of amber that as the light shifted matched the brown of her eyes or the yellow of her hair. A white orchid was her only other ornament. She needed no makeup.

Her father stood at her side—forty-odd, six foot four, barrel-chested, perpetually tanned. He had the same flat stomach, and the same broken nose, he'd had twenty years ago when an all-conference tackle at Harvard, and he was only a few pounds heavier. He had an amiable, at-ease look. Unlike most of his peers and his apolitical wife, he was a proud supporter of Franklin Roosevelt and the New Deal.

Her mother sat to the right of them both in a large wing chair. Her figure and features—her fair skin, her long graceful neck, her aquiline nose—were a mature version of Agnes's. The resemblance was enough to reassure any young male inclined to worry how Agnes might look in middle age. A native of Richmond, Hallie Spalding was a staunch, if not aggressively devout, Presbyterian, convinced that her superior station had been fixed by divine authority. She did not share her husband's social concerns. She was not unaware of evil, poverty, and injustice, but she did not believe it her responsibility to deal with them; her duty, as she saw it, was to maintain a fur-lined nest for her family. She acknowledged charity as a deplorable but obligatory virtue. Despite the enormous store she put on good manners she viewed almost everybody with slight condescension. The expression was there now as she gave a welcoming hand to Agnes's guests.

Behind them was an enormous fireplace, with a small fire set more for decoration than for heat; it was by no means a cold evening. On the mantel was an arrangement of pine cones, set in a cradle of oak and maple leaves. Above it was an original Corot landscape.

It was a large room. Considerable ingenuity had been required to keep it from looking institutional. Close to the hearth was a sofa with end tables facing the fire. An enormous sideboard was in pride of place against the west wall. An equally large table of solid rosewood was in the middle. Normally it held only a big Imari platter. Tonight the platter had been removed and replaced by a large crystal punch bowl with matching cups and a silver ladle. The table was edged with small pumpkins and Indian corn. Set at intervals were small dishes of roasted walnuts, cheese straws, and potato chips. (Later, about ten-thirty, a full buffet would be served in the grand hall—ham in biscuits, fried oysters, scrambled eggs, grits souffle, toasted pound cake, coffee and hot chocolate.) At some distance from the table's left was a grand piano.

Agnes straightened as Damon approached, delighted to find his eyes on a level with hers.

"Oh, Damon, I'm so glad you could come," she said.

Taken aback by her unexpected warmth, Damon stammered, "I'm so glad you asked me."

"Will you dance with me?"

Damon felt his legs go weak. "Of course," he managed.

She gave him another smile and turned to her father. "Daddy, this is Damon Krueger. He plays trombone and is in my civics class."

Mr. Spalding gave Damon a handshake that hurt. "It's good to have you with us, Damon," he said, as if he meant it. "Do you like civics?"

"I've been interested in politics ever since my dad had me passing out leaflets for Al Smith."

"So I take it you're a Democrat."

"A birthright Democrat, sir."

Mr. Spalding let out a laugh worthy of President Roosevelt. He gestured him toward his wife. "Hallie, this is Damon Krueger. He's a Democrat and a trombone player."

Mrs. Spalding looked less than enthusiastic. "Well, Damon, what does your father do?"

Agnes heard her and blushed. "Mother!"

"Hold your shoulders back, dear," Mrs. Spalding told her sternly. "Has your family been in Atlanta long, Damon?"

Damon was beginning to squirm. "A little more than two years. We moved here from Hastings."

"Hastings is a fine town, but Atlanta's better," Mrs. Spalding said definitively. "I assume you're liking it here."

"Yes, ma'am."

She dismissed him with a movement of her eyes. Damon did a clumsy about face, yielding to a pretty girl who'd been standing quietly at his left. Relieved, he walked to a vacant spot at the entryway and leaned against the doorjamb to wait for Ben before going for more punch. The room was filling up rapidly. He counted roughly fifteen boys and almost as many girls—ranging in age between thirteen and fifteen. Most had been brought and deposited at the front door by fathers or chauffeurs. Some walked in together, arm in arm. Some entered alone. None, however, looked self-conscious or uncomfortable or in any way awed, as Damon was, by the splendor of the Spaldings' home. On the contrary, they somehow conveyed the sense that they were accustomed to going in and out of it freely, as if it were communal property. They were laughing and shouting greetings as if they'd known one another from birth. The girls were in party dresses and high heels, the boys in their best suits, and as their numbers increased the clean comforting smell of burning hickory was gradually corrupted by a potpourri of perfumes, Vitalis, Old Spice, and perhaps a hint of Dentyne.

Many of these friends of Agnes Damon recognized as classmates from O'Keefe; none gave any sign that they recognized him. Heretofore he had seen them only in class or during recess, occasionally on the playground—and despite their tendency to dress alike each had struck him with enough distinction to register as a personality. Now, they seemed to have lost their identities and to have acquired a common attitude of self-satisfaction. He saw them not as individuals but collectively as an emblem, though of what he couldn't say. He lacked the insight to see them as the social invention, the cultural anomaly, that they were, or as a smart-alecky social anthropologist from Emory would later classify them: "Adolescents, elite. Peculiar to northside Atlanta. 1934. Protected species. Amenable to programmed conditioning. Traumas to come."

Uncustomarily jealous, Damon yearned to be one of them. At the same time, he wanted to curse them and turn his back on them—perhaps because he lacked the insensibility to feel right in their company (deep down, he knew he was too good for them); perhaps because he knew they would never accept him, for his family had neither wealth nor name. He reached in his right pants pocket and felt the rough seam where his mother had patched it. He winced as his fingers touched a quarter and a dime—all he'd had to bring with him. Suddenly he was overcome by the injustice of his circumstance and an intense, toxic resentment of his father. What was really wrong with his father? Was he really all that sick?

He was aware that Ben had joined him. Together they moved to the punch bowl.

"Do you know everybody here?" he asked Ben.

"Almost. Except for a few girls from North Fulton. And a few older guys. I think they must be from Peabody or USB." He was referring to two private schools for boys.

"I see a lot of people from O'Keefe," Damon said. "But I still feel like a stranger."

Ben gave a friendly laugh. "You shouldn't," he said. "Not the way Agnes has been looking at you."

Satisfied that everybody had arrived, Agnes poked her father who, in a voice meant to be heard, announced that dancing would begin in five minutes. Agnes took her father's hand and, leaving her mother by the fire, walked with him through the crowd into the grand hall. The quintet struck up with "Ain't She Sweet." Her father, happy to do his duty, danced this first number with her, then kissed her sweetly on the forehead and surrendered her to the first young boy at her elbow.

There was a drum roll and Kirk de Vore was saying, "First No-Break. Young ladies, choose your partners."

A moment later, Agnes was tapping Damon on the shoulder. "Dance with me."

Surprised, he gulped, returned her smile, took her hand, and when the music began led her into the dance. For moment they were silent, although he was having trouble keeping his breathing down. The tune was "Night and Day." It wasn't 'Stardust" but he remembered his mother's advice and tried to look soulful.

Agnes was singing softly: ". . . you are the one. Only you beneath the moon and under the sun."

"Don't I wish," he said.

Her eyes opened more widely. "Why haven't I seen you at Margaret's?"

"Margaret's?" He faltered. "Oh, Margaret Bryan's." How could he tell her the family budget couldn't cover dancing lessons?

"You ought to try," she said encouragingly. "At least come to the open sessions Saturday mornings. It's fun. Some of us practically make a day of it. We go from Margaret's to lunch at the Frances Virginia and then on to a movie. Have you seen 'It Happened One Night?' It's back at the Rialto."

The music stopped. When the quintet resumed it was to play "In My Sweet Little Alice Blue Gown." He stumbled. Something was wrong.

Agnes laughed. "It's a waltz, dummy," she said, joking. "I shouldn't have got your mind on Claudette Colbert."

He tried again. His feet were in a tangle. His heart sank. His mother had failed to teach him how to go from a fox trot to a waltz!

"Excuse me," he said. He dropped her arm and fled from the dance floor through the nearest open door.

Agnes brushed aside the boy waiting to break in and followed Damon into the library. She found him standing in a shadow at the garden window, quivering. She closed the door behind her.

"Are you sick?

He shook his head.

She came to him. She started to put a hand on his arm but thought better of it and withdrew. Rattled, she stood quietly until she thought he'd calmed himself.

"What's the matter, Damon? Did I say something to upset you?"

"Oh no," he said vehemently. "You've been wonderful. But I don't belong here. I think I better go."

"Don't you dare!" She was more bewildered than angry. "You don't like me. Is that it?"

A stricken expression crossed his face. "I like you very much," he said clumsily. "I like you so much it hurts."

"Sit down." She didn't sound like herself. She was speaking in a tone of benevolent authority. She gestured to the swivel chair behind the massive mahogany desk in the center of the room. It was a command. He sat down. She tugged at her long skirt and took a seat in a chair facing him. "What do you mean, you don't belong here?"

Damon turned his head toward the wall. He didn't want her to see the disappointment in his eyes. "I lied to you, Agnes. I can't dance. This is the first dance I've been to in my life."

Agnes's expression changed. She seemed more mature, almost maternal. "You do very well on fox trots."

"I practiced." He brought his head up and brushed a stray lock of hair from his forehead. He tried to smile. Agnes noted the deep blue of his eyes, the sculptured line of his nose, his unblemished skin the color of beach sand. Who was this beautiful boy? Where did he come from? She remembered her mother's question: "What does your father do?"

"Well," she said. "It's simple. Just dance only the fox trots. Sit out the waltzes."

They both knew it wasn't that simple. They sat in silence for a moment. She was the first to speak again.

"I've got an idea."

He raised an eyebrow.

"I'm having trouble with Latin," she said. "You're good at Latin."

"Who told you I was good at Latin?"

"Aren't you?"

He shrugged. "Go on."

"I need help with my Latin. You come over a couple of afternoons before exam time and teach me how to conjugate and I'll teach you to waltz."

"You're serious?"

"I think it's a great idea, and a great bargain for me. Will you do it?"

How could he possibly say no?

She got to her feet, leaned across the desk. and gave him a light kiss on the lips. The impulse startled them both. His pulse racing, he kissed her back. She slapped him gently and, laughing, guided him back to the dance floor.

The quintet was playing "Georgia On My Mind." A fox trot.

IN THE FOUR WEEKS between Thanksgiving and Christmas, Damon visited Agnes five times. He biked to the house, timing himself to arrive about two. Each visit would run about two hours. During the first hour Damon would drill Agnes in Latin composition. During the second Agnes would drill him in the box step and its infinite variations.

For Damon, the visits in the big house on Peachtree Circle were like trips to another country. He and Agnes regularly met on the terrace at the western edge of the tennis court, with the sun behind them. The terra cotta tile on the terrace had been freshly waxed and buffed, the floor swept free of leaves and insects, the wicker furniture dusted. Autumn in Atlanta that year was remarkably benign. The air was cool, pungent with the aroma of chrysanthemums and boxwood, and there usually was a light bracing breeze. With Agnes in this setting, Damon felt intensely alive, aware of his body in a way that he'd never been before.

Promptly at two-fifty, the middle-aged Negro—whose name, Damon had learned, was Joshua—would roll in a tea table with a pitcher of lemonade and a plate of cookies. The table also held two heavy iced-tea glasses and two small Irish linen napkins. (Although inclined to accept without question the Spaldings as models of good taste, Damon wondered if the display wasn't a mite too elegant for the occasion.) Josh would leave briefly, then return with a portable phonograph and a stack of records, which he'd put on a table against the wall where the terrace joined the house. After winding the phonograph, he would wait for an approving smile from Agnes, then leave the way he'd come in. When they were done with the lemonade and cookies, Agnes would put on a record. At the first sound of music, Josh would reappear and, spry as a squirrel, remove the tea table and the two chairs, clearing the floor. The dance lesson would begin.

Damon learned to waltz much faster than Agnes learned to decline Latin verbs. After his third lesson she thought him sufficiently confident and smooth on his feet ("The trick is to keep with the beat") to take him with her one Saturday morning to "Open House at Margaret's." Miss Bryan greeted him with a friendly handshake. "We can always use another boy," she said, meaning thereby to relieve him of any obligation to join one of her regular classes. The girls, most of whom he knew from school, seemed glad to see him. Almost without exception they wore wool skirts, white cotton blouses, saddle shoes and bobby socks. Most of the boys were uniformed in khaki slacks, blue blazers, and striped regimental ties; he was only one of two or three in a sweater. Despite Agnes's efforts to put him at ease, he still felt like an outsider; he knew that he always would. He was nevertheless beginning to learn the ways of the born-rich. Another year, he could pass.

"Welcome back from the land of gracious living," his mother greeted him when he came home some time in the late afternoon. She gave him a light kiss on the cheek. "You forgot to take out the garbage this morning. Three of our neighbors have called wanting to know why their papers are late, and Jet says you promised to help him transplant a dogwood before the sun goes down. On your way to your room to change, look in on your father. He went to bed with a raging headache about an hour ago."

The next Tuesday Damon was saying, "No, Agnes, once again—" when the door to the terrace opened noisily and Adam Spalding appeared, his face red with anger, muttering "Damn, damn, damn." He stopped abruptly when he saw Agnes.

"Sorry, baby," he said sucking in his breath. "I didn't know we had company. I was looking for your mother."

She pacified him with a smile. "You remember Damon, Daddy. This is Mother's afternoon visiting the sick."

"Oh," Mr. Spalding said. "Of course I remember Damon. He's my young friend the Democrat."

Damon stood up. "Won't you sit down, Mr. Spalding?"

Mr. Spalding looked around, bewildered. "What happened to the furniture?"

"Over there," Agnes said, pointing. "We had to clear a space. I'm teaching Damon how to dance."

He noted the Latin text in her hands and looked even more bewildered.

Saying nothing, he eased his frame into a canvas director's chair near the wall. He was wearing tennis shoes, white duck pants, and a short-sleeved, open-collared shirt.

"What's the matter, Daddy?" Agnes asked him.

"The matter," he said sourly, "is the Reverend Tom Oglethorpe. I knew it was a mistake to pick a preacher for a partner. Preachers are no more reliable than doctors."

"About what, Daddy?"

"About keeping to a schedule, that's what. We're supposed to start playing in half an hour. Tom's wife just called to say he can't be here. Some woman in his congregation is sick."

"Well," said Agnes, "I'm sure that woman, whoever she is, didn't choose to be sick just to spoil your tennis game."

"You sound just like your mother."

"So you need a partner?

"Immediately."

Agnes gave Damon a look. "Damon will be your partner."

"Damon here?"

"He's very good, Daddy. He's seeded number one on the O'Keefe tennis team. Aren't you, Damon?"

Damon swallowed hard. "I'd be glad to fill in, Mr. Spalding."

As if he were seeing him for the first time, Mr. Spalding noted Damon's height and studied his wrists and hands. He looked uncertain. "Do you know how to play doubles?"

"Yes, sir."

"My friends play killer tennis."

"I play to win, Mr. Spalding."

Mr. Spalding slapped his thigh and stood up. "Well, by golly, let's try it. Can you change your clothes and get your racket and get back here in half an hour?"

Agnes intervened. "He can if you let Marshall drive him home and back."

Mr. Spalding stepped to the edge of the terrace and called, "Marshall!" A moment later a young Negro appeared. He was wearing a canvas hat, a blue work shirt, and jeans, and he had a trowel in his hand.

"Marshall, Mr. Krueger here and I are going to play a little tennis this afternoon. I want you to drive him home and wait while he changes his clothes. Try to get him back here in a half hour. The car's in the garage and the keys are in the ignition."

Mr. Spalding turned to Damon. "Be as quick as you can. I'll be waiting for you."

Damon stepped off the terrace and followed the black man across the lawn to the garage. Over his shoulder he heard Mr. Spalding call his name.

"Yes, sir?"

Mr. Spalding was smiling. "I forgot to say thank you."

When ten minutes later they reached the house on Penn Avenue, Damon raced up the walkway, shedding his shirt as he ran. He opened the front door yelling "Mother, it's me," but didn't wait for a response. In his own room at the rear, he dropped his pants and shirt on the floor and slipped into Keds and khakis. On his way back he picked up his racquet from the hall closet. He was almost out the front door before he saw his father.

Doug was on the porch about to enter the house. He had his coat off and collar unbuttoned.

"Hello, son. I'm glad I caught you. Izzy cut me a little short and I was hoping—"

Damon rushed past him. "Sorry, Dad. I'm in a big hurry."

Doug turned around and watched Damon run down the walk and slide into the front seat of the Packard at the curb. A moment later he heard the scurrying of little feet. Roger, excited by the sound of their voices, had run up to greet them.

Now, disappointed and abandoned, Doug and the cat stood together and watched the car take off, turn the corner, and move out of sight.

Agnes took her Latin exam ten days before the Christmas holidays. The results were posted on the last day of the term; she got an A-minus. Ecstatic, she phoned Damon that evening. "I owe it all to you," she gushed.

"I'll never be able to thank you enough."

"Even Steven," he said, glowing inside. He paused, remembering how she'd taught his feet to follow the music and how it felt to have her arm around his waist. "I wish we could start all over again."

"So do I," she said in a tone that set his heart fluttering. "Daddy is taking us to Nassau for Christmas. Why don't you come over one afternoon before we leave—say next Tuesday?"

"I will," he said promptly. "And this time I'll furnish the cookies."

"And if it's a cool day I'll make hot chocolate."

Cookies and cocoa? It sounded, he thought, like bedtime for Bunny Brown and Sister Sue.

"We should be in for a treat," Damon said on arriving that Tuesday, a small picnic hamper in his arms. "Yesterday was mother's baking day."

"You go on to the terrace," Agnes said. "I'll get the hot chocolate." She moved quickly down the long hall and disappeared behind swinging doors into the kitchen.

Josh got to the terrace before Damon. He'd draped the wicker table with a white linen cloth and set two places with dessert dishes and small napkins. "Good afternoon, Mr. Damon," he said cheerfully, taking the hamper out of Damon's hands. The greeting was like that to an old family friend. Damon was flattered.

Josh opened the hamper and began placing its contents on a platter. There were chocolate nut cookies, coconut macaroons, banana bread, and Banbury tarts.

Agnes arrived with a chocolate set. "My," she said, taking in the spread of pastries. "Is this what passes for everyday food at your house?"

"Hardly. Mother calls this reward food."

"As opposed to what?"

"As opposed to security food."

"Security food?"

"Oatmeal, soup, scrambled eggs, milk. That sort of thing."

"Well," Agnes said, her eyes focused on the Banbury tarts. "I certainly feel rewarded." She giggled and bit into a tart. "Oh my," she said again. "Mother's got to taste this." She pushed back her chair. "Wait a minute."

She left the terrace. When she returned a minute later her mother was with her.

"Hello, Damon," Mrs. Spalding said. She spoke, as she routinely did to everyone under the age of twenty, as if they were in high chairs and she was on a throne. "What have we here?"

"Here, mother," Agnes said, pushing a tart toward her. "You tell me."

Mrs. Spalding took a bite. Her expression went from royal forbearance to skepticism to wonder to joy. "What on earth!"

"What we've got here," said Agnes, "is perfection. Have you ever tasted anything so good in your life?"

Mrs. Spalding picked up a macaroon and nibbled it daintily. Then she took a big bite and a bigger bite and an even bigger bite. "Goodness," she sighed, licking her fingers. "It's enough to make a person lose her manners." She gave Damon a look that was half command, half commendation.

"Do we have you to thank for these?"

"My mother," he said.

"Your mother! Does she bake for a living?"

Agnes was embarrassed. "Mother!"

Mrs. Spalding covered herself. "What I mean, dear, is that Mrs. Krueger has a talent that shouldn't be confined to the home." She picked up a chocolate cookie and devoured it. "Everything on this table is fabulous. Absolutely fabulous."

"My grandmother had this cook from New Orleans." Damon said. "His father worked at Arnaud's and when he was just a boy he had a chance to see some great chefs at work. He learned a lot and Mother learned from him."

"Maybe," said Mrs. Spalding. "But she'd never have learned if she hadn't had a natural talent."

"Thank you, ma'am."

Mrs. Spalding turned around as if to go, turned back, and picked up a macaroon. "Oh dear, the calories," she said, almost smiling. She moved away, talking between swallows. "Mind, children, don't spoil your dinner." She paused at the threshold and addressed Agnes. "Save a cookie for your father, dear." And she was gone.

"Mother's not free with the compliments, Damon. When she says everything here is fabulous she means it's fabulous."

"My mother will be pleased to hear it," he said.

Josh appeared and cleared the table. "I'll get the phonograph, Miss Agnes."

Agnes held out her arms.

"*Saltemus*?"

Damon blinked.

"Some Latin tutor you are," she said, giggling. "Shall we dance?"

22

The Kruegers spent Christmas in Chestertown with Helen and Dave. They would rather have spent it in Atlanta with Jet and Hortense but Catherine let it be known that she considered it important that what was left of her family be together. "The twins will be home for the holidays and none of us is getting any younger and we may not have many more opportunities." So three days before Christmas, they deposited Roger with the Moneypennys and packed themselves, their luggage. and four sacks of gifts into Catherine's Buick and rode through intermittent rain to Chesterton, arriving at the big and comfortable old house on Confederate Avenue in time for supper.

Helen urged them, not too sincerely, to stay through New Year's. Everybody, however, including Catherine, seemed relieved when Doug insisted he had to be back home in time for a job interview on Friday. There was, of course, no job interview; he made up the story after reading in the *Constitution* that the New Deal was reorganizing some of the relief agencies into works programs and might be recruiting electrical engineers. It nevertheless served as a legitimate excuse and after five days of stress and boredom the four of them expressed their thanks and regrets and fled the house.

"I never dreamed," said Catherine from the back seat once the car had left the driveway, "—I never dreamed I could get so tired of my own child. Or that she'd marry a fascist and I'd be too weak to argue with him."

Doug and Maude had had only two brief visits with his sister and her family during the ten years since Jacob Krueger's death. Catherine had warned them of what they might expect this time. "Try not to talk politics with David," she'd said, "and for God's sake don't talk religion with Helen."

Doug and Maude were nevertheless unprepared for the encounter. Doug had remembered David Nelson as laconic, acquiescent, uncritical, and friendly, physically strong and hard working, a typical yeoman not long off the farm. But with the status and wealth acquired through his wife's inheritance, he had turned into a stereotypical small-town boss. He was president of the Chester County Bank. He had just finished his first term as mayor of Chesterton, he was a past president of both the country club and Rotary, a founding member of the Chamber of Commerce, and the teacher of the adult Sunday School class at the Ephesus Methodist Church. He had led the campaign that swung the county vote to Eugene Talmadge in the July primary and had been rewarded with an appointment to the state highway commission. He subscribed to *Literary Digest, Country Gentleman,* and the *Saturday Evening Post*, and he read and quoted *Life Begins at Forty* like a true believer. He talked with the attitude of a man who felt an obligation to enlighten his inferiors and with the assumption that only the mentally retarded would disagree with him. "It was a mistake to give the nigger boys a high school," he told Doug. "Now they're clamoring for textbooks."

The remark reminded Doug to phone Walt.

"MERRY CHRISTMAS, old friend."

Walt's reply was pleasantly reserved. "Merry Christmas to you, too. Whoever you are."

"How's the mayor of Cabbagetown?"

"Doug?" Now the tone was warm and welcoming. "Where are you?"

Doug told him.

"Any chance we can get together?"

Doug sighed. "You know my sister and her husband. They've bound and gagged me."

"I can believe it," Walt said, laughing.

"How are things with you, Walt? I understand you're now the county superintendent of Negro schools."

"Oh God, yes."

"You don't sound too happy about it."

"Happy? These are hard times, Doug."

"I'm sure. What's the worst problem?"

"Money, of course. Or the lack of it. They've cut the school budget in half."

"Including salaries?"

"Especially salaries. Our teachers have been cut to sixty dollars a month."

"Good Lord!" Doug paused before asking the question he could have guessed the answer to. "How about the white teachers? Have their salaries been cut?"

"Of course not."

"But that's not legal. Haven't they heard about *Plessy vs. Ferguson* in Chesterton?"

"Separate but equal? I give you a hollow laugh."

"You could sue."

"In this county? You've been gone too long, Doug."

A familiar curtain was dropping between them. Doug sighed.

"I suppose when you say they've cut your budget in half you mean the county school board. Who's chairman of the school board?."

Walt laughed again, this time bitterly. "Your brother-in-law."

HELEN WAS STILL the able manager and competent housewife ("A place for everything and everything in its place"). But where she once had fretted over her tendency to put on weight, she had stopped worrying about her figure and had come to look more and more like her humpty-dumpty father. Bigger changes had occurred in her personality. She had developed a talking compulsion and she had become a religious fanatic.

"She's driving me crazy," Maude whispered to Doug as they came down to Christmas dinner. "She's spent all morning telling me God's in his heaven, all's right with the world, and nonbelievers, meaning me I suppose, are going to roast in hell."

"Would you rather have spent the morning with Dave?" he asked her, despairingly. "I asked him how business was and if he said it once, he said it a dozen times: 'Furniture's down, funerals up.' He thinks Talmadge is a savior and Roosevelt a disaster. He kept telling me that Mussolini is the best thing to come along since the invention of internal combustion, and he tells me to keep an eye on a man out in California named Townsend who's about to announce a plan that will cure the Depression by giving everybody over sixty a pension of two hundred dollars a month. He's crazy."

Doug and Maude constituted a fresh audience for Dave. He talked over the Christmas meal as if he possessed the table by divine right. Except for the blessing, which he asked in a voice more appropriate for a eulogy, his monologue was almost entirely a series of self-centered stories and self-supported opinions. Governor Talmadge phoned him often, he boasted, "to ask what I thought about something he's planning to do or to ask how things are going in the county. He's promised to pave the old market road to Newnan. He's being very quiet about it, but it's almost certain that he'll run for the Senate two years from now. I wouldn't be surprised if he asked me to be his West Georgia campaign manager."

"You'd like that?" Maude asked him.

He ignored her. "Ole Gene is one smart politician. When he cut the cost of a license plate to three dollars, he got every farmer and mill hand in the state in his pocket. If the law allowed it, he could be governor for life."

Doug said nothing for fear of saying too much. Gene Talmadge was a race-baiting demagogue, probably a crook and certainly no partisan of the poor. The real beneficiaries of the three-dollar tag were the corporations that had large fleets of cars and trucks. The losers were the rural counties, including Dave's if he only knew it; because of the loss of tag revenue, most of them had to raise local taxes to keep the schools open.

To Doug, Talmadge was a despicable fraud. Sure, he'd been born on a farm and may once have known hard labor. But he was also an educated man, a Phi Beta Kappa graduate of the University of Georgia whose bedtime reading included *The Red and the Black*. In his grasp for power, he had cynically calculated the fears of Georgia's poor-white majority and learned to address them with the appeal of an accomplished actor. Doug had seen him once, two years before during his first campaign for governor. It was at a political rally in Cobb County on a hot July afternoon. Talmadge arrived driving a tractor, dressed in work pants, a white shirt, and red galluses. He was scrawny and his skin was brown and leathery, like that of the dirt farmer he pretended to be. He had a turkey neck and a prominent cowlick that descended almost to the bridge of his glasses. When he started to speak he affected a country drawl as fake as his dusty work pants. He held the crowd in thrall. He could be counted on to protect them from those pointy-headed radicals in Atlanta. He promised to keep their taxes low, the schools free of atheists and Darwinists, the factories safe from unions, and the niggers in their place. Reminded by an opponent that during his term as agricultural commissioner he had been accused of defrauding the state out of ten thousand dollars, he said, "Shore I stole, but I stole for you." The crowd hooted and hollered and banged on garbage-can lids. "You tell 'em, Gene."

Listening now to Dave, Doug slumped in his chair, his head so low that he could lick his plate, his eyes half-closed. He was trying to sign off, to tune out. But Dave's voice was grasping and unrelenting, and its arrogance registered even when his message didn't. Now he was talking about tenant farmers and sharecroppers. "Out in Arkansas," he was saying, "they've formed a sharecroppers' union. They're moving organizers into Tennessee and Alabama. Can you believe it? I've told our tenants that if they even think about it I'll cancel their contracts."

Maude saw the pain in Doug's face and posture. Was he merely restraining himself, forcing himself to silence, as Catherine had advised, so not to make a scene during a family gathering? Or was something else at work? Where was the man once so prone to outrage, once so quick to contest the mean and powerful, once so articulate? It seemed to her that one of the worst effects of Doug's protracted depression was that he no longer had the spirit to fight, to protest, even though his sensitivity to injustice remained undiminished. Of all the things he'd lost since the disease struck him, this might be the worst. What was he thinking now, aside from the necessity to endure? Was he thinking, as she was, that if it had not been for the unaccountable estrangement from his father, he would now be in Dave's position, that under his leadership the political bent in Chester County might be toward a more hopeful future, especially for the long-exploited poor? Was he regretting whatever he'd done to have cost him that chance, to have forfeited it to a mindless, Georgia-bred Babbitt? Was his depression irreversible, or was it possible that some of his old energy, his old passion, might yet be retrieved? She thought of him and of their fractured life and she wanted to cry. Impulsively, she reached her hand across the table and squeezed his wrist.

Every now and again Helen would give her husband a word of agreement, but most of the time she was silent. This was not her usual demeanor. Usually, to Maude's distress, Helen's tongue was as loose as her brain, without monitor or decelerator. She talked about anything and everything—the long summer drought, the Ten Commandments, the black spot that was killing the roses, the need for a bigger church, Mrs. Gordon's hysterectomy, the mercy of God, the profession of faith, the increasing divorce rate, Armageddon, the repeal of the Eighteenth Amendment, the Four Horsemen of the Apocalypse, women's suffrage—with equal emphasis, without provocation or pause. She had a particularly disconcerting habit of asking a question ("What's the matter with Douglas, Maude?") and then skipping to a new subject without waiting for an answer. In Maude's observation, the only time her tongue was not wagging was when her husband was near, at which times she surrendered the floor and followed his every word with an expression of obscene idolatry. It made Maude want to throw up.

Helen's twin daughters did a little to enliven the visit, but not much. For most of the time they were either on the telephone catching up with friends they hadn't seen since summer, or off to the movies. One afternoon, for lack of anything better to do or anybody more "sophisticated" to be with, they invited Damon to dance with them; otherwise, they treated him as if he were a child. Now eighteen, four years older than Damon, they were in their second year at a Methodist-sponsored girls' college, tucked chastely away between two mountains in western North Carolina. They were oppressed by the isolation and by a curriculum heavy on elocution, deportment, art history, the domestic sciences, and bible study. "It's like a prison," Sue complained to Maude. "Like Siberia," pouted Flo. They spent most of the three days whining first to their mother, then their father, lobbying for a transfer to Duke or the University of Georgia "where we could meet boys." If they simply had to go to a girls' school, then at least let it be Agnes Scott, "which is only a couple of car stops from Emory." They were still trying, their prospects still dubious, when the Kruegers left for Atlanta on Thursday.

Catherine apologized once they were settled in the car. "I'm sorry children. I'll never put us through that again." She gave a deep and expressively unhappy sigh. "I must have been a terrible mother."

Back home, Damon found a postcard and Maude a letter from Agnes, both mailed from Nassau. Her message to him was brief: "Miss you. See you next year. Carpe diem." The letter to Maude was written in a careful Spencerian hand, on expensive stationery, and in an almost formal tone: "Dear Mrs. Krueger: The cookies and tarts Damon brought us were a special treat. I have never tasted anything more delicious. I will remember you for your thoughtfulness always. Thank you so much."

Maude gave a broad smile as she read it. "I must say, Damon, your new friend has good manners."

"You'd like Agnes, mother."

"Maybe you'll introduce us sometime."

"She's a lot like you."

"Oh my," Maude said. "That's not a very good sign."

It was a new semester when school reopened a week later. Agnes and Damon were assigned different home rooms and no longer had classes together. They saw each other regularly, however, and they soon settled into a stable friendship, a relationship he shared with at least six other boys, four of whom were as tall as he. On the Saturday mornings when copies of the *Post* arrived early and he could complete deliveries before ten, he went to Margaret Bryan's and, on those occasions when tips were good and he had an extra quarter or so, he would join the group afterward for a Coke and sandwich at Miner & Carter's. Usually, when the rest went on to a movie, he excused himself; he didn't often have the price of admission. At school, he was busy writing for the *Log*, improving his backhand, and rehearsing with the orchestra. With Agnes, he was active in the Young Democrats' Club (it was 1934 and there were no young Republicans in the white South). In the spring, when she decided to run for student body president, he became her campaign manager. She won handily on a ticket advocating more flexible library hours and a better choice of desserts in the cafeteria.

He noticed a change in Anna that grew increasingly more visible. She had lost her buoyancy. She looked tired. There were dark circles around her eyes and she spoke as if it were an effort for her to open her mouth. She panted now lugging her three-quarter bass fiddle to and from home; it was still her treasure but it had become a burdensome love. In March she missed two orchestra classes. She coughed a lot.

Worrying about her, one day during lunch Damon got up nerve enough to ask what was going on with her. She looked first as if she wasn't going to reply. Swallowing hard, she let her shoulders sag in a gesture of resignation. "Does it show that much?" She turned her head and spoke to the steam table, suppressing a sob. "First, they cut my father's wages—"

"Who cut your father's wages?"

"Fulton Bag and Cotton. He's worked there nine years. First they cut his pay, then they fired him."

"Fired him? For what?"

"They said because he belonged to the union. He didn't belong to the union. But they said they'd seen him with a union organizer. Maybe they had. They fired him."

"How could they do that?"

"Oh Damon!" She looked at him in exasperation. "Haven't you learned the first fact of life? What, who's to stop them?"

Rebuked, Damon reached over and took her hand in his. She pulled away. "I'm so sorry, Anna. How've you managed?"

She put a hand to her mouth and coughed. "He may not have belonged to the union then," she said, choking. Her voice was so uneven and low he had to strain to understand her. "He does now. Getting fired made him mad. He's gone to work for the union, full time, and they hardly pay him at all." She coughed again to clear her throat. "He's trying to organize a strike, but it's hard. He says the trouble in textile plants is the men won't stick together. They're afraid they'll lose their jobs and won't be able to get another one."

"That's true, isn't it?"

"It's true—whether you belong to the union or not."

"You haven't answered my question. How're you managing?"

Again, she averted his eyes. "The church helps. The county helps more."

"You're on welfare?"

"What passes for welfare."

"Oh Anna."

"Mother and I are doing piece work for Atlanta Linen Supply. We're hemming napkins, twenty-five cents a dozen."

"You work in the factory?"

She laughed. "You sound as if a factory's—" She caught herself. "—a house of sin or something." She paused. "No, we don't work in the factory. We work at home. At night."

"So that's why you look so tired."

She turned her head and coughed.

"You're not well, Anna."

She shrugged. "It's just a cold."

A week later Anna stopped coming to orchestra class altogether. When he caught her in the hall one morning and asked why she evaded him she said simply that she'd decided to take home economics instead. "It's more practical," she said, feebly.

In July, Damon read in the *Journal* that Eugene Talmadge, one day after his reelection as governor, had called out the National Guard to break the textile strike in Georgia. (Jet, who seemed to know about such things, said it was a payoff to the textile industry, whose leaders had contributed twenty thousand dollars to the Talmadge campaign.) Several thousand strikers had been imprisoned in a hastily built camp near Atlanta. Some of them were pictured behind barbed wire.

One was identified as Henry Freitag, Anna's father. Damon tried to phone Anna. "We're sorry," said an operator. "That number is no longer in service."

Other than in a neighborhood known as Techwood, south of the Georgia Tech campus, he didn't know where Anna lived. He did have her address, however, and he was able to locate it on a city map in the school library. On the day after her father's picture appeared in the *Journal*, as soon as school let out he got on his bike and pedaled off to find her.

He rode through a part of Atlanta he'd never seen before. If he hadn't seen it, he wouldn't have believed it—not in 1934 in a city that billed itself "the spirit of the New South." A block beyond the Tech campus, he took a wrong turn and found himself in a slum. The street was unpaved, pock-marked, littered with tin cans, newspapers and food scraps, and bordered by ditches of stagnant water. Unpainted shotgun houses sat on shaky four-by-fours, their porches sagging and rotting, their shingled roofs clumsily patched. The small yards were nothing but dirt and weeds. There was a clear absence of indoor plumbing; water hydrants were placed between the shacks, apparently one for every two families. Behind the houses ran a row of outdoor toilets. Judging from the few people he saw—two old men in overalls, sitting idly on the porch steps; several women dozing in rocking chairs; three young boys, one of them dramatically blond, playing indifferently with an old tire—Damon gathered that the neighborhood was mixed, the whites too wasted, the blacks too tired, to care any longer about the color of their skins. It was a bright sunny afternoon, leavened by a light summer breeze, but there was no life on this street; it smelled of poverty and defeat. He was appalled and beginning to feel uneasy,

He had hardly swung his bike around and turned back toward Tech when two teen-age boys, one white, one black, burst out of one of the shacks and blocked his path. Both were of medium build, dressed in jeans and sleeveless shirts. They looked anything but friendly. The larger of the two, the white, had a dropped eyelid and an ugly scar on his left cheek. The black had a bulbous lower lip and a pugnacious jaw. He spoke first, thrusting his face so close to Damon's they almost touched.

"What you doin' here, muthafucka?"

"I was looking for somebody," Damon told him, trying to keep the rising fear out of his voice.

"Where you from?" the white boy growled.

"Not far from here. I go to O'Keefe."

"'I go to O'Keefe," the black boy mocked. "You know what I think? I don't think you're from round heah. I think you're one of those Buckhead shits. Don't you Jesse?"

"He shore looks like a Buckhead shit," Jesse said.

"An' we don' like Buckhead shits in this neighborhood. You better get outaheah."

"Wait a fuckin' minute," Jesse ordered. "We can use the bike. You get off that bike and give it to me."

Damon almost panicked, but with a sudden resolve and surprising strength he kicked Jesse aside and moved forward before either could stop him. He was approaching racing speed when over his right shoulder, close to his ear, came a heavy rock. He put his head down and pedaled with all his might.

He found Anna's house in a working-class neighborhood two blocks away. Here the shotgun houses were in good repair. One was freshly painted and the others looked as if they might have been painted as recently as two years ago. The yards were neat and swept. The porch steps were flanked by small shrubs. Here and there were beds of daisies, day lilies, and petunias. In the Freitags' yard a pink crape myrtle was in full bloom. There were no privies.

Damon pulled his bike onto the walk that led to Anna's front porch. He was stopped at the door by a sign:

NOTICE
THIS HOUSE UNDER QUARANTINE
BY ORDER OF THE FULTON COUNTY
BOARD OF PUBLIC HEALTH

Oh no! He moved to the window at the door's left, shaded his eyes, and squinted. The room was dark—the living room, he guessed, or what had been the living room. It looked bare. He moved to the right of the door and looked through the other window. There were no lights anywhere. The house was empty. He knew Mr. Freitag was in Eugene Talmadge's concentration camp. But where was Mrs. Freitag and Anna's baby sister? Where was Anna?

He heard footsteps behind him, turning, he saw a woman in heavy white oxfords, white cotton stockings, and the white starched uniform of a nurse. She was on the walkway heading for the porch. She said "Oh" when she saw him.

"I forgot to take down the notice," she said huskily, passing him. She ripped the quarantine sign off the door. "Are you a friend of the family's?"

"I'm Damon Krueger, a friend of Anna's."

"Anna," she said, not unpleasantly. "Did you know she has TB?"

"TB?"

"Tuberculosis. In both lungs"

Damon began to feel sick. "Where is she?"

"On her way to a sanitorium in Asheville. They left yesterday morning."

"I didn't know." Damon said. "Where are her mother and sister?"

"Her mother went with Anna. The little girl is being sent to her aunt's somewhere in Ohio. Mrs. Freitag will join them later, I understand. So will her father, we hope. Our social worker is trying to get him out of that pen they've got him in. It's a hardship case."

Damon couldn't take it in at once. "You've known the Freitags long?"

"Only since they put me on the case. Two months ago." There was a badge on her collar. Her name was Meg Crandall.

"Miss Crandall?" He was having trouble holding back the tears.

"Yes?"

"What's going to happen to Anna?"

Miss Crandall sighed. "Let's pray she gets well."

"How long?"

She shrugged. "Who knows?" She began to walk away, as if she had nothing more to say, but at the edge of the porch she paused and returned to face him. "It's hard," she said. "I don't always like my job. I grew very fond of the Freitags. It's a loving family. Anna breaks my heart."

Damon swallowed. "They can't have any money," he said awkwardly. "And it must cost a fortune to be in a sanatorium."

Miss Crandall agreed. "Mrs. Freitag told me she has a brother in Pittsburgh. A lawyer, dotes on Anna. He's promised to do what he can. But for the immediate—" She shook her head. "They had to sell most of the furniture. They had a few antiques, brought over from Germany, most of them. And some valuable musical instruments."

She moved down the steps and down the walkway to the street where her car was parked. Damon ran after her. "But I can't just forget about Anna. I can write to her, can't I?"

"Of course," she said. "Call me at the office about nine tomorrow morning and I'll give you her address." She handed him her card.

He was well on his way home, pedaling fast, desperate to get back to the security of Penn Avenue, before it struck him.

Anna had sold her irreplaceable three-quarter bass. She'd had to sell her "hair-loon."

He wrote Anna. After a worrisome wait he got a short, sad note in reply.

"You were sweet to track me down and write. I miss you, too.

"No, I'm not in pain. I'm just weak and tired. Oh Damon I can't tell you how tired I am.

"Forget Camille. Consumption is an ugly, disgusting disease. I don't know what to expect. I'm getting a pill once a day, something that tastes like quinine. Other than that, the only treatment seems to be rest and fresh air. I guess they figure the disease simply has to run its course—if it doesn't kill you first.

"The air here is marvelous. I keep trying to take deep breaths, but it's not easy. I spend most days on a glassed-in sun porch, reading and dozing and watching the mountains, which seem to come and go with the clouds. It's all very beautiful, but there are days when I wish for a hard rain and thunder to break the monotony.

"I'll write more when I find the strength.

"Don't forget me."

Next day Damon bought a fifty-cent get-well card and got every member of the O'Keefe orchestra to sign it. He dispatched it to Asheville in a tin of his mother's sugar cookies.

23

On the last day of May in 1935 Damon was graduated from O'Keefe with an A average, the Henry Grady cup for editorial achievement, and a five-dollar gold piece for winning the all-Atlanta spelling bee. That summer he almost found sex and also almost lost God.

He went to work on the Skyland Bakeries wagon only a week after his graduation. He got the job through Maude's acquaintance with Andy Flaherty. Maude had come to depend on Andy for the thin white bread she needed for canapés, and on occasion Andy would linger in her kitchen watching her work. One afternoon he complained that his boss had extended his route down South Boulevard into a area occupied almost entirely by three-and four-story apartment buildings. His legs weren't what they used to be and climbing all those stairs was beginning to be real punishment. "I told him I needed some help on the Boulevard deliveries and he said he'd give me an extra ten bucks a week if I could find somebody who'd work part-time at thirty cents an hour—as if that would be a problem."

"How about Damon?" she asked him. "He'd be happy to work for thirty cents an hour, any hours you like. Until September, when he has to go back to school."

"How old is he?"

"Fifteen. And he's strong and healthy and used to hard work."

"Can he start tomorrow?"

Andy and Damon bonded quickly. Andy was a cheerful man, even-tempered, plain-spoken, and kind. The only time Damon saw him angry was once when he caught some kid throwing pebbles at May Belle. Although he routinely sold day-old breads without marking it down to the company's discounted price, pocketing the difference, he also routinely set aside some of the day-old stuff and gave it to his poorest customers. He rarely talked about himself. It was only in pieces that Damon learned that he'd been born on a farm near Athens, that he'd enlisted in the Army when he was seventeen ("I spent two years in the U. S. Cavalry and here I am driving a goddamn bread wagon"), that his wife worked at the candy counter of the Tenth Street Woolworth, that he had no children, and that he dreamed one day of having his own pastry shop. He taught Damon how to handle May Belle, how to identify the trees along the route, especially one kind of pine from another, and how to distinguish the call of a thrush from that of a catbird. He also taught him a lot of dirty jokes. Damon couldn't decide whether to think of him as his scoutmaster or as a maverick uncle.

On the afternoon of the fourth or fifth day that Damon had been on the job, Andy pulled the wagon into a shady alley. They had just crossed Ponce de Leon and were heading south down Boulevard where both sides of the wide road were lined with look-alike three- and four-story apartment buildings. "It's time for a half-hour break," Andy said. Damon didn't know what he meant; they'd not been accustomed to taking breaks of any length. "I'm going to visit a friend for a while," Andy went on, putting the feed bag over May Belle's neck. "Here," and he gave Damon two loaves of bread, one of whole wheat and another of rye. Take these to 401, Apartment 39. Her name's Thelma."

Damon moved to leave with the bread when Andy called him back. "Thelma's pretty horny, but I think she's too smart to try to seduce a minor. All the same, don't let her lure you inside. Plant yourself at the threshold and don't budge." He paused. "If Thelma asks about me, tell her I had a conflict. Tell her I'll see her Tuesday," He walked away, whistling.

A few minutes later Damon stood at the door of Apartment 39 waiting for Thelma to answer his knock. He was breathing heavily, partly from the four-story flight, partly in anticipation. "Give me a minute, sweetie." The voice was husky. "I'm working on a treat for you."

There was the sound of a latch turning. She was standing in the doorway, eyes closed. "Kiss me."

"Ma'am?"

Damon got a glimpse of a young woman, no older than thirty, a bit plump, red-haired, fair-skinned, green-eyed. She was wearing salmon-colored silk pajamas and a thin, transparent robe of the same color, unbuttoned to expose two exquisitely firm breasts. "Oh," she said, seeing Damon and hastily closing her robe. "I thought—"

"Andy had a conflict. He said to tell you he'd see you Tuesday."

She opened the door more widely, as if to invite him in. "It's a long time till Tuesday." She was disappointed, and also peeved. "And who are you?"

"My name is Damon Krueger. I'm Mr. Flaherty's new helper."

"Well, Damon Krueger, how about taking the bread back to the kitchen? I might be able to give you—" She paused. "A cookie or something."

Damon's head was spinning. "Thank you, no," he croaked. "I'm not allowed to cross the threshold."

She looked skeptical.

"Company policy," he said

She sighed and took the bread from him. "Company policy never seemed to bother Andy," she said. "I guess it has something to do with insurance." Before stepping to the kitchen, she dissected Damon with a look that traveled slowly from his head to his fly. Whatever she saw, she seemed to approve. "Tell me, Damon. How old are you?"

"Fifteen, ma'am. I'll be sixteen this November."

She gave him a light kiss on his cheek and moved toward the kitchen. "Come back to see me," she said over her shoulder. "In about five years or so."

BACK IN THE WAGON WITH ANDY, Damon struggled with mixed feelings. Should he be glad that he had saved his virginity or mad with himself that he had missed the chance to have first-time sex with an older woman?

"Thelma behaved herself?" Andy asked him.

Damon nodded. "She seems like a nice woman."

"She's not the brightest kid on the block," Andy said. "But she's nice all right."

"She seems lonely. Her husband's in Panama."

"I know," Andy said. "An oversexed woman should never marry a soldier." He grew unusually solemn. "Sex can be a trap," he said. "But I don't know why we've made such a problem of it, why we feel so guilty even talking about it. It's one of the normal, natural body functions. It ought to be as easy and natural as breathing."

Damon thought about that. He wasn't sure that even in a perfect world sex could be that simple. "What about love, Andy?"

Andy bit his lower lip and gave another snap of the reins. "Love's another thing entirely. It has very little to do with sex."

DAMON HAD A LOT OF QUESTIONS about sex and he would like to have asked them of Andy. He didn't, partly because he didn't want to expose his ignorance and partly because Andy, whenever moved to talk around or about the subject, flattered Damon by assuming he knew the answers. So, as with most of his generation, what Damon knew about sex was learned in bits and pieces from sources that had little in common. Most of it came from conversations with older boys and his more advanced peers, supplemented by obscene comic books, graffiti on the walls of public toilets, and stories about coming-of-age ceremonies, liberally illustrated with photographs of naked women, in National Geographic. The first admonition he heard against masturbation appeared in the Boy Scout Handbook, although it was not immediately understood that masturbation was what the editors were talking about; the word "masturbation" was never used. (The article appeared under the heading "Conservation" and referred tantalizingly to "the sex fluid" in every male that must be conserved until adulthood, but it never explained how or why.) Somehow, almost everything he was told and read would have him believe that nice people didn't talk about sex and that, while the sex act itself might be the closest thing to rapture mortal man might ever experience, it was a scarlet sin if performed outside marriage and without God's blessing. One would, therefore, properly approach the subject with fear and apprehension.

Last year, however, on his fifteenth birthday Damon received from his father, along with a Bix Beiderbeck recording and an Irish fisherman's sweater, a copy of *What Every Young Man Should Know*. "I want you to read this, son," Doug told him, clearing his throat. "Then talk to me if there's anything you don't understand." The gift held the promise of future man-to-man talks, but none ever came. In the nineteen thirties, sex was not an easy subject for fathers to raise with their sons and it was an even more embarrassing one for sons to discuss with their fathers. Nevertheless, though hardly to be commended for its fidelity to science, *What Every Young Man Should Know* did serve to correct the myths and misinformation he'd been acquiring, and Damon was forever grateful to his father for giving him the book.

It did not, however, free him of the shame and subliminal guilt that afflicted the South of his time. That the culture equated sin with sex was popularly attributed to a natural conspiracy among God-haunted preachers, wayward men, and frustrated women school teachers. But Damon had cause to blame his own inhibitions primarily to one person: his Great Aunt Sarah.

Aunt Sarah was Jacob's older sister. She had married as a young woman and had lived with her husband somewhere in Montana or Colorado (Doug could not remember which) for perhaps two years before returning home and to her father in Alabama; whether she was widowed or abandoned was a matter of polite conjecture within the family. She never spoke of her husband or of her experience out west and made it clear that she did not want to be asked about it. What was also clear was that the experience had left her suspicious of any male over the age of twelve.

She spoke in an accent peculiar to north Alabama. She rhymed aunt with "saint." She pronounced closet "clawset" and she said "they's" when she meant "theirs." It was a mistake, though, to discount her intelligence, for she was well-read and politically acute. She was, moreover, despite her unhappy marriage, neither a whining nor a self-absorbed woman. Back home, she got a job as piano accompanist at the Palace in nearby Edwardsville and held it until the coming of talkies in 1928, after which she became choir director at the Pentecostal One Seed Baptist Church. In addition, she busied herself helping her aging father handle the family farm and all the tenant accounts. After his death she managed the properties even more competently than he had. Although humorless and inclined to few words, she seemed eccentric only in her obsession with religion and the Old Testament.

Sarah had shown up for Jacob's funeral in 1922. Doug had seen her only twice since then. So it was something of a surprise when he got a note from her saying that, having lost her job at the Palace, she was free for a while and would like to see him and his family "before it's too late." She then must have been in her mid-seventies.

When she arrived, Doug hardly recognized her. She was barely five feet four, pencil thin, all bone and muscle. Her face was smooth and unwrinkled, and her gray hair was cut in a boyish bob. Spry and alert, she looked serious and concentrated, as if she were ready for the starter's gun. Maude was a bit intimidated by her.

Sarah said she meant to earn her keep. During the week she weeded, dusted, scrubbed, and swept. She was up at six every morning and had breakfast on the table before seven. Protesting at first, Maude gave up and let Sarah have her way. When, playfully, she asked Sarah how she accounted for her abundant good health, the very serious reply was, "I stay right with the Lord."

For the first four days of her stay, Damon was sick in bed with a fever and a bad stomach. Her first words to him, as he lay nursing a headache, were "Well, young man, what have you been doing to bring on this punishment from God?" He thought she was kidding. She wasn't.

She visited his room several times a day, usually with clear soup and unbuttered toast. Invariably, she would sit at the side of the bed for a few moments, regarding him reproachfully with a kind of unsolicited grace. Once he asked her what she was thinking. "Did you know that you're the first Krueger not to be born on a farm?" she said evasively. "Everything is changing. City people are taking over the world. It's going to be Sodom and Gomorrah everywhere." He made the mistake of saying he didn't know about Sodom and Gomorrah. That led her to start reading to him from *Hurlbut's Stories from the Bible.*

Not knowing quite what to make of Sarah, Maude asked Doug if he thought it was an altogether good thing for her to be spending so much time with Damon. "For Damon, I mean." Doug dismissed her with a laugh. "Sarah's harmless," he said. "I just think she's decided Damon's young enough to be saved."

Damon wearied of Hurlbut and asked Sarah if she'd mind reading from something else. "All right," she said, obviously disappointed. "I'll read a chapter from my favorite book." She proceeded to read from *Little Women.*

The next afternoon, she put aside *Little Women* and picked up the Bible. "How old are you, Damon?"

"Eight, going on nine."

"It's time you learned the Ten Commandments."

"Must I?"

"Do you want to suffer fire and brimstone? Do you mean to commit your soul to the Devil?"

He pulled the bedsheet over his eyes and whimpered. She opened the Bible to Exodus. "Then repeat after me."

And so, at eight going on nine, Damon memorized the Ten Commandments. For good measure, Sarah taught him the Seven Deadly Sins, although he never got straight the distinction between envy and covetousness. To these classic sins she unhesitatingly gave her own interpretations and added a few to be sure that Damon would recognize the forces of evil in the everyday world: "Thou shalt not swear, cheat, smoke, tell tall tales, gamble or play cards, take of strong drink, or dance on Sunday." Although brief and painfully discreet on matters of sex, she managed to convey the idea that intercourse was for procreation only. She also warned him against "pleasuring himself"; it would cause fur to grow on his palms, she explained, and if done too frequently his "male member" would drop off. He had never thought about "pleasuring himself." It was not until he was eleven or twelve that he came to understand what she meant.

Aunt Sarah described hell in vivid and terrible detail, enough to give Damon occasional nightmares. "God keeps a big book. He knows everything you do." The idea that God kept a book with his name on it filled Damon with fear and foreboding but it made a faithful churchgoer of him.

Aunt Sarah was not a 'round-the-clock fanatic. Once, after a dissertation on good and evil, she shifted in her chair and said "Now for a little entertainment." She got to her feet, took several deep breaths, and without pause recited "Casey at the Bat" in its entirety, with gestures. When she packed to leave at the end of the week, Damon hated to see her go. He wasn't sure but that he'd come to love her. "No, no," she said when he begged her to stay. "My parting lesson for you," and she almost smiled, "is that good guests never out-stay their welcome." Just before she stepped into the jitney that would take her to the depot, she gave him an illustrated copy of *Treasure Island*. He gasped. She gave a light laugh and kissed him on the cheek. "You thought it would be the Old Testament, didn't you?"

That was his last memory of Aunt Sarah. She died the next year of pancreatic cancer. The scare of perdition and hellfire she'd bequeathed him began to fade. Still, he figured, it wouldn't hurt at all to have a good score in God's big black book. For three years in a row he won the gold star for perfect Sunday School attendance.

24

He was reminded of Aunt Sarah one morning when he climbed into the bread wagon to take his seat beside Andy. He found an Andy he'd never seen before, an off-putting, frowning Andy who greeted him with little more than a grunt. Damon waited. Finally, Andy gave a heavy sigh and said, "Jane's got a feather up her ass."

"Your wife?" Damon asked timidly.

"She says we have to start going to church regularly. She says something awful's going to happen to us if we don't."

He gave another long sigh. "I don't know what's come over her. She's been listening to some nut on the radio, I think." Abruptly, he turned to Damon and asked. "Do you believe in God?"

"I'm scared not to," Damon replied, thinking of Aunt Sarah.

"Well," said Andy, giving a snap to May Belle's reins. "I'll be goddamned if Jane's gonna scare me."

One day in mid-June Damon got a postcard from Anna. "I'm doing better, they tell me. Gaining weight, breathing more easily. My counselor wants me take up the violin. I studied violin when I was a child and I may do it."

A month later he had a chance to see her at the Asheville sanatorium. For some time he had been a member of the Epworth League at St. Mark Methodist church and in the spring of 1934 he was elected president. Shortly thereafter, the church offered to send him, all expenses paid, to the Methodist Conference Center at Lake Junaluska in western North Carolina for a five-day workshop in Christian leadership.

"Can you spare me?" he asked Andy. "Maybe I could get Ben to take my place for a week."

"Now that seems like quite an honor," Andy said. "And don't worry about me. May Belle and I will do fine. But we'll miss you."

It was Damon's first trip away from home by himself. He was proud for having been chosen but uneasy at the prospect of being on his own. He checked his bag twice before leaving, for fear he may have neglected to include enough underwear, and kept feeling for his wallet, afraid he may have failed to return it to his pants pocket. It was a six-hour bus ride from Atlanta to Junaluska and for reading matter he took the most recent issues of *Haversack, American Boy,* and *Literary Digest.* To fortify him, Maude gave him a thermos of sweet milk and a box lunch. She also gave him a fresh Blue Horse notebook and four number-two, razor-sharpened Ticonderoga pencils. "Write down everything," she instructed him. "I'll want to hear about everything when you get back."

The Greyhound deposited him at the Center's administration building about four in the afternoon, in time for him to register and wash up before supper in the dining hall. Classes were not due to start until the next afternoon. In the morning he hitch-hiked twenty-five miles to Asheville to see Anna.

The sanatorium, Salisbury House, sat in the middle of five acres at the eastern edge of Asheville. It was ringed by three mountain ranges—the Blue Ridge, the Smokies, and Balsam—and the view from any one of its five verandas was of a kind to reduce visitors to silence. It had thirty-eight rooms, of which twenty-four were reserved for patients. It was a sprawling white-frame structure of eclectic architecture, with dormers, cupolas, and turrets that might have come from some enchanted village of a child's imagination. It had been designed to bring in as much natural light as possible. The central lobby had an enormous skylight and every private room had at least one floor-to-ceiling window. The common rooms were sparsely furnished, mostly with unmatched Victorian pieces donated by patients and their families. The inside air smelled faintly of Lysol. Everything looked obsessively clean and germ-free.

Damon introduced himself to the receptionist sitting at small desk in the lobby. "Oh yes," she said, smiling. "Miss Freitag has been expecting you." She picked up a telephone. He seated himself in a wicker chair and waited.

His first glimpse of Anna was through the grill of the door of a clanking elevator as it slowly descended to the lobby floor. She stood straight and still but he thought he detected an expression of excitement in her eyes. He met her, arms outstretched.

"I'm contagious," she warned, her voice trembling. "But do give me a hug." She wiped at a tear. "Oh Damon, dear Damon."

He pulled her into his arms and brought her face to his chest. Then, gently, she pushed him away and guided him to a side porch. "We can talk here."

When they were seated, facing each other, he studied her before he spoke. He thought she looked healthier than when he'd last seen her eight months ago. There was color in her cheeks and she had gained a few pounds. She looked years older, as if she had grown too soon into a maturity for which she was unprepared. He felt somewhat estranged by the added difference in their ages but there was now a waiflike quality about her that could break his heart.

"You look better than I expected," he volunteered.

"I'm stronger, I guess," she said. "I've stopped hemorrhaging, although I still cough more than I'd like. And I still have fever every evening."

"I want to know what they're doing for you. What your prospects are. But maybe you'd rather not talk about it."

She shrugged. "I don't mind talking about it. But there's an awful lot they don't know about TB and nobody seems to be able to tell me anything very encouraging."

"How did it start?"

"With a cough. You remember. I thought it was just a bad cold. When I began to lose weight, I went to the clinic at Grady. They were late diagnosing it. By then I was coughing up blood. I was also having night sweats."

"Were you in pain?"

"More miserable than in pain. I was terribly tired. I could hardly make myself move"

"How'd you catch it?"

"It's some form of bacteria. You catch it by inhaling droplets of sputum—that's a disgusting word, isn't it?—from the cough or sneeze of somebody with an ulcerative pulmonary tract. Also, I'm told it can be hereditary."

"You sound like a doctor."

"I ask questions."

"What kind of treatment are you getting?"

Anna smiled sourly. "Lots of bed rest. A cool climate and pure clean air. Dr. Salisbury says good nutrition is also important; he's got us on a high-protein diet. They haven't figured much of anything else to do."

Damon hesitated. Anna guessed what was on his mind. "Is it curable? No." She spoke with distressing finality. "It can be arrested, never cured. You stay contagious all the rest of your life. Even though you look okay and may be able to work again, there's always the danger that the infection may return."

Without warning, her eyes flooded and she was crying. He reached over in an effort to console her. She brushed his arm aside. "I'll be all right in a moment," she said. "Something just comes over me every now and again." She dabbed at her eyes with a handkerchief. "I don't have many friends left, and I'm so lonesome. I'm scared."

A lump formed in Damon's throat. He couldn't speak. He took Anna's hand and squeezed it.

"We have to hope," he said stupidly when he recovered his voice. "They may find a cure soon. In a laboratory somewhere, right this minute—. We never know."

She nodded and cleared her throat. "It's time for lunch. I reserved a plate for you."

In the dining room they sat down at a plain table with an oilcloth cover. "Dr. Salisbury thinks linen attracts germs."

A heavyset, almost compulsively maternal, black woman appeared with a tray. They were served beef and noodle soup, a large green salad, thick slices of whole wheat bread, hot tea with lemon, and Bavarian cream for dessert.

"It's good to see where you live now. It can't be inexpensive, though."

"No," Anna said. "But my father's got a good job now with Ford. They just negotiated a health insurance plan for employees and their families. And my uncle—a trial lawyer in Pittsburgh—pays the difference."

"But you had to sell the bass, didn't you?"

She nodded and looked as if she might cry again.

"I'm sorry, Anna. I've upset you."

She looked at him tartly. "You haven't upset me. You're one of the few people I know who cares."

She took a long look at him. His hair had darkened a bit and he might have grown an inch taller and put on weight. He also seemed to have grown more callow than she remembered him. Or was it rather that she had grown faster, into an early adulthood that reduced to trivia most of the passions of her contemporaries? She didn't like what she was thinking.

Damon similarly was aware of the changes that the past several months had brought. He felt more acutely the fact that she was almost two years older than he was and that she no longer deferred to the myth of male superiority. He was aware, too, that the two different worlds they occupied had become separated by something more than class. Now, in her eyes and carriage was a history of suffering and residual pain. It had removed her all the more from his own experience. It did not make him proud to acknowledge, but wherever her spirit lay now he did not want to go. He felt a sudden disengagement.

"Have you made any friends here?" he asked, stumbling to break the silence.

"A few. There are twenty-five of us. They come from all over, but mostly from the south and northeast. One man from Michigan. I'm the youngest. I don't have much in common with them. They're all so rich."

"That can make a big difference?"

"Of course," she said impatiently. "For one thing, they hire tutors. It's all I can do to pay for a correspondence course."

"A correspondence course. In what?"

"American history and political science." She sighed. "You asked if I'd made any friends. There's one especially. His name is Tony."

"Oh."

She took a swallow of tea. "I saw that picture of you with Agnes Spalding, at some party or other. The picture that ran in the *Journal*."

"Do you know Agnes?"

"Doesn't everybody?' He detected a touch of envy. "She and I were lab partners in home ec."

"Do you like her?"

"As much as I like anybody in that Northside crowd."

"I wish you could know her better. She's not like most of the girls in that crowd."

Anna nodded indifferently. "If you say so." She paused. "You'll be going to Boys' High this fall?"

"Un huh. They tell me I'll like it, but I'm not so sure. I liked O'Keefe, but a lot of what I hear about Boys' High—it's so competitive."

She patted his hand sympathetically. "You'll do fine. Will you be joining a fraternity?"

"If I can afford it.'"

She grew contemplative. "I guess it's just as well that I'm no longer living in Atlanta."

"Come again."

"Oh, come off it, Damon. Fraternity boys have no time for girls like me."

ABOUT ONE HUNDRED AND FIFTY earnest young Methodists were at Junaluska that week. They were from every state in the Southeast. Listening to them in the dining hall, Damon realized how ridiculous it was to think of *a* Southern accent. He counted at least five different accents; he had to retune his ear any time someone from other than his native Piedmont opened his mouth to speak. Boys and young men predominated, although there was an ample smattering of girls, in glowing good health and many of them quite pretty. They ranged in age from the mid-teens to the mid-twenties. Among the participants were a good number of theology students and an even greater number of pre-ministerial undergraduates.

Each was a leader in his or her Sunday School class. Many were teachers. They saw themselves as the future of the church and the assumed their roles very seriously. There were creationists and fundamentalists among them, and some sought to re-argue the Scopes case of 1925 as if evolution was still an issue. Most of them, however, called themselves Modernists, and it was clear that the liberal wing of the church had been influential in the planning of the Junaluska curriculum. For every session of prayer and every traditional worship service emphasizing the life hereafter, there was an almost belligerent program designed to relate Christian teaching to the here and now: "Good Christians and Good Citizenship"; "Christians and the Rights of Labor"; "Can a Good Christian Be a Good Soldier?"

Although the content was grim, the mood of Damon's workshop was friendly and casual. Breakfast was followed by a devotional and after that a lecture on the history of Methodism (with little emphasis, as Damon later recalled, on the issue of slavery that created the Methodist Episcopal Church South in 1845). Before and after lunch, a team of educators from Methodist headquarters in Nashville presented a series of model programs, many of them designed for easy adaptation by Epworth League leaders in their local churches. Each session opened with a spirited hymn, led by an aging and spectacularly buxom contralto who was said to have once sung in Chicago opera. The hymns were familiar, chosen to make the point that Christians were diligent—"Work for the Night Is Coming," "Bringing in the Sheaves," "One More Day's Work for Jesus." Once during lunch the lady was asked to give a solo and she obliged with "I Love Life" with such joy and passion that water glasses shook on the tables. Each evening after dinner there was a sermon, delivered by a visiting dignitary. Finally, toward the end of the day, came an open forum, led by one of the ardent young Modernists, on "The Christian's Role in a World in Conflict." However heated or contentious the discussion got, the evening always closed with a singing of "Now the Day is Over," the Doxology, and a benediction. Damon embraced it all uncritically and with enthusiasm.

On Damon's third day at Junaluska a Negro guest showed up. On first sight, Damon didn't recognize him as a Negro. He was dark-skinned and his hair was short and crinkly, but he spoke better English than Damon had ever heard before and he was dressed in a business suit. Staff members shook his hand when he arrived and set a place for him at their dinner table. Until that moment Damon had never seen a Negro wearing anything other than work clothes except at a funeral. From birth he had been conditioned to believe that no white person ever shook the hand of a Negro; to eat at the same table with one, except in the kitchen, was unheard of. Nevertheless, here was a Negro, and here were all these white Methodists treating him as an equal.

Rattled, Damon went off by himself to think, and after a while he'd figured it out: If the Methodist church was sending him to Lake Junaluska to learn something, then obviously the church thought there was something this colored man could teach him, Damon decided he'd better listen to him.

His name was Channing Tobias. He was then head of the national Negro YMCA. (Years later he was to become chairman of the board of the NAACP.) When he spoke at Junaluska that first evening he did not mention racial integration; in 1934 segregation was the accepted order. He spoke instead of "racial tolerance" and "equal opportunity." He spoke without emotion; he was there not to convince but to inform. He compared the dollars spent on Negro schools with those spent on white schools. He enumerated the jobs closed to Negroes. He contrasted white and Negro infant mortality rates. He cited the figures on Negro hospitals, Negro housing, and Negro voting as evidence of systemic, corrosive discrimination.

At the close of his presentation, Tobias challenged his white audience to go color blind, to extend to every Negro the natural rights of every human being and to judge him on his merits, Damon recognized that he'd been handed a shining truth. He could hardly wait to take the fight for equal opportunity back to the congregation at St. Mark.

Among the model programs offered that week, several were done as playlets or staged readings. Two affected Damon deeply. One was on the horrors and futility of war. The other was on racial discrimination. When Damon returned to Atlanta, he had with him the scripts for both.

"Ugly things are happening," he told Epworth League members, "and it's time we were paying attention." He then announced that the next two Sunday meetings would feature two special programs. He passed out parts and busied himself collecting props and arranging the lights. He was awaiting the first rehearsal when a call came from Rev. Irving Duncan, the assistant pastor.

The pastor asked how he liked Junaluska. He said he'd heard that Damon had come back brimming with ideas. Could Damon see him in his study at five tomorrow?

The next afternoon Damon asked Andy to let him off a half hour earlier. His face expressed such anticipated pleasure that Andy immediately agreed. He went a half mile off the route to deposit Damon at the right car stop. Damon arrived for his appointment on time humming "Love Lifted Me."

The smile on his face disappeared the moment he entered Mr. Duncan's office.

The Rev. Mr. Duncan was not yet thirty but already there was about him the mark of obeisance as if at some critical point in adolescence he had decided that his best chance for survival was to do what he was told. He clearly did not like what he was having to say to Damon this afternoon. He kept getting up and walking around his desk, and coming back to sit down again, talking about the times he'd spent at Junaluska and the friends he had on the staff there. Finally, he broke off in mid-sentence and forced himself to say: "Damon, you can do the pacifist play. But the one on race relations—" for a moment he faltered—"no. We can't let you do it."

Damon couldn't believe what he was hearing.

"Why?" he was able to ask after a while. "Why not?"

His eyes down, the Rev. Mr. Duncan appeared to be studying the carpet. There was a long pause. He coughed.

"Some day, Damon," he said, hardly lifting his head. "Someday, when you're older, you'll understand." That night Damon phoned members of the cast and told them the program on race had been canceled. None of them expressed surprise or disappointment.

Some things about the episode Damon came to understand quickly. The next Sunday four of the girls were conspicuously absent from Epworth

League. Later, when Damon saw one of them at Hawk's Drug Store she turned her head before he could speak. The others did the same whenever he ran into them. Much later, one of the girls told him her mother had ordered her never to be seen with him again; he was a bad influence.

It was only by pressing Mrs. Pinckney, the pastor's guileless secretary, that he learned what had happened. The girls' mothers, infuriated after reading the parts assigned their daughters, had called on Pastor Adkin in protest. The playlet's message, they insisted, was "radical and obscene." Pastor Adkin, in turn, had told the Rev. Mr. Duncan to "take care of it."

The evening after his talk with Mrs. Pinckney, Damon joined Maude and Doug in their bedroom, where Doug had gone earlier to suffer through his predictable nocturnal depression. Damon showed them the script.

"Do you see anything radical and obscene in this?" he asked after they'd had time to scan it.

"Excuse me," Maude said abruptly. "I've got something on the stove."

"What I can't understand," Damon said to his father after she left them,"—the church sent me to a conference to be taught how to be a better leader. Now they're telling me I can't do what they asked me and paid me to learn."

Doug was having trouble following what Damon was telling him. "Back up, son, and go slower."

"I'm so sorry," he said when Damon was done. His son was confronting the ugliest reality in an environment that was not likely to change in the course of his life. And it was one of those times when a father could help a son grow and draw wisdom from the experience. But Doug was finding it hard to concentrate. He struggled to think of anything helpful to say.

"You know why Mrs. McGee and those other ladies did what they did, don't you?" he said after a long while.

"I'm not sure."

"They were frightened."

"Frightened?"

"How shall I say it, Damon? For these women the idea that Negroes and whites are equal in the eyes of God is life-threatening. It challenges practically everything they believe in and everything they live by."

"I don't know what you're talking about."

"Some day—"

"I know, when I'm older. That's what the preacher told me. You know what?"

"What, son?"

"Mr. Duncan talked as if race was like sex—something nice boys don't talk about, like something I'll discover for myself when I get older."

"Exactly," Doug said. "Those mothers—I bet you they can't think about race without thinking about sex either."

"But what's sex got to do with giving colored people a fair shake?"

"Those mothers aren't thinking about justice, or equal opportunity, or whatever your Mr. Tobias called it. They're only scared. They're scared that if any of the bars come down some black men are more likely to seduce their daughters." Doug realized he was dealing too thinly with an extraordinarily complicated subject, but there was a sharp pain in his temple and it was the best he could do.

"That's hard to believe," Damon said.

"Believe it," said his father.

"But what about Pastor Adkin and Mr. Duncan? They didn't have to do what those ladies asked them to. The script came from church headquarters in Nashville. Why should they pay more attention to these ladies than to Nashville?"

"Another fact of life, Damon. Do you know who Mrs. McGee is?"

"I know she's rich."

"She's the daughter of the founder of Southern Atlantic Railroad and the wife of the president of Cherokee Life. She's contributing a half million dollars to the church building fund."

"Does that make her right?"

"No, Damon, it makes her powerful."

Damon shrugged. "You know what else, Daddy? I understand a lot more about sex than I do about race. Or power."

Despite the ache in his temples, Doug laughed. "In time, Damon. In time."

"But what should I do, Daddy?"

"What can you do?"

"I don't know. I've thought about putting on the play anyway."

"Where? With whom? And why? You want to be a pariah?"

"What's a pariah?"

Doug rubbed his forehead. "Look it up," he said wearily.

"I think I'll quit."

Doug looked at him sharply. ""You mean resign from the Epworth League?"

"Yes."

"I wish you wouldn't."

"Why not?"

Doug sighed.

"Because that's what I would do."

Damon frowned. "Because that's what you would do?"

"Don't press it, Damon. Just don't resign."

Damon sensed that his father was fading. He got up to go. Doug gestured him back. "You have every right to feel good about what you've done, Damon. Try not to worry that you weren't able to do more. Some things, it's only right to resist and fight. Others you have to recognize are just too big, too strong—at least for the now. Fight them, and it's not too long before you're in a wilderness, a martyr for a lost cause. I'm not saying martyrs are unimportant, but being a martyr can be lonely. You know what I'm saying?

"I guess," said Damon lamely. "But I don't think I'll ever feel the same way about the church again. And where was God when this was going on?"

When his father didn't answer Damon shrugged and rose from the chair to leave. At he bedroom door he paused, turned, and asked his father one last question. "Daddy, do you believe in God?"

Doug's temple was throbbing. He eased his head on the pillow and closed his eyes. "Later, Damon," he muttered. "We'll talk about that later."

25

"Zooka!" Jet said when Damon told him what had happened. His tone conveyed more disgust than surprise. "That's enough to sour you for life." He paused. "We mustn't let it."

"So what do I do? Daddy says I shouldn't quit Epworth League."

"Your father's right. You don't want to give Mrs. McGee another reason to think she's won."

Damon looked resigned. "What would *you* do, Mr. Moneypenny?"

"Me? I might just try to draw what lessons I could from the experience and get over it. Tell me, Damon, what's this rejection—this *betrayal*—by the church taught you?"

"That it's not enough," Damon said, frowning, "That it's not enough to be physically strong, mentally alert, and morally straight. "

Jet laughed. "True. The Boy Scout manual is hardly a complete guide."

"What is? The Bible?"

"I'm afraid not, Damon. The complete guide is yet to be written."

"I don't feel good," Damon said. "I don't feel like myself."

"No wonder," Jet said. "It's only natural when you're trying to find your place. And that's what I think you're doing, trying to find your place. In fact, I think you may have just found your place. "

"My place?"

"I tell you this somewhat sadly, Damon. You're learning how it feels to be a member of the white minority."

Damon decided not to tell Andy. He and Andy had never discussed war or race. Damon felt that if they were to talk about either subject seriously would put their friendship at risk. Andy would probably say, "pacifists are cowards" and "colored folks are all right in their place," and take it for granted that the church had the right to permit advocacy on one issue and prohibit it on the other. Damon assumed that Andy, as bright as he was, lived within the confining prejudices of his class. That such an assumption might be a symptom of Damon's own prejudice never occurred to him.

HOWEVER ANDY MAY HAVE VIEWED NEGROES in general, he had nothing but admiration for a young Negro boxer from Chicago. His name was Joe Louis and in August he'd knocked out a favored heavyweight contender, King Levinsky, in the first round. Andy had two other heroes: Lou Gehrig, who also in August had set a new record with his seventeenth grand slam, and President Franklin D. Roosevelt, who had just signed the Social Security Act. Aside from women and the weather, these three were about all Andy talked about during the brief interludes between stops and deliveries. He did mention that he was reading a new book by Sinclair Lewis that Jane had forced upon him ("to improve my mind"). Its title was *It Can't Happen Here.* During that same month Ethiopians began evacuating Addis Ababa in advance of invading Italian troops, the Third International ended in the Soviet Union, and Adolf Hitler heated up his campaign against "Jews and other reactionaries." If Andy read of these events, none seemed of any interest to him. "If you can't see it," he once told Damon merrily, "if you can't see it or feel it, if you can't eat, drink, or screw it, why bother? That's my motto."

Andy had the manner of a man who had never known poverty, never been sick or wounded, never seen a friend in pain, never lost a loved one. But Damon suspected—no, he knew—the manner to be a mask. Even at fifteen, Damon knew that no man who'd fought on the Western Front could have been untouched by suffering.

On a Wednesday morning a week before Labor Day, Damon went to the corner to wait for Andy to pick him up. Andy did not come. Damon waited a half hour, fighting a growing panic. After another ten minutes, alarmed, he phoned the dispatch office of Skyland Bakeries.

"Mr. Flaherty has had an emergency."

"What kind of emergency?"

"He didn't say. He was calling from Grady Hospital."

From the doorway to the hospital's trauma unit, Damon saw Andy slumped on a bench against a wall in a small waiting room. He was unshaven. His hair was uncombed. His nose was running, his eyes were red, and his hands were shaking. He had on the top to red-and-blue striped pajamas, with khaki pants pulled over the bottom. Damon had caught him in psychic pain and for once Andy was making no attempt to pretend otherwise.

Damon sat down beside him and took his right hand. "What's happened, Andy?"

Andy gave him a nod in recognition. He struggled to speak. "It's Jane. She tried to abort herself."

Andy put both hands in his face and began to weep in great heaving sobs. "We've always been careful. I didn't even know she was pregnant."

Damon was confused. Abort? He'd never heard the word before. He didn't know what to say. Clumsily, he moved closer, put his arm on Andy's shoulder, and waited for the sobs to subside.

After a while, he pulled his arm away and stood up. "There must be a canteen on the floor," he said. "I'll get us some coffee. And then we'll talk."

When he returned, he found Andy with a doctor. "We're putting it on the record as a miscarriage," the doctor was saying.

Andy looked puzzled. "This is Georgia, Mr.Flaherty. You don't want your wife to go to jail, do you?"

Andy took a deep breath and suppressed a sob. "Is she going to be all right?"

"So far she's free of infection. We've given her a mild sedation. When she comes to and we're satisfied she's not likely to harm herself, you can take her home."

The doctor left. Andy accepted the cup of coffee Damon offered him. "I guess you heard."

Damon nodded. "Andy, I'm so sorry. What can I do to help?"

Andy straightened his shoulders. The expression on his face struggled between embarrassment and appreciation.

"I don't like anybody seeing me like this." He gulped. "But I'm glad you're here, Damon."

Damon repeated, "What can I do to help, Andy?"

Andy's thoughts were elsewhere. Why had she done it? Whatever had possessed her?

"I'm sorry, son. What did you say?"

"May Belle must be worried. Can't I go and start her on the route?"

"That would be good of you, Damon." He was about to cry again. "Phone the office and ask for Miss Hicks. She knows about you. She writes your paycheck. Tell her I want you to take May Belle and make the deliveries to our regular Wednesday customers."

"Will I find the list in the wagon?"

"In that little drawer under the dash. Tell Miss Hicks I'll be back on the job tomorrow."

"You may have more important things to do tomorrow. Don't worry. May Belle and I can manage without you. I'll get Ben to help me."

Andy stood up and grabbed Damon's shoulders.

"Is there anything else, Andy?"

"Yes." He pulled Damon to his chest and gave him a rough male hug.

MAY BELLE WAS CLEARLY RELIEVED to see him but the worried look in her eyes remained. She nuzzled on Damon's neck and whinnied. He gave her a carrot and rubbed her mane. "Andy will see you soon, May Belle. Maybe tomorrow. Right now you and I have to fill today's standing orders."

She lowered and lifted her beautiful head. She pawed the stable floor, anxious to get started.

Wednesday's route started at Fifteenth and Peachtree and wound through most of Ansley Park. Once May Belle recognized where she was, Damon let down the reins. She led him from stop to stop without error. He had only to check the order list in Andy's record book, make the specified delivery, and mark it as done. May Belle, he figured, must have an IQ of at least 120.

The afternoon went fast but not fast enough to distract Damon from thoughts of Andy and his wife. "Abortion" was not in Damon's vocabulary. He could only assume, from what Andy had told him and from what he'd overheard the doctor say, that it ended pregnancy and that it was illegal—in Georgia, a felony. But what had driven Jane to do it? What would drive any woman to do it? How did Jane do it, and when had she done it that Andy couldn't have stopped her in time?

Once home, after freeing May Belle of her harness and giving her a last carrot of the day, he went immediately to the bookshelf and pulled down *Webster's.*

Abortion. n. the expulsion of a human fetus before it is viable.

He put the book back in its place on the shelf. "That's a big help," he said to himself. "I'll go ask Daddy."

Maude met him on the stairs. "Your father's had a bad spell. He's lying down. I've given him a pill, and closed the bedroom door. Let's hope he sleeps."

"Oh," Damon said, crestfallen. He turned on his heels and headed for the front door.

"Where are you going, Damon? I'll have supper ready in fifteen minutes."

"I won't be gone long. I'm just going next door. I want to ask Dr. Moneypenny a few questions."

Damon did not resign as president of the Epworth League. The anti-war play was staged and well received. Although the four girls never came back to the evening services, League attendance increased, and by mid-September when his term expired the to-do over the race play was almost forgotten. After that he gradually stopped going to League meetings. He had found another interest.

A week or so before he was to enter his freshman year at Boys' High, a team of six well-dressed, well-mannered boys called on him and his parents. They were the rush squad for Alpha Rho and they were inviting Damon to pledge.

"A *high-school* fraternity?" Maude said to Hortense, unbelieving. "They have fraternities in high school in Atlanta?"

"Thirteen or fourteen of them," Hortense said. "And four sororities."

"What do they do?"

"Well, for one thing, during the season, they provide the paper with a half page of society news every week."

"The season?"

"From early fall till late spring. One of them puts on a formal dance, a dinner-dance, every Friday. Sometimes a tea dance on Saturday. We always carry the names of the members with their dates. We can count on their filling at least two columns."

"You mean they're organized just to sponsor dances?"

"And whatever else fraternities and sororities do. In Atlanta they constitute an early blossoming of a snob culture. To be a member you have to live in the Northside—Damon qualifies on that score, but barely. If you're a boy, you can go to Boys' High or to North Fulton High, but if you go to Tech High or to Commercial High, forget it. For girls, membership is confined almost entirely to students at Washington Seminary, North Avenue Presbyterian, or North Fulton. That's the territory, I'd say. If your family lives in the Northside and if you go to one of those high schools or to a private school your chances of being recruited are about one in ten. It's all terribly exclusive."

"That doesn't sound too good."

"It can be awful. Three or so years ago a girl didn't get a sorority bid because when the rush team came to call it found her father mowing the grass in his undershirt. She tried to kill herself."

"My Lord. Is membership all that important?"

"To some. The mothers are worse than the daughters. They're not above bribing the rush teams. They think there's no higher honor than to have a daughter who gets bids from all four sororities. Not many do."

"What about the boys?"

"It may be easier for boys, if only because there are so many more fraternities. And maybe with boys, being 'in' doesn't matter so much. But there are some risks." Hortense winced, remembering. "Boys at that age can be sadists, you know. Some of them. The fraternities have rituals they call 'beating-ins' and beating-outs.' A beating-in is when the pledges are initiated, a beating-out at the end of the spring term. All the new boys come forward, one at a time, bend over with their hands on their knees, and one by one the upperclassmen strike them with paddles. Some upperclassmen aren't too gentle. Tony Nichols still suffers from a damaged kidney because somebody who couldn't aim well struck him in the back with a sawed-down baseball bat."

"How often does something like that happen?"

"Often enough that some people are wanting to put an end to the whole business. A couple of months ago the School Board passed a prohibition against fraternity meetings at Boys' High. It also started disciplining members if they showed up wearing insignia on school premises. Fraternities and sororities can no longer be mentioned in school yearbooks either. But the system will undoubtedly continue, just as long as the parents permit it, and I think most parents think of it as a good way of channeling all those raging hormones."

Maude demurred. "It sounds more like an early introduction to class and caste."

"Undoubtedly," Hortense agreed. "But for the 'in' group it may be the most marvelous time of their lives. It's like a fairyland, where all the girls are queens and all the boys are princes. No worries. No cares. The Depression is unknown or unmentioned. The idea is to have fun, be popular—dress well, dance well, be attractive. It's all one Great Long Dance—silks and satins, orchids and gardenias, endless stag lines, and intermission at the Varsity, where everybody orders toasted pound cake and chocolate milk." Catching herself before being carried away, she laughed. "Joe Cumming, a newspaper friend of mine, calls it 'a land of concupiscent innocence.'"

Maude didn't feel like laughing. "Even if we can afford it," she said, "I don't think we ought to let Damon join."

"Oh no sweetheart," Hortense said with conviction. "Damon would never forgive you."

26

Boys' High, as Damon soon discovered, had an attitude. It was not an attitude of arrogance but that of an institution whose record had earned it the right to be proud and saw no need to defend it. The attitude was derived in large part from the school's history. It was conceived at a time when the South's educational facilities were in ashes as a result of the Civil War and when there was wide concern that unless they were restored and improved the South would be additionally vulnerable to post-war exploitation by an educated North. This at least was the rationale advanced by a far-sighted doctor and alderman named D. G. O'Keefe who introduced the municipal ordinance that in 1869 established Atlanta's first free public school system (for whites). A high school was to be an important element in this system, but Boys' High almost didn't make it. Originally the school was to be coeducational and it was only at the last minute that the Board of Education decided to separate the sexes.

Moreover, there was strong opposition at the time to the idea of any kind of high school. Many parents, especially those not long removed from the farm, held that high schools benefited only the children of the rich; children of the poor customarily dropped out of school after the grammar grades and went to work. So when Boys' High opened in February 1872 its future was dubious, the predominant view among taxpayers being that the school was an unnecessary expense and a gift to the privileged. That image persisted well into the twentieth century.

Over the next twenty-four years Boys' High was moved no fewer than seven times. On three of these occasions it shared space with Girls' High, for several years occupying the basement. In 1883 it was shut down for a month because of insufficient funds. But by 1896, with a student body now numbering almost four hundred, it had apparently proved its worth, and with a change in the School Board it got quarters of its own—a brand-new, red-brick, four-story building at Gilmer and Courtland streets. In 1909 its workshops and engineering labs were transferred to the newly founded Tech High. Eight years later its business sequence was combined with that of Girls' High to form Commercial High. It thus emerged, finally and exclusively, as a college preparatory school.

Fate, however, brought two more moves, the second its last. In January 1924 the building at Gilmer and Courtland was destroyed by fire. After a stay of several months in makeshift quarters in an elementary school, it settled on a campus of two hundred acres on Parkway Drive near Piedmont Park. To almost nobody's satisfaction, it shared the campus with Tech High, which occupied the main part of an existing brick building. Although the School Board's announced intent was to give Boys' High a new and modern facility of its own, most students went to classrooms in portable wooden buildings, adapted from surplus World War I army barracks. These "temporary" structures were home thereafter as long as there was a Boys' High.

The years of adversity had given Boys' High the cachet of a wounded but triumphant survivor. Its unique identity had been shaped further by a classic curriculum and by principals who modeled themselves after Victorian headmasters and regarded excellence as a minimum standard. The curriculum, significantly influenced by the eastern academies, included Latin, Greek, German, French, physics, geography, philosophy, American history, European history, rhetoric, composition, and grammar; as late as the mid-twenties proficiency in Greek was required for graduation. In the three years that Damon was a student there, its principal was a magna cum laude Harvard graduate, a Shakespearean scholar who wrote sonnets for a hobby. Among public high schools of its day Atlanta's Boys High was a monumental aberration.

Boys' High gave Damon a secular secondary education that qualified him for almost any college he chose. It did not, however, teach him much of anything about Asia or the American Civil War, two subjects that later came to be enormously important to him. In American history, there was hardly a mention of the Civil War and Reconstruction, and absolutely nothing was said of slavery and Emancipation. In Damon's memory, the only time the Civil War ever came up in class was on one Confederate Memorial Day. Apparently incensed by something he'd read in the morning paper, the patrician and normally soft spoken Mr. Moseley, a devout alumnus of Washington and Lee, was moved to say: "It's not The Civil War. It was not a civil war, young gentlemen. It was a war between states. It is The War Between the States, and it will remain The War Between the States! Do you hear me, young gentlemen?"

Damon's record at O'Keefe had preceded his arrival at Boys' High. He was invited to join the band and the staff of *The Tatler*. Still, for a long while Boys' High remained unfamiliar terrain. Of the seven or so boys from O'Keefe who entered the freshman class with him, Ben was his only close friend. And it took getting used to, being exclusively with males for six or more hours every day. The faculty was entirely male, most of whom had the voices of drill sergeants. The only two females on the staff were the middle-aged dietician and the younger but matronly registrar.

The student body was divided into three uneasily compatible factions. Damon felt estranged from all of them. There were the boys from West End, who piled off the trolley every morning after a forty-minute ride and chased one another to class. There were the Jews from the south side, quiet and bookish, friendly but only when spoken to first. And there were the Northside boys of the upper middle-class, with their cultivated languor and their cashmere sweaters and cordovan shoes and their Fords and Chevrolets and hand-me-down Packards that dominated the cinder parking lot.

As for the classrooms, at first sight they looked more like rustic vacation shacks than places for learning. In the fall they had a smell hard to identify—partly of smoke from the pot-bellied stoves by which they were heated, partly from the Octagon soap with which the pine floors were scrubbed every night, partly from blackboard chalk, partly—perhaps mostly—from the sweat of thirty or more restless adolescents. Every now and again one of the boys would throw a handful of rubber bands on the stove, creating a stench strong enough to clear the room. Nor was it unusual for one of the West End boys on the front row to toss a lighted match into the metal waste basket while the teacher was facing the blackboard. When the teacher turned and began to stomp out the fire, the boy would rush forward with a pail of water and drench him. A teacher's lot at Boys' High was not a happy one.

The fact was, a student body of four hundred boys between the ages of fourteen and seventeen under the influence of surging testosterone had more energy than it could contain. The school administration tried earnestly to diminish the excess with football and through sustained rivalry with Tech High ("Boys High Forever!" "Fighting ever, giving never.") And in this effort it must be said that high-school fraternities played a significant if unacknowledged part, draining off a lot of energy that otherwise would have been spent on activities more harmful than dances, pop-calling, and hay rides.

At the kitchen sink helping with the supper dishes, he asked his mother: "Why do you suppose they want me?"

Maude answered with a question. "Why shouldn't they want you?"

"I'm not in their league. They've got money. If they're over sixteen they've got cars. They dress better. They have more than one suit. Some of them have tuxedos and tails."

"Maybe they just like you."

"They don't even know me."

Maude scrubbed harder at a food stain on the frying pan. "Money and clothes aren't everything, Damon."

"You know what I think? I think they want me as an exception to the rule."

"Come again?"

"Well, you know their reputation. The school board wants to outlaw them because they're undemocratic, a bunch of snobs. Maybe having a few members like me will be good for their reputation." Maude dried her hands and laughed lightly. "I agree," she said. "You'd certainly improve the tone of any group. I doubt, though, that the Alpha Rhos are inviting you because they need to make a better case to the school board." She gave him a kiss. "It's more likely they need somebody who can take good minutes or who can write up their parties for the society pages. Maybe they know you live next door to Polly Peachtree and can get them a mention in Peachtree Promenade. Or maybe they've seen you with Agnes Spalding. My goodness, Damon, I can think of all kinds of reasons why any fraternity would like to have you as a member."

"But I don't have a tux."

"We can get you a tux."

"But mother, if I'm invited to take a date to one of the sorority formals, I'll have to buy an orchid, or at least gardenias."

Maude sighed. "That could be a problem," she said.

Maude had her own reservations about Damon's membership in a high school fraternity. That night she expressed her misgivings to Doug. "I don't much like the idea of Damon's running around with a bunch of young snobs," she said.

"I don't either," Doug responded. "I guess it'll put us to a test."

"Us?"

"We'll find out how well we've taught him."

She snorted. "It's hardly an even contest. Don't underestimate the power of peer pressure. I don't want Damon turning into a lounge lizard."

"And that's how you see his so-called peers?"

"More or less."

"Well, I guess we'll just have to trust Damon."

"But I also don't want Damon being made to feel inferior, that he's not as good as they are."

"So?"

"I think we'd better let him join."

JET GAVE DAMON A TUXEDO he'd outgrown. After Maude took up two inches in the waist, it fit Damon perfectly. His father gave him black silk socks, a black bow tie, and a pair of suspenders. Maude gave him a dress shirt and the set of gold studs and cufflinks her father had left her. Catherine gave him twenty dollars for the initiation fee. He was able to pay his first year's dues with fifteen dollars from what he'd saved that summer on the bakery route.

"My!" said Hortense on seeing him dressed for his first formal dinner dance, "aren't you the jelly."

Maude looked puzzled. "Jelly?"

"A jelly is a boy, a Northside boy who dates girls from Washington Seminary, NAPS, or North Fulton. The girls are called pinks. "

"Why are they called jellies?"

"I know," Damon volunteered. "It's from a Phil Harris song."

He sang, a bit uncertainly: "He's a curbstone cutie/His mama's pride and beauty/They call him Jelly Bean/Parts his hair in the middle/Plasters it down/And jellies, jellies, jellies/All around town.'"

Maude frowned. "'Jellies all around town,'" she repeated. "That song doesn't make sense."

"Well, it rhymes."

"And where does 'pink' come from?"

"Lord knows," Hortense said. "I asked somebody at the Atlanta Historical Society and was told that Henry Grady may have been the first to use it, in a speech praising Southern women. She could be right, because one of the definitions of pink in Webster's is 'anything or anybody of superior quality.' I looked it up."

Damon was humming a tune. "There's an old English courting song," he said, pausing. "It's in my practice book. It goes: 'I guess you think, my pretty little pink, that I could not live without you—"

Hortense finished the verse with him. "'Well, I've just come by to let you know, I don't care a fig about you.' Damon, that's it!" She gave him a kiss. "You just gave me the lead for my Monday column."

"Why We Call 'Em Pinks" was the headline over Hortense's Peachtree Promenade when it appeared. Always scrupulous to give credit, she named Damon in the second paragraph but, in innocence and with the best of intent, did him no favor. "Thanks to Damon Krueger," she wrote, "my young neighbor and the smartest boy on anybody's block . . ."

Embarrassed, he went to school on Tuesday expecting the worst. But when it came it came not from his classmates but from his European history teacher.

Clarence Tucker was notoriously short of temper. He was tall, dark, and surly, with features vaguely remindful of Basil Rathbone's. He was relatively new on the faculty but he had been there long enough to show a prodigious intelligence and an equally accomplished talent for sarcasm. "Well, young gentlemen," he said at the opening of class that Tuesday. "Today we continue our study of the Crusades. But first, we might see if the smartest boy on the block is also the smartest boy in the class." While the class snickered, he gave a sour smile and turned to Damon. "Tell me. Mr. Krueger, what was the name of the Pope who called for the First Crusade?"

Damon blushed. His throat went dry.

"Come, Mr. Krueger. Tell us, who called for the First Crusade?"

"I don't know," Damon said, swallowing hard. "I thought it was Richard the Lionhearted."

"A good guess, Mr.Krueger—better Richard than Robin Hood."

The class broke out in a chorus of snickers, as if uncertain that laughter was called for but confident that Mr. Tucker expected applause. Damon felt an anger for his teacher that he'd never felt before for anybody in his life. Hurt and humiliated, he sat frozen, waiting for the ridicule to end.

"No, Mr. Krueger," Mr. Tucker said, picking up a piece of chalk. "It was Pope Urban II." He wrote the name on the blackboard. "A Frenchman. The year was 1095. You might tell your friend Miss Peachtree, if she'd care to know."

Mr. Tucker went back to his desk and over the laughter directed the class to page 309. But before he could resume, a quiet voice spoke up from the rear. The mood in the room was suddenly changed.

"Mr. Tucker?"

"Yes?"

"With all due respect, sir—" It was Ben Aycock. "That was uncalled for. Damon didn't deserve that."

Mr. Tucker went red in the face.

"Are you trying to tell me how to run this class?"

"No sir, I just think you should not have spoken to Damon the way you did."

Mr. Tucker's face got redder. "This is outrageous," he said, choking with fury. "I want you to leave this room immediately."

Ben picked up his books and moved toward the door.

Damon rose and opened his mouth to protest.

"You too, Mr. Krueger."

Damon rose shakily and followed Ben. He was almost at the door when he heard the footsteps behind him. One by one, all his Alpha Rho brothers were leaving with him. And behind them, slowly at first but quickening, came the members of Eta Sigma Psi and Zenax and Alpha Mu and Kappa Tau—every fraternity boy in the class.

Next day when the class reconvened Mr. Tucker was absent. In his place was H. O. Jones, the principal. "Mr. Tucker has resigned," he said by way of explanation. "I'll be substituting until we find a satisfactory replacement." There was a murmur of surprise and disbelief. Mr. Jones ignored it, opened the text, and said, "Now, where were you? Oh yes, the Crusades."

FOR DAMON, the incident validated membership in Alpha Rho and to cement a lifelong friendship with Ben. It also made him feel more accepted in a social class theretofore alien to him. But he didn't feel like a Jelly. He was at band practice while his brothers were at the curb near Washington Seminary waiting for the girls to come out. Too young to drive legally, he had to bum rides to the fraternity functions. With so little pin money, he dared not join the others in the crap games that went on in the locker rooms during the dances at the country clubs. He wore corduroy; they wore wool. He wore pants from Sears and shoes from Thom McAn; their clothes bore labels from Muse's or Zachary's or Brooks Brothers.

Damon's passage into the magic kingdom was eased by an older boy, Chip McLauren, who became his Big Brother in the draw of names after the beating-in. Chip's mother had died of an inoperable brain tumor when he was eight and he had been reared by his father, an orthopedic surgeon with a taste for fine wines and natural blondes. Now sixteen, Chip had a maroon 1934 Pierce-Arrow sedan, a wardrobe that included custom-made shirts and fishermen's knit sweaters from Ireland, and a seemingly inexhaustible weekly allowance. Some mothers thought him a bit wild and dutifully warned their daughters, but the daughters by and large found him exciting. He was the best dancer on the floor. Very few things seemed to alarm or surprise him. Maybe because he'd read too many of his father's anatomy books, his face conveyed a studied cynicism from which girls inferred an advanced knowledge of sex. He was almost too short—barely five feet six—but his hair was black and curly, his complexion clear and dark, his chin strong, his nostrils slightly flared. He had the appeal of a sleeping colt.

Aware of his deficiency in height, Chip stretched every vertebra in his spine to hold himself straight. Nevertheless, he managed somehow to look so at ease, his manner so calm and controlled, that most adults credited him with a dignity his behavior didn't always support. During his freshman year he had organized the Boys' High Rose Fanciers, which editors of the yearbook accepted and listed as a legitimate school activity. In truth, it was a fan club for the exotic Miss Rose La Rose, an artist of the strip tease who customarily played Atlanta for a week every November; not Atlanta exactly, because an Atlanta ordinance forbade "corrupting acts of nudity," but in a roadhouse-theater just over the Fulton County line off the Marietta Highway. In the year of Damon's initiation he was invited, at Chip's expense, to join the twelve Fanciers on first-row center. At the first note of "Poor Butterfly," following Chip's instructions they rose like a troop of courtiers and threw American Beauties at her feet. Whereupon Miss La Rose danced to the apron, leaned over, exposing more than the audience paid to see, and gave Chip a big kiss on the mouth.

Chip introduced Damon to cigarettes and three-point-two beer. Usually quiet and miserly with words, from time to time he would shed his Silent Chip mode, take on an avuncular tone, and offer his younger friend appropriate advice. "Keep your nails short and clean. There's nothing a pink hates more than a boy with long or dirty fingernails." "If you're going to smoke, try not to smoke more than half the cigarette. All the poisons, the tars and stuff, are in the last third."

Chip was a good driver but so fast there were times when Damon was scared to be in the same car with him. On many an early Saturday morning, after the Friday night dance when the downtown streets were deserted and no longer patrolled, he would challenge another boy to a race down Peachtree Street, from Pershing Point to the Capital City Club, pushing the needle up to sixty miles an hour or more. He also made a game of seeing how close and how fast he could drive past one of the street-car islands without hitting it. The only way Damon could bear it was to slump down in the passenger seat, close his eyes, and hold his breath.

But there was another side to Chip, which Damon saw for the first time when grades were posted for the fall semester. Chip was listed number one in his class.

Damon was awed. "I never thought you had time to study."

"I have a lot of time after midnight," Chip said, in a strange, almost apologetic, tone. "Which reminds me," he went on, skipping over whatever it was that reminded him, "You play the trombone. I've got a new record of Brahm's Horn Trio. How'd you like to come over Saturday afternoon and hear it?"

"You like classical music?"

Chip shrugged. "Can you come this Saturday?"

Damon went. Chip lived in Ansley Park on The Prado, within easy biking distance. Damon was surprised to discover the house to be a modest white-framed bungalow, and equally surprised on entering to see how large it was. The foyer led to a high-ceilinged living room with deceptively simple looking furniture; Maude, hearing his description of it, told him it must be Shaker—"very expensive." The walls were painted oyster white and on the far one facing the entry was an enormous canvas, an abstraction in bold brown and orange stripes. Damon sensed correctly that the painting had been done by Chip's mother, who obviously had also designed the house decor. The beauty of the room almost took his breath away.

He was met at the door by a short, slender woman who identified herself as Chip's aunt. "Do come in," she said, shaking his hand. "I had to send Chip to the store for some vanilla extract. Please, go back to the study"—she gestured toward a door to the rear left—"and make yourself at home. He shouldn't be more than five minutes." Her eyes were the same deep brown as Chip's and her smile as welcoming. Damon assumed she was a maternal aunt.

"Excuse me," she said, "I have something about ready for the oven." She left, obviously to return to the kitchen.

In the study, he stood for a moment, his eyes exploring the bookshelves, the coffee table, the sofa, the two end tables, the walls, for clues to the house's occupants. It was comfortable room, a man's room. The sofa and the one easy chair were upholstered in leather. The walls were paneled in pecky cypress. There was a pipe rack beside the chair and the tables showed rings where glasses had been set down wet. Against one wall was a console radio and next to it was the latest model Capehart phonograph with automatic record changer and a cabinet full of records. On the coffee table were copies of *The New Yorker, The Golden Book* ("John Erskine, this month's guest editor"), *National Geographic, Lancet*, the *New England Journal of Medicine*, and the *AMA Journal*. On one of the end tables was a book-marked copy of *Lamb in His Bosom* ("The Pulitzer-prize winning novel by Georgia's own Caroline Miller"). From the coffee table Damon picked up an exquisitely illustrated edition of *The Rubaiyat*. The flyleaf was inscribed, "To my beloved Frances on her birthday, 1923." Feeling like an intruder, he shut the book hastily and moved to the wall behind the sofa to look at a tryptych in tempera—scenes of a weather-scarred beach house and a calm, subdued sea. The tiny signature on each read "Frances McLauren, 1926." They would have been painted, Damon figured, the year before she died.

He sat down and reflected. The room's contents humbled him. He had grown up with books, music had been an integral part of his education, and he was not unfamiliar with the Old Masters or insensitive to modern art, to which his grandmother had exposed him early. But his reading had been from libraries and the art he had seen was in galleries and the music he heard came mostly from the radio. To have a private library like this, to own all this, represented a scale of affluence, a degree of what?—sophistication?—beyond his imagination. At this moment, Chip seemed far away, like a benign stranger.

He heard a door slam and the sound of quick footsteps. "Aunt Julia!"

A moment later Chip was in the study.

"Hope you haven't been waiting long," he said. "Aunt Julia ran out of flavoring at the last minute."

"She made me feel right at home."

Chip went to the record cabinet. "She's pretty wonderful. My mother's older sister." He found the records he was looking for. "I think you'll like this." He put the two records on the spindle. "Some day," he said while they waited for the first record to drop to the turntable, "somebody's going to invent a record that'll have a complete concerto, maybe a complete symphony, on one side. There's no reason that a record has to turn at seventy-eight RPMs. That could be cut in half, at least."

"Why don't they?"

Chip shrugged. "Probably because the record companies have too much invested in seventy-eights. Here now, here we go."

When the record finished, Damon sat quietly for a moment before he spoke. The music conveyed an ambiguity that matched his own search for certainty.

"I'm glad you chose Brahms," he said, hearing himself sound more pretentious than he meant to be. "He speaks to me, although I'm not always sure what he's saying."

Chip was impressed. "That may be the secret of Brahms's appeal, and why he was so hated until people got used to him."

"Do you listen to records a lot?"

"Enough," he said. "When I'm alone and feeling sorry for myself."

"You feel sorry for yourself?"

"Don't everybody?" He was dusting the records and putting them back in their jackets.

A knock on the door announced the arrival of Aunt Julia. "Snack time," she said cheerfully. She put down milk and cookies on the coffee table.

"She lives with you?" Damon asked after she'd left the room.

"She came a month after mother died. Without her, I don't know what Dad would have done—with me, I mean."

They finished the cookies. Damon rose to go.

"Don't leave," Chip said. "Daddy will be home in about a half hour.

We're going to the S&W for supper—Daddy, Aunt Julia, and me—and after that to the Grand to see *The Painted Veil*."

"*The Painted Veil*?'"

"The new Garbo movie."

Chip was full of surprises. "You like Garbo?" Damon asked.

Chip looked not a bit defensive. "Garbo was my mother's favorite," he said.

"Chip sounds like a nice young man," Maude said one evening." Your father and I would like to meet him. Why don't you bring him to Sunday dinner?"

Two weeks later Chip arrived in his Sunday best and with a dozen yellow roses for Maude. He ate with impeccable table manners, talked knowledgeably with Doug about the Civil War in Spain, and charmed the three of them with an account of a Christmas holiday in London with his father. None of what he said sounded planned to impress; he was altogether lacking in pretension. ("This," Maude said to herself, "must have been what Jefferson had in mind when he wrote of a natural aristocracy.") He obviously enjoyed the meal and showed no reluctance to accept seconds. He commented, however, only when he took a spoonful of Maude's banana pudding. "This may be the best meal I ever had in my life." His eyes were bright with pleasure, and then, as if a cloud had passed over, the delight was gone. He looked at Maude with an expression of longing. "I can't tell you how much I envy Damon," he said.

Maude was a bit ruffled. "Cooking's my one talent," she said, and then hastily, "You must come again."

After he'd left with Damon to go pop-calling, she said to Doug: "There's more going on with that boy than he lets show."

"Like troubled waters?"

"Not quite. But beneath that attractive gloss there's something terribly sad."

Doug, who had long ago learned to trust Maude's intuition, could only say, "Probably."

DAMON'S LIFE WENT FORWARD as if Bach might have scored it. Weekdays were spent in the real world—going to class (he had developed a strong interest in history and civics), doing feature stories for *The Tatler*, practicing with the band, competing for a spot on the tennis team, and after school hours, daylight permitting, helping Jet in the garden and doing whatever chores Maude had for him.

Weekends he spent in Never Never Land, a magic kingdom populated by perfumed sub-debs, their parents and chaperones, and endless stag lines. There were almost four times as many high-school fraternities as there were sororities—about twenty in all—and almost every Friday from October through May one of them put on a formal dance at one of Northside Atlanta's four country clubs. The dance, to which all members of the In Group were invited, ran from ten to two. It was preceded by a four-course sit-down dinner exclusively for members of the host fraternity and followed by a full breakfast at an accommodating restaurant on Peachtree Street called Peacock Alley. After that, laughing and giggling, the tireless pinks and adoring jellies would snuggle into cars and drive to Stone Mountain to watch the sunrise. Conversation in large part was conducted through oohs and ahs, rarely rising above the level of gossip except when some lovestruck adolescent was moved to wonder aloud about love, God, and destiny.

On those few Friday nights when no formal dances were held, there would be hay rides or wiener roasts. Saturday afternoons would frequently be taken up with tea dances. Any vacancies left in the frenzied schedule would be filled by private parties staged by mothers eager to advance their daughters in what amounted to an unorganized popularity contest. On Sunday afternoons all the mothers were taxed, because it was then that the boys came pop-calling in clumps, expecting to be fed. The mothers consequently found themselves forced into competition to see who could put out the most appetizing spread; merely to invite the boys to raid the refrigerator was considered stingy and tacky.

This well-orchestrated social system was easier on the boys. Uniformed in tuxedos, they had no other clothes to buy whereas most of the girls felt deprived if they couldn't have a new evening dress for every dance. The boys had only to worry about keeping their shoes shined and gasoline in the tank, and having enough money for movie tickets, snacks at the Varsity during intermissions, and a corsage perhaps twice a year during the season. The girls had to keep their hair done and their nails manicured and their weight down, and they had to be forever on their best behavior to make sure of having enough escorts. At the annual dance sponsored by her own sorority, a pink customarily had three dates—one for dinner, one for the dance, and one for breakfast. Each wore at least three orchids, one from each date. (Gardenias were acceptable but were a sign of lesser means if not of lesser regard.) If the young lady happened to be an officer of her sorority she could expect to get an additional corsage compliments of Betty Longley, the favored florist, and perhaps still another from Kirk de Vore, the bandleader. It was not always possible to find enough room on the dresses for all the corsages, so many of the pinks arrived carrying flowers on their wrists and in their hair. To Damon so much flora had the effect of protective armor and he usually approached such bedecked girls gingerly, dancing at arm's length. This fairy kingdom was not without tension or heartache, but the ambience was lighthearted and the rules that governed it were contrived to promote an attitude of endowed privilege and self-assurance. For the minority who danced and played within its walls, life was exciting, safe, and ordered. It was easy to surrender to it, as Damon did.

He got postcards from Anna fairly often. But in the thrall of this determinedly carefree society he thought of her less and less frequently. The postcard messages were brief, touched with a poignance of which she was clearly unaware, and contradictory. She was breathing more easily; her breathing was harder. She was less tired; she was more tired. Her doctors were hopeful; her doctors were guarded in their prognosis. He liked better her reports on what she'd been doing. "Tony and I drove over to Junaluska and saw *Dinner at Eight* at the outdoor movie on the pier." "Am reading *Brave New World*. Scary." "My counselor has persuaded me to take up the violin again. If I can hold my concentration, I think it'll be good for me." "Have discovered a soap opera called 'Ma Perkins.'" She never failed to say in closing, "Miss you."

He rarely replied with news of his own. He could think of little to tell her about himself and his friends that wouldn't make her feel bad and bitter. Weeks went by when he didn't write. Gradually, the correspondence all but stopped.

Throughout their high school years Damon thought of Agnes as his girl. Agnes, however, thought of him as only one of the more favored among a clump of boys attracted to her, almost all of them more than five feet nine. This was partly because her mother adamantly opposed the idea that any girl under the age of nineteen should have a "steady," and partly because she unashamedly enjoyed the flattery. She was naturally his date at the annual Alpha Rho formal and he was one of her three escorts to the Phi Pi dinner dance.

Nevertheless, he was not altogether sure where he ranked in her affections until in her junior year at Washington Seminary she was invited to join an exclusive club of sub-debs called the Vamps. To be tapped for membership in the Vamps was like being summoned for honors at Buckingham Palace. It was no small matter, then, that she chose him to take her to the dinner and costume dance at the Driving Club following the initiation ceremony.

"Will you?" she asked.

"What a foolish question," he said. "Of course."

But there was a problem. Earlier, he'd promised Anna to be in Asheville on a no less special occasion, to be held the same night. "Dr. Salisbury has arranged for me to have my first violin recital," she wrote. "He thinks I'm ready, although I myself have misgivings. Anyway, I'm very nervous, and it would mean everything to have you with me." Without a second thought, he had written, "I'll be there, come hell or high water."

An hour or so after saying yes to Agnes, he realized his mistake.

Sweating, he went to his desk and composed an apology to Anna. "Anna, dear: I spoke too soon. I can't make it to Asheville for your recital. In my excitement at the prospect of seeing you, I forgot that I have mid-terms that day and—"

"Damon!"

It was his mother at the door. She'd been waiting for him to join her in the kitchen to help her pack an order for canapés.

"Just a minute, Mother."

Then she was at his side, tapping her foot impatiently.

"Come on, we're running late. What's so important that you can't do it later, after we get this order off?"

She looked over his shoulder and read what he'd written. "You're turning Anna down?"

"Well," he said, his shoulders sagging. "I can't take Agnes to the Vamps party and be in Asheville at the same time."

She began to get angry. "You promised Anna first."

"I know," he said. "But I'd rather be with Agnes."

She was shocked. "What you prefer has nothing to do with it," she said, her voice rising, "except to say something about how easy you find it to lie and how indifferent you can be to somebody else's feelings."

"Oh, Mother!"

She sucked in her breath. "Do you really mean to do this, Damon?"

"Why not?"

"If you don't know the answer to that, you're not my child."

"But Anna will have other recitals I can go to. This may be the only chance I'll ever have to go to a Vamps function."

"It's also the only chance you'll ever have to go to Anna's *first* recital." Maude said sternly. "And if you're not careful, you'll go to neither."

"Mother!"

"I'm very serious, Damon. You're going to Asheville and give that sick girl the support she wants and deserves from you. Or you can stay home and sulk."

He dropped his jaw, convinced now that she meant it.

"I didn't raise my boy to be a self-centered snob. I'm ashamed of you, Damon. For the first time in my life, I'm ashamed of you."

She turned on her heel. "Are you going to help me in the kitchen or are you not?"

She said no more to him during the time they were together packing the canapes. He couldn't bring himself to say anything, although he yearned for some mitigating word. Stung and embarrassed and disappointed, he packed the box, sealed it, and took it to the car for Doug to deliver when he arrived a few minutes later. He excused himself abruptly and went back to his room.

It was not until after supper and he was at the sink with Maude washing dishes that he was able to speak. "I've phoned Agnes."

"How did she take it?"

"She said she was disappointed but that she understood it was the only decent thing I could do. She said she'd send Anna a good-luck card."

Maude turned on the faucet to rinse a glass. Her tone was noncommittal. "It's nice to know somebody who's got good manners, isn't it?"

"I'm sorry, Mother."

She looked at him intently. "Are you, Damon? I want you to think hard about what you almost did. It's no trifling matter."

On a Friday two weeks later Damon hitch-hiked to Asheville. Anna met him in the lobby of the sanitorium. She looked a bit keyed-up but there was no doubt of her delight in seeing him. "I've arranged for you to have one of the guest rooms here. It should be ready for you now and Martin will show you up." She paused, a question on her face that she immediately canceled. "We'll have a chance to talk later. There's to be a reception after the recital. We can talk after that, if not before. Right now I want to get to my room and be quiet."

"How do you feel about the recital? What're you going to play?"

"The andante from the Mendelssohn concerto. I have a wonderful accompanist. I guess I'm excited."

He kissed her on the cheek. "I'll be leading your claque." She gave him a weak smile and headed for the elevator.

The recital that evening went well. There must have been more than a hundred in the audience and each of them appeared at the reception to congratulate her. Behind her at the receiving line was a lean handsome man in his mid-twenties whom she introduced as Tony.

It was at least an hour after the reception that they were able to be alone. They sat opposite each other in one of the small consulting rooms. She looked tense and nervous.

"I wanted very much to have you here tonight. Not only because I knew I'd play my best knowing you were here but because I have something special to tell you."

"You're well and they're going to dismiss you?"

She shook her head. "I've fallen in love. With Tony. He's asked me to marry him, and I think I will, in about a year."

He couldn't believe it. "But you're not old enough to get married."

"I'll be eighteen next January."

"I didn't mean to say that, Anna. I'm flustered. What I mean to say is I'm happy for you."

"And I have your best wishes?"

"All of them." He gulped. "And all my love."

"I've asked Tony to join us. He'll be here any minute. I want you to get to know each other. He's a wonderful man, Damon. I think it may help that he too has had TB."

Tony turned out to be a warm, open man. The fact that he was nine years older seemed to make little difference. The three of them sat up late talking, easing their way into what was to be an enduring friendship. Nevertheless, when Damon said good-bye the next morning and walked alone to the junction to start the hitch-hike back home, he felt as if something had been taken from him.

HE RETURNED SOMEWHAT sobered but still easily seduced by the synthetic, sequestered world of Atlanta's advantaged teens. He forgot about Channing Tobias. Thoughts of Anna came less frequently. He was hardly aware of the sporadic violence in the nearby textile mills. Washington reported almost eleven million unemployed, and in Yugoslavia King Alexander was assassinated, but such extramural events hardly touched his consciousness. It was as if a charitable Fate, aware of the shocks and sorrows in store, had granted him a few years of grace; he had no serious decisions to make, there was no necessity for independent judgment, no cause for worry. For these few years his main obligation was to himself.

A tuxedo, Damon learned, was a great equalizer. In starched shirt, black tie, and jacket, he looked as well-endowed as any other boy on the dance floor; he never felt more like a legitimate member of the In Group.

His sophomore year went by like one extravagant weekend, savored and remembered for the milk-fed beauty of the girls, the sweetness of their scented breaths, the softness of their cheeks, the squeeze of their hands, the tilt of their shoulders and the cadence of their voices ("Hey there . . . Enjoyed it, you come back, hear?") And also for the smell of smilax in the halls and the fresh polish on the ballroom floor, and for the ten-piece band, delivering soliloquies on love found and lost with more respect than the lyrics deserved. There were almost six hundred boys in the fraternity set. Damon knew most of them on sight. The relationships, however, were shallow ("Hey!" "Good to see you." "Be good." "Don't do anything I wouldn't do.") It was only with Ben and Chip that he felt any firm and mutual affection. The Butler twins made a bid for his friendship, but the Butler twins, it turned out, were troublesome.

Fred and Gregory Butler had arrived in Atlanta from Chicago about two years before, shortly after their father had been named regional vice president for Sears Roebuck, which had a big mail-order operation on Ponce de Leon avenue. Atlanta by now was a town where position was as important as ancestry and where one came from figured less significantly than what one did and how much money he was paid to do it. Mr. Butler's status as a Sears executive, and the fact that he was able to buy a Neel Reid house in Druid Hills, were enough to win him acceptance by the Piedmont Driving Club and enough for his twin boys to gets bids from three or four high-school fraternities. Damon met them when, the first week of the fall term after their arrival, they were pinned to Alpha Rho and showed up for practice with the Boys' High Marching Band. They were immediate favorites of the band director because each came with a brand-new bass drum at a time when the director was having trouble raising enough money to repair the one bass drum that belonged to the school. They were good-looking redheads and big for their age, which was the same as Damon's. They occupied positions at each end of the last row, separated by a tuba, a sousaphone, and three trombones, and their power and energy gave the band a distinct flair. They had learned to do spectacular movements with their drum sticks; they could toss them high, juggle them, swirl them around their ears, and then pull them from the air without missing a beat. They became a popular feature with football crowds at half time and their outgoing dispositions attracted a solid cadre of friends at school. But somehow they put Damon off. It may have been that he was more than a bit jealous, not merely because they were so talented but because they had expensive clothes and a car of their own, a red Pontiac convertible. But it was more than that. The Butler twins seemed almost too eager to please. In a compulsive effort to identify themselves with everything they thought Southern, they never missed an opportunity to say "ma'am" or "y'all," they said "nigger" freely, they made a thing of ordering fountain Cokes with lime, and in the cafeteria at lunch they showed a conspicuous preference for collard greens, yams, catfish, hushpuppies, black-eyed peas, corn bread, and sweet potato pie. On the heads of their drums they had a local sign artist paint "On To Victory" across an image of the Confederate battle flag. When the Georgia gubernatorial campaign warmed up in the spring, they came to classes sporting red suspenders like those worn by Ol' Gene Talmadge. Damon thought it all a bit too much.

But the twins were oblivious to Damon's opinion of them. Every afternoon after band practice they would offer to drive him home. If there was enough daylight left they would invite him and perhaps two other boys to go joy riding. It was too late to catch the Seminary or NAPS girls leaving for home at the end of the school day, but the twins had learned that the Girls' Glee Club at North Fulton High practiced every Tuesday and Thursday afternoons till five and could be met at "the circle" coming out of the auditorium. To meet them, however, required that the twins drive up north Peachtree at a speed considerably over the lawful limit. While most of the gang found the ride exhilarating Damon sat holding his breath and his body rigid, sure that the car would spin out of control on the next curve and he'd be left unconscious on the road. Blessedly, no such accidents ever occurred, but Damon still wondered if the trip was worth the scare. Usually, by the time the Butlers got to the circle those glee-club girls who weren't waiting for a family chauffeur had already been picked up by other boys and carried off to the Pig 'n Whistle for fudge cake. The joy ride nevertheless became something of a late afternoon ritual. It gave Damon a peculiar satisfaction to be included.

One afternoon, coming back from North Fulton, Gregory invented a new game. He would race down the side of the road, as close to the curb as he could get, scaring the daylights out of any pedestrians who might be standing there waiting to cross, and then swerving the car back into the traffic lane. At the corner of Peachtree and Collier, a knot of Negro women were standing at the car stop waiting for a ride home after a day's work. Each had a bag in her hand containing leftovers from her employer's table. They all looked tired. One of them had moved off the curb and was peering intently up Peachtree, hoping to spy an oncoming streetcar, which was late coming.

Whish! Gregory had brought the convertible within inches of her feet. Frightened, she let out a scream and jumped. Fred, on the passenger side, thrust his head in her direction and yelled, "Get back there, you nigger bitch." He and his twin brother then burst out in loud laughter as the car moved ahead. The two other boys in the car laughed with them.

On the back seat, Damon was silent. He could not bring himself to say anything, but he realized that he'd been an accessory to a mean and dirty act. He felt corrupted.

27

For the better part of a year, Arabella Perdue had been busy organizing the fact-finding project for the League of Women Voters. At the same time, she was working secretively on a project of her own.

"She's writing a book," Bessie told Maude.

On days that Catherine could spare her, Bessie was now helping Maude in the kitchen two afternoons a week. On this particular afternoon she had just returned from a trip to Arabella's after delivering two dozen coconut macaroons. (Arabella had a standing weekly order for the macaroons; "I read somewhere that coconut's good for coronary arteries.")

"A book? What kind of book? "

"A story book."

"A novel? How do you know?"

"Angie told me."

"Angie being Arabella's maid?"

"Miss Arabella don't want anybody to know, but Angie says she's almost finished it."

"Do you know what it's about?"

Maude couldn't be sure but she thought Bessie was blushing.

"Angie says it's about a colored man and a white girl. She says it's a love story." Bessie hung up her coat before she spoke again, and this time Maude was sure she was blushing. "And you know what, Miss Maude? Angie says Miss Arabella uses the word."

"The word? What word?"

"You know, the word nice folk don't use."

"Oh I'm sure it's not Arabella who's using the word. It must be a character in the novel, some white-trash character."

"I don't mean that word." Bessie corrected. "The other word. *That* word."

BY FALL Arabella had raised the thirty thousand dollars needed for the fact-finding project. She had in hand the twelve papers she'd charmed or bullied as many experts to write. What she lacked was an editor who could turn the papers into readable essays for discussion.

"Doug's available," Maude suggested.

"Your husband?"

"He's a good editor. Also a good writer. And he's had experience working with printers."

So Doug went to work for Arabella. They occupied two desks at right angles to each other in a small office in the headquarters of the League of Women Voters. She was busy compiling mailing lists while he took the papers, all done by academics, and turned them into plain English.

"How're you coming?" Arabella would ask, it seemed to Doug about every twenty minutes. Every now and again, she would leave her desk, come to his, and look over his shoulders. "Mmm," she would say, in a tone that expressed neither approval nor disapproval, and it almost drove Doug crazy.

Finally, he caught on.

"You're nervous, Arabella, and you're bothering the hell out of me. You're afraid I may go too far and oversimplify things, don't you? That I'll change and distort what your experts have written."

She looked sheepish. "You can't imagine how important it is to me that we get everything right."

"It's important to me, too," Doug said. "But I need your confidence. Why don't we wait and see what Dr. Wilson thinks of what I've done to his piece. I've almost finished my edit. I'll get it over to him this afternoon."

She let her shoulders sag. "You're so right, Doug. I'll try to relax."

She did not relax, however, until the manuscript came back from Wilson with a hand-written note: "Many thanks and congratulations. You've done a marvelous job of translation. I'm afraid that over the years I've succumbed to academic jargon without realizing it. Except for two comma faults, I find nothing to correct. Appreciatively, DW."

After that, Arabella let Doug alone.

She arrived at the office early every morning prepared for her day's rounds. She dressed tastefully, usually in suits from Bonwit-Teller. Her clothes always looked fresh from the cleaners and her hair as if it had just been done by Antoine. She was a striking woman whose manner could alternate, as her audience required, between the charm of a Charleston matron and the crisp efficiency of a businessman. Over the several weeks that Doug worked with her she called on virtually every man of influence in Atlanta—every minister, priest, and rabbi, every corporation executive, the president of every civic club, the heads of the three parent-teachers associations, every union leader and the directors of every trade and professional association—that is, every man with a constituency. She converted them all. By the time she left their offices, she had pledges from every one of them to devote at least one membership meeting to a discussion of some relevant finding of her fact-finding committee.

On occasion, when she had no luncheon appointment, she would return to the office for a brown-bagged sandwich with Doug. Usually, however, she spent the noon hour, without explanation, in the library at Atlanta University doing research on something that had nothing to do with her fact-finding project. The only clue Doug had to what she was doing came one morning when a young black man from the University showed up looking for her. Told that Arabella was out of the office and not likely to return until mid-afternoon, he then handed Doug two slim volumes, each wrapped in brown paper. "She was looking for these. Tell her we found them misfiled in the stacks. Tell her to keep them as long as she needs them."

Doug put the books on Arabella's desk where she would be sure to find them and forgot about them until Arabella saw them a few hours later. As if fearing exposure, she picked them up nervously and tried to cram them into her pocket book. One fell to the floor and the loose cover came off. Doug stooped to retrieve it. It was a typewritten monograph bound in heavy cardboard. The title was handwritten in ink: "I Saw Them Lynch My Daddy."

Arabella almost grabbed the volume from him. "Thank you," she said, making it clear that she meant to say nothing more.

Every afternoon Arabella was busy on the telephone while Doug was editing and rewriting. Her conversations didn't distract him at all; from his days in the Signal Corps he'd learned how to concentrate completely on the job he'd been assigned. He was not, however, unaware of her afternoon achievements, it being her habit, by way of clearing her agenda for tomorrow, of giving him a report every day at quitting time.

What she was doing, Doug recognized, was organizing nothing less than what came to be Georgia's first statewide program in adult education. She obtained endorsements from almost every civic club and interest group in the state. Her only rejections came from the Chamber of Commerce and the Georgia Association of Manufacturers, both of which declined "for internal policy reasons." (In truth, their directors were scared stiff that Arabella's white-gloved project might kick off a contentious anti-Talmadge movement.) She persuaded Ralph McGill to do a column in the *Constitution* commending the project. She pressed the *Journal* into running two supportive editorials. She got the Georgia Press Association to do a brief on each subject for publication in the state's 159 county weeklies. She booked every expert for radio interviews and talks at luncheon clubs. When WSB rejected her proposal for public-service time for a dramatic series, "What Georgians Should Know About Georgia," she got a foundation grant and bought the time. Using every wile and appeal in her arsenal, she talked the Secretary of State into contributing use of the Great Hall of the General Assembly for a public symposium, "Let Us Reason Together," at which each expert would present a synopsis of his report. A press conference would be held on the afternoon before.

Observing her as she worked, hearing her wheedle, flatter, tease, cajole, or simply state her case, Doug was awed by her energy and inventiveness and no less by her administrative skills. Were it not a man's world, he decided, she could be running General Motors if not the country.

By mid-August Doug had sent the last of the discussion guides to press. Satisfied now that the booklets would be delivered on time, Arabella scheduled the public symposium for the Friday after Labor Day.

About two hundred and fifty Georgians showed up for the symposium, at which Doug's discussion guides were on conspicuous display, as they had been the day before at the news conference.

"A lot of people worked hard to bring us this far," Arabella said in her introductory remarks. "I have in mind most particularly the distinguished men and women of our fact-finding committee. But this morning, as we move from fact-finding to fact-facing, I want to give special thanks to only one, for you will not find him listed or credited on the program. His name is Douglas Krueger. He's the man who edited and produced every one of the papers on the subjects we'll be discussing throughout the state this next year. He wrote the pamphlet that summarizes them all. I think it fair to say that without his contribution we would not be here today."

The symposium served as an effective kick-off to the League's year-long colloquy. Except for one predictable dissent, the press reception was enthusiastic. The Talmadge organ, *The Statesman* ("Editor, The People"} called it "nothing more than a cry-baby orgy for pointy-head liberals in Atlanta." It went on to say:

> The League of Women Voters is calling for a change in everything from the soup in our school cafeterias to the way we handle rapists and arsonists in our state prisons. In the guise of democracy, it is gleefully hanging out our dirty linen and proposing reforms that if enacted would raise taxes beyond anybody's ability to pay. And as for the man credited with editing, if not actually writing, the Commie-slanted discussion papers, what do we know about him other than that his name is Douglas Krueger? He calls himself a consultant in electrical engineering, but as far as we can find out he has no known clients and no visible means of support.

28

October had always been Doug's favorite month, and in 1935 in Atlanta its blessings came in abundance—clear blue skies, cool nights, bright sunny days, temperatures that never went below seventy or higher than eighty. There was a fresh smell in the October air that revived an old anticipatory mood; although his melancholy persisted, he was almost persuaded that something good was on its way. And indeed it was. Early in the month Strut, whom he hadn't seen since Thanksgiving the year before, had phoned. Would he and Maude be up to having company over the weekend of the Tech-Georgia game? If so, he would drive over with Gertrude and Alice in his new Ford and be in Atlanta in time for supper Friday evening. They could stay through noon Sunday, if that would be convenient.

"If I didn't know better," Izzy said when Doug arrived for his afternoon session, "I'd think I was seeing a happy man."

"An old and good friend, maybe my best friend, is coming for a visit."

"Strut? The man who brought you out of the woods?"

"In more than one sense. And more than once."

Izzy leaned forward, trying to read Doug's expression. "Are you sure it has all to do with Strut?"

"What, my relatively good cheer? What else have I got to be happy about?"

Izzy opened his mouth to speak, changed his mind, and then said simply, "I hesitate to say." He shifted his seat in the chair to signal a new subject. "I have something to tell you."

"Good or bad?"

Izzy saw the sudden apprehension in Doug's eyes and hurried to reassure him. "I'm going to have to rearrange my hours and cut back here at the office."

"You mean, spend more time at the hospital?"

"And at the med school. I'm going to be the lead psychiatrist on a team some of us have been trying to organize for years. We've finally got the University to see depression as a legitimate subject for research and the Coca-Cola Foundation to fund us."

"The team, I presume, will be interdisciplinary?"

"Exactly. Besides me there'll be a clinical psychologist, a brain surgeon, a neurologist, a pathologist, a pharmacologist, a sociologist, probably a cardiologist, maybe a philosopher."

"A philosopher?"

"Depression may have a lot to tell us about free will. About the individual's ability to confront fate, about the limits of our own power to plan and control."

"Maybe you ought to include a poet."

"Why not? I bet if Emily Dickinson were still around she'd be very helpful."

"If you could get her to talk."

"I suppose."

"And what do you mean to research?"

Izzy sighed. "God, what we don't know about depression." There had been an excitement in his voice when he spoke of the team; now the excitement was gone. "It may be the oldest affliction in recorded history, older than Job. It's a lot more common than society cares to admit—how common we hope to find out. Most of it goes undiagnosed, or misdiagnosed, or untreated. Somehow, to confess to depression, or to acknowledge it in a member of the family, is a mark of failure, a character flaw, a disgrace." He laughed sourly. "Luckily for us, the manager of that foundation behaved with exceptional intelligence. But I bet we'd still be looking for a grant if his own mother hadn't come down with it."

"Where will you begin?"

"With an acceptable definition, if we can develop one. Which won't be easy." Izzy sighed again. "Is depression a psychic disorder? Of course. But is it also a disorder of the brain? Very likely. Autopsies on cadavers of people who had dementia show lesions, perforations, new and abnormal pathways in the brain. Some of us are convinced that autopsies of depressives would show similar abnormalities. But which comes first, the organic affliction or the brain's response to circumstance? And if depression proves to be as much a brain disease as a psychological dysfunction, will it be any easier to cure—with chemicals, say, or with surgical repairs to the circuitry? This is what I'm personally most interested in, what I mean to concentrate on. If we could only establish that depression is a physical disorder, we'd go a long way to abolishing the stigma and initiating a brand-new approach to therapy."

Doug sat silently, fascinated. He waited for Izzy to go on.

"What's the difference between simple depression and major depression?" Izzy reflected. "Is it only a matter of degree? We know that response to loss is a common denominator, but why is it that some of us take our losses and get over them and others are defeated by them? Why is it that some victims suffer only a brief single attack, others a protracted misery before miraculously recovering, and still others have recurrent episodes throughout their lives? Why is it that depression gives some patients chronic insomnia and makes others want to sleep all the time? Why is it that some patients are angry and aggressive, sometimes to the point of being dangerous to themselves and their families, while others are so passive they're practically catatonic? Why, in the majority of cases, does the disease in time just wear itself out and the victim go on to live a normal life?"

Doug was having trouble absorbing it all. "What do you plan to wind up with? An encyclopedia?"

"At least. But I don't expect we'll ever wind up really—certainly not in my lifetime."

"Well, it sounds as if you won't have time for the likes of me any more."

Izzy reached for his journal. "Let's come back to that. First, let's talk about you. How do you think you're doing?"

Doug wasn't prepared for the question. He tried to answer it honestly. "Better, maybe. I think I may have progressed from depression to resignation."

"Headaches?"

"Haven't had a bad one in a month."

"How're you sleeping? Have you cut back on the Mickey Finns the way I suggested?"

"Yes. I'm off them almost altogether."

"Good. You sleep well then?"

"I still dream a lot."

"Nightmares?"

"Not always. Sometimes I have rather pleasant dreams—about people I haven't seen in twenty years, and places I used to go, sometimes places I've always wanted to go."

"And when you have nightmares, do they have a theme?"

"A theme?"

"Do you dream often about the same thing, something embarrassing or demeaning? Like going naked to a dinner party?"

"Not often. In most of the nightmares I'm looking for something—like the house keys, or my wallet, or my income tax records, something I've lost. In the one I have most often, I've parked the car somewhere, say in the lot at Grant Field on a football Saturday, and I can't find it. I spend hours walking around, getting more and more into a panic, never finding it. The most horrible dream I can remember—thank God I've only had it once—Damon is still a baby and he's in his pram and I'm walking with him and the pram gets away from me and starts rolling faster and faster down a hill. When I woke up I was shaking and in a sweat."

"Are the nightmares increasing or diminishing?"

"I'd say I'm having fewer and fewer."

"Good." Izzy turned back to his journal, flipping pages until he found what he was looking for. He read to himself for several minutes.

"Do you realize that you haven't talked about your father in more than a year?"

"I'm not surprised. I don't think about him much any more."

"That's interesting."

"How so?"

"With many depressives the loss or absence of a father is a principal cause."

"I don't think it was with me. I was more relieved than grieved when he died." Doug thought back to his childhood and recalled the vacancy and the deprivation he had felt whenever he and his father were in the company of his classmates and their fathers. "I guess mostly, growing up, I felt I never had a real father."

"So if you felt a loss it was for some idealized figure of a father?"

"Possibly. But I got over that once I went into the army."

For a moment the two of them sat quietly, each with his own thoughts. Izzy stirred. "You know what occurs to me?"

"About my father?"

Izzy nodded. "In the classic story line a son fights to win his father's approval. He lives to fulfill his father's expectations. He doesn't want to let his father down."

"Yes?"

"With you and Damon, it's just the opposite. You, the father, want nothing so much as to win your son's approval. You live in worry that you'll let **him** down."

"So?"

"How do account for that? This reversal of roles?"

Doug shrugged. "Obviously because of my relationship to **my** father. The last thing I'd ever want is for Damon to think of me as I thought of Jacob."

"Do you think that's a rational fear? Enough to be depressed about?"

"I can't help it."

"Okay, let's change the subject. How about Azalie?"

"Azalie?"

"Did you love her?"

"Yes. I thought so at the time. We were awfully young. I loved her, but not the way I've loved Maude."

"And when you found she was pregnant but you couldn't marry and she went to Chicago and you never saw her again? The loss of her didn't bring on any sense of depression?"

"No. Certainly not immediately. At the time I was mostly scared, and mad with my father and the unfairness of the whole thing."

"Exactly," said Izzy. "But, clearly, it was the death of your son, whom you'd never seen, that drove you over the edge. Why?"

"It made no sense for him to die. He'd done nothing to deserve to die. I'd done nothing to suffer his death. It was like some capricious act of God."

Izzy thought he may have surfaced a critical insight. "You've had what most of us would consider an intolerable series of losses—the loss of your father, the loss of your sweetheart, the loss of your savings, the loss of a child, the loss of more than one job. But have you thought that there might be something else at work here?"

Doug frowned. "Isn't that enough? These dreadfully wrong things, these unfair things had happened, were happening, through very little fault of my own, and I couldn't do anything about them."

"Go on." There was a pause. "Go on, Doug. You were mad and you felt impotent. Mad about what?"

"Everything, I guess." He spurted it out. "Goddamn it! The injustice!"

"Injustice? Now we've got a name for it. Whose injustice, Doug?"

Doug raised his eyebrows. "I don't know." He appealed for help. "God's?"

Izzy had his elbows on the desk and his hands at his lips, the fingers touching to form a steeple. He waited, expecting Doug to say more, but Doug settled into silence. Neither said anything for a while. Izzy swung in his swivel chair to a bookshelf behind his desk and pulled off the Bible. When he found what he was looking for, he began to read aloud: "'Did I not weep for him that was in trouble? Was not my soul grieved for the poor?'"

"Come again?"

"'For he addeth rebellion unto his sin and multiplieth his words against

God . . . I am become like dust and ashes. Wherefore do the wicked live, become old, yea, are mighty in power? I cry unto thee and thou dost not hear me.'"

"I recognize it now. The book of Job? I remind you of Job?"

"More than somewhat."

Doug squirmed a bit. "The Book of Job is a reactionary folk tale. I never found any comfort in it, and I don't understand people who do."

"Why? Is it because you have no faith?"

"No faith! I should believe in a God who'd set Job up and then when Job starts asking questions tells him to keep quiet? Who does, or gets Satan to do, what he does to Job and then claims never to afflict without cause? Who hears Job's complaints, practically invites them, and then tells him that by questioning God he's committed another sin? You know what I think? I think the God of Job is a bully and a tyrant."

Izzy laughed. "You never expected God to be a democrat, did you?"

Doug relaxed. "Anyway, you can take that back. I'm not like Job. He capitulated."

"You mean repented."

"No, I mean capitulated. Job capitulated. I'm not capitulating."

"You're a good man, Doug. Maybe a bit too good for this world." Izzy grew quiet again; he felt the conversation moving into a treacherous thicket. "Maybe we ought to move on. Theology's not my field."

"Maybe you ought to add a theologian to that team of yours."

Izzy laughed again. He thought of the theologians he knew. "I don't think so," he said. "Now—"

Doug waited. Izzy was abandoning his indirect manner. He was as close as he ever came to offering a convinced judgment and a tacit prescription.

"Let's assume," he began. "Let's assume that you're coping with your losses better. Next thing, you've got to learn how to live with your justified resentments. You've got to learn to live with reasonable comfort in an unjust world where the wicked flourish, where the poor and deprived are further abused, where good deeds go unrewarded."

"What you mean is," Doug added, thinking of segregation and the

Scottsboro Boys, "I've got to learn how to stay sane in an insane society."

"Precisely."

"And how do I do that? By just signing off, by ceasing to care?"

"Oh no!" Izzy said. "Your intolerance of duplicity, your allergy to bullshit, your passion and your righteous indignation—all that's admirable. I wouldn't want you to change any of that. I just want you to be better able to control it, to make better use of it, to be angry and resentful without making yourself sick."

"And how do I go about doing that?"

"I'm not sure. That's why we're talking." Izzy grew thoughtful again. "I think it takes a lot of discipline, a lot of self-discipline. The few successful reformers I've known have all been smart about rationing their energy. They choose their shots very carefully. They spend themselves fighting the battles where the chances are at least even that they can win. They don't undertake anything where the odds are hopelessly against them. Lost causes can serve a purpose, but they're not very emotionally satisfying, are they?"

Doug was stung. "So what do I do?"

Izzy picked up his date book. The hour was almost over. "Beginning next week, I'd like to see you only on Tuesdays and Fridays, same time. From now on I'll be spending Wednesdays at Emory with the team. Do you think you can manage with only two sessions a week? I'll always be available in a crisis."

"I'll manage," Doug said, more confidently than he felt.

"I have only one more thing to suggest this afternoon. I think the time has come—that is, I think you're well enough—for you to go back to work at a regular job, one at your professional level."

"I'm glad to hear that. But jobs aren't easy to come by, times like these."

"I know. I'll do what I can to help."

"Strut says I'm constitutionally unable to work for somebody else. He thinks I should go into business for myself."

"That's an idea. As an engineer?"

"Probably. I'll check the prospects with my old prof at Tech. He's always been helpful."

Izzy rose. "I'll see you next Tuesday."

Doug was at the door when Izzy spoke again. "You are making progress, Doug. Believe it."

That night Doug slept till dawn without waking. He dreamed of white corrugated beaches and swooping sea gulls and marching bands and barefoot dancing girls in long skirts and billowing sleeves. Early in the morning, lying on his right side at the edge of the bed, he became slowly aware of a warm damp nose pressing on his; Roger was giving him a rare wake-up kiss. Pleased, he whispered "Good morning, baby," and in his half sleep scratched the cat on the top of his head, starting a purr that Henry Ford would have envied. Leaving Maude undisturbed, he swung his feet to the floor and followed Roger into the kitchen. He warmed some leftover hamburger for the cat before putting on water for coffee, and then went to the refrigerator for eggs.

It was as he was opening the refrigerator door that he realized that for some time he'd been humming: "Who's afraid of the big bad wolf, the big bad wolf, the big bad wolf? Who's afraid . . ." He put his fingers to his temples, amazed to confirm an absence of the pain that had been there every morning for the past six years. Breathing heavily, he moved quickly to the cupboard and looked into the mirror on the door. The face it reflected was smiling. And it was his.

He fell into a chair and put his face in his hands. Could it be? Izzy had said that depression sometimes disappeared spontaneously. In some cases the disease simply, mysteriously, ran its course. Was this the beginning of the end for him, the first sign of a gradual but sure recovery? Oh dear God, let it be. Please let it be. He stood up and looked at himself again in the mirror. The smile broadened.

He turned and ran back to the bedroom, Roger at his heels.

"MAUDE!"

29

Bessie's hand shook when she poured coffee after lunch.

"Excuse me, Miss Catherine," she said. "I didn't sleep too good last night."

"Are you all right? Maybe we ought to get you to Dr. Samuel for a check-up."

"I don't need no doctor," Bessie said emphatically. She cleared the table and carried the dishes noisily to the kitchen.

"I fret about her," Catherine said to Doug, who had joined them for dessert on his way to his Tuesday session with Izzy. "She's been looking worried lately, almost distraught, as if her mind is somewhere else."

"What does she say when you ask her?"

"That she's just getting old."

"She's not all that old, is she?"

"She's sixty-two. Hardly an old woman."

Doug took a last swallow of coffee and pushed his chair back. "Well, we can't let anything happen to Bessie. I'll speak to her."

He found her at the sink washing the lunch dishes.

"What's troubling you, Bessie? Is there anything I can do?"

She dropped the dish rag and turned, her face full of anguish. Taking him by surprise, she buried her head in his chest and began to cry.

"Oh, Mr. Doug," she said when she'd recovered enough to speak. "It's Walt."

"Walt? What's he been up to?"

"Nothing to deserve what Mr. Dave's trying to do to him."

"Dave Nelson? My brother-in-law?"

She wiped her eyes on her apron.

"He's tried to get Walt fired and he'll try again, I just know. And now he's threatening to foreclose on Walt's house because he's three months behind in his mortgage payments."

"That doesn't sound like Walt. How'd he let himself get so far behind?"

"Oh, Mr. Doug. It's young Teddy, Walt's boy. He's caught polio and Walt's eaten up with doctor bills." An uncharacteristic bitterness was in her voice. "There ain't no Warm Springs for colored folks."

He took her elbow and directed her to the breakfast table. "Let's sit down, Bessie. Tell me everything you know." He helped her into a chair.

"I think Mr. Dave may have just got too full of hisself. He's the mayor now, you know."

"I know," Doug said. "And also president of the bank and a director of the Chamber of Commerce."

"I think he wants to drive Walt out of Chesterton."

"But why, Bessie? What's he got against Walt?"

"You know Walt, Mr. Douglas. He can't stand things the way they are. First time I knew anything was crosswise between him and Mr. Dave was some time last year when Walt brought in a new high-school teacher from Philadelphia. He was to teach history and civics. Only they no longer called it history and civics. Walt and this new teacher, they changed the course. They made it more about current events and called it social studies, or somethin' like that—and Mr. Dave accused Walt of trying to stir up the children with wrong ideas."

"He tried to get Walt to drop the course?"

"Uh-huh, and when Walt said no Mr. Dave took it to the school board. He made a motion to fire Walt if he didn't."

"What happened then?"

"Walt went before the school board and described the new course. The board said they didn't see anything in it to get excited about. To keep peace in the community, though, they told Walt to go back to calling it history and civics. He agreed. The teacher resigned and went back to Philadelphia, and I thought that would be the end of it."

She dabbed at her eyes. "And that's when Mr. Dave got real personal.

Said Walt was no fit person to be with children. Called him an uppity nigger to his face. And now he's threatening to take his house away."

"You think he means it, Bessie?"

"I know he means it."

Doug looked at his watch. "I've got a doctor's appointment. We'll talk again later." He forced himself to convey an optimism he didn't feel. "Meanwhile, I'll see what I can do to get Dave to lay off Walt."

He squeezed her hand. "I know it's hard, Bessie. But try not to worry. I'll see if something can't be done to get care for Teddy, too."

Her lower lip was trembling.

"I'm so sorry, Bessie. So terribly sorry."

"God bless you, Mr. Doug."

"MY BROTHER-IN-LAW is proving to be as big a sonofabitch as my father," Doug said to Maude when he told her of his talk with Bessie.

Maude's eyes flashed. "It's dreadful," she said. "What can we do?"

Doug sighed. "I can start by talking to Dave."

"Tonight?"

"Now." He was leaving the dinner table when Damon called him back.

"Daddy?"

"Yes, son."

"Is it true that Warm Springs has no place for Negro patients?"

"I'm afraid so."

"Is there no other place for Negroes to get treated for polio?"

"That we'll have to find out."

"I know where to start," Damon said. "With Mr. Spalding. He's on the board of the Infantile Paralysis Foundation."

"Good for you. Ask him as soon as you can."

DOUG WENT TO THE TELEPHONE in the back hall. Maude joined him, pulling up a chair behind her. "Mind if I listen?"

He kissed her. "I'll need all the support I can get."

He asked for the long-distance operator and gave her the number in

Chesterton. "It's ringing," Doug said. Maude observed him nervously.

"Dave? It's Doug Krueger. How's the squire of Chesterton?"

She could hear Dave's laugh and after that, "To what welcome event do I owe this call?." It sounded like the canned response of a politician.

"The family all right?" Doug asked him.

"They're fine. Everybody's fine. How's Maude?"

"Fine. Just fine."

There was an awkward pause. Maude held her breath.

"Dave, I'll come right to the point. What's this I hear about bad feelings between you and Walt Seymour?"

"You mean the nigger school superintendent? What have you heard?"

"That you've tried to fire him. That you're going to foreclose on him for being in arrears with mortgage payments."

Dave spoke warily. "You've got it right. He's a bad, uppity nigger. We don't need him in Chester County."

"What's he done that's so bad?"

"Meeting with the head of the state NAACP for one thing."

"That's bad?"

"I don't want any agitatin' niggers in my town."

My town?

"But you can't fire a man just because he's exercising a constitutional right."

"How's that?"

"The first amendment, Dave."

Dave's voice was rising. "Don't be a smartass, Doug."

Doug took a deep breath. He took another tack. "But you can't do this, Dave. Walt's Bessie's boy. He's family."

Sharply: "Maybe your family, Doug, Not my family."

"Did you know his son has polio?"

"What's that got to do with it?"

"Are you seriously trying to fire Walt?"

"Absolutely. The school board overruled me last month and saved his job. But I'll find a way. So long as I'm mayor of this town, we'll have no troublemakers in our school system."

"And you're going to foreclose on him?"

"If he doesn't make at least two payments in thirty days, the bank will have his house."

"What can I do to change your mind?"

"My mind's made up."

Doug could think of little more to say.

"Well, Dave, I'm glad we talked. Thanks for being so open with me."

Dave reverted to his political persona. "My pleasure, Doug. Give my love to Maude and the boy."

Doug turned to Maude. "Well, at least I got through that without showing my temper."

"You did fine," she said, giving him a kiss. "Now what?"

He rose. "What else? I'm going to call Strut."

HE RANG STRUT early the next morning. "Does Dave have the legal right to do this?"

Strut answered with a question. "Have you talked with Walt?"

"Not yet. Only with Dave. He's stubborn. He won't listen to reason."

Strut sighed. "Oh my dear naïve and innocent friend. Do you seriously expect a bigot to listen? People like Dave aren't moved by persuasion. For that matter, very few people with set minds are moved by persuasion."

"If not persuasion, what?"

"Pressure. Power. The law. Sometimes by violence, or the fear of violence. Even then, they're likely to change only their behavior. Whether they've changed their minds is problematical."

Doug all but despaired. "If that's true, I suppose the fact-finding project and all the work I put into it, will be in vain."

"That depends."

"On what?"

"On how many people in Georgia have open minds."

"You intrigue me, Strut, but spare me the lecture." Doug took a deep breath. "I need to talk with you about Walt."

Strut paused before attempting an answer. Then, "—I doubt if Walt has a contract with the school board. Few black educators do, not in these parts. But see if he's got anything in writing, say from a member of the school board—a letter commending him for his job performance, or maybe an evaluation report, especially if it recommends lifetime employment. And check out his mortgage agreement. See if it provides a grace period for hardship."

"Anything else?"

"About Walt's meeting with the NAACP and the charge that he's introducing radical ideas in the classroom and is a first-class troublemaker—we may have to get Walt a civil rights lawyer. Do you think Dave would like to see a federal case made of all this?"

"I doubt it, as much as he might enjoy the publicity. He's a coward at heart, I think."

"Well, we can hold that as a threat." Strut began to sound as if he was running out of time. "I've got a client waiting, Doug. Call me tomorrow and tell me what you've found out."

A telephone call to Walt produced little but Walt's appreciation. The closest thing Walt had to a contract with the school board was a letter establishing his salary for the coming year. His mortgage agreement gave the bank unilateral authority to cancel after three consecutive failures to pay his monthly premiums. Hearing this, Strut sighed and said seriously. "This calls for blackmail."

"You mean we should blackmail Dave?"

"Exactly."

"But how? What have got to blackmail him with?"

"I don't know. I'm sure there's something. I've never known a small-town politician who wasn't into some sort of hanky-panky and would be scared to death of disclosure. We'll just have to find out what Dave's done or doing that he doesn't want to make public."

"I'll start first thing tomorrow."

DOUG STARTED WITH TOM LUCK, executor of his father's estate and Catherine's lawyer.

"You're asking me what kind of record Dave Nelson has made as mayor?

Or are you asking what I think of him?" Mr. Luck laughed. "What I think of him is easy. He's an ass and a bore. But his record and his reputation? He's clean as a hound's tooth. The worst thing I've ever heard about him is that he's stubborn and pathologically resistant to a new idea."

"I'm grasping at straws, I guess," Doug said. "But Dave's behaving very badly to Walt Seymour and I've got to find a way to stop him."

"I'd like to help," Luck said, meaning it. "I'm general counsel to the bank. I'll do some digging and get back to you."

SINCE HE LEFT FOR COLLEGE and the army almost twenty years before, Doug had lost touch with most of his friends in Chesterton. There were only two that he felt sufficiently close to that he could approach with a certitude of confidentiality. One was Tom Johnson, who'd inherited the drug store on the square, and the other was Ed Hines, the projectionist at the movie house. Both were glad to hear from him but neither had anything significant to say about Dave. "He's straighter than an arrow if only half as sharp," Johnson volunteered.

Who else? Doug was at a loss until he thought of James. Of course. If anybody in Chesterton knew if Dave Nelson had a secret life, it would be James.

He caught him in the embalming room on the fifth ring.

"James? Are you alone?"

"Yes, Mr. Doug."

"We must be very careful, James. I know Dave would fire you, or worse, if he thought you were spying on him. But I need you to tell me everything you know, everything you can think of or can find out that we might use to stop him from going after Walt. Anything. Has he been cooking the books at the store? Has he been giving company funds to the Talmadge campaign? Has he been cheating his tenants, the way my father used to cheat his? Has he been playing favorites with bank loans?"

"You know I'll do what I can, Mr. Doug. But I don't know nothin' about Mr. Dave's bank business."

"But you've been with him every day at the funeral home and at the store, for how many years now? If he's the man I think he is—or isn't—he will have done more than one thing on the shady side during that time. Think hard and try to remember. It's important, James."

"What's he so mad with Walt about?"

"You know the answer to that, James."

"Yas, sir, I think I do."

On Thursday Doug got a call from Tom Luck.

"After we talked," Luck said, "I decided to have a look at loan records for the past two years. I found nothing illegal."

"Oh," Doug said, disappointed.

"But I did find something curious. In April last year Dave authorized a mortgage loan to a woman in Newnan at two percent interest, the lowest admissible rate and one, I need not say, rarely offered. Then, in January and February of this year the account went unpaid."

"So?"

"Wait. In March the account was credited with two mortgage payments. There was a note saying they'd been paid by a third party."

"And the third party was?"

"Dave Nelson."

Doug's pulse was racing. He sucked in his breath. "Do you have the woman's name?"

"Her name is Trixie Wilson. Her address is Highway 70, RFD 2017, Newnan. My young associate here says she runs a whorehouse."

James reported nothing to suggest that Dave was anything other than a straight-and-narrow businessman. He did, however, suggest a bizarre change of behavior that he thought Doug might want to look into. "I hadn't thought to tell you this when we talked yesterday," James said when he phoned as promised. "But Mr. Dave's been spending a lot of time in Newnan. About six weeks ago, on a Wednesday, he came back after his lunch with the Rotary and said he had business in Newnan and would be gone the rest of the day. Same thing the next week, and the week after that. Then he told me not to schedule any memorial services on Wednesdays from now on less he say otherwise."

"Do you have any idea what he's doing in Newnan on Wednesdays?"

"No, suh. But it sure is reg'lar and whatever it is it's mighty important to him."

"He left no phone number where he might be reached if you needed him?"

"No, Mr. Doug. He just say he'd be checking in with us from time to time, as if he might be gone longer than the one afternoon."

So his brother-in-law was having regular assignations. And with a woman named Trixie, for God's sake!

"James?

"Yes, Mr. Doug."

"You may have found just what we've been looking for. But we'll need proof. Today's Tuesday. Can you get somebody—somebody we can trust—to follow Dave when he leaves the store tomorrow?"

"I REALLY THINK I ought to confront Dave face to face," Doug said to Maude. "Maybe I ought to drive over to Chesterton."

"Please don't," she said. "Whatever you two have to say to each other can be said just as well over the telephone. And I want to be where I can hear you."

He didn't try to dissuade her. Plainly, Maude was concerned with more than that Dave Nelson got his comeuppance, and it had to do with him. Was she testing him?

"Have you thought about how you'll approach him?"

"I've thought about very little else for the past eight hours."

She gave him a hug. "It's ten-thirty. Dave should have finished his business at city hall and be back at the store."

They went to the phone in the center hall. Maude pulled up a chair beside his. A few minutes later Dave had picked up, answering in a voice cultivated to reassure his constituents that God was in his Heaven and all was right with the world.

Doug gulped and swallowed hard. "Dave? This is Doug. Are you alone?"

The voice shifted to wariness. "Yes. Why?"

"I don't think you'll want anybody else to hear what I'm going to say. Are you sitting down?"

"Yes."

"You may want to take notes."

"What's this all about?"

"I'll get to the point, Dave. I want you to apologize to Walt Seymour. I want you to cancel all your charges against him, waive his delinquent mortgage payments, and see that he gets a raise."

"Are you out of your mind? Why should I do any of that?"

"Because if you don't I'll let it be known where you've been spending your Wednesday afternoons."

Dead silence.

"Dave?"

"I'm here. What do you mean, where I've been spending my Wednesday afternoons?"

"You know what I mean. I'm talking about your long affair with Miss Trixie Wilson of the House of Tricks."

"You're crazy. What makes you think I've been having an affair with anybody?" Now the voice was shaky.

"Don't try to bluff your way out of this, Dave. I have witnesses. It may come as a surprise to you, but there are some people who don't like you and who, given a chance, would be glad to tell what they know about your Wednesday afternoons with a prostitute. Besides"—he took a deep breath. God, please don't strike me dead.—"I have photographs."

"And if I don't do what you're asking me to do?"

"Then I'll make sure everybody important to you is aware of your little dalliance. Starting with Helen."

"You wouldn't dare."

"Try me. And including the man who ran against you for mayor three years ago and plans to run against you next year."

"You're trying to ruin me."

"Exactly. And with cause, which is more than you've had for trying to ruin Walt Seymour."

"My own brother-in-law!"

"There are higher loyalties, Dave. Now, write this down. This is what you're going to do."

Dave Nelson's voice registered confusion and defeat. "I'm writing."

Doug reached in a pants pocket and took out a hand-written draft. He referred to it as he talked. "Tomorrow or next day you'll be getting a letter for your signature from Tom Luck. The letter will be typed on your official mayor's stationery. What it will say is this: 'Dear Mr. Seymour: I have reviewed the record and have concluded that I have been grossly in error. I am, therefore, instructing the Chester County School Board to withdraw all charges against you. I am requesting further, in recognition of your exemplary performance as superintendent of Negro schools and in compensation for the emotional distress this controversy has brought you and your family, that you be given a raise in salary of five hundred dollars per annum, effective with the start of the new fiscal year next month. Sincerely, and so forth. P.S. In my capacity as president of the Chester County National Bank, I am also authorizing a waiver of all arrears in your mortgage account.'"

Pause. "Is that all?"

"That's all, Dave. You'll sign that letter and get it off to Walt. And you'll make a carbon copy for me. As soon as I'm satisfied that Walt has it, I'll forget about you and Miss Trixie and you'll be off the hook."

"You're asking a lot."

"Are you saying you won't agree to sign Luck's letter?"

There was the sound of a man struggling to control his anger. "No, Doug. I'll sign it. What choice have you given me? I just never suspected I had a nigger-lover for a brother-in-law."

Doug hung up and turned to Maude, his palms wet, his mouth suddenly dry. The question was in his eyes.

She stood up to embrace him. "You were marvelous." She could not restrain the tears. "Oh Doug, my dearest. You were like your old self."

30

Two days before his sixteenth birthday Damon came down with a bad cold and aching joints. Maude canceled the small party she'd planned for him. She baked him his favorite lemon cheesecake, but he was unable to eat a bite. She nursed him with aspirin and orange juice and chicken soup; it was all he could do to keep any of it down. He spent two days in bed with the curtains drawn, in pain, wanting neither to speak nor be spoken to.

By the fourth day his temperature had returned to normal, his head was clear, and he was able to open his gifts—an Argyle sweater from Catherine, a foulard tie from Agnes, a copy of *Seventeen* from Jet and Hortense, and a pair of flannel slacks from his parents. To his surprise, there was also a package from Andy—a clumsily wrapped copy of *Webster's Collegiate Dictionary* with a note:

"For Damon, my friend and partner. May he always be as caring and as good at heart as he is at sixteen. Happy Birthday."

Damon got a lump in his throat. His mother was holding her hand to his forehead and speaking, but for a moment he couldn't form words to respond.

"There's also a cake for you, from somebody named May Belle. A Skyland Bakery cake," she was saying. "We can have a turn at it after you've had a taste of the one I made for you." She swept the presents off the bed and put them on his dresser. "Fever's gone but we mustn't overdo; we can look at these again tomorrow. We'll have a proper celebration one day next week when the Montagues are here."

HE WAS CALLED STRUT not because he walked like a rooster but because his little sister couldn't pronounce Stewart. He had been an anchoring presence in Doug's life since the two met as freshmen at Georgia Tech and tried out for positions with the Yellow Jackets. Doug was passed over; Strut went on to become an All-Southern tackle. He was stocky, though at five feet eleven taller than he looked; barrel-chested, square-shouldered, his biceps large and firm, his hands big and his fingers almost long enough to encircle a football. His hair was thick and black and his eyebrows heavy; his body, surprisingly, was hairless. He looked powerful and to a facimg lineman menacing, but there was a gentle quality about him that, with his demonstrable strength, made him appealing to most girls and like a faithful big brother to his male classmates.

It was a mystery that he chose to study engineering. Without Doug's tutoring, he would have flunked algebra and he had a hard time remembering the first principles of physics. Perversely, he made straight A's in English, Southern history, and ethics, courses that the state legislature in an unlikely but inspired moment had made compulsory at Tech despite the fact that most of the student body and many members of the faculty thought them irksome distractions. It was no wonder, then, that a year after graduation he decided engineering was not for him and enrolled in the University of South Carolina law school. The day after he passed the South Carolina bar he married sweet, plump Trudy Fisher, his childhood sweetheart, with Doug as his best man. Back from the honeymoon, he entered his father's law firm, Hastings's most prestigious, where by 1935 he'd been a partner for the past three years. It was Strut who steered Doug and Maude to the house across the street and for the next ten years the two families lived almost as one. Maude and Trudy were pregnant the same year; Alice was only a month younger than Damon.

The prospect of their visit was like a tonic for Doug and Maude. Damon, however, acted as if he couldn't care less. "What's the matter, Damon?" Maude asked him. "Aren't you looking forward to seeing Alice?"

Damon shrugged. "She's fat."

"She's what?"

"She's too fat."

Astonished, she looked at him disapprovingly.

"There are times, Damon, and this is one of them, when I'm sorry they ever voted you 'Best-looking Boy.' You ought to be ashamed."

"I had other plans for that weekend."

"Such as?"

"I was going to take Agnes to the movies."

"Well, you can forget about it. You're going to the game with Alice and the rest of us."

Damon pouted.

"What's come over you, Damon?" Maude scolded. "Isn't Alice good enough for you anymore?" She didn't wait for an answer. "You haven't seen her in a year. Something has gone to your head and it's time you got a grip on yourself."

"Okay, mother," he said, still pouting.

"And stop pouting. It's very unattractive and it makes you look ugly."

For several days before the Friday the Montagues were due, Doug and Maude, with reluctant and occasional help from Damon, vacuumed and waxed the floors, aired the guest bedroom and put on fresh sheets, scrubbed the bathroom, polished the silver, cut the grass, swept and washed down the porch, washed the car, and put two dozen or more books back on the shelves where they belonged. The house had not been cleaner or more inviting since Christmas. When they were done, they were both whistling.

They decided to have Catherine and the Moneypennys in for dinner Saturday evening. In preparation, Maude made a casserole of diced chicken that could be heated up after the game. That, a tossed salad, a Cabernet, and dessert, she thought, would make an eminently satisfactory supper. By Friday noon everything was in order. She and Doug relaxed and waited.

Sometime around two that afternoon they got a phone call from Strut. He was still in Hastings, he said. Court was running late and it might be another hour before they would be free to leave. "Expect us about nine," he said, "and save me a piece of pie." He could hardly wait to see them; the Ford would knock their eyes out. He laughed heartily.

Shortly before sundown a thunderstorm struck and a heavy rain followed for the next hour, subsiding into a drizzle. Nine o'clock came and the Montagues had not arrived. Ten o'clock and they still hadn't come. Maude and Doug reassured each other that they'd been held up because of the rain.

Sometime after eleven they heard a car in the driveway, followed by the sound of the doorbell.

"They're here, darling," Doug shouted from the living room where he'd been sitting. The bell rang again. He got to his feet and ran to the door. Opening it, he faced two uniformed state troopers.

"Mr. Krueger?"

"Yes?"

"Are Stewart and Gertrude Montague friends of yours?"

Doug's heart sank.

"May we come in?"

He opened the door wider and gestured to two chairs. The troopers sat down. Maude joined them.

The older of the two men cleared his throat. "We have bad news for you." Doug, his knees buckling, sank into a chair. "An accident just outside the city limits on Route 40. A front tire blew. Mr. Montague apparently lost control and the car spun into an oncoming truck. Except for the driver of the truck, there are no survivors. There was a young girl, I'd say about fourteen."

Maude moaned and grasped Doug's right arm. They clung to each other, fighting nausea and shock and a descending blackness. "We found this in the wreckage." The trooper held out an envelope. It was Doug's letter to Strut in which he'd sent directions to the house.

They sat wordlessly for a minute or so. The only sounds were of Maude's weeping and Doug's heavy breathing and the ticking of the grandfather clock.

After a while, the older officer spoke softly. "Mr. Krueger."

Doug raised his head.

"We need you to come with us. We need you to identify the bodies."

Doug nodded and rose to get his raincoat. Maude rose with him. She wiped her eyes and said, "I'm going with you."

The younger trooper demurred. "That would not be a good idea, Mrs. Krueger."

Doug knew what he meant. He hugged his wife to his chest. "You stay here, Maude."

"But this is too much for you."

He squared his shoulders and shook his head. "No, baby. I'll be all right." There was fear and anguish in her eyes. "Please, darling, try not to worry—not about me. I'll manage. I promise."

He left her on the porch, Damon by her side. They were both sobbing.

Two hours later he signed the last of the three certificates and left the morgue, expecting one of the troopers to drive him home. Instead, he found Damon and Jet waiting for him in the foyer.

"We wanted to be with you," Damon said, pulling his father toward him.

Doug couldn't speak. He gave Damon a rough embrace and Jet a look of profound appreciation. They drove silently to Penn Avenue. Maude was on the steps in her heavy blue robe, the collar buttoned tightly at the throat to protect her from the midnight chill. "I've got a drink for you," she said, her voice shaking.

He kissed her. "Maybe some tea."

Damon followed her into the house. Jet stood with Doug on the porch. "Is there anything—anything at all—I can do, Doug?"

Impulsively, Doug threw his arms around Jet's shoulders. "You've already done more than I—" His voice cracked. "Thank you, dear friend."

Jet nodded, gave him a pat on the arm, and left.

He went to the kitchen. "I've changed my mind, Maude. I don't want the tea. I think I just want to be alone for a while."

She turned off the burner under the tea kettle. "I put on fresh sheets for you. Would you like a hot shower?"

"I'll take one. But I have this strange feeling. Like being outside myself, like being somewhere else looking on. I can't think a shower or anything else is going to help much." He put his hand under her chin and kissed her on the forehead. "I can't believe what's happened."

"Nor can I," said Maude, beginning to blubber.

"Oh Maude. I should be comforting you."

"No," she said. "How I feel is nothing compared to how you must feel. I just want to lie by your side and hold you."

"Give me an hour," he said.

The shower washed away some of the tension, but he was still feeling somewhat disembodied when he went to the bedroom. Maude was at the door by the light switch. "I'll join you in an hour, darling," she said as he got into bed.

She was in the act of closing the door, meaning to leave Doug by himself, when from the hall outside came the sound of scampering cat feet. Roger darted into the room, a moment before the door closed and almost caught his tail. Doug was lying on his side, his eyes closed, trying to hold back the tears. Roger jumped on the bed and placed his warm, soft body against Doug's thigh, For the next half hour he lay there purring, while Doug cried his heart out.

MAUDE LEANED ON THE KNOB of the closed door, listening to Doug's sobs. Good Lord, how much more could he—could *they*—bear? And why, oh Lord, did it have to happen now? Doug had been showing such promising signs. Orenstein had even suggested that his incapacitating depression might soon be behind them. Why now, oh Lord? Not again, oh Lord. Why?

Trembling, she made her way downstairs to the living room to turn off the lights. At the front door she noticed an envelope on the entry table, apparently overlooked in the afternoon mail—a small pink envelope addressed to her. It was a note from Catherine:

"My dearest Maude: I am in bed unable to sleep, thinking of you and Douglas. I have you in my heart all the time.

"I'm thankful for your strength. I'm confident that because of you things will get better. We just have to keep in mind that we have come to a bad stretch, not to the end of our world. Remember, this family is 'like a tree, standing by the water.' It can be hurt, but it won't crash."

31

Catherine was dying. That September, not long after a stressful visit with her daughter in Chesterton, she'd come down with a cold. The cold persisted, progressed into bronchitis, and then into pneumonia. Her fever spiked to 103 before stabilizing at 100. She never entirely recovered from the pneumonia. It left her weak and with chronic arrhythmia. She lost twelve pounds and almost overnight changed into an old woman. For six weeks or more she kept to her room, rising twice a day on doctor's orders for fifteen-minute walks up and down the hall with Bessie at her elbow, after which, wheezing and gasping for breath, she would return to her bed, where on most days she lay fretfully until her next meal of broth and oatmeal. She took aspirin three times a day, largely because, in the absence of any known cure, it was presumed to be harmless. In the thirties there were no antibiotics and medical science knew nothing more than to prescribe bed rest, check vital signs regularly, and hope that the body's natural recuperative powers would somehow conquer the infection.

Bessie was in constant attendance. Helen came over from Chesterton and stayed for a week. Maude and Doug visited daily, Maude in the morning, Doug in the early afternoon. Damon made a habit of dropping by on his way home from school. Although many times she showed no signs of distinguishing one visitor from another, she invariably smiled when touched or kissed, and it was obvious that she welcomed company.

One afternoon Doug arrived to find her surprisingly alert, propped up on pillows with a small wicker chest on her lap. She was removing items one by one and savoring each for the memory it evoked. Coming closer, Doug recognized his blue baby blanket, a baby tooth, his old Boy Scout knife, the tin cookie cutter he'd made for her in shop class, the gold medal he'd won for coming in first in the hundred-yard dash, the blue ribbon he'd won in an essay contest ("Why I'm Glad I'm an American"), a pressed white rose from the corsage he'd given her one Mother's Day, a collection of report cards, and the letters he'd written her from Fort Monmouth. He watched in silence until she raised her head and spoke.

"You caught me," she said, her voice high and cracking. "An old lady, counting her blessings."

He leaned over and kissed her on her hot forehead, pulling up a chair to her bedside. "Your blessings? I've been nothing but a burden to you."

She looked angry. "I don't know what went wrong with you," she said, as if she was winding up to deliver a long-suppressed maternal lecture. "But it's time you stopped."

"Stopped what, Mother?"

"Stopped deprecating yourself. Stopped feeling so unworthy."

"Unworthy? Of what, Mother?"

"Of love, I guess." She looked at him intently. Her eyes were watering. "What's been the matter, baby?"

He didn't know how to reply. "I don't know," he said haltingly. "Here I am, almost forty, out of a job, a failure. I'm a disappointment to myself and to everybody I care about. Why deny it?"

"Come closer, Doug."

He did. She slapped him hard on his right cheek.

"Now you cut that out," she said. "Stop abusing yourself. You're too old to still be masturbating."

"Mother!"

"My language offends you?"

"I was startled."

"Now listen to me, Douglas. I'm talking to you like your best friend."

He took her wrist and held it in a profound desire for connection.

"I'll try to make it quick, for it's hard for me to talk. I adore you, Doug. You have meant the world to me. For more than thirty years you've given me what life I've had."

"How can you say that, Mother? I've been nothing but a drain on you, as long as I remember."

She was about to cry. "Oh my dear one. What have I done to make you think that? I've been so proud of you."

"Proud?"

"Do you think I don't remember that time you saved the colored boy from the Klan? The time you befriended little Irma Rubinstein? The time you jumped in the pond, with your clothes on, to rescue the kitten? Do you think I don't feel blessed that you married a girl like Maude, that you've given me such a dear and remarkable grandson?"

Doug swallowed hard and closed his eyes. For a moment he could almost believe it. That night, for the first time in recent memory, he slept soundly.

Several days later Catherine appeared stronger. She was waiting for him, sitting upright in a fresh gown, her gray-free brown hair done in a bun at the neck, rouge on her cheeks and a drop of perfume behind each earlobe. She returned his kiss with a smile.

"Do something for me," she said. "Pull out the top right drawer of my dresser and reach way back. Under my slips you'll find a manila envelope. Bring it to me."

He did as directed.

She opened the envelope and showed him its contents. It held a torn Chatauqua program dated June 13, 1892, and a faded photograph of a young man.

"That's your father," she said.

He looked puzzled. "I can't believe Papa ever looked like this."

"I said your father."

He had a flash of comprehension.

"My father?"

"His name was Olaf Petersen."

"You're serious?! This man was my real father?"

She patted the bedspread. "Come closer, darling."

He sat on the edge of the bed. She was showing little emotion. There was only the suggestion of remembered sorrow in her eyes and a slight catch in her voice.

"I know it's hard for you to think of me as having ever been young," she said. "One doesn't think of a parent as being moved by passion. But there was a time—"

She sighed deeply and put her slender fingers to her brow. "I was twenty-four. Helen was not quite two. Chautauqua came to Chesterton that summer and Olaf was one of the lecturers. He was mesmerizing. He had a program for young people in the morning—five lectures on Great American Presidents—and one for adults in the evening, Great Issues in American Democracy. You can't imagine today how exciting Chautaqua was for us in 1890. It was like Grand Opera and a Broadway theater and a three-ring circus and a university classroom and Carnegie Hall, a different attraction every day, all in one. And Olaf was the star attraction. My, was he good!" She paused.

"I went to all ten of his lectures. I tried to take notes but I got so hypnotized by his performance I forgot I had a pencil in my hand. He roomed that week with the Smiths across the street. I'd watch from my upstairs bedroom window and each morning when I saw him leave the house I'd run to catch up with him and we'd walk together to the fairgrounds. I fell in love with him."

Doug studied the portrait. He assumed that Olaf Petersen had been blond but since the photograph had been printed in sepia it was impossible to tell the true color of his hair. He had a high forehead, long lashes over friendly eyes, and a nose just askew enough to blemish an otherwise handsome face. "What color were his eyes?" he asked.

"Brown. Deep brown. Like yours."

"And his hair?"

"Sort of reddish blond."

"Also like mine. How tall was he?"

"About six, maybe six feet one. He had wide shoulders and a marvelous physique. He took good care of himself."

"You saw him only during that week?"

"I saw a lot of him that week. We invited him over for dinner one night. Jacob picked a quarrel with him—about William Jennings Bryan and the rights of labor or perhaps free silver, something like that. It was very unpleasant, but Olaf was a perfect gentleman. Never raised his voice."

"What did he do when he wasn't touring summers with Chautauqua?"

"He taught history at the University of Minnesota. When Chautauqua was over and he left Chesterton he and I wrote but I thought I'd never see him again."

"You did?"

"A year later he came back to Chesterton, meaning to stay for good. He'd been offered a job on the faculty at West Georgia. Why he decided to take it when at least two Ivy League schools were after him I don't know."

"Could it have had something to do with you?"

"Maybe. It was that fall our affair got serious. I'd never before known what it was to be truly in love, or to be loved. I couldn't help myself. I knew what I was risking. I had a child. I had a husband that—"

"You didn't like."

"That I could tolerate."

"Olaf was single?"

"A widower. He'd lost his wife in childbirth."

"And the child?"

"A little girl. She lived in Minneapolis with his parents when he was away."

"What happened? Did you mean to divorce Papa—I don't know what else to call him—and marry Olaf?"

"That's where things were headed."

"But it didn't work out."

There was a long pause. Before continuing she raised herself higher in the bed and took a long breath.

"He was a very good teacher. The students liked him. After his first semester, so many registered for his lecture courses the classrooms couldn't hold them. Some of the faculty were probably jealous of him but not enough to cause trouble. He started writing a column for the *Herald* that became extremely popular, and all in all things were going swimmingly for him until the next summer. It was 1893 and Tom Watson—you know who Tom Watson was?"

Doug frowned. "Of course. He was a race-baiter. The worst kind of demagogue."

"Not in 1893. That was before he turned sour and went crazy. He—" She was halted by a distracting thought. "I had a professor at Emory who thinks the story of Tom Watson is the real American tragedy."

"I don't understand."

"The young idealist who takes on the powerful, is defeated, becomes embittered, then corrupted, and then goes mad. That story."

"You knew Tom Watson?"

"No, but Olaf did." With difficulty, she took a deep breath. "I have a lot I want to tell you and before you came I rehearsed it in my head. I want to be as succinct as I can because after a while it hurts to breathe. So listen, and try not to interrupt me."

She smiled wanly and resumed. "Watson in those days was just about everything you'd want in a politician. He was honest, he was smart, he hated the high and mighty, and although he may not have loved them, he fought for the poor. If they were poor and hard done by, he didn't care what color they were. What he wanted was to bring together farmers and workers in the South into an alliance with the West and break the hold that the banks and railroads of the East had on the rest of the country.

"Olaf was fascinated by him. Even more by his ideas. He subscribed to Watson's paper, read his speeches, followed his record in Congress, and before long Olaf's column in the *Herald* began to sound like Watson. In the beginning his column had been largely—what do you call it?—human interest. He wrote mostly about early American history—the Lost Colony, Jamestown, little-known facts about the presidents, what it was like to live in a log cabin, that sort of thing. Then he began to concentrate on local history, I think hoping people would think of him less as a Yankee. He did a lot of research into Chester County when it was populated only by the Creeks and into the settlement of Chesterton before it was incorporated. As long as he stuck to flora and fauna and Indians and life on the frontier he was in fine shape.

"Then he began writing about things closer to now, closer to home. He went out into the county, into the backwoods, talking to farmers, and wrote about what he saw and heard. Some of it was funny and some of it touching, but a lot of it was grim and unpleasant and it didn't set too well with some people, including Jacob. It got worse. From Watson's speeches, Olaf learned about the lien system and it outraged him. You know what the lien system was?"

"It sounds like a diet."

She arched her eyebrows. "Not lean. L-I-E-N. It was a—" She raised her arm and made a gesture of futility. "You should look it up. I never understood it, although Olaf tried hard to explain it. All I know is that it was a system controlled by bankers and the men who sold feed and fertilizer and farm equipment and it worked so they got everything at harvest time and the farmers nothing. Men would work for a year and sell their crops and wind up even more in debt.

"It was a terrible time in Chester County. Cotton, I remember, was selling for four cents a pound. The courthouse door was covered with notices of sheriff's sales. There was at least one foreclosure every day. Hundreds, maybe thousands, of acres of our best land was overgrown in weeds because there wasn't enough money to work them. The roads were full of homeless Negroes begging for food.

"Olaf would report all this, at first without comment. Then he began to editorialize. Conditions like these, he'd write, were a disgrace in a country founded on principles of equality and justice. 'Those privileged to have money and food and roofs over their heads are obligated to share with those who do not; the powerful have been commanded by God to use their power for the common good.' He was very good with words."

For a moment she was quiet, gathering her thoughts while she took another deep breath. Continuing: "I need not tell you, the 'powerful' in Chesterton took all this personally. The plight of the farmers was greatly exaggerated, they said. Olaf should go back to Minnesota where he came from. He was an unwanted agitator, a communist. When Watson lost his seat in Congress in 1892, Olaf wrote a really stinging piece in which he charged the Democrats with election fraud and with gerrymandering Watson's district in favor of his opponent. That upset the old guard so much that they called on the *Herald*'s editor in a body and insisted that Olaf be fired. The editor didn't fire him; Olaf was popular with the farmers and the farmers constituted more than half the *Herald*'s subscribers. Then they went to the president of the college and demanded that he dismiss Olaf from the faculty. The president refused, I guess because he was afraid that if he did he'd be faced with a student uprising and probably be accused by his colleagues of violating academic freedom and the first amendment. Olaf made no effort to restrain himself. Next he wrote a piece to the effect that Negroes and white farmers are natural allies, and they were kept divided only because it was in the interest of the rich and powerful to keep them divided. That aroused the righteous people of Chesterton to go after him in earnest. He got letters calling him an seditious alien, an atheist, a carpetbagger, an agent of the Devil, a nigger-lover, a spoiler of Southern womanhood. They burned a cross in the front yard. One morning he found his effigy hanging from the limb of an oak tree."

Doug couldn't resist interrupting. "How did he manage during all this?"

"He just continued to do his work and to speak his piece. He simply didn't believe that Chesterton people were as mean and hateful as I knew they could be. For all I knew, they were planning to tar and feather him. Seriously."

Doug waited for her to go on.

"Tom Watson had written him a thank-you note after that column about his being cheated in the election. A few weeks later Watson invited him to come to Augusta for a meeting. Olaf went and came back with a new slogan: 'Not a revolt but a revolution.' It scared me.

"Watson toured the state that summer, holding rally after rally. He was no longer claiming to be a Democrat. He called himself a Populist. Everywhere he went—and was he ever a spellbinder!—he attacked the Democrats. He said they'd sold out to the Eastern corporations. He said the time had come to organize a new party.

"When he came to Chester County, he asked Olaf to introduce him. The rally was held on a Saturday on the fairgrounds, where Olaf had first appeared in Chesterton when he was with Chatauqua. People from four counties came—farmers and poor blacks and quite a few workers from the cotton mills. All told, about two thousand of them. Chesterton had never seen such a crowd. Before Watson spoke it was like a big family picnic. There was barbecue and fiddles and banjos and a lot of country singing. There was a big platform and behind it an enormous American flag. Olaf was on the platform with Watson, and so was a Negro preacher from Newnan. Everything quieted down while the preacher led the crowd in prayer. Then Olaf introduced Watson and you never heard such shouting and stomping."

"You were there?"

"Fifth row center. In the grandstand."

"Was Papa with you?"

"Oh no. He had to deliver a body to Bullochsville. I went with a young neighbor, Lulu Ransom, who'd been in one of Olaf's history classes."

"Do you remember the gist of Watson's speech?"

"The gist of it? Farmers are good. The railroads are bad. Workers are good. The banks and corporations are bad. The Democrats have sold out to the Eastern capitalists. The time had come to rebel and organize a third party."

She frowned. "Two things stick in my mind." Her breath was short and she spoke so softly it was sometimes hard for Doug to follow her. "He said the Populist Party would make lynch law 'odious' to the people.' Odious was the word he used. I wondered at the time how many people in the crowd understood what he meant, but the Negroes sure did."

"This is the same Tom Watson who egged on the mob to lynch Leo Frank?"

"That was twenty years later. By that time Tom Watson had become an altogether different man." She rose on her elbows and shifted her weight. "That day in Chesterton, in 1893—. Some things you never forget. He said that although the Populist Party didn't advocate 'social equality'—that was the first time I'd ever heard anybody use that term—it stood fairly and squarely for political equality. And he went on to say something to the effect that 'the accident of color can make no difference in the interests of farmers, croppers, and mill hands.'"

"It's a wonder somebody didn't kill him," Doug said.

His mother nestled her head deeper into the pillow and closed her eyes. She was silent for so long that Doug thought she may have fallen asleep. When she resumed, her eyes still closed, she spoke as if in the grips of a bad dream.

"What I remember, even more than what he said, was how he looked and sounded. He was lean. His skin was sun-dried and wrinkled, the color of an overripe peach. He had this narrow rawboned face. His cheeks were sunken and he had dark eyes, so intense they seemed to pin down everything they lit on. His voice was not at all pleasant. It was high and shrill and raspy, like an angry bird, and he had a jutting jaw, as if he were daring you to strike him. He had astonishing vitality. He gestured a lot—he'd whirl and sway and toss his head—but his gestures were timed so precisely to his words that watching him was like listening to band music, a march. He was so earnest, he spoke with such sincerity, he simply carried you away."

She opened her eyes and reached for a handkerchief. He poured her a fresh glass of water.

"He was winding up for a close when—" She gulped and took a long sip.

"When what?"

"From all sides of the field there came a tremendous shout, what I suppose was meant to be a rebel yell. There was a loud crack of gun shots and then, rushing into the crowd came I don't know how many men on horseback, in white hoods and sheets. The men had whips and they started lashing out at everybody they could reach. The crowd scattered. I stood up on my seat in the grandstand and saw two men whisk Watson and the colored preacher away. The Klansmen surrounded the stage. I lost sight of Olaf."

"My God!

She dabbed at her eyes with the handkerchief.

"It lasted only a few minutes. Five at the most. The Klansmen raced away, yelling and shooting at the ground or in the air. People picked themselves up where they'd fallen or been pushed, too stunned to do anything. Everybody went home."

She turned a sorrowful face to him. "Olaf was supposed to see Mr. Watson off on an afternoon train. We'd agreed that I would wait for him, with a few of his college friends, at Jenny's Diner and have a light snack. We got there, one by one. Olaf never showed up. I waited until I thought Jacob would be back from Bullochsville and couldn't wait any longer. I went home, fixed supper for Helen and Jacob, hoping to hear from Olaf, yet realizing that he could hardly reach me without making Jacob suspicious. Midnight came and I was sure that something awful had happened. About eleven the next morning two men in a rowboat found his body in the fairgrounds lake. His head had been split with an ax."

He put her hands in his and held them tightly. "I hardly know what to say."

"I wanted to die myself," his mother said.

He kissed her on the forehead clumsily. "What did you do?"

"Two days later I found I was pregnant. I decided to live."

"All these years," he said, not quite sure what he meant. "Did Papa suspect?"

"If he did, he never let on. I was a Southern lady, remember. As a matter of male pride, he had to keep me on my pedestal. I counted on that."

Catherine looked tired, drained. "I'd like to nap now." she said weakly. "But don't leave me. I feel better, just knowing you're with me."

She closed her eyes and a moment later she was fast asleep. Doug rose quietly to adjust the window shade. On his way back to his chair he picked up the envelope where he'd left it on the bed, meaning to put back the photograph of his father and the old Chautauqua program. Raising the flap, he saw that he had overlooked a newspaper clipping. He sat down to read it. It was from the Chesterton *Herald* of January 12, 1891:

AROUND AND ABOUT

By Olaf Petersen

A prominent Methodist divine has chastised me for predicting a big Populist turnout in next year's Congressional elections.

"Be not deceived," he writes. "A Populist victory in 1892 would result in negro supremacy, mongrelism, and the destruction of the Saxon womanhood of our peerless wives and daughters."

Does his Eminence think white men too anemic to defend their wives and daughters should they need defending? Would he have us believe that in a fair contest Negro men would naturally prove superior? Are our "peerless Saxon women" so easily seduced, or do they simply find Negro men more attractive?

The implications are ludicrous and they are insulting to white men and women alike.

My churched correspondent is appealing to the same fear that the rich and mighty have always aroused to keep poor whites and poorer Negroes enslaved. Were we once and for all to bury this fear, the truth of Tom Watson's perception would be clear: "The accident of color makes no difference in the interests of farmers, croppers, and laborers."

Henry Grady, the distinguished editor of the Atlanta *Constitution* speaks of a New South, of Atlanta's "wonderful advancement," of business miracles and rising stock-market profits. Meanwhile his rival in Atlanta, the *Journal*, reports that in the workers' district of the Exposition Mills "famine and pestilence are making worse ravages than among the serfs of Russia." Mill workers are paid the magnificent sum of thirty-six cents a day. Eight, ten members of a family, crowded in a single room, are stricken with pneumonia and flu and abandoned. There is no sanitation, no help or protection from the city, no medicine, no food, no fire, no nurses—nothing but biting hunger and death."

If not Tom Watson, who will speak for our exploited poor? If not the Populists, who?

Doug returned the clipping to the envelope and sat motionless. So this was my father! How eloquent, how true. How foolhardy and naive. How, in some critical ways, so like me.

He leaned over to kiss Catherine good-bye. With a slight murmur, she roused herself and smiled. "Douglas, dear."

"Yes, Mother. I'm right here."

"One more thing." She took a deep breath. "I've revised my will. I'm leaving the house to you. Along with all my stock, mostly Coca-Cola and Atlantic Ice. When I go—"

"Oh Mother. You're not going anywhere."

She smiled wanly. "I just ask that you take care of Bessie."

He gripped her wrist. "Of course."

"The stock's not worth what it used to be. Maybe no more than forty thousand."

32

"So how do you feel," Izzy Orenstein was saying, "now that you know who your real father is—or should I ask, now that you know the man you always called Papa isn't?"

Doug returned his smile. "Relieved. Gratified. Proud. Also very sad."

"We've made great progress," Izzy said, making a note. "Has it occurred to you that you may have just passed a phenomenally long identity crisis?"

"How long would that be?"

Izzy laughed. "How old are you?"

"Forty."

"Well, I submit you've been in crisis since Papa threw you overboard and told you to swim."

"I was five."

"Thirty-five years with the wrong daddy," Izzy said. "That could have been tough."

"It was."

"Do you think you might be over it now?"

"God, I hope so."

Izzy glanced at his wristwatch. "Time's about up. I'll see you Tuesday. Meanwhile, I want you to do some homework."

He handed Doug a book.

"*Anna Karenina*? I've read *Anna Karenina*."

"Then maybe you'll remember that Levin had this thing, this compulsion. He insisted that Kitty read the diaries he'd kept when he was a single man, before their courtship."

"And?"

"I think you and Tolstoy may have had the same problem."

"What problem?"

"Oh come on, Doug. The problem you brought up last week."

"You mean whether should I tell Maude about me and Azalie?"

"Or, as Tolstoy saw it, what an honorable man feels obliged to tell his betrothed about his sinful life as a bachelor."

"I never thought Tolstoy had a sinful life."

"I want you to read the passage I've marked. Pages 252 through 258. Carefully. We'll talk about it next week."

ON THE FOLLOWING TUESDAY, Doug had hardly taken his seat when Izzy opened the subject. "I gather," he said, referring to his notes, "that you think you ought to tell Maude but are scared of the consequences."

"Wouldn't you be?"

Izzy ignored the question. "It may be right for you to tell Maude, or it may be better if you don't. The important thing is that you understand why you tell her—or don't—and live with it."

Doug opened the book to the passage Izzy had marked. "Is that why you gave me this to read?"

"Right. Levin is Tolstoy, you know. *Anna Karenina* is about as autobiographical as he ever got."

"Well," Doug said a bit defensively. "I'm not Tolstoy and Maude isn't Kitty. And this is 1935, not 1876."

"So?"

"For one thing, I don't have Tolstoy's worry about disbelief. Maude couldn't care less. Neither of us is oppressively religious. And another thing, it says here that Levin 'had resolved to tell her two things in the very first days—one, that he was not as pure as she was, and the other that he was an unbeliever.' And when he told her, when he gave her his diary to read, it was only after she'd sworn not to renounce him. See?"

"And you're afraid that after seventeen years Maude might not agree to renounce you before you confessed? And that she would renounce you afterward?"

"Maybe."

"What I find interesting about this episode," Izzy said, "is that Levin thought Kitty would be more upset to be told he was a disbeliever than to learn how 'impure' he was, which I presume means, among other things, how many and what kind of women he'd slept with."

Doug referred to page 253. "Not only that. In the beginning Kitty was eager to hear it. 'You absolutely must tell me.' she says. 'I must know everything.'"

"And when he tells her, what happens?"

"She goes to pieces. It says here, 'The confession made her weep bitterly. Only when he saw her tear-strained, pathetic, and dear face, miserable from the irremediable grief he had caused her, did he understand the abyss that separated his shameful past from her dove-like purity.'"

"And he felt horrified at what he had done. Right?"

"Yes. He asks her if she can forgive him. She says she'd already forgiven him, 'but it's terrible.'"

"And then what?"

Doug thought long and hard. "I think Levin lost. Tolstoy has him believing he's no good, he's dirt."

"Read it to me."

"'After that he considered himself even more unworthy of her, bowed still lower before her morally, and valued still more highly his undeserved happiness.'"

"So what do you think?"

"I think Levin was a fool."

"So you've decided not to tell Maude."

"I didn't say that."

Izzy waited, expecting Doug to go on, but Doug said nothing more.

"All right," Izzy said, sighing slightly. "It's review time." He put his elbows on his desk and laced his fingers, hoping his body language would convey no sign of his growing exasperation. "Tell me again why you think it might be a good idea to tell Maude about you and Azalie and Douglas."

"Well." Doug felt a tension in his shoulders. "It could be liberating."

"Um, you mean for you."

"Of course for me. It's not very comfortable keeping something like this to yourself."

"And what are you afraid might happen were your near and dear to find out?"

"They'd think me contemptible, I guess."

"Contemptible? Why?"

Doug had asked himself that question more than once. His answer sounded like a recitation.

"One, I had a premarital affair and fathered a child. Two, the woman I fell in love with is a Negro. And three, I abandoned her and the baby."

"And so in a very difficult situation you think you did badly."

"Yes."

Izzy looked at his notes. "Maybe it would help if we talked about these three things, one by one. You grew up in a place where nice boys aren't supposed to have sex before they marry and where white men aren't supposed to get it on with black women. The fact that you did both doesn't mean that you behaved badly. It only means that you did something thousands of other young males have done and that a sick, sick society has permitted, maybe even encouraged, as long as it's done in the dark and nobody talks. Has it occurred to you that maybe your motives, your feelings, were far more worthy than the thousands of others who did precisely what you did and yet managed to live comfortably with their 'sins'?"

Stunned by Izzy's unexpected eloquence, Doug dropped his jaw and looked at him wide-eyed. "You sound as if I just shouldn't bother about it."

Izzy shrugged. "It's hard not to get impatient with you, Doug. What I'm trying to do is to get you to stop blaming yourself. You may have made a mistake, but you've been consistently emotionally honest. If I can believe you, what started with you and Azalie may have been lust, but it developed into a genuine, caring relationship. Your biggest sin, at least in the eyes of the hypocritical, God-mocking, soul-killing society you were born into, is that you came to love her—or whatever passes for love when you're only eighteen."

"You really believe that?"

"I wish you could."

Doug was silent, reaching back into memory for his feeling for Azalie twenty-two years before. There was hurt and unreconciled guilt in his eyes.

"I did love her," he said. "Why then did I agree never to see her again, never to see my own child, and let Papa support her? Why didn't I go with her to Chicago, whatever the cost? That would have been the honorable thing."

Izzy had to tell himself to remain professional, that it was not his job to tell Doug what to think but to get him to think for himself. "Have you thought how hard that might have been on you and Azalie? Am I right? You had no money, you had no job and you probably would have had to go to work doing hard labor in a stock yard or packing house, and you weren't even old enough to vote."

"It might have been hard, but maybe I could have made it in Chicago. Chicago isn't west Georgia."

"No, but it's Chicago. Would you really have wanted your family to live in poverty? It takes an almost impossibly strong love to survive in poverty."

"Azalie said something like that once. She said we'd probably have ended up hating each other."

"And even if in time you were to get a job, let's say a good job, you'd be facing ostracism and discrimination. What kind of life would that be for you? What effect do you think that would have on your boy? Miscegenation may be legal in Illinois but the population is hardly hospitable to mixed marriages."

"That sounds like rationalization."

Izzy was having trouble thinking of something more to say. He sighed. "All I can do is to ask you to think about it. You were victimized by bad luck and a sadistic father, or a man you took to be your father—and if knowing that doesn't make you feel better about yourself, then we've got another problem in addition to your depression."

Doug raised an eyebrow. "You think I'm masochistic?"

"What else?"

They sank into a long silence. When Doug spoke again, it was to return to the question of opening up to Maude.

"I agree with Levin, or Tolstoy, about one thing—that there shouldn't be any secrets between husband and wife."

Izzy laughed. "Are you kidding? How many marriages do you think could exist with full disclosure? How many wives do you think really want to know everything about their husbands? How do you think Maude would react were you to tell her about you and Azalie? You don't think she'd take it like Kitty?"

"Oh no."

"Do you think she'd react differently if Azalie were a white woman?"

"I don't know," Doug answered honestly. "Maude is a pretty emancipated woman, but still—"

"As I remember, Tolstoy implies that one reason Levin feels bad and cheap after telling Kitty is that he'd been thinking only of himself. He'd not put himself in her place. How much have you thought about what effect your so-called confession would have on Maude?"

"I don't understand."

"Let's say she hears you out, considers the circumstances, and says it's all perfectly understandable, it's in the past. She still loves you, so forget it."

"I think I'd feel like a released convict. I'd feel like a carload of coal was off my back."

"Is there any chance that she might react otherwise? Would she leave you?"

"I don't think so."

"But she might stop loving you. That's what you fear most of all, isn't it?"

"I couldn't stand it. I'd rather be dead."

"But still you're inclined to think you'd feel better if you told her. Am I right?"

"Yes."

"Do you think she'd feel better?"

"No. Probably not."

"Probably? You're not sure?"

"No."

"There's another possibility, isn't there?"

"I can't think of it."

"Women are full of surprises," Izzy said. "By and large I think they may be less prudish than men. How well do you think you know Maude?"

"As well as any man can know a woman. Women are full of surprises. You just said that."

"Exactly," said Izzy. "Is it likely that, more than anything else, she may be just provoked?"

"Provoked?"

"Not provoked by what you've told her. But provoked by the revelation that after all these years you know her so poorly that you thought she wouldn't understand and were worried that she might not forgive you. Forgive you for what? As far as she's concerned, there may be nothing to forgive."

"In other words, I may only make her mad with me."

"It's a possibility."

"I could live with that. Maude doesn't stay mad for long. I know her that well."

"Well," Izzy ventured as a last suggestion, "before you decide to tell Maude anything, do what Levin didn't do. Put yourself in her place."

The session was over. Doug rose to leave when Izzy called him back.

"I've never told you properly how sorry I was to hear about the death of Strut and his family."

"I appreciated your card. There's little more that you could have said or done."

Izzy frowned. "We ought, however, to recognize it as another milestone."

"A milestone?"

"Marking your way out of depression. Has it occurred to you that had this happened even six months ago you would have hit bottom again?"

"I almost did."

"The important thing is, you didn't. From my observation, your reaction was only a normal grief." He coughed to clear his throat. "I'm very admiring of you, Doug."

"That's good to know. I can't tell you how glad I am to hear that."

Izzy got out of his chair and walked with Doug to the door. "Have you made any progress on the career thing?"

"Not much. I've sent out new resumés and had long talks with my old mentor at Tech. Jobs at the professional level are still hard to come by."

"I know. But of the possibilities, if you had your choice, what would you like most to do?"

Doug thought hard. "I think I'd like to go back into radio."

"In management?"

"Or as owner."

Izzy frowned, not quite sure what Doug meant. He opened the door to admit his next client. "That sounds promising," he said hesitantly. "WSB could use some competition."

LEAVING IZZY THAT AFTERNOON, Doug was in a peculiar state of suspense. It was ridiculous but the only comparable feeling he could remember was the anticipation he'd felt as a child on Christmas morning when it was too early to go down to the tree and too late to go back to sleep. Something good could be in store for him, or he might be tearfully disappointed, as he was the time he'd asked for an erector set and instead got a copy of *Peter Pan.* Though his situation now was nothing so trivial, it held the same promise of fulfillment or frustration. His pulse was racing and he felt the urgent need of exercise.

He looked at his watch. In a half hour Damon would be quitting band practice. There would be time for at least one set of tennis before dark.

He drove to the house, changed his clothes quickly, packed a canvas bag with Damon's tennis shorts and sneakers, and picked up two racquets and a can of balls. The house was quiet. This, he remembered, was Maude's afternoon to be at the church kitchen, making beef stew and apple dumplings for the homeless. He was glad, momentarily, for her absence, for he had not yet decided how much, if anything, to tell her of his session with

Orenstein and he didn't want to run the chance of saying something on impulse he might later regret. He wrote her a note saying he was on his way to meet Damon and that the two of them would be home in time for supper. Band practice was over and Damon was strapping his trombone to the rack of his bike, preparing to ride home, when Doug drove up beside him at the edge of the Boys' High drill field.

Damon was surprised to see him. "Are you all right, Dad?"

"Rarely better," Doug assured him. "Leave your bike here. We'll pick it up later. I'm in bad need of some exercise and I thought a set or two of tennis might do us both good. Hop in."

Damon looked puzzled, then pleased. "Swell. I won't be a minute." He rolled his bike over to the parking rack in the shade of the band room, ran back, threw his trombone on the rear seat, and climbed into the old Ford next to his father. Doug put the car in gear and turned right onto Parkway Drive toward Piedmont Park.

Damon gave Doug a wide grin. "What's happening, Daddy? This seems like old times."

Doug patted him affectionately on the shoulder. "Not old times, Damon. New times."

Damon sensed something hopeful in Doug's response but he was hesitant to press. "You look tense," he said, noting the firmness of his father's grip on the steering wheel. As he spoke he scrunched down in his seat and began pulling off his ROTC uniform, changing into a short-sleeve pullover shirt and tennis shorts.

"Maybe a bit keyed up. Not tense."

Damon laughed. "You're going to beat the pants off me."

Nature was showing its benign face that early December afternoon. The sun was out. The air was cool and of a sweetness rather to be drunk than breathed. The leaves were turning but had not yet fallen, so the clay court was clean and dry. Doug was invigorated, invested with an energy he had not known in years. Something magical was going on in his body. It was as if all his pores had opened and released the poison from a long-festering infection. He dared not think about it for fear it couldn't stand analysis, but whatever was going on inside him was inspiriting. His serve was strong, his backhand never better. He covered the court with no strain, retrieving Damon's best-placed shots shamelessly. Before the sun had dropped behind the sentinel pines they had played two sets. He won them both, six-three and seven-five.

"Gee, Daddy," Damon said, wiping the sweat off his cheeks with his sleeve. "What's come over you? Have you been practicing secretly?"

Doug laughed. "Would that it had done as much for my head."

Damon gave him a puzzled look. "What?"

"All that practice, if you want to call it that. All this exercise."

Damon still didn't understand.

"Dr. Orenstein prescribed exercise as part of my therapy," Doug said. "Remember? I run, I walk, I go bowling with the support group. And I play tennis with your mother, and when she's not available anybody I can find, at least twice a week."

"But not like this afternoon," Damon said. "You and I played tennis just last Saturday, or have you forgotten? I beat you six-two, six-one, and six-four. Something's happened to you."

"Let's hope so." Doug said cheerfully. "Shall we try again next Saturday?"

BACK IN THE CAR, before starting the ignition, Doug turned in his seat and studied Damon thoughtfully. He felt a surge of pride. Damon's face was free of pimples; his complexion, obviously a contribution from Olaf, was smooth, the color of fresh-roasted peanuts. There was a becoming beard line and strong cheek bones, which he, Doug, credited to himself. He had his mother's dark brown eyes and long lashes. He was getting broader in the shoulders and heavier in the chest. No longer of an age to be called a boy, Damon was turning into a young man, and a rather handsome one. Fleetingly, Doug wondered what he might need to know about sex. He must remember to ask him.

For supper that evening Maude had fixed a cheese soufflé, tomato aspic, green beans with almonds, cornbread, and a lemon meringue pie. Each was a favorite dish of his. What was the occasion? Did Maude know something he didn't?

His mood of exhilaration passed into a feeling of ease, and the unaccustomed sense of well-being continued throughout the evening. They were eating in the breakfast nook, as they often did when the dining table was loaded with the utensils and ingredients for a party Maude would be catering the next day. (Seeing them, Doug told himself that he must really get on with conversion of the back porch into a room for food preparation. Maude's business was growing and clearly the small kitchen would no longer do.) He was sitting across from his wife and son, listening bemusedly to Damon's account of their tennis game. His eyes were on Maude. The flesh under her eyes might be a bit plumper. Daily baths in cake batter and hot water had changed the color of her hands from white-pink to coral. Otherwise, her skin was as firm, as glowing as the day they met. She was wearing her hair longer, with a slight under curl at the edges; thank God bobbed hair was no longer the fashion. She was smiling now, pleased with whatever Damon was telling her. There was a tease around the lips as if they held a dirty little secret she was finding difficult to keep. He'd like to know what was going through her mind, for he was convinced it had something to do with him. He said nothing, however, and was just about to pick up the last forkful of soufflé when it hit him—such a poignant flood of awe and appreciation and love that he got such a lump in his throat he could not have spoken had he wanted to. His eyes watered. For a moment he felt as if he might break into sobs. What an extraordinary woman he'd married! How blessed and lucky he'd been! In all their years together he could remember not one crucial quarrel. In reality it must surely have been different, but at the moment the most serious dispute he could recall was whether the toilet paper should roll off the spool from the inside or the outside. The memory almost brought him to laughter.

His train of thought shifted and he found himself reflecting on the many times he'd failed her. For a moment he half-expected his familiar nocturnal demon to return and smite him on the head. This evening, however, he did not sink into his old well of despair. His mind and heart were in conflict to a discomforting degree, yet now he could tell himself, and believe it, that however bizarre his behavior had been it had not been his fault. Maude must have understood this from the beginning. How else could she been so patient, or forgiving? That she could sustain such undeserved trust in him over all the years must, he decided, be what Orenstein would call a sex-linked characteristic. Whatever, he was profoundly grateful.

He had decided to tell her. Soon, but not now. Not tonight. For a whit longer, let him wallow in the relief and joy that had so recently overcome him. All understanding, even Maude's, had its limits. Later he would be prepared to risk its loss. But not tonight.

After supper he remained unusually alert, alive with undefined promise. Later in their bedroom he undressed and decided to take a shower. Emerging from the bathroom in his pajamas, he saw Maude, in a thin cotton gown with machine lace at the neckline, standing in silhouette at the moon-lit window on her side of the bed. He went to her, drew her bosom to his chest, and gave her a long kiss on the lips.

"Mmm," she murmured. "What's all that about?"

He took her right hand and placed it between his legs.

"I have a surprise for you," he said.

She closed her eyes and murmured again. "Doug, dear—"

"I'd like to try," he said.

The sex was the best they'd had in years. An hour later, it was more leisurely and even better. They fell asleep in each other's arms, reassured and renewed.

Doug slept until about three, when, as he had been habitually doing, he woke up. This time, however, he did not feel drowsy or half-sedated, caught miserably in a troubled state of the semi-conscious. Very much to the contrary, he came wide awake almost in an instant, more eager than anxious, with an acute sense of unfinished business. Careful not to disturb Maude, he eased himself out of bed, pulled on his slippers and robe, and went quietly to the kitchen, where he brewed himself a cup of tea. He took the tea with him to the breakfast nook and for the next half hour sipped it slowly, hardly tasting it, while he thought.

The question for him now was not whether to tell Maude but how best to tell her. He knew that he was over the worst of it; magically, biology and psychology had intersected in some obdurate chamber of his mind and erased the guilt, the self-debasement, and the chronic premonition of defeat. But he also knew that his recovery could never be complete, that his marriage would never be truly and fully consummated, that he could never be at peace with himself, until he'd disclosed to Maude the events of his late adolescence and their prolonged trauma.

"Darling?"

Maude was at the entry to the breakfast room. It was chilly and for warmth she was pulling at the sash to her robe with one hand and buttoning the collar with the other. Startled, Doug got up to give her a hand, for she looked sleepy and unsteady. She sat down on the banquette across from him.

"I knew you were up when I heard the water running. The walls in this house are so thin—"

"Would you like a cup of tea?" She nodded and he got up to freshen the kettle.

"You couldn't sleep either?" he asked.

"I was too happy to sleep," she said. She accepted the cup of tea, took a sip, and said. "What was the matter with you?"

"I was happy, too. Happier than God knows when. But after I woke up I guess I had too many things on my mind."

She leaned across the table and took his hand in hers. "Is it possible, baby, that the horror is behind us?"

"O Lord, Maude, let's hope so. At this moment, I'm so high I can't believe I was ever down."

She was reading his face. "You look as if you were about to say more," she said. "You've got something on your mind."

He squeezed her hands. "I never loved you more than I do this minute."

She arched her eyebrows. "Never? I guess I can believe that." She put an index finger under his chin and lifted his eyes to a level with hers. "But that's not what you were going to say. What is it, darling?"

"Two things. One of them, I think, will surprise you, and it may please you." He took a deep breath. "The other—I only hope won't make you love me less."

She looked puzzled. "Give me the good news first."

"Papa—the man I've always called Papa—Jacob Krueger is not my real father."

"What?"

"My real father was a man from Minnesota named Olaf Petersen. He and my mother fell in love when he came to Chesterton with Chatauqua about three years before I was born."

Except for an occasional murmur of disbelief or sympathy, Maude sat quietly while he told her what Catherine had told him. When he was done, her first reaction was to say, "Poor Catherine," and then, "I guess that could explain a lot, couldn't it?"

"About me, I guess you mean."

"About you, and also about Papa Krueger's behavior toward you."

"Of course."

They lapsed into silence. After a moment or two, she shifted in her seat, as if to mark a transition, and asked him about "the other thing." He too shifted, hesitant to begin. His face grew solemn.

"There's an important part of my life I've never told you about," he said. "I want to tell you now."

"Why only now?"

He shrugged. "For a long time—until Papa Kreuger died—I was pledged not to tell anybody. After that, maybe I was just too ashamed."

"Ashamed? Why should you be ashamed to tell me anything?" Had Doug killed somebody?

"Well, it's not the sort of thing a man can be exactly proud of." He cleared his throat. "It started when I was seventeen."

He put his arms on the table and laced his fingers, all defenses down. She gave him a reassuring pat on a forearm, and he proceeded. He told her everything in detail, ending with the death of Douglas Junior. When he was done he sat quivering.

"You don't have to say anything now," he told her when she gave no immediate reaction. "Maybe you ought to think about it. But Maude—oh

Maude, if you should hate me—"

"Don't be silly," she said impatiently. "I don't need to think about it, and I don't hate you, for God's sake. I just want to ask a few questions."

He must have looked confused and pained. "And don't look like that," she said irritably. "You're not in a dock."

"I'm waiting," he said.

"All right, you and Azalie and the baby—. This all happened a year or so before we met?"

"That's right."

"So it has nothing to do with you and me, does it? What I mean is, with your feeling toward me."

"No."

"And you haven't seen Azalie since?"

"No. I've been in touch with her, maybe three times over the past fifteen years. I've not seen her since she left Chesterton for Chicago and I went off to Tech."

"Then why should I care? Except that it's obviously been such a trial and a burden for you, and kept you in hell when you didn't deserve to be. Why should I care except that I care for you? Have there been any other women since we married?"

"No. Absolutely not." He bit his lip. "It doesn't matter that I'd slept around a bit before we married?"

"Oh Doug, don't be a simpleton. Who do you take me for—Elsie Dinsmore? Rebecca of Sunnybrook Farm?"

"Or that Azalie is colored?"

She slammed her hand down on the table. The teacups rattled. "Now that does make me mad—that you'd ever think race or color could make a difference to me. After almost twenty years together and you don't know me any better than that?"

"But honey—"

"Don't honey me. There are just some things a man and wife ought to take for granted about each other."

"I'm sorry, sweetheart. I really am. I should have known better."

"Indeed you should have. And I'll be a long time forgetting."

"But you still love me?"

She broke into a broad smile. "You're so pitiful, Doug. And so dumb. Of course I love you. I love you like mad."

She stood up, collected the empty tea cups, and started toward the kitchen. She paused in the doorway and turned back toward him. "I'm also thinking about Azalie. It must be terrible for her, losing the boy." Another pause. "And for you. It's unforgivable, what Papa put you through."

She continued to the sink. She said nothing until she'd run hot water over the cups and dried them with a dish towel. Then, swiveling to face him, she spoke gravely. "Tell me, Doug. Why did you think it necessary to tell me all this?"

"I couldn't stand it any longer, not telling you."

"You weren't testing me?"

"Testing you?" He remembered Orenstein's parting admonition: "Put yourself in Maude's place." Had he made a mistake?

"Testing my love. How much more I could take."

"That never entered my mind," he said. "If anything, I was tired of testing myself. I'd come to the point where I had to have somebody I could confide in."

"Surely you've run through this with Orenstein."

"Of course, but that's different. I had to tell you. I needed you. I'd come to feel more and more that telling you would bring us closer, even though I also felt that telling you might tear us apart."

"You mean you didn't feel we were close enough?"

"Oh come on, Maude, you know that isn't what I meant."

"And do you feel closer now?"

He went to her, swung her around, and held her tight.

"If we were any closer, we'd share the same heartbeat."

"Oh my God," she said, moved suddenly to laugh. "I married a poet." She looked over his shoulder at the Big Ben on the counter. "How about waffles for breakfast?"

And that was that.

33

On the night of the Boys High-Tech High game, Damon was out of the house early to play in the band at the pre-game rally in Piedmont Park. After that he was to go to Ponce de Leon stadium and march in the half-time ceremony ("Boys' High Forever!"). After the game, he would join Chip and as many other boys as could be packed into the Pierce-Arrow and be off to God knows where for what they expected to be a victory celebration. He explained all this to his parents and told them not to worry.

Doug had no appetite that night. Shortly before supper he began to get a headache that got progressively worse. He feared a return of his old despair. There had been nothing in the day to be depressed about. If there was anything that depressed him, he decided, it was the realization that his problem was probably one of a bad chemical mix in the brain, inexplicable, unpredictable, and resistant to anything he knew to do. After a bowl of soup and crackers, he gave Maude a good-night kiss, took two aspirins, and went to bed.

About two o'clock the phone rang. He heard Maude stir and then her voice. "Officer who?" Pause. "He's not well. He's sleeping. Can this wait?" Pause. "Oh. Certainly. I'll put him on."

She shook him awake. "It's for you. The police, I think."

With heroic effort, Doug got out of bed and walked unsteadily to the phone. "Yes?"

Maude waited. She was quivering and breathing heavily. "I'll be there as quickly as I can. Yes, I'll bring my checkbook."

She looked at him, worried and scared.

"It's Damon," he told her, trying hard to mask his own anxiety. "He and some of his friends are in trouble. A prank that got out of hand I suspect. They're being held at the station."

Maude got off the bed and started to dress.

"No, no," Doug said. "I'll handle this. This is something for me to work out."

"But you're not well, darling,"

"Damon needs me," he said. He took off his pajamas and went to the chest of drawers for underwear and a shirt.

She got up again, determined to dress and accompany him.

"I said no, Maude. This is something between me and Damon."

She looked puzzled.

"Damon's my son, too."

He kissed her on the forehead. "And you're my wife. And I mean to take care of you both." He pulled on his trousers. "Please, Maude."

She subsided. "Will you phone me as soon as you know anything?"

"If I can find a phone. I shouldn't be gone long."

He picked up the water glass beside the bed and took two more aspirins. He gave her another kiss and left, forcing himself to walk without wobbling.

By the time he got to the police station on downtown Courtland Street his headache had eased and he was wide awake.

He gave his name to the desk sergeant. He was told to take a seat, the lieutenant would see him shortly.

He had to wait for no more than five minutes. Damon was brought in, rocking slightly to keep his balance, behind a uniformed, middle-aged police officer whose face registered the relaxed authority of a veteran. Damon sat down on a bench, his head drooping and his eyes staring at the floor. The lieutenant gestured Doug to the desk, where he consulted the night's log. "We picked up your boy with five others about the same age and in the same condition."

"Condition?"

"They'd been drinking. Quite a lot. Very good stuff. Premium grade Bourbon, I'd say."

"Where'd they get any Bourbon?"

"One of the boys broke into his father's liquor cabinet."

"And then?"

"They decided to visit Myrna."

"Myrna?"

The lieutenant smiled indulgently. "I thought every male in Atlanta over the age of fifteen knew Myrna. She runs a whore house, on Baker Street. Has for years. We bust her about once every month or so. We busted her last night."

"And my son was there?"

"With his friends." The lieutenant looked as if he anticipated Doug's next question. "No, we don't think so. Myrna says she told them to sober up and come back."

Doug was breathing somewhat easier. "Are you booking them?"

The lieutenant shook his head. "No. They're young and we have no interest in putting anything on the record. But we thought it might be a good idea to scare the shit out of them. If you could contribute twenty dollars to the police fund."

Doug wrote a check. The lieutenant put it on the desk and shook Doug's hand. "You two can go now, Mr. Krueger." He moved away, but before he disappeared into a back room he turned and said, "Don't be too rough on the boy."

Doug went to Damon, slumped on the bench. "Well, son," he said, putting his hand on Damon's chin and lifting his head up. "I take it Boys' High won."

Damon grunted and made an effort to stand. With Doug's support he made it to the car. On the way home he made sounds like fragmentary sentences. Straining, Doug made out what sounded like "hell fire and brimstone."

"Don't try to talk, Damon," Doug told him. "We can talk later."

"Hell fire and brimstone," Damon repeated. "What you gonna do with me?"

Doug restrained a chuckle. "First, I'm gonna take you home. Then I'm gonna sober you up. Then I'm gonna put you to bed."

"Um, um."

Maude was under the porch light waiting for them, a robe drawn tightly around her neck. It was turning colder.

"Is he all right?"

Doug held Damon up and thrust him through the door. Maude followed them. "No permanent damage," he said.

"Oh Doug, he's drunk!"

She began to cry.

"I'm afraid so. I think Damon's training to be a good ol' boy."

"Don't try to be funny, Doug," she said between sobs. "Shall I make him some coffee?"

"No," he directed her. "I'm taking him to the bathroom. Bring me two raw eggs in a glass."

After Damon threw up, Doug got him into pajamas and to bed. Every now and again Damon made sounds as if he wanted to speak, but Doug discouraged him. "Sleep it off, Damon. We'll talk tomorrow." He gave him a pat on the shoulder, raised the shade enough to admit a shaft of moonlight, and left him snoring. Going to the master bedroom, he found Maude sitting up, two pillows behind her head, sniffling into a handkerchief.

"He's sleeping," he told her as he undressed. "He'll be all right, maybe a bit of a hangover, but all right by the time we've had breakfast. Try not to fret. I'll speak to him in the morning."

"But where was he? What was he doing? Why did the police call?"

Doug didn't answer till he was in pajamas and beside her.

"He and some of his friends were celebrating after the game. The police picked them up for reckless driving and disturbing the peace. They were in Chip's car, so I suppose it was Chip who was driving. The cops took them in but didn't charge them, out of consideration for their age and the circumstances, I suppose."

"Oh Doug, do you think Damon is growing away from us?"

"Damon, sweetheart, is fifteen going on sixteen. He's growing up, not away."

She wiped her eyes with the sleeve of her gown. He took her in his arms. "What would I do without you, darling?" she said and kissed him sweetly on the lips. She put her head down and closed her eyes. He lay there sleepless, holding her fast, rehearsing what he would say to Damon tomorrow.

ABOUT TEN IN THE MORNING, after a late breakfast with Maude, Doug roused Damon with a cup of black coffee. "Drink this, son."

Damon groaned and raised himself on an elbow.

"Take these, too." Doug handed him two aspirin tablets. "Get up and get dressed as soon as you can. Your mother has breakfast waiting."

Damon took the aspirin with a full glass of water and followed with a swallow of coffee.

"That should help," Doug said sympathetically. "I'll see you later."

He was leaving the room when Damon called him back. "Are you ashamed of me?"

Doug thought for a moment. "I may be more surprised than ashamed." Damon started to say something more but Doug cut him off. "We'll talk later, son. Now go on, take a shower and put your clothes on."

When fifteen minutes later Damon came into the kitchen, Maude put her arms around him and gave him a strong hug. She found it difficult to talk. She had a second cup of coffee while he ate his eggs and toast in silence.

Doug left the two of them and went to the bathroom to shave. He could not account for the way he was feeling. His headache had left him hours ago. He was wide awake, alert, and though he was uncertain how the coming talk with Damon might go, he was not crippled by his usual morning anxiety. He was in control, confident in a way he'd not felt in years. It fleetingly occurred to him that if indeed his depression was ignited by a neural dislocation in the brain, maybe events of the past several weeks had worked like electric shock. He would remember to ask Izzy.

He went to the breakfast room as Damon was finishing the last bite of grits. Maude poured a fresh cup of coffee for him and left after giving him a weak smile she meant to be encouraging.

He sat down and faced his son. "Damon?"

"Yes, sir."

"Are you ready to talk?"

Damon squirmed. "I don't know what to say."

"You might start by telling me what happened last night."

Damon inhaled audibly. His lips were drawn and his eyes looked on the verge of tears. "First, tell me, does Mother know?"

"She knows that you were drunk. I told her the cops picked up you and your friends for drunken driving and disturbing the peace. She does not know the cops found you in a house of prostitution, and I hope she never does."

"Thanks, Daddy." Damon began to weep. Doug waited.

"Now tell me what got into you. You've not made a habit of drinking hard liquor, have you? I've never smelled it on you before."

"The first time. Nothing stronger than ale ever before."

"So?"

"Chip had lifted a bottle of Bourbon from his father, and after the game we just started riding around town and drinking and singing 'On to Victory' and yelling 'To hell with Tech High,' till one of the guys suggested we call on Miss Myrna. I'd never seen the inside of a—a whore house—and I went along. By the time we got there all of us had had too much to drink, I guess."

"I guess," Doug agreed sourly. He took a long look at his son before resuming. "Let me tell you how I feel, Damon. First, I'm relieved. Very relieved. We've never lied to each other, and I know you're telling me the truth. I was much more troubled by the fact that you were found drunk than that you were found in a whore house. You're too young to start drinking and, believe me, liquor can be a problem. I don't want you visiting whores, for reasons I hope you understand, but let's not make too much of it." He paused, wondering what to say next. "But you knew what the gang was doing was wrong. Driving while drunk is illegal. It's also stupid and dangerous. And you're probably under the legal age—if there is such a thing—to go to a whore house, although the cops seem to take a peculiarly lenient attitude toward all the customers regardless of age. It's the poor whores who get fined and sometimes put out of business. You do realize, I hope, how lucky you are, don't you? You could be in jail right now."

He saw fear and guilt in Damon's eyes. He remembered what it had been like for him when he was fifteen. He must be careful not to be too forgiving. "Now, what I want to know is, when Chip started passing the bottle around, why didn't you just say no, get out of the car, and come home?"

Damon now looked bewildered; the answer, he thought, should be obvious. "Why? I guess because I didn't want them calling me a sissy."

"You're better than that, Damon. Nobody's expecting you to be one of the boys, especially the other boys."

"I don't know what you mean."

"Well, some of us—by birth or experience or personality—are leaders. Others aren't necessarily fated to be followers, but most of us are content to play follow the leader all our lives. You're leader material. Can you believe that? The other boys will take their cue from you. You don't ever have to betray yourself to be one of the boys."

"I wonder sometimes exactly who or what I am." Damon was speaking in gulps, his eyes fixed on his empty plate. "Help me."

Doug leaned back and lowered his tone, hoping to ease the tension. "There's an episode in *War and Peace*," he said, thinking how odd that Tolstoy would once again, and so soon, enter his mind so instructively. "There's a place in *War and Peace* where the French enter this small village on their way to Moscow. The mayor is trying to rally the people and protect the village, but he's making a serious mistake. He acts as if he's an ordinary citizen. 'I'm one of you,' he keeps saying. The people booed him and threw fruit at him and finally chased him from the town square. The thing was, they didn't want a mayor who was one of them. They wanted a mayor who was better and a lot smarter than they were. They wanted a leader, not a peer. Do you understand what I'm saying, Damon?"

"I shouldn't try to be like the other boys?"

"Exactly. You should be yourself. You should accept the fact that you're smarter, more talented, more sensitive. You've got to learn to live with your natural superiority and take responsibility for it."

"But I don't feel superior."

"Good. I'm glad. I'm not saying that you should act as if everybody else is your inferior. The trick, I guess, is to behave modestly, to be comfortable with the fact that you're gifted, that you were born with a better brain and a more attractive body than most of us."

Damon sniffed. "You're just trying to make me feel better."

"Of course I am. But not *just*. Any time you act as if you're just anybody's son, not my son, I'm disappointed in you."

Damon raised his head and his voice in a flash of defiance. "Are you saying you've never given me reason to be disappointed in *you?*"

Doug sucked in his breath. "No, son," he said quietly. "But what you may not know is how much I've tried, how it's hurt ever to have failed you."

Damon began to weep. "I know, Daddy. I shouldn't have said that. I really do know. I didn't mean what I said."

"Oh yes you did, Damon. And for good reason." Doug sighed heavily. "But if it can make you feel any less disappointed in me, please remember that even when I've been at my worst, impossibly self-absorbed, I've thought of you. I've loved you. I'll always love you."

Damon squirmed. "I think I've always known that."

Doug reached over and patted Damon on the arm. He laughed nervously. "I guess that's enough of that. The question now is, what do we do to get beyond this."

"You mean, what are you going to do about me?"

"I don't think there's anything much to do. It's not as if you're in danger of becoming an alcoholic or a whoremonger. And I've tried to tell you plainly what our expectations are of you. From here on I think it's a matter of your setting your own expectations and living up to them."

"You mean you're not even going to ground me for a week?"

"Would it make you feel any better to be grounded?"

Damon smiled and shook his head.

"I tell you what," Doug said. "It cost me twenty dollars to spring you."

"But I don't have twenty dollars."

"Some day," Doug said wryly, "when you're older, you can pay me back."

SHORTLY BEFORE NOON, Doug got a phone call from Charles McLauren. "Chip will be calling to apologize for last night," Dr. McLauren said. "But I thought first it would be good to get our stories straight. How much have you told Mrs. Krueger?"

"Only that the boys were picked up for drunken driving and disturbing the peace."

McLauren laughed. "Good. That's what I told Chips's Aunt Julia. Nothing about the call on Miss Myrna?"

"Nothing."

"Chip feels terrible."

"So does Damon."

"Chip thinks he's flunked as a Big Brother."

"Let's say he's just slipped. My wife and I are very fond of Chip."

"And he is of you. I think that's what may be troubling him the most. That Mrs. Krueger especially may not like him anymore."

"She'll take care of that. I married a very intelligent woman."

The line went silent for a moment. "I guess that does it," McLauren said awkwardly. "Except that I'd like to meet you. Perhaps you and Mrs. Krueger could join me for dinner one night."

ON WEDNESDAY AFTERNOON the next week Damon again went joy riding with the Butler twins. Once again Gregory behaved like a recent initiate into the Junior Klan.

A very skinny black woman was standing at a car stop. She was wearing a long plaid coat, probably a discard from her employer's closet, and she was carrying a brown paper bag full of leftovers, which would be her family's supper. She was tired. She had been working since six that morning and her body was sore from heavy lifting, for it was fall-cleaning time and the lady she worked for had had trouble figuring how she wanted the furniture rearranged. Every now and again she would rub her left shoulder, where the pain from a strained muscle was concentrated. Otherwise she was motionless. To Damon, from his position in the back seat of the Butler boys' convertible, she appeared to have her eyes closed, the better, he guessed, to catch the sound of an approaching streetcar.

Whush!

"Get back there, nigger!"

Alarmed, the woman opened her eyes and jumped back. The paper bag fell from her hands and broke on the sidewalk below. She looked at the mess of potatoes and greens and ham at her feet. She broke into tears.

"Stop the car," Damon shouted over the Butler twins' laughter. "Stop!"

Fred slammed on the brakes, responding without thinking to the tone of command in Damon's voice. Damon reached for his trombone case and let himself out of the car. From the curb, he spoke angrily. "That wasn't funny. You owe that woman an apology, and the cost of her dinner, too."

"Go to hell," Gregory said.

"If you won't apologize, I will." Damon turned and started moving toward the car stop, where the woman was still shaking and crying. Behind him, he heard Gregory say, "I never knew you were a nigger-lover!"

Damon turned and faced him. "Now you do," he said forcefully. "Don't wait for me. I'll walk from here on."

At the sight of Damon the woman pulled her coat up around her neck and stepped back. Fear was in her eyes and her cheeks were damp with tears.

"Please don't be afraid," Damon said. "What happened—I can't tell you how sorry I am."

Bewildered, the woman frowned. She said nothing.

Damon reached into his pants pocket and pulled out three quarters and a dime. It was his lunch money for the rest of the week. He pressed the coins into her palm. "Please, take this." He stooped and picked up an apple and a piece of cornbread that had survived the fall to the sidewalk. He gave them to her. She took the food silently, as she had the coins. She was confused now. She nodded in a gesture of dubious appreciation.

Damon floundered. "I can't speak for my—" He caught himself, realizing that he was about to say "friends." He stammered. "They don't understand," he heard himself say. "They're Yankees."

THE NEXT AFTERNOON, Damon went early to band practice. The Butler twins were there ahead of him, waiting. They came over to the brass section, pulled up two straight chairs, and sat down facing him. Their eyes had the uncommonly alert look of someone who couldn't sleep and Damon expected a confrontation. Instead, Gregory spoke contritely. "We've been thinking."

Damon wanted to say, "That must have been hard for you." He kept quiet.

"We think you were right yesterday," Gregory went on.

"That was a mean cheap thing we did," said Fred.

There was something different about them. Damon didn't know what it was until Greg spoke again. They had dropped the fake Southern accents.

"We won't do it again."

"And we won't say nigger again, either," said Fred.

Damon couldn't believe his ears. "What came over you?"

Gregory blushed. "We saw you talking with that colored lady—"

"She was crying."

"We began to feel bad."

"And last night Daddy started a big fuss with us."

"He'd noticed the scuff marks on the tires and wanted to know how they'd got there."

"We told him we'd hit the curb, and he said it looked like more than once."

"Then he asked us if we'd been racing."

"We said no, but then we told him what we had been doing, and I must say he was some put out."

"It made him mad?"

"As mad as I've ever seen him," said Gregory. "What he said was, we'd been trying too hard to act Southern."

"Or what we thought was Southern."

"He said we should cut it out."

"He said we should be ourselves, not to hide that we come from Chicago."

They paused, waiting for some expression of approval from Damon.
"We should listen more to our fathers," Damon said thoughtfully.
Gregory put out his hand. "Can we still be friends?"

34

With passage of the 1934 Federal Communications Act, Congress created the Federal Communications Commission, which promptly announced its intent to license more radio channels. Now, with the renewal of his old entrepreneurial spirit, Doug called on Professor Hunter.

"Atlanta could use another radio station. I'm thinking about organizing a corporation and applying for a license. Would Tech be interested?"

"You mean interested in owning a nonprofit, public service station?"

"Oh no. That battle's been lost. I have in mind a commercial station. Tech would be the principal shareholder. The station would be advertiser-supported. Tech would commit its share of profits to public service."

"And what would your position be, Douglas?"

"I'd be the second biggest shareholder and chief executive officer."

Jack Hunter was sixty-one, almost completely bald and grown a bit portly. His eyes failing, he wore wire-rimmed glasses with thick lenses and he sometimes had the look of a startled fawn. He was a kindly man, fond of Doug, and this afternoon, after a light lunch at his desk of chicken salad and milk, in a particularly receptive mood.

Of the several hundred male students Hunter had taught electrical engineering in his twenty-five years at Tech, Doug was one of no more than a handful that he remembered distinctively and with affection. Not only had Doug made straight A's; he had also demonstrated an enthusiasm for problem-solving and a brilliant talent for innovation. Hunter could recall in remarkable detail the sound-and-light effects Doug had designed for the senior-class production of *Dracula*.

He listened now with partisan interest. "That's an intriguing idea. How much of a dollar investment are we talking about?"

"Maybe as much as thirty thousand for start-up."

"And how much of that would you expect from Tech?"

Doug drew a deep breath. "Perhaps all of it. I'd handle all the preparation on deferred compensation, taking it in shares. The thirty thousand would go for hardware—the transmitter, the studio, broadcasting equipment, that sort of thing."

Hunter sighed. "We'd have a hard time getting the Regents to put up thirty thousand dollars on speculation."

"Not even with the reasonable expectation of a ten percent first-year profit?"

"A reasonable expectation?"

"The average profit for the industry last year was fourteen percent. WSB earned twenty percent."

"Are you sure?"

"If you can believe the *New York Times*. We could be even more profitable. It's only a matter of time—perhaps only a matter of months—before there's a third network. They're going to need an Atlanta affiliate, and it could be us."

"You sound very convincing, Douglas. How easy is it to get a license?"

"With Tech as a petitioner? It shouldn't be difficult. Provided our application is up to snuff."

"Hmmm."

"This will be my second try for a license," Doug said. "I filed some years ago, in Hastings. I was turned down in favor of the *Courier*. Here, look at this." He reached into his briefcase and pulled out a file folder. "I was so disappointed at the time I was ready to burn the records. But Maude, bless her heart, insisted we save them."

They sat quietly, the silence broken only by an increasingly frequent number of "Hmms" from Hunter as he turned the pages. When he was done, he smiled and said, "That's an impressive piece of work, Douglas." He swiveled in his chair, looking vacantly out the window. Doug waited, his pulse quickening. After a punishing amount of time, Hunter turned to face him. “How long will it take you to prepare the application?”

“Three weeks. Perhaps two if you could lend me a couple of bright students to help me update the technical data.”

Hunter consulted his desk calendar. “The Board of Regents meets on November 11, five weeks from today. I’ll ask Brittain—President Brittain—to put you on the agenda. Can you be ready?”

The Regents approved his proposal, with an appropriation of thirty thousand dollars. The only caveat was that programming be strictly nonpartisan.

With that, Doug turned his attention to the application. “The Georgia School of Technology,” he began, “proposes to invest in a private for-profit corporation for the development and operation of a 500-watt commercial radio station. It will be the principal shareholder. All profits received from its shares will be donated to the Tech Foundation for the Advancement of Science, Education, and the Arts.”

He had completed the rationale and was assembling the relevant exhibits when he got a call from Alan Spalding.

“Mr. Krueger? To my regret, we’ve never met. I’m Agnes’s father and your son’s tennis partner.”

Doug immediately took to the voice. Alan Spalding sounded like a man of reason with a sense of humor. He said, “Damon speaks of you often. We have a lot to thank you for. Especially now, for finding a bed in that polio hospital in Alabama for my friend Walt Seymour’s boy.”

“Don’t thank me,” Spalding said. “Thank Mrs. Roosevelt. She was the one who insisted that we create a facility for Negroes.”

“Still, you got him there, and the family is eternally grateful to you.”

“Glad to have been of help,” Spalding said, clearly impatient to change the subject. “Now, let me tell you why I called.”

“Yes, sir.”

“Damon tells me you’re drafting plans for another radio station in Atlanta.”

“Well, it’ll be Tech’s station. I’m handling the application for a license.”

“Damon says you’re totally involved. It’s your idea. When the corporation gets chartered you'd be chairman, and when you go on the air you'll be general manager. Right?"

"That's how I'd like it."

"Well, let me know when you issue stock."

"You mean it?"

"Absolutely. I'd like to be your first public investor. The town could use another station."

Doug's cheeks went warm and his throat tightened. He couldn't speak.

"Mr. Krueger . . . ?"

"I'm still here. I think I must have choked up." He recovered himself. "It's very generous of you, Mr. Spalding."

"Call me Alan. And it's not generous of me at all. I pride myself on being a good businessman."

"I'd like to meet you."

"And I you. How about lunch Thursday at the Capital City Club? Say twelve-thirty."

"I'll be there."

"One other thing, Doug—if I may call you Doug. Wouldn't it be a good idea to include, say as an endorsement of the proposal, the signatures of twenty or more civic leaders. I don't mean to be immodest, but people like myself?"

"Indeed it would."

"You draft the statement and I'll get the signatures."

Doug choked again. Before he could speak Alan Spalding had another question.

"Do you know Bob Carmichael?"

"The Congressman? No, I'm afraid I don't."

"He could help. I'll speak to him."

Two weeks later the application, with endorsements by twenty-five of Spalding's friends, augmented by signatures of fifteen Copernicans, was in the mail to the Federal Communications Commission.

Shortly thereafter Doug got a receipt saying that the assignment of new channels would be made and announced in January. The notice came from a commissioner named Smith—the same D. G. Smith who nine years earlier as a Commerce Department staffer had called Doug's rejected proposal "superb."

35

Doug heard the phone ringing as he was opening the front door. He caught it on the fifth ring. "Douglas?" He had trouble recognizing the voice. The accent seemed both sharper and flatter.

"Azalie?"

"I'm calling from an apartment on Boulevard. I've been here for six weeks or so, but I haven't been able to bring myself to call you."

"You've been in Atlanta six weeks?"

"That's right. I've been a library consultant at Atlanta University, helping plan a special collections department."

"But why have you waited so long to let me know? I'd love to see you."

Azalie coughed.

"Have you got a cold?"

"Just a frog in my throat." She paused. "I didn't call sooner because I really think we ought to get over it, just get out of each other's mind."

"Oh God, Azalie. If only I could."

Another pause.

"Anyway," she resumed, "I'm leaving tomorrow afternoon and I've decided I'd like to see you. I have something for you. Can you come over tomorrow morning, say about ten?"

He had promised Maude he'd put up the Christmas tree that morning, to be decorated before they left for Arabella's party; Maude was of a traditional mind and did not believe in putting up the tree before Christmas Eve. Now he made his excuses. "I just learned. There's a job opening in Decatur. The county works department is hiring an inspector. Tomorrow's the last day for interviews, and the office closes at noon."

He saw the disappointment in her eyes. "I'll bring in the tree before I go," he said. "I should be back before one and we can spend all afternoon together on the trimming."

"Will the job pay more than the WPA?"

He took a deep breath. "Twice as much."

He got up early and with Damon's help brought in the tree from the garage where he'd been keeping it in a bucket of water hoping it would stay as fresh as Maude demanded. It was a handsome balsam fir, fully seven feet tall, with thick, spreading branches. It took the two of them only fifteen minutes to bring it in the house but forty-five minutes to get it standing straight and, after several tries, in a place in the living room that satisfied Maude's perfectionist eye. When they were done Maude gave them breakfast of fried eggs, bacon, and pancakes. Doug then drove Damon to the corner of Boulevard and Ponce de Leon, where Damon was to be picked up at eight-thirty by Andy Flaherty for a day on the bread route.

Doug breathed easier once he was on his way. He didn't like having to lie to Maude, but any reference to Azalie, he believed, was likely to summon ghosts and it would be just as well if Maude didn't know where he was going this morning. Azalie had said ten. He had an hour to kill. He spent it in the wood shop at Tech sanding and putting a last coat of polish on a bookcase.

Azalie was quick to answer his knock. They embraced, kissed, and stood back at arm's length, each to get a good look at the other.

"You've still got that gorgeous hair," she said.

"And you those incredible eyes."

There was a small fire going from gas logs. She directed him to a chair on the right of the hearth while she sat down in a matching chair on the left. She laughed nervously. "Would you like some coffee?"

He shook his head and tried to relax.

"Well!" he said.

"It's been a long time," she said.

She was wearing a dress with a mandarin collar that drew his eyes to her long neck. She was as beautiful as he remembered. Her wiry black hair was cut close to her perfectly proportioned head, her skin was the color of café au lait, her lips full, her teeth even and white. It had taken generations of miscegenation to make her. "You haven't changed a bit," he said.

"Don't look too close. I'm a lot older."

"And wiser?"

"Maybe." She was about to run out of small talk. "The apartment belongs to the head librarian at Spelman. She had an extra room and offered it to me for the time I'd be on assignment here. It beats camping out in a hotel."

"It's very pleasant."

She straightened her shoulders and took a deep breath, "I'm leaving the country, Doug."

"For the holidays?"

"I mean I'm leaving the country for good. Paul is in Liberia. He's taking over as dean of the law school there. I'm taking the train to Chicago this afternoon and this time next Monday I'll be leaving to join him in Monrovia. We'll be married immediately after I get there."

"In Liberia?"

"He's been after me to marry him for five years. I don't know why but I never seemed ready in Chicago."

"And now you do?"

"I think so." She smiled. "Somehow it seems right, getting married in Liberia."

He recalled what little he knew about Liberia: on the west coast of Africa; founded before the Civil War by black freedmen; a republic modeled after the United States; population probably less than three million.

"It should be a great experience for you."

"I've got a job with the State Department. In the cultural affairs office."

"What does that mean you'll be doing?"

"Bringing American artists and writers and scholars into the country for lectures and performances. Staging exhibitions of one kind or another. Promoting native arts and crafts for export. Things like that. The great thing is that the concept's so new I'll have a chance to develop the program from scratch."

"I'm terribly pleased for you," he said.

She shifted in her chair and changed the subject. "And you, Douglas? How's it been with you?"

He told her. "I'm coming out of it, I think. At least I can work now."

"I never realized. It must have been awful for you."

"The awful part—all these years I've lived feeling I should have behaved better by you and our child."

She fixed her eyes on his. "What do you think you should—could—have done differently?"

"I don't know exactly." He told her what he had told Izzy earlier. "Maybe I should have said to hell with Papa and taken us to Canada, or France, where we might have had a chance for a life together."

She sighed. "You've always had trouble being practical, haven't you, Douglas?" There was a hint of exasperation in her voice. "What can I say? How in the world could you—how old were you, eighteen?—how could you have found the means to take us to Canada or Paris? In the circumstance, there was absolutely nothing else for you to do but what your father was telling you to do. There've been times, believe me, when I've felt almost blessed by him." Now she spoke in sorrow and anger. "You have no idea what it's like to have to live with prejudice and discrimination. At least your father spared you that. And as for me, thanks to your father I got an education, a Ph.D. no less, and have been able to live well and raise a child in comfort for ten years. Without you."

"But haven't you ever wondered how it might have been with me?"

"Of course. But let's not romanticize or sentimentalize our affair—our very brief affair, I remind you. We were very young. We were infatuated. But I'm not sure we were truly in love. I'm even less sure that whatever we felt for each other could have lasted."

He shrugged. "Sometimes I think you're too Goddamned practical."

She grew solemn. "I went through some bad days after Douglas died. I kept blaming myself. If I'd only recognized the symptoms and gotten him to a doctor sooner."

"But isn't that the thing about meningitis, that the early symptoms are so deceptive?"

She ignored him. "If it hadn't been for Paul I don't think I could have gotten through it." She plucked at a bit of lint on her sleeve distractedly. "Anyway, it's all behind us now. We should try to be content with the memory and get on with it." She paused and looked vacantly at the fake flames from the gas logs. "I don't expect to see you again."

"Is that how you want it?"

"Damn it, Douglas. That's how it's got to be."

He closed his eyes. She had relieved his heart of a great and corrosive weight.

It was time to go. He started to rise from his chair, then remembered. "You said you had something for me?"

She picked up an envelope from the coffee table and held it, momentarily uncertain that she should give it to him. "I found this while I was sorting through things and packing before I left Chicago. Douglas was about seven when he wrote it. I didn't send it to you at the time because I thought it would be too painful for you." She looked dubious. "I'm still not sure."

He reached across the table and took the envelope from her. He opened it, his fingers trembling, and unfolded a faded message written in pencil on a ruled sheet torn from a school boy's tablet:

> DEAR DADDY, I have BEEN THINKing about you and WONDERING. WHAT iS it like IN HEAVEN?
>
> MAMA SAYS I SHOULD be good aND BrAVE LIKE you. I TRY.
>
> I LOVE YOU.
>
> YOUR SON,
>
> DOUGLAS KRUEGER, jr.

He couldn't speak.

"Oh Douglas. It was a mistake. I shouldn't have given it to you."

He gulped and wiped his eyes. "No, no. It might be the dearest thing you could have done for me. It makes me feel proud. And loved, in a way

I never thought anybody could love me." He suppressed another sob. "You were good to give him that image of me."

"I told him you were missing in action and buried somewhere in France, an unknown soldier."

"Now I'm beginning to feel like a fraud."

She studied him, not sure that he was serious. "I guess the important thing is how Doug Junior was made to feel."

"Of course."

He pushed the chair back and rose. She followed him to the door.

"I wish you—and Paul—everything good. But I don't know quite how to think of you in Liberia. Are you sure it's safe?"

She laughed softly. "Safer than Chicago."

He opened the door and stepped into the hall, then turned back and pulled her into his arms. He hugged her tightly and gave her a full kiss on the lips.

It was then that Damon turned from the door of Apartment C-34 at the far end of the corridor after delivering two loaves of rye bread to old Mrs. Yancey.

MAUDE AND DOUG GOT BACK from Arabella's party shortly after midnight. On the whole it had been Maude's sort of party. The company was small and familiar. The talk was congenial and not of a kind to raise anybody's blood pressure; the gossip was benign. Those whom the hard liquor moved to reminiscence told stories mostly of happy Christmases past, and there was general agreement that Roosevelt would run against token opposition and be reelected in a landslide. Arabella's supper, for which Maude had contributed a date nut cake, was hot and sobering. And, thank God, nobody had wanted to play games.

Toward the end of the evening the party had turned into a celebration. Looking shy and embarrassed, Arabella announced: "I guess you all ought to know." She held up what looked like a paperback book in a brown wrapper. "I've written a novel and found a New York publisher, and yesterday the publisher sent me this bound copy of page proofs." She went on, speaking over the applause. "I'm told it'll be out sometime in May." Then she paused and took a deep breath. "The title is *Sex and Segregation.*"

(Little did Arabella imagine, when the book came out five months later it would be immediately banned in Boston as obscene. A week after publication it hit the *New York Times* bestseller list and stayed there for eight months. Bessie had been right. Arabella had used "that word" no fewer than four times.)

Maude had never been one to dwell on old injuries and disappointments, nor was she one who counted her blessings in public. She was even-tempered by nature and under the guidance of her Lutheran father she had cultivated an analytical mind that did not easily blow a fuse. Moreover, from childhood she had been taught to think of herself as one among equals, even though she was transparently superior in every way that mattered. Her father would have agreed with Izzy: "Self-pity is the eighth deadly sin."

This Christmas morning she could not go to bed until she had made the three pounds of butter mints for Mrs. Norcross. She encouraged Doug to go on to bed without her, but he refused; if she wouldn't let him help her pull the mints he would just sit there and watch her do it. She didn't try hard to dissuade him, for it was sweet for the two of them to be together, just the two of them, in the quiet of the early morning. She allowed herself to feel almost happy. Doug had gotten through the evening without any signs of returning despair. Moreover, he had had his first Scotch in three years. He had nursed the one drink throughout the party with apparently no desire for a second and with no ill effect. She could not help believing that the worst was over.

Damon slept until almost ten Christmas morning. His father had left the house a half hour before, to be with Catherine so Bessie could have a Christmas visit with her daughter on Auburn Avenue. The plan was for Maude and Damon to join him at noon for eggnog with Catherine, then at two or thereabouts, by which time Bessie would have returned, the three of them would go back to Penn Avenue for Christmas dinner.

His mother was in the kitchen. The turkey was in the oven and everything else was waiting to be put on the stove: rice, cranberries, sweet potatoes, okra (battered for frying), pole beans with almonds, and corn bread. The pies—mincemeat and pumpkin—Maude had baked yesterday and needed only to be warmed. She was at the sink washing her hands, singing to herself what she could remember of "Good King Wenceslas" when she heard Damon come in. She turned and gave him a kiss. "Would you like a full breakfast or would coffee and a cinnamon roll hold you?"

"That and a bowl of cornflakes," he said, yawning. The kitchen heat seemed to start at the waist and dissipate into the ceiling. He pulled his robe tighter around his knees. "I'll get going as quickly as I can."

"No need to hurry," she said. "Just make sure you get back by eleven-thirty."

"Grandmother's in a coma, isn't she?"

"I'm afraid so. And I don't think she's likely to come out of it."

"And she can't recognize us?"

"No."

"Then what should we do while we're with her?"

Maude looked at him sharply.

"You sound as if you don't want to go."

"I didn't mean that. It's just so sad. And awkward."

"Make no mistake, Damon. None of us has any idea what your Grandmother can feel, or sense. But don't assume she can feel nothing. Quite possibly she can hear. So while we're there we'll talk to her, and we'll hold her hand, and we'll kiss her and, of course, tell her how much we love her. Over and over. It will mean more to her than we have any way of knowing."

"If I've got the car how did Daddy get to Grandmother's?"

"Hortense left us the keys to her Nash."

Damon thought about his grandmother and then about Strut, Trudy, and Alice. "It's not going to be a very merry Christmas, is it, mother? This is the first Christmas I can remember when there were only the three of us for dinner."

"I know." She moved impulsively to give him another kiss. "I had hoped the Moneypennys might join us, but Hortense's parents insisted they spend the holidays with them at Sea Island." She sighed. "We'll have to do our best. We can at least be glad we've got one another, the three of us." It was a feeble thing to say. She tried to do better. "Your grandfather used to say joy never comes but what grief is sure to follow, and vice versa. Just a moment ago I was thinking how happy I am."

"Happy?"

"That we're together. That somebody wants to buy my butter mints. That we've got such good neighbors. That Doug is getting better."

"You think he's getting better?"

"Don't you?"

"Maybe. I haven't seen enough of him to notice. He hasn't had much time for me."

"I would have said it's you who hasn't had much time for him."

"You think I've not been as close to him as I should?"

"Let's just say I don't think you understand his condition."

"His depression? I guess I don't. Sometimes I think he's just given up, and I don't understand why. Most of the time he looks perfectly normal to me."

"Oh Damon!"

"I know. Someday, when I'm older, I'll understand. I'm tired of being told that. What is there about depression I don't understand?"

"Just about everything. That it can come without warning, that it's disabling, exhausting, painful, and frightening—and a lot more that nobody understands. But don't make the mistake of thinking your father had given up. He may be the bravest man you'll ever know."

BUT WOULD DEPRESSION account for betrayal? What was his father doing in the apartment of that colored woman? And who was she? From his observation of their intimacy as they were parting in the doorway, it was no brief acquaintanceship. What had brought his father to do this? How could he be carrying on with another woman? How could he do this to Maude? The thought produced a touch of nausea. Should he tell his mother? Of course not. Should he confront his father? He might.

His mother was speaking. "Maybe the time has come for you to have a talk with Dr. Orenstein."

Damon took a last bite of the cinnamon roll. It seemed to calm his stomach. "That might be a very good idea," he said. "There are times when I look at Dad and wonder, why doesn't he just pull himself together and—"

At that she raised her voice. She was screaming, mocking him. "Why doesn't he just pull himself together?" Her eyes watered. "I'm ashamed of you, Damon. I thought you knew better. I thought you were more caring." She sniffled and cleared her throat. "You don't know what you're talking about."

Damon pushed his chair back and rose. "Maybe I ought to get going."

"Yes," she said, her lips drawn in suppressed anger. She put the tin of mints in his hand and left him.

IT WAS A SIX-MILE DRIVE to the Norcrosses' house on West Pace's Ferry Road. Except for an occasional jitney, the streets were clear of traffic. Damon remembered that the street cars were on holiday schedule, running only every two hours. All the stores were closed and, according to denominational tradition, Christmas services were either over or would not begin for another hour. He decided to go straight out Peachtree, although on a normal day it would have been quicker to go by Piedmont Avenue. He turned onto Peachtree at Fifth Street and proceeded through neighborhoods that progressively delineated the caste system of Northside Atlanta—first, the modest nondescript homes of lower middle-income families; next the larger brick bungalows of the stable middle class; then the old Georgian-style houses, some of them residuals of antebellum estates, of the upper middle class; and finally the relatively new mansions of the very rich. He drove past the Tenth Street Theater ("Back by popular demand, *Dinner at Eight*"), past the meandering, sixteen-room green-frame Windham house set back on four acres near Thirteenth Street, past Peacock Alley and the far entrance to Ansley Park at Nineteenth Street, past Brookwood Station, and from there to Peachtree Hills, Garden Hills, and Buckhead. It had rained lightly just before sunrise. Now the air was clean and cool and bracing. (Years later during World War II, choking on the dust of New Guinea, he would think of Atlanta's air with acute homesickness; Atlanta to him would always mean clean air and even cleaner water—water that went down like liquid silk, so soft that you had to be careful in the shower not to use too much soap; so pure, in fact, that some druggists eschewed distilled water and preferred to mix prescriptions from the tap.)

Buckhead, west of Peachtree, had developed slowly in the early twentieth century with the coming of the automobile and an accompanying urge among the newly affluent to move beyond the confines of Druid Hills and Ansley Park. Most of the early residents had prospered from the industrialization and explosive commerce of Reconstruction, and in a time of low or no taxes they had acquired both great wealth and an obsession to display it. They built enormous mansions, most of them neo-Colonial or Italianate, on twenty- to forty-acre lots fronted by meticulously tended lawns. Almost without exception each property was defined by a magnificently hospitable tree—a giant magnolia or a tall spreading oak or a sentinel pine, and not uncommonly the big trees sheltered stands of dogwoods, maples, and poplars. It was winter now and the denuded oaks and poplars stood in the landscape like abstract sculptures. But bordering the houses and their dependencies was a profusion of evergreens—boxwoods and yews and hemlocks. Many of them were decorated and lit for the season, as were some of the large pines, their colors diminished but not entirely lost in the mid-morning sunlight.

Unlike the Italian Baroque style of its neighbors, the Norcross house was English Regency, a sedate wood-frame mansion that sat at the end of a hundred-yard driveway. The exterior was painted yellow to enhance the white portico and green shutters. Its central portion had a pristine Palladian motif and a wrought-iron railing above the doorway. Approaching the house, Damon felt smaller and smaller.

Dry-mouthed, he stood at the doorway, rang the bell, and waited. The face of an attractive young black woman appeared at a window. She smiled. "Would you mind goin' 'round to the kitchen? I just mopped the hall." She saw the question on his brow. "That way, honey. 'Round to the left, then right. It'll be the second door."

The tin of mints weighed no more than six pounds, but the walk to the kitchen was a long one. The house was flanked by twin recessed bays each the size of a studio apartment, and by the time Damon reached the kitchen he was winded. He was met at the door by a heavyset black woman who greeted him like a member of the family. "You're Damon, the Krueger boy," she said. "Your mama is an angel, but I guess you know that." She took the tin from him. "Can't tell how obliged I am for getting the mints to me today. Miz Norcross was some put out when she learnt I'd left the mints off our order."

Before Damon could speak, she was asking if he'd like a cup of coffee. She looked genuinely disappointed when Damon said no, he had to get back home as soon as he could. She gave him a ten-dollar bill and a fifty-cent piece. "The half dollar is yours."

Turning the corner of the house on his way back to the car, he crossed paths with a middle-aged man tossing a ball to a collie. The man was dressed in gray corduroy trousers, a red flannel jacket, and a gray cap. From the indifferent way he was playing with the dog and from the unhappy look on his face, Damon figured that either he had a hangover or his wife had shooed him from the house.

The collie gave a sharp bark and ran to Damon hoping to be petted. Damon squatted and obliged. "Merry Christmas, baby," he said.

"His name's Bobby," the man said, brightening, as if pleased to have company for the moment. "I'm Tom Norcross."

"I'm glad to meet you sir," Damon said, rising and taking his outstretched hand. "I'm Damon Krueger."

"I was at Tech with a Krueger. Doug Krueger."

"My father."

"Your mother must be Maude Krueger, the caterer."

"Yes, sir."

"I'm lost track of most of my old schoolmates. How long have you and your parents lived in Atlanta?"

"We moved here from Hastings four years ago."

Tom Norcross had a soft. friendly voice and an attitude of wistful resignation.

Here it comes.

"And what does your father do?"

Damon gave him his rehearsed answer. "He was an electrical engineer in Hastings. He hasn't done so well here."

Mr. Norcross asked no more questions. "These are rotten times. No time to start a new business."

He threw the ball into the middle of the lawn. Bobby scampered after it. "I'll walk with you to the car."

They walked in silence, enjoying the air and their new friendship. Damon didn't know quite why, but older men often seemed quite drawn to him.

"Mr. Norcross?"

"Yes, son."

"What was my daddy like when you knew him?"

"I didn't know him well. He was a couple of years behind me. I was studying business administration and he was in engineering. He was a Phi Delt, I think. I was a Chi Phi."

"But you knew him."

"Yes. I remember him as very bright, very good-looking, very talented. He did all the sets and wrote some of the songs for our annual show."

"He wrote songs?"

"Well, the lyrics anyway."

"Do you remember any of them?"

Mr. Norcross frowned. "One of them." He laughed. "But only a couple of lines." He sang in a parody of Gilbert and Sullivan: "Although they have the urge'n'all, Atlanta pinks stay virginal."

"My daddy wrote that?"

"Indeed he did."

"And he's never told me. That's what we say about Seminary girls today, in just those words."

Mr. Norcross laughed again.

"I guess there are just some things we fathers don't want our sons to know."

They had come to the car. "It was good talking with you, Mr. Norcross."

"My pleasure," Mr. Norcross said, closing the door after Damon had settled into the driver's seat. He called for Bobby, turned, and walked, Damon thought a bit sorrowfully, to the rear of the big house.

ON THE WAY BACK DOWN West Pace's Ferry Road to Peachtree, Damon again passed through Atlanta's sanctuary for the rich. (A labor agitator—a Communist, probably—once called it "a perfumed ghetto.") At this hour on Christmas morning, Damon seemed to be the only creature stirring. The vast lawns were deserted, the air was still, there was the sense that life was suspended between revelries. He scanned the houses as he drove—all architecturally distinctive but collectively a statement of money, station, and power. They conveyed pride but, curiously, pride without arrogance. There was about them, in fact, a natural assumption of class and birthright privilege, and a further assumption that their position would be admired and respected; there were no gates, no security staffs, no fear of intrusion, much less of burglary. Lord knows what went on behind their walls but Damon sensed that the pampered and insulated residents, certainly those of his generation, lived lives of innocence and sweet ignorance, unaware of or indifferent to the families only a few miles away who struggled daily against the corrupting evils of poverty and disease, and inevitably lost. Yet Damon envied these pretentious, self-invented new aristocrats more than he resented them. Bitterly, he told himself, this is where he too belonged; he would be here now had his father not gone to pieces. Someday, he vowed, he would own a house like one of these, if not in Buckhead then in a neighborhood equally orderly and elegant.

He had gone several blocks down Peachtree when the car started sputtering. He pumped the accelerator. The old Ford sighed, and died. There was barely enough momentum for him to get to the berm. He was out of gas.

Damn him! Obviously, his father had forgotten to put in four gallons yesterday as Maude had asked him to do—something that the three of them regarded as vital since the gasoline gauge had been broken for months. Now what was he to do? Any filling station within walking distance was closed for Christmas. It would be at least fifty minutes before a street car came by. There was no Samaritan in sight. Angry at his father, frustrated, helpless, he pounded on the dashboard with his fists and let out a cry of desperation. He took a deep breath, relaxed in defeat, and waited. Time passed.

He had been sitting for perhaps twenty minutes, his eyes half closed, head down, when he heard a pick-up truck pull up beside him and stop. He raised his head. At the window stood a young black man in overalls and a knitted skull cap, with a thick mustache that didn't quite hide a scar. Damon's stomach turned. Now he was going to be robbed! Without thinking, he felt in his pocket for the ten-dollar bill.

The man rapped at the car window. Hesitantly, Damon lowered the window.

The Negro smiled. "You in trouble?"

Damon could not return the smile. He swallowed hard. "I'm out of gas."

"I figgered," the black man said. "Don't fret. I'll have you going again in a jiff."

Damon watched as the man reached into the back of the pick-up and pulled out a five-gallon can of gasoline. A moment later he was pouring gas into the Ford. Damon got out of the car and stood with him, listening with inexpressible relief to the sound of the gasoline gurgling in the tank.

"You think a gallon will get you where you're going?"

Damon nodded.

The man looked thoughtful. "Let's give it a bit more just to make sure."

Damon found his voice. "Do you always drive with a spare can of gas?"

The Negro laughed. "When you're colored and—," he paused and shrugged, "you travel prepared."

Damon reached in his pocket. "How much do I owe you?"

"Nothin' a-tall, man. It's Christmas." The black man returned the can to the truck. Damon reached to shake his hand. The Negro paused, puzzled, then accepted the handshake.

"I don't know how to thank you," Damon said. "I got fifty cents for a delivery. Won't you take it?"

"Now don't you go spoilin' my good deed." The man gave Damon another broad smile and a friendly pat on the arm. He climbed into his truck and turned on the ignition. The truck moved forward. Damon ran to catch up and yelled over the sound of the motor. "What's your name? I don't even know your name."

Without turning, the stranger waved his hand and shouted, "Merry Christmas!"

"Merry Christmas," Damon said softly. He was choked with gratitude and with a quivery feeling that he'd been the beneficiary of something beyond human generosity.

IT WAS AFTER ONE O'CLOCK by the time he got home. His mother had changed into her best dress. His father was absent—still with Catherine, Damon assumed. Or maybe not. Maybe he'd taken a detour and stopped for a quickie with that woman. The thought almost nauseated him.

"We won't have time to see Catherine before dinner," Maude was saying. "Maybe we can run out there before you have to leave for your party."

"I ran out of gas."

"But—"

"I know. Daddy was supposed to have put in two dollars' worth. He didn't."

She grimaced. "Oh my dear. How'd you manage?"

"A black Samaritan came by. He gave me more than enough gas to get home on."

"How lucky." She didn't like the expression on his face. "Stop looking so sullen, Damon."

"I'm not sullen," he said sourly. "I'm mad. I could still be sitting there if that Negro hadn't come along."

"Your father just forgot, Damon. He has a lot of things on his mind."

"I bet," Damon said, and started to move away. "Here. Here's the ten dollars for the mints. I'll go change."

As he bathed and dressed he tried to get his father off his mind. He didn't like what he was thinking. Whatever good there was in him he owed his father, if not his mother. From his father he'd learned honesty and fair play and modesty and to be comfortable with himself. He couldn't square the virtuous man he'd always taken his father to be with the deceiving, unfaithful man he'd discovered his father to be only yesterday. What happened? How could it have happened? And as for his father's prolonged depression, his so-called sickness, what had brought that about and why couldn't he get over it? There were too many times when his father seemed perfectly normal; it was hard to believe that he couldn't cure himself if he truly wanted to.

He shook his head and put his mind on Bertha's birthday party that evening. Bertha had been blessed or cursed to have been born on Christmas day. How to observe her birthday in the midst of Christmas festivities had always been a problem for the family. This year, her parents were giving her a quiet dinner party to which no more than a dozen of her "very special" friends were invited. (Of the dozen, only Agnes wouldn't be there; as usual at Christmas she was somewhere abroad with her parents, this year in London.) Bertha's mother had appended a note to the invitation: "Please bring only your love and friendship."

Damon hadn't taken the request literally. He had made—or written—Bertha a gift far more memorable, far more personal, than anything he could have bought her. He had composed what he called "Merry Birthday: A Portrait of Bertha in Four-Four Time"—a duet for trombone and flute, Peggy Hirsch, Bertha's best girlfriend, supplying the flute. Bertha had yellow hair. She loved animals, baseball, and roses. She was studying art seriously and showed signs of becoming an accomplished painter, especially in watercolor. Out of such attributes Damon found it fun and relatively easy to construct a medley of tunes that captured her:

"Girl With the Flaxen Hair," "Pictures at an Exhibition," "The Carnival of Animals," "Take Me Out to the Ball Game," "My Wild Irish Rose." He laced them together in three different keys, sometimes his trombone dominating, sometimes Peggy's flute. For the close he fashioned a duel between "Jingle Bells" and "Happy Birthday." He and Peggy had rehearsed it a half dozen times. If all went well, Bertha should be as pleased with it as he was himself.

He was tying his tie when he heard a car pull up in the driveway. From wherever he'd been, and surely he couldn't have been all this time at Grandmother's, his father had returned.

THROUGHOUT CHRISTMAS DINNER Damon studied his father for signs of guilt or shame. He found none. On the contrary, after reporting somberly on his visit with Catherine, Doug seemed as relaxed as Damon had ever seen him. Moreover, he seemed buoyed by some anticipated joy. "This," he said more than once, "is going to be a Christmas to remember."

"Where were you?" Maude asked him. "What kept you?"

His father's eyes twinkled. "I had to run an errand," he said, and then, sorry that he'd said anything, "I'll tell you later."

By "later," it turned out, he meant after dessert when, as was their Christmas custom, they moved into living room and sat around the tree and opened their presents. Roger, as lovely as any ornament, was sound asleep under the tree.

Doug strove valiantly to keep his secret but when he could stand it no longer he burst out. "Let me go first." Astonished, Damon and Maude stared at him and waited.

The words came tumbling out. "After leaving Mother, I went by Dr. Hunter's house to wish him a Merry Christmas. While I was there a phone call came from Congressman Carmichael. The FCC, Carmichael says, has approved our application for a broadcast license."

Above the hullabaloo that followed—as much hullabaloo as three people could make—Doug shouted: "I feel like myself again." His pride had been restored; his turn of fortune had come not from charity or from a bequest but from his own initiative. "In a month or less I'll be president of Georgia Tech Broadcasting and general manager of Station WGTI."

Maude began to weep. She went to Doug and gave him a big kiss. Damon watched them, bewildered.

After they'd recovered they turned to their presents, saving to the last their gifts to one another. Damon's gift to his mother was a box of embroidered handkerchiefs, to his father a plaited leather belt. From his mother he received a pair of gray suede gloves. He found nothing under the tree from his father.

Finally, making a little fanfare, Doug gave Maude a clumsily wrapped package. Opening it, she found a hinged, beautifully carved recipe box made of chestnut and lacquered to a high gloss. The craftsmanship took her breath away.

"Oh Doug," she said, giving him a kiss on the lips. "This may be the most beautiful thing I ever saw in my life."

"Do you like it, darling?" he said, beaming. "I made it over at the Tech wood shop when you thought I was out for my afternoon walks."

Damon watched the two of them, feeling strangely isolated. Then his father turned to him. "Your gift is still in the car. You'll have to help me bring it in."

They went to the driveway and from the back seat of Hortense's Nash they took a sizable piece of carpentry wrapped in butcher paper and tied with a bow of red and green ribbon. Back under the tree, Damon unwrapped it. It was a bookcase, made of the same chestnut wood. Under three shelves were two drawers, each large enough to hold a ream of manuscript paper. He pulled out one of the drawers. On the bottom was an inscription, burned into the wood:

"For the best boy in the world. From his Dad. Christmas 1935."

Damon couldn't speak. His eyes misted. He stood up and went to his father and gave him a big bear hug. At that moment, washed in love, he decided that whatever mysterious and suspect thing his father had done, there had been an honorable reason. Someday, when he was older, he would understand.

About the author

Calvin Kytle has worked as a newspaperman, as the senior public relations executive for an insurance company, as deputy director of a federal civil rights agency, and as a Washington, D.C., communications consultant. During the fifties and sixties he was an irregular contributor to such magazines as *Coronet, Saturday Review.* and *Harper's*. He is the author of *Gandhi, Soldier of Nonviolence,* a biography for young people, and co-author (with former Congressman James A. Mackay) of *Who Runs Georgia?* In 1976 he founded Seven Locks Press, a small Washington-based publisher of nonfiction, mainly in the fields of politics, public policy, health, and race relations. Shortly after selling the press in 1987, he moved with his wife Elizabeth to Carolina Meadows, a continuing care retirement community in Chapel Hill, North Carolina. Born in 1920 in Columbia, South Carolina, he went through public schools in Atlanta, Georgia, and was graduated from Atlanta's Emory University in 1941. *Like a Tree* is his first work of fiction.

Printed in the United States
124575LV00002B/3/A

9 781603 060363